KU-476-177

ALSO BY AYANA MATHIS

The Twelve Tribes of Hattie

The Unsettled

The Unsettled

Ayana Mathis

ALFRED A. KNOPF
New York 2023

THIS IS A BORZOI BOOK
PUBLISHED BY ALFRED A. KNOPF

Copyright © 2023 by Ayana Mathis

All rights reserved. Published in the United States by Alfred A. Knopf,
a division of Penguin Random House LLC, New York.

www.aaknopf.com

Knopf, Borzoi Books, and the colophon are registered trademarks
of Penguin Random House LLC.

Library of Congress Cataloging-in-Publication Data
Names: Mathis, Ayana, author.
Title: The unsettled / Ayana Mathis.
Description: First edition. | New York : Alfred A. Knopf, 2023. |
Summary: Identifiers: LCCN 2022058917 (print) | LCCN 2022058918 (ebook) |
ISBN 9780525519935 (hardcover) | ISBN 9780525519942 (ebook) |
ISBN 9781524712594 (open market)
Subjects: LCGFT: Novels. Classification: LCC PS3613.A82847 U57 2023 (print) |
LCC PS3613.A82847 (ebook) | DDC 813/.6—dc23/eng/20221220
LC record available at https://lccn.loc.gov/2022058917
LC ebook record available at https://lccn.loc.gov/2022058918

This is a work of fiction. Names, characters, places, and incidents
either are the product of the author's imagination or are used fictitiously.
Any resemblance to actual persons, living or dead, events,
or locales is entirely coincidental.

Jacket images: (tree) enterphoto; (birds) Ihnatovich Maryia; both Shutterstock
Jacket design by Kelly Blair

Manufactured in the United States of America
First Edition

For my mother

Who can sleep when she—
hundreds of miles away I feel that vast breath
fan her restless decks.
Cicatrice by cicatrice
all the links
rattle once.
Here we go mother on the shipless ocean.
Pity us, pity the ocean, here we go.

—ANNE CARSON, "Sleepchains"

"How long will you be gone, and when will you return?"

—NEHEMIAH 2:6

The Unsettled

Prologue

TOUSSAINT WRIGHT STEPPED onto Ephraim Avenue with a backpack slung over his shoulder and a bleeding cut on his cheek. He was thirteen years old. Two years before, a fire had consumed 248 Ephraim Avenue, where Toussaint used to live. The fire destroyed most everything he loved. Nothing remained but a few girders inside the charred hull of the house and a scorched old oak tree out front.

Toussaint had passed through many homes since then—group homes and foster homes, the rectory of a pastor he knew—but he always busted out of them. Now he stood a long time on Ephraim, watching browned leaves falling from the oak. The gutter pipe on 248 came loose and bent with a metallic shriek that sent a flock of sparrows flying off into the night. Toussaint had not eaten in two days. He had run most of the way, stopping to catch his breath behind parked cars or in alleys. His heart was beating too fast; his blood ran like water. He touched his hand to the cut on his cheek and felt something small and hard protruding. Glass.

Earlier, in another part of the city, some boys who hung around the same corner Toussaint had been hanging around had asked him a couple of questions: Why you always alone and why you don't never talk? You ain't got no mama? Or a grandmama or something? The answers to these questions were unbearable. Sometimes grief came on him like a sweeping numbness, up from his toes and along his neck so he couldn't swallow. Other times, it was a column of rage rising along his spine. In answer to the boys' questions, he picked up a brick. He picked up a brick and threw it through the glass window of an abandoned storefront on the corner. He ran.

On Ephraim Avenue, he stomped his feet to warm himself. His sneakers thudded against the asphalt. The sound rang in the cold empty air, so he stomped again, harder this time. The block was all shadows, as though the night was more night there than anywhere else. He pried off a piece of plywood nailed over the doorway of 248. This took the last of his strength. He ducked through the opening he'd made and entered the house. "Yo, yo, yo!," he called, just to hear his voice echo down the hallway.

Toussaint settled in the warmest corner with a blanket, a sandwich he'd taken off a passed-out drunk, and a sheaf of letters from his mother, who wrote to him every week from Holmesburg Prison even though he couldn't stand to go and see her. He had letters from his grandmother too. Her name was Dutchess. She lived in a place called Bonaparte in Alabama. He was on his way there. He was really going this time. Toussaint fell into a jerky shivering sleep and dreamed of throwing the brick through the window all over again. Filaments of glass caught in the streetlight glowed as they fell. The glass rain sparkled like tinsel.

1985

. . .

PHILADELPHIA

. . .

Cherry Street

IT TINSELED DOWN on Ava Carson clutching her two suitcases in front of the Cherry Street Intake Center for the Homeless. Ava cried out and dropped her bags. The latches unlatched when they hit the pavement and the suitcases popped their guts like a melon thrown from a great height. Visions are not real, or they aren't real yet, but they do terrify.

"Toussaint!" Ava called out.

He was standing right behind her, just as he had been before the vision struck: a little boy of ten, small for his age, with both hands around the handle of his own suitcase. There they were, on a late August morning: mother and son, with three cases between them and a black trash bag bulging with their belongings.

"What were you doing on that street? Why did you . . . ?" Ava paused. She was shrieking, she realized. "No," she said. "Nothing."

She had never heard of Ephraim Avenue. Hallucinations. This is the sort of thing that happens when you haven't slept for days and you're so exhausted that your vision goes black at the sides where the peripheral ought to be.

Ava got to her knees and scrabbled at the things on the ground: pajamas and her silk top with the tie at the collar, and a couple of nice skirts she had managed to pack, Toussaint's good Buster Brown school shoes and his sequined Michael Jackson glove, a few

Avengers comic books. She stuffed them back into the suitcase fast as she could, only they wouldn't fit like they had before.

"Ma! You have to fold them. Ma, they're just falling out again."

Brisk feet stepped around them. A pair of scuffed black lace-up shoes stopped next to one of the suitcases. A woman's head lowered into view.

"You need some help, miss?" she said.

Ava shook her head.

"Let me help you." Her hands swung down and hovered over Ava's things, cracked palms, ashy knuckles, dirt under the nails.

"No!" Ava said. "I mean, that's all right."

"Mmph," the woman said. Her heel went down on a pair of slacks as she walked away.

Inside, Cherry Street smelled of sweat and stale junk food and hair.

The waiting room was big like the DMV, with rows of plastic chairs bolted to the floor. The man at intake kept calling Ava and Toussaint up to the window to ask a single question: Names? All right, sit down. ID? Okay. Take a seat. It was grim, but it was busy. The people working there had an urgency about them, like they were fixing things, phones pressed to their ears and their desks piled with folders. In the corner of the waiting room a skinny lady rubbed Vaseline on her kid's elbows like her life depended on it. That was a comforting sight. One monkey don't stop no show, like the saying goes. Ava squeezed Toussaint's hand. "Maybe we won't have to wait too long," she said.

But they did wait. An hour passed, then two. Afternoon came, or Ava guessed it was afternoon because the sun turned white and the room was broiling. The intake man called them up again to give Ava a stack of forms attached to a clipboard. When they turned back to their seats, a go-head-say-something kind of woman was sitting there next to a kid with his arm deep in a bag of Doritos. Not a free chair left in the place. There wasn't anywhere to be but leaned up against the wall with their bags at their feet. The thick air pressed on Ava's chest and stomach till she heaved a gob of sick into a used wad of tissues she picked up from the floor. A woman sitting at the end of a nearby row frowned and looked away. Who is going to help, Ava thought, if there's nobody here but these women and their kids, all of them poor as cracks in the floor? People who ain't got nothing can't do nothing, like her mother used to say.

"Ma, you want me to hold it?" Toussaint asked. Ava couldn't balance the clipboard against the wall and the papers kept slipping to the floor. Her boy put his hand on her arm. His eyes were big as plums and flitted from one thing to the next: a nut-brown baby slung over a shoulder, a little girl who kept undoing her barrettes till her mama popped her one, a lady shaking her papers at the intake man. Ava swallowed back another wave of sick and focused on the forms.

The forms had questions like: Last address. 245 Turnstone Pike, James Creek, New Jersey. Next of kin. N/A. Marital status: Married. Separated. Emergency contact: N/A. What circumstances led you to seek assistance at Homeless Services? Two weeks ago, my husband Abemi Reed threw us out of ~~our home~~ his home in New Jersey.

Then she wrote: Last night me and Toussaint were sitting on a bench in a bus shelter across the street from a lady's house out in the Northeast. She had a pitcher of iced tea on her table. It was dark in the bus shelter, then the streetlight came on right over us and we were lit up. That woman in her kitchen saw us so I didn't think we should stay there. And we were so tired. I spent nearly all the money on a motel. In the morning my son asked where we'd go after we left there. Are we going to spend the night here again, is what he said. I got him an egg sandwich at the McDonald's down the street. We sat in the air-conditioning and watched some kids on the slide in the PlayPlace. I had put aside enough for bus fare, so that no matter what, we could get somewhere. We used the bus fare and came here on the El.

Ava ran out of space and had to write down the margins. She knew that wasn't the kind of answer they wanted, but she had to tell somebody. The man at the intake window was talking on the phone and didn't even look up when she pushed the clipboard through the slot. She stood with her arms at her sides and waited. After some time, he glanced up at her and sighed.

"Come on, miss. Take it easy." He picked up the clipboard. "You can't cry in here. You need to calm— Gloria! Come out here cause this lady is . . . Don't put your hands all on the glass, miss."

Gloria was noisy coming out of a side door: "Okay. You got to be easy or we can't . . ." But it wasn't just Ava—half people in there were crying, or trying not to. Wouldn't any of them look each other in the eye though.

Gloria assigned Ava and Toussaint to the Glenn Avenue Family Shelter. She gave them carfare—tokens and paper transfers, not cash. Three hours later they were back out on the street. The skinny-boughed Center City trees drooped in the heat, and the business ladies' hair-sprayed dos were limp. Ava and Toussaint dragged their suitcases and trash bag down Broad Street to the subway. They took turns hauling their things down the subway stairs: Toussaint guarded the stuff and Ava took two suitcases down. Then switch. Then switch. People stared but nobody helped. A dark collar of sweat spread around Ava's neck. Toussaint's eyes were glazed and his lips were whitish and dry. The other passengers kept their distance, even though they were sweating too, even though some of them were taking up too much space with shopping bags and laundry carts. People are funny like that.

Ava and Toussaint got off the subway, took two buses, and at last found themselves trudging through the streets with their bags. The directions said walk four blocks to Tulpehocken. Turn left. They walked five blocks, then six. Mosquitoes buzzed in their ears.

"Ma? Ma! Is this it?" Toussaint asked of every building they passed.

They arrived at an intersection. Around the corner, a one-story gray building sprawled in the middle of the block, big and sad-looking the way government buildings are. There was a tumult in the U-shaped driveway in front, and a tangle of women and children; so many you'd think kids and mothers were the only people bad things happened to. Some of the mothers needed to take out their rollers, and some of the kids had stained T-shirts, and some of them needed haircuts. Ava didn't notice the boys with their pants neatly ironed or the women with their hair and nails done up nice. All she knew was she couldn't walk in there. But Toussaint was slumped against a tree. He couldn't take another step, or not many more.

"Stay close," she said, picking up the suitcases. She got a grip on the trash bag even though the handle dug into her wrist and her shoulder strained in its socket. "Stay right by me." A woman by the door tried to say something, maybe hello or maybe she wasn't even talking to them. Ava couldn't call up any words in response. Just inside the door a tubby security guard stood behind his desk and said, "Who goes there?" with a grin that could have been a leer.

"You want to go run around, champ?" he said to Toussaint while he checked Ava's paperwork. He told her they had a nice playground for the kids, with monkey bars and a slide. Ava hated him for standing there and for the kitchen and bedroom waiting for him when he got off work, and for all his talking and talking. His name was Melvin. Ava wanted to slap his face. "You can go out there for a little bit before they close it up for the night." If his stomach weren't cramping, Toussaint would have liked to climb on the jungle gym and hang off the bars and scream like he was scared of being upside down but really he'd just be screaming. He looked at his mother to see if maybe . . . but her face was clenched like a fist.

"Mondays," the guard was saying, shaking his head. "It's crazy here Mondays." He jerked his thumb in the air behind him. Probably was going to be a minute; everybody was gone for the day except Miss Simmons.

"She been backed up since morning," he said. "You can leave your stuff in there." He pointed to what looked like an empty office. Ava shook her head. She would not leave their things in an unlocked room. She would not let Toussaint run with these raggedy children. Wasn't there anything to eat, for her son, she wanted to know.

"Well, miss, this ain't Pizza Hut," he said. Then: "I'm playing. I'm just playing. Dinner's over, but you can ask Miss Simmons. They usually got something for people that get here late."

Ava and Toussaint sat on the chairs in the hallway and tried to keep their suitcases out of the way. A woman sitting across from them rolled her eyes. Like there was anything they could do about having stuff. Like that woman wasn't sitting there with her legs spread open like a man, cow chewing a wad of gum, Ava thought. The hallway was dim and too warm. The knobs of Ava's spine pressed into the hard back of the metal chair. Toussaint fidgeted.

"Don't scratch," she whispered. "We don't have . . . don't scratch." He had a raw-looking spot just above his elbow.

Toussaint sat on his hands. "It's not so bad, Ma," he said. "They put up all these decorations. See?"

The corridor was plastered with construction-paper cutouts, the kind kids make at school. And a big smiling apple with a slogan written across the middle. A food pyramid with pieces of bread that had legs and little hats. But there weren't any windows, and the cinder-block walls that ran down to a dead end were taped over with official-looking signs and notices.

"See?" he said again.

Snatches of conversation floated out to them from the pay phone near the guard's desk: "And what about Miss Jeanie? What she doing? She been over?" Ava hit at a mosquito on her leg. Down the hallway coins clattered, followed by a thunk when the soda machine dropped the can down the shoot. The pay phone rang every instant there wasn't somebody talking on it.

"Don't scratch, Toussaint."

"Don't *you* scratch. You're scratching," he said. Ava's thighs burned with mosquito bites. She itched so bad it felt like panic. She jumped up from the chair, then sat down again.

A lady with her ends curled into a pageboy led them into an office and introduced herself as Miss Simmons. She sat down and moved her mouth around while Ava's thighs burned. Miss Simmons had perfectly mauve nails, oval, and she tapped them against the desk while she talked. No drugs and no alcohol and no men. *Tap.*

Counseling was available. *Tap*. Every resident must actively seek employment. Ava should sign up at the job center by the end of the week. Failure to follow the regulations—strictly!—would result in immediate termination of their stay. No questions asked. *Tap tap*. Ava rubbed her legs through her jeans. Was Miss Carson tired? Miss Simmons asked. Had she used any substances? She looked a little out of sorts. Drug-treatment counseling was available. Mealtimes were strictly observed. No food in the rooms. No drugs and no alcohol and no men. Every resident must be out of the facility by nine a.m. on weekdays; residents can return for lunch. Curfew is nine p.m. unless special permission was received. Section 8 vouchers were available if they found housing on their own. Residents should make every attempt to find housing.

Ava's eye twitched. She was so tired she could have lain on the floor. Miss Simmons led them on a tour of the facility. The TV room is locked at nine p.m. The door to the right is one of five family bathrooms, each with five shower stalls, sinks, and toilets. Was Miss Carson all right? She should come for a mental health assessment at one p.m. tomorrow. She should come for her general intake at ten a.m. They'd finish the tour tomorrow. The boy looked a little tired. They descended a half flight of stairs and went down a long corridor to arrive at room 813. Miss Simmons produced a key from the pocket of her blazer. No drugs. No alcohol. No men. Then she was gone.

The walls in room 813 were dingy mint green. High rectangular windows faced a yard of trampled grass, beyond which a parking lot was just visible across a busy street. Ava's sandals stuck to the gummy linoleum. The room smelled of dirty mops and all the bodies that had lived in it: kids with flaky rashes and years of women giving their armpits a quick rub in the little sink in the corner—how many women over how many years?—and dirty clothes and an ammonia stink over all of it. Toussaint stepped forward. Ava put her arm across his chest to stop him from walking farther into the room. A wooden desk stood at the back with a couple of plastic hard-bottomed chairs alongside. A metal shelf and mirror were mounted on the wall over the chipped, shallow sink. There were two single beds on metal frames pushed against opposite walls. A half-dead roach on the mattress. Toussaint leaned against her arm.

"Sit on the chair, honey," she said. "Don't sit on that mattress. Don't touch anything. We can't stay here. We're not staying here."

After a few hours, the traffic on Tulpehocken slowed. Ava and Toussaint had not moved from the chairs by the battered old desk. A baby cried somewhere down the Glenn Avenue hallways. A wall clock ticked into the silence. Ava looked up to check the time only to discover that the hour hand quivered over the 10 like a fluttering eyelid. Ava climbed up on the chair, then onto the desk. She grabbed the clock with both hands and tugged. "Come on," she said out loud.

Toussaint jerked awake and looked around red-eyed.

"Ma?"

Ava climbed down. Toussaint sat with his head leaned on his palm, but his elbow kept slipping on the desk. "Ma," he said. "Ma, can I please lay down?"

"Soon, honey."

"I feel sick, Ma. I think I need to lay down."

"I know, baby. I know. We'll lay down soon."

The next minute he was sprawled across the desk again. Ava bent over him and rested her cheek on his head. His hair was damp. He did need to lie down. But not here. Only there was nowhere else to go. She had, they had, no place and so they were in this place instead of a park bench or a subway station. She leaned on the desk to steady herself. Maybe we could . . . a thought leapt across her brain like a cat over a wall. It might have been a good idea, the one that could save them, but Ava was too slow to catch it.

Toussaint yelped like he was being kicked in his dreams. Okay. Okay. Ava stood. She didn't have anything to clean the mattress so she used both sets of sheets to make the bed that didn't have the roach. Her back ached, but she managed to heave Toussaint up from the chair with both arms and guide him across the room. She draped him over the bed like Abraham's Isaac.

Ava angled her chair toward Toussaint to guard him against anything creeping out of the corners to crawl up his neck and lay its eggs in his ears. She shivered with exhaustion but as soon as she closed her eyes, she felt legs skittering on her ankles. The overhead light buzzed and the room was suddenly bright white and washed out, like an overexposed photograph. Another vision coming down on her. Or the Holy Ghost or her pop's spirit streaming through the fluorescent light on the ceiling. Whatever it was calmed her. Ava rested her head against the wall and after some time, she slept.

Frayed Social Networks

"HAVE YOU FELT SAD in the last two months, Miss Carson? Or wanted to hurt yourself or other people?"

Miss Simmons sat across from her 1 p.m. appointment, Ava Carson. She had given her an additional two days to settle in before this second assessment. Some of them took their arrival here harder than others. This Carson woman seemed a little fragile; plus there was something odd about her. Could be a secret boozer though she didn't look it. Clear eyes. Or a user but she didn't look like that either. Psychiatric problems maybe, though the psych social worker said she'd passed the evaluations. But that didn't mean anything. People could be depressed, couldn't they? They could have something seriously wrong and still know the day of the week and who was president. She's *fine*, June had said after the evaluation. June was a little put out about that. June didn't like a pretty, well-mannered woman taking up her time if she wasn't a little out of her mind. Fine with me, Miss Simmons thought. I'll take the Ava Carsons of the world any day, even if she is a little strange. Just yesterday a resident had told her very calmly that she left her previous place of residence because her father, who was apparently a bastard—and dead—had taken control of the hi-fi system and was talking to her through the speakers. It seemed this father could now be heard through the radio on Miss Simmons's desk. And the stink coming off her. Hadn't washed in God knows how long. This while she bounced a two-year-old on her lap. So.

"Miss Carson?"

"I mean, sure I feel sad. We don't have anywhere to go."

Miss Simmons didn't care for crying though it was unavoidable in her line of work. She didn't want this Carson woman welling up and spilling tears down her front. She did not like when things overwhelmed their boundaries. Her job was to impose order on chaos so these women could get out of there and live like other people.

"You have reported that the cause of your departure from your previous place of residence in—" Miss Simmons consulted Ava Carson's file. "In New Jersey was domestic violence."

"No! I mean, yes but it wasn't like—"

"Police reports?"

"What?"

"Do you have police reports?"

Ava Carson shook her head. A shame, Miss Simmons thought, and crossed out Shelter House, Hill of Hope, and the Women's Rescue Mission. Those places were nicer for kids. Day care and such. None of them had beds anyway.

"Nearest next of kin?"

"Alabama."

"No nearby living next of kin?"

Ava shook her head.

Not even the boy's father? A Cassius Wright was listed on the birth certificate.

"Any other connections? Maybe somebody you hadn't thought of, that might be able to offer assistance?"

813 took a deep breath and clenched her jaw. Well, don't get mad at me, Miss Simmons thought. Somewhere along the line Miss Carson had done some things, or failed to do some things, that left her on her own twisting in the wind. They don't end up here because of lost jobs or bad boyfriends. They end up with me because of what the new city guidelines called "frayed social networks." They had nicer terms for things now.

"And you have listed total assets as eleven dollars?" 813 nodded.

"Nothing besides cash? No car? No property in your name even if you don't have access to it?"

"I was married . . . Abemi, my husband, was, uh, religious, so I was . . . I stayed home and took care of the house. But it didn't turn out the way I . . . It didn't work out."

"So. Last employment, three years ago."

"Yes, but—that's when I got married and I stopped working. I always worked before that. Always. I had a few hundred dollars saved and I put my money in his account." Ava paused and took a breath. "But he didn't add my name like he said he would."

None of them ever kept their accounts, Miss Simmons thought. What she said was "That's pretty common in a marriage."

"That men keep their wives from having their own money?"

"Joint bank accounts, Miss Carson."

Ava pursed her lips; just barely, but Miss Simmons caught it.

"It wasn't joint, Miss Simmons. I just said he—"

"James Creek, New Jersey," Miss Simmons said, looking at Ava's address forms. "That's a nice area," she said. "Apartment or single-family?"

"Single-family."

"I see. All right. So . . ." Miss Simmons said.

813 took a deep breath, jaw clenched tight as a vise. It's nothing personal, Miss Simmons thought. Don't get yourself worked up.

"Most recent form of income was this job at Kelly Girl Services? Is that correct? In 1982?"

813 fixed her gaze somewhere beyond Miss Simmons.

"Miss Carson?"

"Born: 1940. Dutchess and Caro Carson. Parents."

"Yes, we have your biographical information, Miss—"

"Philadelphia. West Oak Lane. Pale yellow dress. Empire waist. September 1982."

"Excuse me?"

"Well, since you're reviewing things I already wrote on those forms you have there, and on the forms before those forms, and what I discussed with the other social worker, I thought I would save you the trouble of asking any more questions. And then you know, people always like to hear about weddings."

"Miss Carson, are you all right?"

"Oh, yes. Fine."

Miss Simmons took her glasses off and gave Ava a hard stare. She had found this often helped to discourage unhelpful behavior. Clearly the woman had been through something. She had written some mess on her intake forms about the husband watching TV or eating chicken or something while she tried to get back into their house. But what was Miss Simmons supposed to do with all these people's sad stories? If the information couldn't get an emergency housing voucher, Miss Simmons didn't want to hear about it. She changed tack.

"Is the marriage still active? No divorce or divorce proceedings in progress? No alimony or child support?"

Ava cleared her throat and straightened the bow at the neck of her blouse. It was a nice blouse. She'd be presentable at a job interview. She had that going for her, and nicely spoken. All 813 had to do was what Miss Simmons told her. Simple.

"Miss Carson, let's not waste time. I don't imagine you want to be here any longer than need be." Miss Simmons tapped a cinnamon nail—once, twice. "So. Alimony or child support?"

"No. Nothing like that," Ava said softly, looking down at her palms.

Pork and Beans

"WE CAN'T DWELL on negatives," the new chick in 813 was saying. She and her boy, he had a weird name—Too or Two—something like that? Anyway, they were at a table near the back of the Glenn Avenue cafeteria when Melvin made his lunchtime rounds. The boy shoveled that food in. Musta been hungry to eat that shit so quick—Melvin never touched a thing they made in that kitchen. Today they didn't even get the pork and beans right, lukewarm but burnt, with little black bits suspended between the squares of pink meat.

Two big standing fans pushed the canned-bean air around the room. It was so humid the tape on the kids' drawings had come unstuck and the paper flapped against the walls. 813 gulped her water, looking a little green. She was light-skinned enough to turn colors, which wasn't really Melvin's thing, quiet as it's kept. His wife was on the yellow side too, which was his right and his privilege as a man with a city job with a pension. But he liked a brown woman, or at least cinnamon. Kinda gave him the willies when he could see all kind of veins underneath a person's skin. 813 was pretty in her way. Prissy hippie style. She had on what they'd call a blouse, short-sleeved with some kind of nice little pattern on it, and a jean skirt that was a little tighter than you'd expect with that churchy top.

"We have to banish him from our thoughts," she was saying when Melvin passed by again going the other direction. Banish!

Who said banish? Schoolteacher, maybe. You'd be surprised who all ends up at Glenn Avenue. He shook his head. She was probably talking about her boyfriend or somebody. All these women in here had a man who had fucked them up some kind of way. By Melvin's calculation there were sixty women in the cafeteria that afternoon, so that was at least sixty, or maybe a hundred and twenty, dudes that had something to do with them being there. And that's exactly why Melvin had one kid and one kid only. Two Trojans in the wallet at all times. Switched them out every three months. Of course, they always got used before that. Always! Point is, none of his boys were swimming upriver with a sidepiece. Nope.

The yellow chick was up on her feet holding her son's tray and looking a little confused, like she all of a sudden didn't know where she was or what happened to her.

"Ma?" the boy said. He wasn't in such good shape himself. Circles under his eyes. Runty. Poor little man looked all set to bawl. She should take him back to their room and give him a hug or something. Melvin wasn't a barbarian. He figured it was fine for boys to cry up till they were eleven, twelve. They had to stop that shit after that though.

Melvin leaned against the wall, surveying the room. Lunchtime was nice, peaceful. Most of them were out doing whatever bullshit they got up to—supposedly looking for jobs, but you know—which meant Melvin could take it easy. He had learned a thing or two since he got here. When he was hired, he thought the ladies would be easy. It was true that the respectable types kept their heads down and minded their business. But them other ones? Mmmph. First, if they're high they got strength like Godzilla. Second, it's ten times worse breaking up a fight with them than trying to get between two niggers. Women'll use anything—nails, teeth, hair pulling. Melvin had seen one of them stab another one in the cheek with a broke-off bobby pin. A bobby pin! Fairer sex, my ass. Just yesterday he stopped a fight by the pay phones. They were beefing over . . . Well, speak of the devil. Public Enemy Number One walked into the cafeteria. "What up, Tess," Melvin called, so she'd know he was there.

The day before he nearly got his eye put out pulling her off somebody. He and Renee agreed Tess had won, but she had three deep nail scratches down her cheek. Today she was looking a little sad. Usually, she was loud and holding court: "Tess ain't got time for the bullshit." Or, right before she got them scratches yesterday: "Tess not trying to stand here while a bitch talk a whole hour on the PUB-LIC phone." New chick came in from outside and had to pass by while they were scrappin. You know what? She wasn't even scared. The little boy looked like he was gonna piss himself, but when they got close to the action 813 put herself between him and that fight and walked on by looking like she wanted to spit on them. Nose in the air. She stopped for a second all clenched up, like she was thinking about catching hands herself. Now, that was surprising.

813 was leaning forward and whispering hard, her whole body tensed. "But, but . . ." the kid was saying. She said a name, at least Melvin thought it was a name, and shook her head. Then the little boy wanted them to pray so they joined hands across the table but only the kid bowed his head. She stared in front of her all rigid. Intense was a word for her.

Tess made her way up to the front and stood there mugging the whole room, and who do you think she mugged the most? No surprise she didn't like the looks of 813. Tess is about six foot tall and a little bit German shepherd in the face. Not in a bad way, exactly.

"You need something?" she yelled across the room.

Uh-oh, Melvin thought.

"No ma'am," 813 says. Oh, but the shade she put on that "ma'am." Plus, she flashed a big Miss America smile while she said it: mouth only, hard eyes. Kinda scary.

"You sure about that?" Tess says. But even hothead Tess realized this was a battle for another day. She and the woman she came in with sat at a table near the front and tucked into their pork and beans. Tess started in with one of her monologues after a few bites, like it wasn't the scratches on her face that made her sad, or anything about life, it was just that her batteries were run down and the pork and beans fixed her right up.

Bedtime Rituals

ON THE FIFTH DAY at Glenn Avenue, Ava got sixty dollars in emergency funds—rushed through, Ava was informed, by Miss Simmons herself. There was a lot of to-do about signing for the money, but once Ava was through with all of that, she went out and got a few things she and Toussaint needed. Two cans of Raid, for starters. She emptied both in one go and room 813 stank so bad their eyes watered for two days. Every morning they found roaches twitching on their backs on the window ledge, on the floor, half-dead bugs dropping from the ceiling. Toussaint was a good boy. He acted like he didn't see them. But at least they could sit on the beds. Ava took the sheets to the Laundromat and washed them on the hottest setting, two times through.

Their suitcases and trash bag were still closed up tight in the corner of the room. Only one closet in there: the metal hanger bar rusty and bent in the middle, a layer of something sticky on the single shelf, and a sweaty shoe smell that turned Ava's stomach. She shut the door fast, and shut it stayed. She was almost glad their other things were safe from that filth. But maybe that stuff wasn't safe either, left behind in New Jersey. What would Abemi do with their keepsakes and winter clothes and bed linens? Rage through the rooms, throw it all out onto the highway, make a bonfire of every precious thing he could find: the snapshot of Toussaint in his little paper crown on his first day of preschool, her teaching certificate.

Five days at Glenn Avenue and already routine began to impose itself on them. Even in that place they went on needing to eat, and to sleep, and to go to the bathroom. The family bathroom was foul: mildew reek, wads of hair and wet toilet paper all over the floor, shit unflushed in the toilets. She and Toussaint only went in when they couldn't hold it anymore. Ava wouldn't shower in there; they washed up at the little sink in their room.

She made some rules: lights on at all times. Ava slept three or four hours a night in her chair. She smashed roaches and silverfish. She used napkins from the cafeteria to wipe the insect gobs off the green walls. Toussaint wrapped himself in the sheets when he got into bed, you couldn't see an inch of flesh. He was a mummy tipped onto the slab of rubber-covered mattress. He sweated in the night and woke with the sheets wet and his head pounding.

Another rule: no leaving the room at night. That guard Melvin was a joke. Anybody could get in the building. Anybody did. Ava had heard men's voices in the hallways late at night.

"I got you this juice bottle," she told Toussaint. "For at night."

"What?"

"For when you have to go to the bathroom at night."

"That's nasty."

"I know," she said. "I know it is."

He was too old to sleep six feet away from his mother. They were both embarrassed. Their bodies had done them a mean turn, with all the parts that dangled and secreted and swelled.

"Tell me something, Ma," he said. "I can't get to sleep."

Ava told him bedtime stories about her childhood in Bonaparte like she had been doing all his life. He pretended to be comforted. Maybe he was. They made Ava feel better, too. The stories reminded her that room 813 wasn't the only reality that ever was. They sat opposite each other in the plastic chairs by the desk in their room.

"Muscogee mostly," Ava said.

"With feathers?" Toussaint asked.

"No feathers, Toussaint. Just hats."

"Oh. Well, what else?"

"Boots."

"Ma! You know what I mean."

What else? The creak in the wide board on the porch when you climbed up into the swing. Also, Poarch-Creek farmers and Choctaw traders coming into Bonaparte to barter shoes and all manner of supplies for Bonaparte's tobacco (grown or stolen), or salt pork, or corn liquor. They stopped in to see Miss Tillie on business little girls weren't supposed to know about, then bedded down by the riverbank and were gone by morning. Like it was 1820, like anybody else in the whole world still bartered this for that with Indians in 1947. Ava's pop said Bonaparte was a place for free people; they and the Indians had been helping each other stay free for a hundred years. Also, Pop steadying the rifle on Ava's shoulder when they went hunting. Hold, hold, then the shot exploding and the wingbeat when the spooked osprey flapped out of the trees and the shot wild pig crashed into the crispy summertime underbrush. The taste of roasted pheasant, fresh killed. A pleasure Toussaint had never had. And flood years when game was the only food because the fields got washed out and everything rotted or never grew in the first place. Dutchess at her piano in the front room, playing and cussing.

Toussaint's next question would be about her, this grandmother he had never met, who lived in a place so strange and far away it might as well be a fairy tale, at least in Toussaint's mind. Dutchess didn't know she had a grandson.

"Bonaparte was the second Negro incorporated town in Alabama," Ava said. "1868!"

"You always say that, Ma."

"It's important."

"I *know*. What else?" he said. "What about my grandmother?"

Ava couldn't ever tell Bonaparte the right way. It was like this, she would say, but that wasn't how it really was—it was just her memories playing tricks and making pretty stories. What she should say was: When I was a girl, I watched my pop sprint across

Bonaparte's fields of sprouting peanuts, head down, arms pumping. The bullet burst came from behind. Pop fell chest-down into the green shoots. The crickets stopped singing. No tricks there, see? Could be if Ava could tell it straight, she'd see the whole long line of her life, clear as newsprint. Maybe room 813 had been waiting for her since she was born, since before she was born. Could be that "now" is already curled up inside "then," like a family's generations already inside a woman's body. What a terror. And what sweetness too, like some hand had laid it all out for you, lovingly, like you might lay out a child's clothes.

"What?" Toussaint said.

"Nothing. Sorry. We should go to sleep."

Into the Wolf's Mouth

AFTER TOUSSAINT FELL ASLEEP Ava called Abemi. "Where are you?" he asked. "Why are you calling if you won't tell me where you are?" He tried to sound like he didn't give a damn. "I guess you're still seeing him. I guess that's where you went when you left here." He'd be yelling in a minute. Ava's throat tightened, like a hand was squeezing from the inside. His face floated up in her mind's eye: mouth twisted, those wet, angry baby eyes. She hung up before he could say anything else.

Back in her room she paced while Toussaint slept. There was something she needed to do before she could figure out how to get them out of there. But she couldn't get her thoughts in line, they scuttled away from her like silverfish.

A couple of coloring books sat on the desk. They'd given them coloring books. For a boy Toussaint's age! Ava took up a nubby pencil. Maybe, she thought, if I write things down. If I make a list of everything that has happened, maybe it'll straighten out in my mind. She'd include every detail: Abemi and New Jersey. Cass. She'd have a full record and when it was done, she'd see where things had gone wrong and know what to do next.

She wrote:

We have been in the Glenn Avenue Family Shelter for 5 days.

No, that wasn't right. Not far enough back. She could start when she got married. Or maybe she should begin with how things were before she got married. When it was just her and Toussaint against the world. Only the world required money and Ava didn't have any.

Right before me and Abemi got married Toussaint asked me why we couldn't stay just the two of us going on our trips to the Please Touch Museum and the zoo on weekends. But the zoo cost a mint, what with the entrance and the popcorn and hot dogs and McDonald's after to keep the good feelings going. Then Monday would come around and all I had left was $12 in the bank. There was the rent at that one-bedroom on Upsal Street that got to be too much so we left there, and then the efficiency on Camac. After that the other efficiency, on Gratz. No trees—just a lot of roaches and the kind of kids who would try to fight my boy and he didn't know anything about fighting, or being tough. I got us back to Germantown. We rented a room from Mrs. Crawford on Pulaski, her and her good-looking husband who I did my best to ignore. But he didn't ignore me and so we were out of there in a couple of months. Then Mrs. Tagliaferro's place . . .

No, that wasn't it either. That was just a laundry list of the when and where. Maybe it began with Toussaint and the day she'd come from the doctor's office with the news she was pregnant. *Me and Cass were already broken up by then but—* She couldn't finish the sentence. Too much Cass talk was like falling into a hole in the floor.

I met him at a Panther meeting in 1971. I don't remember how I started going to things like that. I never cared much about all that stuff, really. I never thought being black was some kind of political statement like they always made it out to be up here. Black just *is,* like a butterfly is or a river *is.* In Bonaparte we just were. Still and yet, back then going to meetings was the thing to do. Standing room only. You squeezed yourself into these basements or living rooms or community centers. Little silver sparks shooting off the people and whipping around the room. I felt a little like I was back home—everybody had that same tall walking way people had in Bonaparte. I had never met any other black people like that up here. Black people here talk so much mess like they're better off than we were at home but I'm not so sure they're as free as they think. This one meeting Cass walked in and stood at the back. I swear the room stopped. Everything hushed for a minute. He's the same tawny gold color all over: eyes and skin and hair. It nearly hurt my eyes to look at him.

After the meeting we went to a diner. Why did you come, he asked. What are you looking for? He never took his eyes off my face. We didn't do anything but talk that night, or the next night or any of the nights after that for a couple of weeks. I was high on him. Delirious. You know that feeling? I didn't sleep and didn't need to. We kissed the first time in the hallway outside his apartment door. The feeling of his mouth on mine thrummed up through the crown of my head. We managed to get ourselves inside, half-dressed, but didn't make it past the living room. I couldn't get enough of anything—not Cass, not even the air. I left my body and entered into his. I have never felt that way before or since. I don't suppose I ever will.

We stayed together two years. Cass and his endless tumblers of Chivas, smoking and sipping and going on about Fanon and Lumumba and Gramsci at every late-night Panther, CORE, whatever meeting. He was always standing in a corner while the party slowly tilted toward him like planets around a sun. Tie always straight despite the lateness of the hour. And the women. My God, the women. On top of everything else, he had the nerve to be a doctor. Women draped all over him, practically laid out in front of him, panties around their ankles. But at the end of night, it was always me and him leaving together. We'd go flying back to my place in his little Saab. After three or four hours of sleep off he'd go to the hospital for his rounds. Sometimes he came back the next night and sometimes in a few days and sometimes in a week. Without warning, the little Saab would pull up to the curb. I was always watching for him, at least that's how I remember it—half surprised he came back. And a little bit terrified. I can still see myself standing in the doorway to my apartment while he climbed the stairs. I felt his footsteps in little shocks against my skin.

Ava put the pencil down and pushed back from the table. "Oh," she said out loud. Thinking about him was like putting her hand in a wolf's mouth. Blood blood blood.

She needed to start again, with the earliest beginning she knew. Hard facts. She wrote:

I was born in a boardinghouse in Natchez, Mississippi in 1940. My mother's name is Dutchess Carson. My father was Wardell Lyons. Dutchess met him when she was performing on the road. I never knew him. He died overseas in the war. My pop was Caro Carson. Pop and Dutchess got married in 1945 and we moved to Bonaparte, Alabama. Dutchess quit singing. We lived in the house my pop's pop built in a clearing at the end of Sundown Road. Dutchess is still there. My pop is dead.

Clear and simple. Abemi was always telling Ava she was all muddled up. Your family's muddled and you're muddled right along with them. What sort of person says things like that? He didn't talk to her like that in the beginning. It was all right between them for a while. It was fine, they started off fine.

A Full Record

AVA AND TOUSSAINT MOVED to New Jersey right after the wedding. Abemi had never been a husband before, and she had never been a wife. They would figure it out as they went along. That's what he'd said when he asked her to marry him: the two of them were grown and needed to settle down. Not the most romantic proposal, more like an offer, really, but it was honest. Ava was eager to move to the little house he'd bought, to be a wife in a house with a front yard on a quiet road. Wifeness was solid, not drifty like being forty-two with a little boy to raise on your own.

It wasn't the prettiest house you ever saw. Ranch-style in a ramshackle kind of way, and every inch of the ranch smelled like the cows were still there. Haha. Actually, it was more like mothballs and mildew, and the carpet was a little squelchy. Outside, poop-brown shutters at the windows and the dingiest white siding you ever saw. Abemi said, "Just needs a little TLC!" The next day he went off to the hardware store and came back with two cans of red paint. When he finished, the shutters were sticky-looking and violent against the white of the house. Maybe that was a sign. Like maybe it's not so good if your new husband paints the shutters so they look like a burst blood vessel in an eyeball. That's hindsight for you. And plus, Toussaint and Ava didn't bring many of their things. Ava brought her cane rocker, a photo album, personal papers, and a quilt from Bonaparte. And their clothes, sundry keepsakes, and Toussaint's comics. Everything else in the house was Abemi's. Their stuff ended up at the Goodwill, or Ava supposed it did because she left it all in their apartment. They were living on Broad Street then. It's true, that place was kind of a dump, and half their things were still in boxes and bags. She never unpacked much in any of the places she and Toussaint had lived. They moved so often, and plus she wasn't much bothered about a lot of furniture—she and Toussaint had their beds and a small dining table and a couple of chairs. Nothing wrong with living that way, it just isn't for everybody. It wasn't for Abemi, that's for sure. "Just leave it, Ava," he said when they were packing up. He waved at their stuff like it was something you have to step over on the sidewalk.

The Jersey house was peaceful once they fixed it up, set on a two-lane country highway across the street from a 4-H club with a pond at the far end of the property. Weeping Willows. Their neighbor Mr. Leroy was the 4-H caretaker. He kept a hammock strung between the trees at the far end of the grounds. In nice weather Ava would go back there looking for Toussaint. She'd find him doing something muddy at the edge of the pond and Mr. Leroy swinging in his hammock. He always had butterscotch candies, and he was forever giving them to Toussaint, who was forever spitting them out in the palm of his hands. Sticky, that kid. It's true about little boys. Toussaint always smelled like the outside. Even in winter when he had to stay inside playing in the den. That made Ava proud. She was proud of him just for being in the world with her, alive and sticky and warm. She was proud of him for just breathing the air.

Nine or ten months into the marriage Abemi got it into his mind that he wanted to have a baby. Ava was forty-three by then, and had had all the kids she was going to have, but Abemi skipped right past good sense and wouldn't let it go. Maybe it was all the younger deacons at their church strutting into Sunday service like roosters with their hens and chicks behind them. Maybe it was because

Toussaint hadn't warmed up to him as fast as he'd hoped. He prayed about it. Relentlessly. When it was clear a baby wasn't coming, he sank into a funk, like something had been stolen from him. Then he got mad and stayed that way. Mean.

Ava might be doing the dishes on any random Wednesday or Saturday and he'd start in on her without warning. He'd stand in the kitchen doorway holding a beer. Never mind their church forbade strong drink.

"Who do you belong to?" he would ask. Then he'd shake his head. "Nobody. You and Toussaint just blow in and out like clouds."

Those were the facts, all right. Ava and Toussaint been here and there and nowhere.

"You don't know how to stick with anything," he'd say.

Ava tried to calm him. "We are married," she'd say. "I'm sticking with you."

Sometimes she even meant it. Most times she wanted to mean it.

"You have to pray God teaches you how to love," Abemi would say. "You have to ask God to help you overcome your nature."

His eyes glittered and his voice squeezed and pitched higher. He had never understood a thing about Ava's nature. But he sure knew how to press her buttons. In her private moments she wondered if there was something selfish and inconstant lurking in her. She had turned out to be a drifter like Dutchess was a drifter. Maybe it was in their blood and she would pass it on to Toussaint, who'd grow up to be a restless man rambling down roads and in and out of bus stations.

Ava never knew what might set Abemi off: the thermostat was turned up too high, or she had ripped the Reynolds Wrap wrong and the edges were uneven. Once he came charging out of the bedroom and dumped the folded laundry on the floor because the fabric softener Ava had been using for months was suddenly giving him hives. "You can't even keep the clothes clean!" He shoved one of his shirts in her face so hard the button bruised her chin. Then he was sorry. Weeping-and-wailing sorry. It was all such a cliché it embarrassed her even then. But he never hit her.

After one of these episodes he always wanted to pray.

"Father God," he started up like he was Jimmy Swaggart. Like he was Moses. "We come before you to ask your guidance and healing." And, contrition be damned, he always got one in: "I ask your grace for my wife, who needs your help to conceive and extend our family."

The thing is, Abemi could have had what he said he wanted, if he had really wanted it. He could have got a young woman to pump them out for him. But what he really wanted was someone to lord over, someone to rub their face in it, whatever *it* was. He was sad, really. Lonely and small. Poor thing. When he was at his most pitiful Ava tried to remind herself it wasn't fair to compare him to Cass.

Ava just got on with the business of being married. And she would have kept right on, too. What would have stopped it? Not her, she was ashamed to say—she sure wasn't having any kids with him though. Then Cass came back. Nearly ten years in the wind and he came walking into her yard in Jersey like somebody had conjured him up.

Abemi found out about Cass's visit a week later. He accused Ava of keeping up contact with him all these years. He said she was a liar. She was having an affair with Cass. She had made a fool of Abemi. In his own house. He was on his feet waving his arms around. Charging toward Ava then veering away right before he hit her. He banged his fists on the table. Pulled the jars out of the cabinets and threw them to the floor, at the wall, at Ava.

She barricaded them in Toussaint's room. Her boy sat on her lap in the armchair by the window, both of them shaking. Suddenly it was quiet. Ava clapped her hand over Toussaint's mouth—tight—so he wouldn't make any noise. His eyes flew open and he gasped way down in his throat. Even now she could feel the panicked wet suck of his inhales against her palm. That was unforgivable. She wouldn't ever forgive herself. She didn't know if her boy had.

The quiet deepened. They moved to the narrow bed and sat with their arms around each other until Toussaint fell into a restless sleep. Ava stayed awake listening. No footsteps. Abemi must have been out there, sitting in the rubble of the kitchen. At early light a chair scraped the linoleum; glass crunched under his heavy tread. His footsteps closed in on the bedroom door. Ava leapt from the bed and grabbed Toussaint's school scissors. She gripped them in her fist, all the tremble gone out of her. But he moved past the door and Ava heard the water turn on in the shower. Twenty minutes later he left for work like it was any other day.

When he was gone, Ava packed up their most important things in a couple of suitcases, plus a garbage bag for the overflow. She went over to Mr. Leroy's, where she took a long time explaining things to his wife, Miss Lucille. She couldn't catch her breath and she kept getting so tired she had to sit down for a bit before she could go on. "We only have ten dollars," she said. Miss Lucille made Toussaint a ham and fried egg sandwich. She took a fifty-dollar bill from a tin on the highest shelf in her cabinets and pressed it into Ava's hand.

When Ava went back to the house Abemi was there. Barely noon but already back from work, sitting at the kitchen table eating a piece of chicken. All the mess still on the floor around him and the cabinet door hanging off the hinge. He'd locked all the doors. Ava went around to the side of the house and banged on the kitchen window. She pounded. She yelled. Abemi didn't so much as glance in her direction. Ava threw pebbles against the window. A few seconds later, the back door opened and suitcases flew out one by one. Trash bag last. A spectacular rage came down on Ava. She was ten feet tall; she was invincible with fury. Pathetic, she called him. Hysterical. A sorry excuse for a man. Oh, she was blazing. You could have seen her a mile away. Abemi stepped onto the back steps with his fists balled. She wished he would. "Do it," she said. Go on. She'd take a chunk out of his shoulder with her teeth; she'd bash his head in with a rock. But he just stood there heaving and grinding his jaw, then he said, "You've been wanting to go. So, go." He turned his back on her and locked the door behind him.

Miss Lucille didn't say a word during the ride to the bus station in town, her fingers white-knuckled around the steering wheel. She wasn't much used to driving. They crept along so slowly it hurt. Ava kept expecting Abemi to appear around a bend and run them off the road. Miss Lucille let them out at the station and said, "God be with you." She squeezed Ava's hand.

In 813, the evening passed into predawn with Ava trying to get at that thing flickering in the periphery of her mind: the real story. Or maybe it was a memory, a sense, no, a whiff of dirty diaper from down the hall. No, a black water bug on the green wall. The night ticked toward dawn. She fell into a restless sleep and dreamed she called her mother. "Come get me," she wept into the phone. But Dutchess just sat in the old house in Bonaparte, drinking whiskey from a jelly jar.

BONAPARTE

. . .

IN THE BEGINNING was the Alabama River. Sunrise, dusk, starling flight. Gators, sunfish, Spanish moss, live oak, mountain lion, lark. Muscogee. Alabama. Choctaw. Bonaparte wasn't yet Bonaparte because all the niggers were still in Africa not knowing they was going to become niggers. No *Huntress* or *Isabella* full of Africans sold to Quakers, no *Clotilda* sunk off the coast of Mobile. All the white folks still up in their cold places fighting each other. They sure was coming though. And when they did! They wanted to conquer death and time. They came down on the world like the rain came down on Noah. They wanted to *be* the rain and Noah, and God too.

What they don't know is God helps people invent the God they deserve. White folks have Zeus. Popes. Dollars. Big motherfuckers that suck the bones of tender things. Scared all the real gods into hiding with their cannon fire, burning forests, whales trailing blood under all the oceans, death howling everywhere at once. Big teeth chomping up all the Indians, every wood and plain. Ships filthied the waters with our mothers sealed below the decks. Topside, the sails clapped and the wind blew the crews' hair and whipped their lice into the foaming water. Their souls went too. Damnation haunts their generations.

Bonaparte is how the white people called this place on the banks of the Alabama River. It was green and greener, even after they got some bodies to fell the trees. Some bodies planted cotton, planted sorghum. More cotton. Them motherfuckers didn't know what they was doing. Could have asked the Muscogee but they drove them like dogs to Oklahoma. Could have asked the niggers, but you know. The earth turned on them (told you they was cursed) and sent plagues of insects. *We* had our kitchen gardens, we had our chitlins and pig feet, we know how to eat around little bones. Floods came. God said float. Niggers made rafts out of wood. First master drowned, washed up covered with leeches. Second master, smallpox. Third, tuberculosis. Fourth master's three sons all died on the same full-moon night. Shiiiit. The spirits don't play. Our mothers neither. Massa so shook up he come down to the cabins, his thing soft and in his pants for once. "What happened to my sons?" he wants to know. "Should have put blood on your door," Old Rea said. He gave her the bit, sure. Three weeks later he was dead too. Heartbreak, you reckon.

After that there was a lull in masters. The story goes that Old Rea took to standing on the river's edge looking across the water. One's coming, she'd say every decade or so. Then she turned her back and walked into the woods. Wouldn't nobody see her till that new master grew a goiter on his throat and strangled, or got burnt up in a slave cabin, the brown girl in it with him outside warming her naked self by the flames. The War came and went. Evidently, we all got freed, but nobody in Bonaparte heard about it until long after because by then wouldn't no white folks blight our shorelines or our woods or our fields.

Bonaparte farmed. People made shiny-eyed babies with minds quick as rabbit traps. Old Rea kept watch on the shore. One day— who could say how many decades passed—one day Rea said, "One's coming." White folks troop up the road, big-eye staring cause they never saw the like. Our men with no yassir in their mouth. The women looking em in the eye. Fields neat as ironed handkerchiefs, big fat cows everywhere. The white men say they got new plans for a new time. New time? says Bonaparte. Nineteen and thirty-six, they say. The plans say the government decided to give Bonaparte to the people, even though the people already had it. Rea said, "Let em. But don't tell em nothing."

So it went. They did their surveys and drew up their deeds. Everybody signed. When it was done Bonaparte gathered by the river at dusk. Rea said: Everything born on this land, Everlasting knows by name. Anything come for us, God rise against it. Through us. We are God's vengeance and blessing. Then Rea, she was something old by then, raised her arms up to the woods and up come a flock of starlings swelling the sky. They're still there, every night, a wave surging black across the twilight. You should see them. Oh, you really should.

It's nobody left here now.

Cows. Graves. Me. There's not but a thousand acres of Bonaparte left between us: Carter Lee and his wife, Juniata, Memma and Nip LaPrairie, and Erma Linner. Bonaparte was ten thousand acres once upon a time. Ten thousand free nigger acres. Hear that. The records are across the river in Bodine at the Pauline County Court House—all of us Carsons, Moores, Bennys, Dukes, Linners, Jameses, Coopers, Billupses, Bells, Petes, LaPrairies, Hundleys, Greens, Camdens, and Richards—our deeds and property surveys and tax records, alongside the records of the white folks' thieveries, which they call bills of sale or sometimes foreclosure depending on how they do the stealing. That's nine thousand acres lost, if you can stomach the count. Nobody left around here can stand to hear it. You can't blame them. Erma Linner used to have six hundred acres all on her own, but her no-account crackhead sons sold them off piece by piece so they could suck it up a pipe, gamble dice, and then move to Washington D.C. where, if it's any justice in the universe, they are dead in an alley. I do my best to keep up morale and get us to stick together, but you know, you can lead a donkey right down to the water's edge but the motherfucker still might kick you in the head.

One thing is the same, Carter Lee is still the postmaster even if he is 194 years old, and it's just him riding geriatric on his moldy motorboat to get the mail from the depot in Bodine across the river. Over there it's just white folks far as the eye can see, with a few lost Negroes ain't have better sense than to come to Bonaparte years ago when they still had the chance. Maybe they gloat now Bonaparte's a ghost town. Probably. Niggers love a comedown.

Back in the day, they foaled and foaled round here. "Dutchess," they used to say, "you ain't gon have but that one? Aww." Then the kids grew up and went off and the mamas sat up on their porches in their sackcloth and ashes mooning over pictures of the grown children. I used to say, What did you expect? Nothing for a young person to do around here but watch the kudzu grow over the fence. Now we are just a rutted red dirt road between two Live Oaks. Trailing off into the woods like a whistle in the wind. Addio, Bonaparte.

We had a town placard: BONAPARTE, ALABAMA, NEGRO INCORPORATED TOWN, ESTABLISHED 1868. Used to be Caro re-did it every few years and kept it staked on the road by the Oaks. Till a few years ago the white folks never touched it, they thought it was cursed. White folks ain't scared of nothing as much as they scared of niggers with spells. Progress Corp. pulled it up like a weed and threw it facedown in the dirt. Me and Carter Lee moved it to the front of the old Bonaparte General Store. Yeah, we had a store too. Nothing in there now but the shelves, but we're still proud of what it was. We have our little four-family town meetings in there too. This is our church, Carter Lee said one time. Stupid Juniata shushed him up like God was going to strike him. After that me and Carter Lee repainted the lettering across the front. BONAPARTE GENERAL. Took us two weeks and our old behinds nearly met our maker, but we did it. Memma and Nip sat in folding chairs and watched us. Lazy coloreds. At least they brought lemonade.

Few times a year white boys come down my road sizing up my acres, licking their chops. Last week it was three of them, I let them get almost to the house then I went round the back and shot off a few rounds. An Alabama cracker, even one in nice shirtsleeves, is tougher than few bullets in the air. That's how I knew them white boys were from Progress; they ran away down my road like God and dignity had deserted them, which I guess it did. Scavengers. We used to dig traps for the kind of creature, man or beast, that would steal your chickens. Can't catch these though, most time they do their dirt with letters.

Carter Lee brings them from Bodine by the bagful. I see the Progress logo and I don't even open the envelope. I let them pile up till they get on my nerves then I take and burn them out back. I'm not a stupid hayseed, talking about "I ain't a-scared of sumnun with they book learnin'." Please. Here's the thing, all those years ago we made the mistake of deciding to play by white folks' rules. But if that's the game, I know my rights. I pay my taxes. We all do. My three hundred acres ain't going nowhere. This is the last big land parcel left in Bonaparte, and Caro's birthright. If I don't keep it there won't be any Bonaparte left.

I ain't one for the kooks and spooks, but hear me on this, you can vanish a place and time. You can vanish it so hard nobody can't get back to it even in memory. Whatever good it had goes with it. We were free in Bonaparte. Every time I step off this land a yoke comes down around my neck. Not that I leave much anymore. I'm scared I might cross the river with Carter Lee and time would knit itself so tight around this place I couldn't get back home again.

The starlings come up at sundown like always. They lift up from the treetops and swoop across the sky like black ink poured in a glass of water, curl and uncurl then the night falls down on Bonaparte like somebody dropped it. I walk back to my house from the edge of my woods with my lantern—not that I need it. I have Delilah with me and she'd rip the throat out of anything comes near me. I know every rock, every tree root sticking up out the dirt. Night is when I like to be alive. People always saying this or that about the night being lonely, but nothing's lonelier than the sunlight bright-ing down, showing every little scratch and smudge on your life. I ain't scared of nothing at night. I was brought up to be brave at night and watchful in the day. And so I am.

You got be. Watchful, I mean. This morning Juniata come by my place with the post because Carter Lee was down with his bad leg which he has because he was already old when the Everlasting was a child. If I told him once I told him a thousand times don't give none of my mail to goddamn Juniata, I know she your woman but she nosy and I don't like her. We don't get the mail but every two weeks anyhow, wouldn't hurt me to wait another week. But Carter Lee says he has a duty to deliver the mail in a timely fashion, even if he can't deliver the mail, so here comes Juniata. Even after all these years I still can't get over how ugly that woman is. Just bug-looking. Carter Lee must wake up in a fright some nights.

She started up like I knew she would: "You ain't been down to be sociable in a while. How you keeping?" See that? I have never gone to see her one day in my life, and she knows it. And she knows how I been keeping cause my lights come on every night which means I ain't dead. "All right, Juniata," I say.

"Well," she says. "I got this here gonna make your day." And then she pulls out this letter she was holding behind her skirt. "It's from Ava!" Smiling all over me. "Maybe she has settled down somewhere at last." And she stood there looking at me, waiting for my face to change.

Ava's letter's right on the table where I left it this morning. A little thing like a letter can take up so much space in a room. Even Delilah was eyeing the thing from her spot by the front door. Maybe she could smell Juniata's fingers on it. Probably tried to steam it open. Caro used to say, "Dutchess, you got to have patience with em. It ain't everybody can go hopping trains with a guitar on they back, baby girl." Caro hadn't got around too much either, but he could go anywhere in his mind. When I would get mad, he'd take one look at me and say, "Imma get out of here. There be dragons!" Where does a deep woods Alabama nigger come up with some shit like that?

Juniata and all them thought I was crazy for sending Ava off. They thought you ought to keep at least one daughter behind, to mind you in your old age, and if you only had one daughter . . . well, too bad for her. By the time she left, Caro was dead. Bonaparte was leaking sons and daughters like a hole in a bucket. I wanted her to go, no work for her here anyhow. She's not the minder type, you know. She can't hardly take care of herself. It's like her own self is always jumping out at her. Anyway, she finished her high school and she went to college in Birmingham. Didn't last more than a couple of years, but I knew she wasn't coming back. She drifts. Or she did. She been in Philadelphia for a good bit now. Before that I used to get these letters: California, Nevada, Arizona. Chicago. I'm glad she's seen some of the world. I have too. I been my fair share of places. Sung on my fair share of stages. High and low. Mostly low, I guess.

Caro built furniture. He used to load up his truck and drive his tables and credenzas to a place in Selma—set it all up in an open lot, so the white folks could come and look at it without having to go in a store in the colored parts of town. They couldn't come here because we didn't allow them in Bonaparte. Plus, they had to have cash in hand. Caro wouldn't take credit from a white man. Niggers, he practically gave the stuff away. Things supposed to be beautiful, he would say. Every day we need some beauty. Caro was the most beautiful I ever knew. He looked like the chairs he made: clean lines, brown as, slim as, glowed in the light. I used to reach out and touch his cheek while he was sleeping, run my hands down his arms and legs. Those nights! The cicadas singing, the half-moon caught in the square of open window, the leather wood dust pine smell of him, the heat coming off his skin.

You know what people don't talk about old widow ladies? Getting some. I miss it. I will till I go in my grave. It gets so bad some nights I think about trying Carter Lee, but surely he has forgotten his thing has any use but pissing. And Nip LaPrairie? That would be like humping a rotten potato. If I think all of these years of empty nights ahead, and how many I already passed . . . I think it's doing something to me, drained the color out of the world. Nothing is any less beautiful than it ever was, but the beauty is all surface—skin-deep and goes by fast.

I used to feel like the world was too much. Some days it hurt me just to look at a pear tree in bloom, or hear one of those old Bonaparte women singing while she walked down the road. The sound burst in my brain like it might crack my head right open.

Every thought I had swooped up somewhere I couldn't reach. Caro could see when I got bad. He'd put a cold cloth on my head, whisper in my ear, coo over me. And when that didn't work, he took me for a long walk in the woods. He'd pull up my dress and put me against a tree, make love to me till I didn't have a mind no more. He'd wear me out with coming. And we'd go home bruised and my knees all cut up; then I could sleep. I guess anybody would say it's better now, better to be calm most times. Maybe it is. But I wouldn't wish this flatness on anybody.

Anyway, Ava was working in a school some years back. She said she was sick of being a secretary and she was going to finish her degree and be a teacher. She did get so far as a teacher's assistant. Sent a Polaroid in one of her once in a blue moon letters. I keep it in my box of things from her. Here she is with the blackboard eraser in her hand next to a little boy. "My classroom with Reggie," she wrote on the back. Ain't that something! I thought that was just so fine.

She called me at Christmas that year, and left me her number too. She was renting a room in Philadelphia in a place called Mount Airy. She had a nice place to stay and a job. I was happy she found a normal life that wouldn't rough her up too much. I thought, Well, she'll be all right. She has convinced herself I had it in for her, especially after Caro died. She wants things to be simple, but they never were and she thinks that's my fault. Ava can't let things go, never could. That's no way to be—you just have hounds chasing you through the years.

Anyway, a little while after the Polaroid she went AWOL again. Six or seven months later I got a postcard from her. "Atlantic City!" Nothing else. No return address. I said, "Carter Lee, I thought y'all wasn't supposed to take the mail with no return address." It's eleven years since she sent that picture with Reggie. I've heard from her in the meantime, of course. I don't know why she didn't keep up with the teaching.

I do daydream. To pass the time. I dream of visitors. Somebody stepping out of the trees to . . . to what? I don't know. Counsel.

That's a good word. I feel like I need counsel. I got a little book where I keep my phone numbers and such. I have a list with Ava's numbers—just ten in all these years. There's her letter laying there staring at me from the table, but I don't want to read a goddamn letter. Everybody I want to talk to, it ain't but two people, both of them somewhere I can't get to them. I keep this yellow phone on the wall but I don't call nobody, and don't nobody call me. I flip through my little book of numbers.

First, I dial Byard 6-898, those old-style numbers nobody remembers anymore. Natchez, Mississippi. That woman is long dead, pious old bitch. I guess I call it to make sure she's still in her grave. Then it's the first number Ava had in Birmingham, 765—. Disconnected. I go on calling down the list till I get to a 215 number. That one rings. "Hello?" Can I speak with Mr. King, I say. "No. I . . . you must have the wrong number." I hang up. Husband must be dead. The woman has that creak in her voice like she ain't got none in a long time. I bet you she keeps the light on in her kitchen. The rest of the house is dark. Quiet as a hand over a mouth. Oh, I know all about that.

I wonder what kind of place Ava lives in. I don't know if she has gray hairs yet, or if her bushy eyebrows thinned out like mine did when I got to be in my forties. I wonder what she sees looking out her window, what she can hear from her bed when she lays down at night. I'm done with my dialing but I can't seem to hang up the phone, just keep on holding it like there's somebody on the other end. If I could call her, I would ask if they'd had a cold winter up there. What does your coat look like? I read y'all got a colored mayor! Black, she'd say, not colored, because that's how young people call themselves now.

How you getting on with that man with the funny made-up name you wrote me about a while back? You expecting? Is that why you hitched up with somebody you only knew three months? "You gonna come back here, ever at all, even just a week?" Once I say that out loud, we can't talk no more, so I set the phone back in the cradle and boy it's so quiet in this house I think I might die of it.

Delilah just sitting across the room looking at me. She doesn't cock her head like most dogs, she just look at you straight on like she's going to shake her head. Like: Dutchess, you a mess.

"Well, girl. Let's read this letter. It's no point in saving it up anymore."

I got myself a little jelly jar of the whiskey Carter Lee brings me from Bodine, and went round back with the letter and a cigarillo. I set up one of Caro's little round tables and sit on the big tree stump, right in the beam from the floodlight at the back of the house. Delilah paces around me, in and out of the light, watching for bogeys in the dark. You can't hardly hear her paws touch the ground, the wolfy thing. On her hind legs she's tall as me. She's in a mood tonight. "Ain't you, D? All right, you ain't got to cut your eyes at me."

It was a funny-feeling night. It wasn't humid, but the air was heavy. Delilah had stopped pacing. My little jelly jar weighed in my hand. That thick air held me to my chair, the whole night felt like a hand pressing down on a spring. The letter was all about how Ava and this husband she got was so happy, just a bliss. But smack-dab in the middle there's this stuff about how some cat she used to know had come around to see her, after a long time gone. *No big deal!* she wrote. Huh. That's a peculiar thing to mention if it ain't worth mentioning. Something going on with her. But she won't tell what it is, or why it is. She won't tell nothing. Ever. I was just settling down to fret about it to Delilah when I heard something from the west, carried in on the wind from the direction of the river. It wasn't a sound so much as a hint one was coming. The air hissed. For a minute I thought it was me, like I was so vexed with Ava I had called up a lightning storm pure out of my mind. There be dragons. But then Delilah took off like a shot and when I turned to follow her, I saw an orange glow at the bottom of the sky. I ran to my truck.

I was there in five minutes but it was already too late. "Carter Lee, get the hose," I said. "Erma Linner, don't just stand there. Get some water somewhere! Goddamn you old niggers, do something," I said. "Why don't y'all do something?"

We got the hose turned on the fire. But by then the owls were flapping out of the trees. I felt the animal panic from the woods. For a good while I could see the lettering, BONAPARTE GENERAL, through the flames. A few minutes later headlights swung through the trees, then receded—heading down the road out of town. Everybody who belongs to Bonaparte was already standing with me, watching our store burn. It ain't hard to guess who was night riding through our place. Carter Lee saw them too. I know he did because he reached for the pistol in his holster. Nothing we could do. I think I must have been crying, but the fire was so hot the tears fried right off my face.

PHILADELPHIA

. . .

Family Day

"HONEY!" AVA SAID, sitting up in bed, wild-eyed. "Quick! Get dressed!"

It was already ten-thirty. Toussaint sat cross-legged on his bed across from his mother.

"Today is Labor Day," he said. Ava's hair was mashed in on one side. "Here they call it Family Day. There's a sign in the hallway."

Toussaint didn't like it when she slept late. It reminded him of the mornings after she and Abemi had one of their fights back in New Jersey. Those mornings he spent sitting on the floor by the bed, watching his mother curled on her side as the hours ticked by, eleven, noon, one.

Toussaint had gone to the cafeteria while she slept. Two weeks at Glenn Avenue and this was the first time he'd gone anywhere alone. He had rehearsed the routine in his mind: Take the tray from the stack, just like at school, take the fork, tell the lady what you want, hold the tray steady. Sit. Take the tray . . . But the cafeteria was heaving with people: Red sweatpants and pink foam curlers, hard rollers, black tracksuit, bright green slippers, ashy heels, mother and daughter, gold earrings, edges pressed. Duck pajamas. Toothpaste smudge on a chin. The lady at the counter asked him if he wanted toast, but when he opened his mouth he couldn't form the words. He sat in a corner choking down the rubbery eggs, but at least he didn't cry. And he didn't run away either.

"There's a barbecue," he told his mother. She had gotten out of bed at last. "They were talking about it in the cafeteria," he added when she didn't answer.

"You went to the cafeteria by yourself?" she asked.

After he'd finished his eggs, he smuggled out a piece of toast and a banana to save his mother the trip when she woke up. He pointed at the little bundle sitting on the desk.

"Nobody said anything," he said.

Toussaint peered out into the hallway as Ava brushed past him on her way to the bathroom. Family Day had got itself up and running. New faces in the corridor, most of them smiling. Music playing. Men's voices boomed out of the propped-open doors of the rooms, kids squealed at the fathers and uncles and older brothers who had come to see them. Someone set up a boom box in the playground and propped the door open so the little kids wouldn't get their fingers mashed in the metal doorframe. A teensy potbellied brown girl in an orange shirt was laughing her head off and offering the drooly leftovers of her icey pop to everyone who passed her. Toussaint smiled too.

"What a confusion," Ava said when she returned to 813 a few minutes later. "These people are a mess."

Toussaint thought it was all a little bit joyful, it was just that his mother couldn't see it.

"I think it's fun," he said.

"Oh, honey," Ava replied, shaking her head. "There's no fun here."

Toussaint opened the long windows. He sat cross-legged on top of the desk; if he held his head at the right angle, he could see the edge of the A&P parking lot across the street. He stared at the ankles of the people milling on the trampled grass just outside.

"They're barbecuing!" he said.

The hotdoghamburger holiday smell hung in the air. Earth, Wind & Fire played on the radio in the playground. *"Boogie on down, down, boogie on down,"* Toussaint mouthed. Then just like that he memoried himself all the way back to New Jersey; he could taste the spicy gumbo at his friend Paul's house, and the milk he drank after, silky creamy and cooling his mouth. Paul's mother always had a pot of something good bubbling on the stove. "Call me Jilly," she said the first time they met. "No 'Miss,' just Jilly." Jilly knew every card game there was. "You don't know how to play nothing? Not even gin rummy?" she'd asked him. "They're Holy Rollers," Paul explained. He didn't mean anything by it. He'd never been to church. Not one time. He asked if he could come with Toussaint some Sunday, just so he could see what it was like.

Jilly taught Toussaint to play blackjack. "Hopefully Jesus won't get mad," she said and winked. She was always laughing and it sounded just like the telephone ringing, bells bells bells. And she was always in a slip when he and Paul got there after school and she smelled like sweet candy, like if you could make candy out of flowers. Her hair was in pincurls and she walked from stirring the kitchen pots to changing records in the living room, back and forth, with the mascara wand in her hand. At some point late in the afternoon she put on a dress and heels and click-clacked out the door. "See you later, babies!" she called on her way out. Jilly was just like a movie. When she was gone, Paul took control of the turntable. They had the whole world to themselves. "You know Sylvester? You know Martha Wash?" Paul asked. He was three years older. He gave Toussaint an education. They played songs ten times, fifteen times till they knew every word, every break in the beat. The house smelled of Jilly's cooking. The setting sun cut the living room into gold and shadow; music thumped in the floors.

Family Day was loud as if it was happening right in their room. Toussaint wondered if people were dancing out in the hallways. "You can do the hustle to just about anything," Jilly had said one afternoon. Toussaint didn't know if his mother could do the hustle. He thought she used to know—before Abemi she probably knew. Maybe she had done the hustle with his father, but Toussaint couldn't picture Cass dancing. Like, Magneto wouldn't dance. *"Aaand gliiide, like a seven forty-seven. And looose yourself—"* he sang under his breath.

Ava sat herself down at the desk with one of those stupid coloring books. *His* coloring books. Not that he wanted them, but still.

"What are you going to do with that?" he asked.

"These gnats!" she said, waving her hand around.

There were only gnats because she hadn't eaten the banana he'd brought her that morning.

"Close that window, honey. It's just letting the bugs in."

"But . . ."

She didn't reply. She was in one of her moods. She was like a big tall mountain with clouds so thick around it you couldn't see the top half. It was cold up there behind those clouds—on a real mountain, that is, which Toussaint knew from geography class. If you tried to climb one, you'd have felt like you were the only person on earth. You'd have felt so lonely you could die.

Renee's Rounds

RENEE WAS ON HER WAY to 813 to ask them to join the Family Day cookout. She was pissed. She wasn't even supposed to be on duty. Of course, 813 were the only ones who hadn't come. That poor skinny boy was probably beside himself. She and Melvin had been sitting at the back table of the cafeteria that morning when the child came in on his own. Snuck out some breakfast for the mother. Melvin hadn't even noticed till Renee said something. Dumbass. He's the whole reason they say niggers ain't shit.

Anyway, the little boy was shaking like a leaf. And that mother of his! Sending that child because she was too missy-miss to come in there herself. "I mean, Melvin," Renee had said. "They end up in here because they trifling in some kind of way. She musta did something."

"Mmm-hmm," Melvin said.

"You know I don't judge. But the point is, she's walking around like she's too good for everybody."

"Uh-huh," Melvin said.

"She just scared and trying to cover it up being snobby. Everybody makes mistakes. You ain't gotta have a stick up your ass."

"I know that's right."

Melvin wondered why she cared so much. Renee was always getting all worked up. He tucked into his pancakes from the McDonald's on Stenton Avenue. Nice and hot. He didn't think much about these people in here. It was just a job. Better than being, say, a CO or the dude that drives the Brink's truck. And it had its benefits. "How you doing, Belinda," he called to a woman who waved as she walked by. Yeah, the job had its perks. Renee frowned at him. Anyhow, that woman with the son was too skinny for his taste. And why she was wearing that Afro in 19 and 85 he would never know. She obviously had good hair! An all right ass though. As for scared. Well, they all scared unless they crazy. Shit, they didn't have no place to live. Damn, Renee.

"Miss Carson?" Renee knocked on the door of 813. "Miss Carson? You in there?" She knocked again. "Miss Carson?" Renee was getting about sick of this. She *could* just open the door if she wanted. She had a key.

"Miss Carson!"

"Yes?" Ava said in a stiff, uppity voice. Who the hell said, "Yes"? Like she was Alexis Colby.

"Uh, yeah. Miss Carson, we got games for the kids on the playground. And burgers and stuff."

"Yes?"

"Everybody is welcome!" Renee got a little high in the octaves when she was uncomfortable. Some people just make you feel so put off, even from behind a closed door. "Come on out!" she said brightly.

"No thank you," Ava said.

"Family Day till five!"

"No thank you," Ava said again.

Renee went on down the hallway. That's what I get for trying. She had a soft spot for the kids. Wasn't their fault the mothers landed them in this shit. She just knew that little boy wanted to come out and have a hamburger. She could feel it through the door. Why couldn't that woman see how easy it would be to give the poor thing a little bit of relief? Just for a damn hour!

Then she spotted that delinquent Tamar bouncing his ball against the wall at the end of the corridor. "Boy!" Renee shouted, but by the time she got up there he had run outside. He got about three years fore they put his ass right in jail. Renee shook her head.

In the Nursery

"YOU SEE HOW a little persistence pays off, Miss Carson," Miss Simmons said. Miss Simmons had called Ava to her office to inform her she'd gotten a job interview. "It's clear you are a nicer kind of woman. I can see you don't have some of the problems others come here with." She leaned forward and lowered her voice. "Some families come and go from here two or three times." Ava knew Miss Simmons was hustling her with all this "between you and me" jazz, like they were in it together. But Ava sure was smiling, feeling like she was better than the rest of Glenn Avenue. A cut above! Ha. Today's nails were burgundy. She must get them done two or three times a week, Ava thought—never chipped or scratched or dull. Miss Simmons smiled a benevolent close-mouthed smile. Her bow collar was white as salvation. "Bell Telephone," she said. "Very promising." She offered Ava a peppermint and sent her on her way.

They'd been at Glenn Avenue for five weeks. The interview was in eight days. Ava could get that job, easy. After a couple of paychecks, she'd rent a room. In a few months she'd get an apartment and all of this would be done with.

When she got back to 813, she emptied the suitcases and garbage bag looking for something she could wear to the interview. Her skirts and blouses were wrinkled and smelled of plastic. Nothing hung right. She tried one dowdy outfit after the next until there was nothing left. "It's like they're somebody else's," she said, looking down at the little heap of church-lady clothes she had bought over the years with Abemi. Mid-calf-length skirts, tops with Peter Pan collars. She suddenly hated the whole matronly pile of them. Ava stood in front of the mirror above the little sink; the knobby outline of her throat rippled when she swallowed. The cross Abemi had given her on their second anniversary glinted. She felt like a hole in a pocket, saggy and losing bits.

Toussaint came in looking freshly showered.

"You didn't go to our secret bathroom, did you?" Ava lowered her voice, as if there were someone else in the room who might hear her. "By yourself? In the middle of the day?"

"I used the family bathroom."

"The family—Toussaint!"

Ava had found a private bathroom just the week before, near the corridor with the administrative offices. She was looking for someplace to sit by herself for a few minutes and there it was—with a busted lock on the door and a sign that said UTILITY CLOSET. Inside was a whole bathroom—sink, toilet, shower stall. Not sparkling but clean enough. Clean in comparison. So what if they had to go before seven a.m. or late in the night.

"We don't have to use the family bathrooms anymore," Ava said.

"I know. I just wanted to take a shower. At a normal time. Not sneaking around and—"

"Okay. Okay."

He sat on his bed flipping through his comics. Ava tried not to stare at his feet. He'd get athlete's foot from that bathroom. She sighed, louder than she meant to, and tried to turn her attention back to the pile of grandma clothes.

"School on Monday," he said.

They were already weeks into the school year and she'd only just gotten him registered. Taft Elementary, it was called. It looked okay from the outside, but when she got in there the paint was peeling in the hall by the principal's office and two scruffy-looking boys were fighting in the hallway. Her baby didn't know anything about that. She didn't want him to have to learn. Now she thought, I'll get this job and he won't be in that place for more than a couple of months.

"Yeah, baby," she said. "I know."

Toussaint let out one of his exhales.

"Why do you have all the clothes out?" he asked.

Ava thought she'd save the job as a surprise for him. She shrugged and began folding the clothes back into the cases. Her reflection flashed in the mirror above the sink as she moved.

"I don't look any different, do I?" she said. "Than before, I mean. Do you think I do?"

"Everything is different," Toussaint said.

Ava set off on one of her walks around the building. She'd stopped trying to get Toussaint to go with her. Five minutes in and he started complaining like they were crossing the Sahara. It was too hot. He hated the Easter-colored hallways. They *were* ugly. Each long corridor of rooms was painted a different pastel: lavender, baby blue, yellow, pink. Theirs was mint green. The hallways extended from a central area in the front with all the administrative offices and the nurse and Miss Simmons and the pay phones near the front door. Ava passed their green hallway family bathroom. She didn't know why Toussaint would go in there. It wasn't safe. Anybody might be in there. You couldn't take off your shoes, even in the showers, especially in the showers. She shuddered and headed toward the front of the building.

At the top of the blue corridor, she checked to make sure the secret bathroom was still unlocked. Then, before anyone saw her, she turned down the lavender corridor toward the nursery at the end. A girl sat in there dozing with a baby on her lap. Ava shook her head. What do you do with a tiny baby in a place like this? Babies need washing. They need someplace clean; they need soft things. Ava had lived in a one-bedroom on Bouvier Street when she was pregnant with Toussaint. She was alone. In the sixth month her blood pressure shot up and the doctor put her on bed rest. She slept and woke round the clock so that the two states were not quite distinguishable and her dreams were like thoughts and her thoughts like dreams. Sometimes when she woke up her friend Connie was in the room with her. Mostly there wasn't anyone. The great bulk of her floated away from the world like a calving glacier. Bye bye, Ava. Bye bye.

The girl in the nursery couldn't have been more than twenty, plump and soft and nearly as innocent-looking as the new baby in her lap. Ava figured the girl had landed in here because she didn't have any high school and some man had done her wrong. Girl, she thought, you have to keep your wits about you. You can get yourself a real bastard, and keep right on with him until you can't anymore. Or maybe the girl had one of those men who turned her out so hard she was nothing but ash in the end. You couldn't recover from men like that. You just had to get away from them. Take it from me, Ava thought. She wasn't cured from Cass. Never would be.

The girl and her baby slept on. She looked a little doomed. Life would grind her up slowly and be done with her. Ava figured most of the people at Glenn Avenue were like that. They were a certain type. Clear as day Ava got a picture in her mind of that girl in the days before she got to the shelter: late at night in a bus station with her little baby in her arms. Then she realized she was remembering the night she and Toussaint spent in the bus depot in New Jersey the night before they came to Philadelphia.

They had to get out of Glenn Avenue. Job interview or not. Abemi's rages or not. They couldn't stay here. Nothing tender could survive this place. She'd call Abemi and make amends; she'd fix it up with him.

The baby shifted and snuffled in her sleep; she wore a yellow bonnet with ducks on it. Ava crossed the nursery; she reached down and stroked the baby's cheek, once, twice. She wanted to kiss her little head, but that would have been too much so she turned and was gone just before the mother woke.

Be the Spider, Not the Fly

"WE COULD TRY COUNSELING. With Pastor Ralph," Ava said.

She sat next to Abemi in his car in the A&P parking lot. The Cadillac gleamed. Abemi had wiped it down that morning. He ran his hands along the dashboard and kept his eyes on all the come and go at the big sad-looking building across the street. They were living over there, she'd told him. That's what happened to us when you threw us out, she told him. She wanted to come back. After everything she'd done. After *she* left, not him. Abemi wasn't going to give her the satisfaction of looking her in the eye. But he stole a couple of sidelong glances. She had a feral look about her. She fidgeted in the passenger seat and kept turning to look out the window. He wasn't sure if she was scared of being eaten or if she was scanning for prey.

The truth is, he didn't much want to go to counseling. The truth is, after the shock wore off, he was relieved she was gone. He had been good to her, or at least he'd tried to be, but he didn't think she could say the same about how she treated him. His buddy Cliff had warned him. Before they got married, he said, "You got a handful there," and laughed and slapped him on the back. But then he got serious: "Watch yourself—right, man? Be the spider, not the fly." Abemi missed Toussaint. He could help the boy. Anybody could see Toussaint wanted a father and a normal life, but Ava wouldn't let him have either one.

Abemi wished he hadn't noticed how pretty she was in her wild state, even if her hair was one side high—those dark cat eyes and toasted-peanut skin, and the high cheekbones with the dip beneath where a little roundness used to be. He sat in the driver's seat with his arms folded, waiting. She had called him, after all. Had been calling him. She'd left him a callback number with no explanation, and every time he called her somebody different answered the phone. He figured it was a boardinghouse, or somewhere she was shacking up with *him*. She hadn't even told him they were in a shelter till the day before.

Ava hadn't told him much about Cass. She made it seem like he was a blip, a mistake she didn't like to dwell on and was glad to put behind her. He had been some kind of doctor, Abemi knew that much. And he was a Panther. He'd disappeared years ago then showed up, out of the blue (so Ava claimed) two months ago. Belched up out of the past like he had made time sick in its stomach. Leroy told Abemi all about it. He was a good neighbor, Leroy—kept an eye on things when Abemi was at work. He told him Cass didn't look like much. Raggle-taggle, were his words. But then he said something strange. He said he was so shabby you couldn't hardly feel that pull he had about him. Like there was more to him, like if he cleaned himself up, he might be somebody.

She sure put one over on me, Abemi thought. She sure did play me. Maybe he had lost his temper a couple of times, but he never hit her. Forty-three wasn't too old to have a baby. People had babies at that age. Two years of trying to get pregnant and the whole time she was sneaking those pills. Everything about her was a lie or a secret. Didn't hardly speak to her mother. She didn't know much of anything about her father. He had tried to help her get to the bottom of that too. But Ava never cared what was real and what wasn't. She would make up a story and live in it and screw everybody else.

"I don't know how Cass got the address," Ava was saying. "I hadn't spoken to him for eight years."

This mess again. "Before you said you hadn't spoken to him in five years," Abemi said.

"I didn't say that."

"That's what you told me, Ava. I'm just telling you what you told me."

She kept her eyes trained on the shelter across the street. Her jaw clenched tighter and stayed that way. A proper-looking old lady with her hair done nice looked into the car and frowned at them on her way into the A&P. Ava rolled up the window.

"Well, look at this. Here I am," she said. "The kind of woman that fights with a man in a car in the middle of the day."

"Nobody's fighting, Ava. I'm not fighting. Are you fighting?" She wanted to, he could see she was squaring up for it.

"I don't know what good counseling would do if you keep on lying," Abemi said. "You did this, Ava. You fucked up." He never cursed like that. It felt good coming out of his mouth. "You out here with some Negro that already left you one time."

"I already told you I haven't seen him—"

Her eyes narrowed like she was thinking something that made her mad, sitting there like she had a metal rod for a backbone. She had been angry the entire three years they were married. Look at her, still mad now.

"Let me ask you something, Ava. What'd you marry me for?"

Abemi rubbed his hand across his forehead. He was suddenly very tired. He wanted to go home, back to his quiet house in New Jersey where he felt safe. Yes, that was it. Now that the place was empty of them—no, of *her*—he was safe.

"I mean, because you don't . . . I don't think you much liked being married. Maybe you didn't even like me. Maybe you like this other cat better. I don't know, but if we're just going to sit here arguing about something you don't even want, what's the point?"

"Look at that building across the street," she said, pointing at Glenn Avenue. "You want to know what it's like in there?"

Abemi shook his head. He didn't want to go around in circles with her.

"I don't want to play games with you," Abemi said. "I came to talk to you about Toussaint. He doesn't have to, you know . . . I can take care of him for a while if that's . . ."

"What?" Ava turned to him. "My son? You talking about my son?"

"He could come anytime he wanted—"

"Have you been talking to my son? Did you talk to my son?"

"I'm offering to help him, Ava! It would help you too while you . . . while you get yourself together."

"My son doesn't need your help."

"Somebody has to think of the boy. You sure the hell aren't taking care of him. Look where you got him living!"

Ava reached over and scratched his face, clawed him down the cheek deep enough he felt the skin tear. For a fraction of a second both of them were too stunned to do anything. The scratches on Abemi's face welled with blood. Then he was at her neck, hands around her throat, her head wobbling. Her face bashed into the Cadillac's window. Once, twice, three times. He had not meant to . . . He let her go. She looked almost impressed. Then the wild in her came out and she was punching him with both hands. He got hold of her wrists and she thrashed like a trapped animal, like somebody in a straitjacket. Like somebody who ought to be in a straitjacket. When the tussling was done, they were both breathing like junkyard dogs. Her face was swelling. He reached over her and opened the passenger door. "Get out," he said. "Get out of my car."

In her hurry to hop out—she didn't even look sorry, she looked like she wanted to dig his eyes out with her fingernails—her sandal caught on the floor mat. She tumbled out of the car and onto the asphalt. The nice old lady looked out through the glass front of the A&P and shook her head.

Abemi pulled off slowly so he wouldn't hurt her. His hands were sweaty and slippery on the wheel. When he looked back through the rearview mirror she was still down there with her hands in her lap, down on the ground with the soda cans and cigarette butts, tears dripping onto her shirt. He almost went back. They could go get Toussaint and they'd all go back to James Creek together. But that was just a fantasy. "I've had enough," he said out loud and eased the car onto Tulpehocken, then Lincoln Drive, and onto I-676 toward home.

Cornbread Rat

THE DAY AFTER THE FIGHT, a bruise spread around Ava's right eye—livid purple wings opened extravagantly along the side of her face from above her blood-red eye to her cheekbones. Her face ached with the effort of talking or moving her head side to side, or yawning or chewing. The ache was so bad Ava sent Toussaint to the A&P where he spent a dollar she couldn't spare on a bag of frozen peas. The cool felt so good against her face it made her weep. "Why you crying, Ma?" Toussaint said. "Does it hurt?"

"No. No, it doesn't hurt right now, honey."

He sat on the bed watching her from behind his eyes. That was a Dutchess phrase. She used to say: Look at you crouched behind yourself staring at me like a kicked dog. You give me chills right on my spine, she'd say. Ava had told Toussaint she got the bruise when she fell on a wet floor in the hallway. He didn't ask her anything more about it, so she didn't ask him if he'd spoken to Abemi. She said, only, "Things are back how they used to be—right, baby? You and me. Just you and me."

Ava took to reading some of Dutchess's old letters in the blurry midafternoon hours when she couldn't get herself out of bed and Toussaint was still at school.

This man you got seems like a sulker. You married him so I guess you figure you stuck with him? To my mind you can always just walk out a door. There's nothing worse than a sulking man. What happened to that one you were going with years ago? I think you said he was a doctor. Seem like you liked him. You run him off? You don't give a damn about none of them nohow. They just something to be mad about.

On she went, grouchy and chastising. Even so, the letters satisfied, like picking a scab. Pick pick pick, but sooner than later Ava would break the skin and bleed all over the place. And plus, who was Dutchess to pretend she was the kind of mother who *advised*. "But the thing is," Ava said aloud in her empty room, "I'm out of options." Her chest tightened when she thought of going back to Bonaparte with Toussaint—back to Dutchess and her 'shine and her dogs and shotguns. Ava could smell the Nu Nile and chicory coffee smell of her. I want my mama, Ava thought. She tried to muster a chuckle at her bitter little joke.

Dutchess quit mothering when Pop died; after they killed him she willed every trace of tenderness right out of herself. How many times had Ava crept into her mother's room looking for a hand to hold when she was a girl? How many times had she said, I'm scared. Or, Why won't you look at me anymore? "Dry your face, girl!" Dutchess would say. "You ain't doing nothing but wetting your dress front." Dutchess left her daughter's care and comfort to their neighbors and the family dogs.

Ava hadn't told her she was pregnant. In the final days of her pregnancy she'd very nearly called her. She was bedridden, with nobody but the hospital nurses for company. But no matter how she rehearsed the conversation in her mind, it always came down to Dutchess saying something like: A baby! You must be kidding. You can't even keep an apartment long enough to get the stove dirty. Mean.

Maybe mean was the best she could do. Well, but. Too late for mending fences. Dutchess was who she was. She couldn't be trusted with a new soul. Ava knew she'd have found a way to get to

Toussaint, and she'd've hurt him without even trying. She couldn't risk her boy. Toussaint was a new dawn. He undid the whole past, whatever came before him couldn't touch Ava anymore.

A bleach smell seeped in under the door of 813. Sooner or later maybe every woman ends up with nobody but her children for comfort—children who are already slipping away, children on the verge of being old enough to know you can't save them from any-thing. A few weeks after they put Caro in the ground Dutchess lay down and didn't get up again—she smoked morning till night, the coffee can next to the bed overflowing with half-smoked cigarillos, match burns on the hook rug. She stopped writing songs, stopped getting food or cooking it, stopped bringing in wood or boiling water, stopped leaving the house.

That was the winter Ava got her period. Everything was uncom-fortable, everything ached and swelled, inside and out. She'd come home from school in need of a refuge, or at least somewhere com-fortable, but the living room was too cold for her to take her coat off, leaves and twigs banked in the corners, ribbons of Dutchess's cigarillo smoke hung in the air like Ava had entered an underworld. The slop pots under the bed stank, worse because she didn't know what to do with the rags from between her legs. Dutchess laid on the bed submerged under the sea of blankets, with her face turned to the window where the weak winter light came in, headscarf slipped back off her forehead.

"Mama?"

Ava sat on the edge of the bed. "Mama, I brought an apple from school. We can share it?" Dutchess did not turn her face from the window. "What's out there, Mama?" Fallow fields, amber in the setting sun. The grandfather clock ticked in the hallway. Ava stretched across the bottom of the bed and turned on her side so she could rest her chin on the blankets through which, layers deep, her mother's knobby knees made little peaks. They lived entirely in that single bedroom. Sometimes Dutchess would rest her yel-lowed fingers on top of Ava's head. "You know you was born in a room with a bed just like this one," she said. "With a hook rug on the floor? Nobody around till the landlady came with a pot of warm water to wipe you down once you were already out and screaming."

One cold afternoon Ava dug into the closet for the fur coats, two of them if you can believe it, that Dutchess ordered a couple of years earlier in one of her electric weeks when she hardly slept and scrubbed the house at three a.m. Caro let her keep the coats. It's just money, he said. What a pair they were. Dutchess catatonic, both of them hollow-cheeked and stinking in the leaf-blown house, wrapped in matching fox coats.

There was a little fatback and some cornbread on the kitchen table, the last of everything. Ava was dazed with hunger. When a rat hopped onto the table and went at the cornbread she sat on the bed and watched it through the doorway. Scraggly and beast hungry, the color of dry-skin ankles. When Ava roused herself to rush at it, it lifted its nasty head and showed its yellow teeth, its whole body tensed like it was going to leap from the table and sink those teeth into her neck.

"Mama!" she called, backing away. "Mama, a rat got in from the barn!"

"Mama! It's a rat eating the cornbread I saved!"

"Mama, it's the last we have."

Dutchess raised herself on her elbows and scooted forward slowly so she could see through the doorway to the kitchen table. She gripped the edge of the blanket like she was going to throw it off. Ava held her breath. Dutchess was going to get up from that bed at last and smash the rat's brain out. But she fell back onto the pillow and turned to the window. Tears brimmed and streamed down her cheeks and kept on streaming. She wouldn't get up no matter how Ava shouted. She jumped on the bed and shook Dutchess by the shoulders. She whipped the covers away but Dutchess didn't move, just sat there with her knees drawn to her chest, shivering in the cold.

After that, there wasn't any point to any of it. No point in trying to rouse Dutchess, who maybe thought the two of them should die along with Caro. No point in shooing the rat, there wasn't any more food for it to eat anyway. No point in doing anything at all except resting. Ava was so tired and she was so cold. She curled next to Dutchess on the bed and pulled the blankets around them. The afternoon sun gave way to dusk and the room darkened. Ava fell into a woozy sleep.

A steady rapping on the door woke her. She bolted upright. Dutchess lay still next to her, murmuring in her sleep. In the months before Caro was killed he hid out in the woods half the time. When he returned to Sundown Road at odd hours to eat or bathe or sleep, the three of them were so happy to be together they piled in the warm feather bed for the few hours till he slipped out again. He always arrived in the deep night, tapping lightly on the door so Ava and Dutchess knew it was him. Ava leapt out of bed. "Pop?" she called, running through the living room. "Pop?"

The porch was empty. The road too. The bare branches of the chokecherry swayed in the wind above Miss Memma's house down the road. Ava was peaceful and cold, like a drowning person who had stopped fighting. She wasn't even shivering and she felt a pleasant warmth around her ankles. She looked down to find a pot sitting on the porch, so close she'd have kicked it over if she'd taken another step. She carried it inside and lifted the lid. Chicken and dumplings. Till her last breath Ava would remember the soft carrots and the chew of the dumplings and the hot salty gravy. She ate it sitting on the bed next to her mother, one spoonful for Ava and one for Dutchess. Her mother opened her mouth like a baby bird.

The cornbread rat came the next day trying to steal up to the pot of dumplings. This time Ava ran to the kitchen. She picked up the big cast iron frying pan with both hands and swung with all her strength. The rat squelched then crunched beneath it. She smashed it till it was a broad flat pulp. She hit it till its brain and guts seeped into the floorboards. The spot dried dark brown and never came out entirely, even after many bleachings.

. . .

Ava folded her mother's letters and put them back into the suitcase. She looked in the little mirror above the sink. She was so dizzy she swayed on her feet. She needed to rest, just a little while. She'd just close her eyes for a few minutes before tidying the room so it was nice when Toussaint came in from school. Just a few minutes.

"Oh! Oh, baby, I'm sorry," she said, some hours later when Toussaint shook her awake. He had fear in his eyes. Ma, he said very quietly, then turned away from her toward the window.

BONAPARTE

· · ·

WE NEVER WERE SCARED of crackers in Bonaparte but I guess Nip and them want to start now. Well, not Dutchess Carson. The white people wrote about the fire in their little Bodine paper: "Bonaparte Blaze Sparks Insurance Fraud Investigation." How you like that? And trying to be funny on top of it. Bonaparte smelled burnt for two weeks. It's just us to clean up the rubble, so most of it's still there. We was in the middle of hauling some of it away when the insurance came down our road. I thought they were Mormons—young blond boys with short-sleeve shirts look like they just finished drinking glasses of Ovaltine.

Me and Carter Lee and everybody stood around doing our best Old Negro People act. Turns out the insurance policy was lapsed for more than a decade. We nodded and scratched our heads like, "Say what now? Lap-sed. What dat mean?" Then the head white boy in charge says, "We will need to investigate the false claim." Oh no, motherfucker. My dumb darky went right out the window. I said, "With all due respect we never filed any claim. We made a request, in writing, to find out the state of our coverage. We have a copy of the letter." It's so easy to shock white folks, all you got to do is speak in full sentences. They went on their way after that.

About a week later I looked through my curtain to find Memma and Nip and Erma Linner out front looking glum. Could be cause it's hard to find room on the porch with all the trumpet vine and wisteria. And the bees! I don't care to make it too easy for folks to come to my door. But there they were, the men stooping to keep clear of the hanging pots and Erma Linner batting away the clematis swinging in her face.

When I got out there Nip says, "Don't nobody own that land, Dutchess." Nip has breath like every grave that was ever dug. And don't know what he's talking about. The town of Bonaparte, that's all us standing here, plus Carter Lee, put that land in Marlin Duke's name and when he died it went to his son, Theodore Duke. "Naw," says grim reaper Nip. "It don't belong to nobody. Marlin ain't have no will, and come to find out Teddy died up North, no kids. So that land don't belong to nobody." Duchess shook her head. Little Teddy. Goddamn. He was a sweet boy, used to say he was gon grow up and keep bees like his daddy.

Memma says, "They got us now."

I can't tell you how bad I want to drown that woman in the river. She has seven children. Look at that, Caro, I used to say every time she littered again—every one of them babies got more sense than their mama and they can't even chew.

"What the hell they got us on, Memma? They ain't wipe all Marlin's family off the face of the earth. The acres belong to somebody. Whoever it is ain't bothered about it so we just go on and take care of it like we always do."

Nobody said the obvious about heir property and tax sale. I was grateful for that.

"We need to track down whoever owns it in Cincinnati—ain't that where they went?—then we'll be all right," I said. Memma and Nip just shook their heads and turned around looking hangdog. Erma Linner said, "I don't know, Dutchess. I don't know." She gave me the eye and went on away too.

Since the fire me and Delilah haven't been ourselves. Now and again, Delilah comes to the back porch with a rabbit in her mouth for us. But she's less and less for hunting and I'm less and less for gutting and skinning. The hot gas insides of animals, the smell of the life under their skin, turns my stomach lately. I don't know why. I used to be like the panther. I hardly cooked the meat, when we had such luxuries. Everybody would wrinkle up their face and say,

Why ain't'cha just chomp the cow while she was still standing in the field.

Everybody round here, except Carter Lee who looks after my bank deposits in Bodine, believes I have the cash to buy that land. They think I had a grand career on all the high stages. I guess I helped them around to that version of things. Truth is, I wasn't never a great singer. Sure did love it though. Most of the little bit of money I got is from songs I wrote. It's still a few royalties coming in but not much to spare after I pay the taxes on this place. I hardly ever get commissions for songs anymore, which is just as well because I can't write nothing these days. It's like chasing the far brightness in the sky, I can see it but when I get there it's already dark. Last night I played "Mary Don't You Weep" till I had the chills down my neck. And Delilah! She's half wolf and half witch so she got to howling.

The only thing saves me from what they call malaise is thinking on Ava. I had decided I wasn't going to write back to her last letter. I don't know why it hurt my feelings so much. It wasn't much different from her usual BS: never asks about me or this place, don't tell nothing about herself. She's in a rage at me. She has been since they murdered Caro. She wants somebody to blame, and not the untouchable somebodies who killed him. She wants an up close and personal somebody she can hurt to make up for her hurt. I keep on hoping she'll work it out. She don't want to sever ties completely, much as she acts like it. Take this dumb letter she just sent, anybody can see she's trying to tell me the marriage ain't going too good. She was always more susceptible to other people's bad nature than she realized. Still, she got a nerve on her, don't she? Damn near twenty-five years since she been here, and more than thirty since Caro died. She doesn't know the fields are mostly kudzu. The asphalt we laid on the roads around town is all broke up and the rainwater puddles breed mosquitoes big as hummingbirds. It's parts of our woods so grown over with pole vine it's like the green that used to be is taking the place back. Like it's turning back into Eden.

Ain't seen Carter Lee for a minute now. He got a good head on his shoulders; he was probably hiding out, weighing up the situation with the store. But I didn't go looking for him right away because I didn't want to hear it, to tell you the truth. *Don't you bring me no bad news.* Like they said in *The Wiz*. I went on my night walks like always; skirting our burnt-out store.

Used to be we sold our Bonaparte Preserves there. Blackberry, pear, orange, and muscadine. We canned it in our canning house down the road and sent it out all over Mississippi and Alabama. People used to drive from Montgomery to buy our preserves and shop in our store with no signs saying who could come in and who couldn't. I put up a sign that said Niggers Welcome but Marlin's wife Ornetta made me take it down. She was a good woman so I said okay. I know it's no point getting moony-eyed over the bygone years of Bonaparte Cooperative Commerce. It's all over and ain't coming back. Plus, it's 1985. We can go to the grocery store now. Once upon a time we grew everything we put in our mouths. Everything from the collards to the chicken legs was raised by our own hands. That work'll break your goddamn back. Here's to the Piggly Wiggly. I guess.

It takes about five minutes to cross through what's left of the center of Bonaparte. All that's left is the burnt-out store, the church, our old townhall, the schoolhouse, a little one-room shack where we did all our bartering and trading, and the Shed. We keep everything with a fresh, or fresh-ish, coat of white paint. Since the fire I make a point of walking with my shotgun. We still got a couple guns stored in the Shed. They're rusted out but we leave them there for our memory.

Once you get out of town the road forks: to the east it runs a few miles past a dozen or so houses left to the possums and the wind, and on through the wood that leads to my place. To the west a mile of asphalt in chunks spits you out onto a slope of high river grass and frog song. Used to be most nights you could see across to the lights in Bodine, but now half the time there's a curtain of mist that rises up over the middle of the river, some spots thick as cotton balls, other places thin like gauze, all of it pearling and shimmering and breaking apart and coming together again, so the white people's shoreline is now you see it, now you don't. I've sat here the night through a couple of times, watching it knit and unknit itself. Silly as it is, round dawn I got a little nervous it wouldn't burn off. I don't like new weather, which is a reasonable position—no such thing as new weather, right? Delilah doesn't care for it either, she paces the shore, growling, ears back, like now. Tonight it looks more solid than last time I saw it, which gives me a twitchy feeling so I check my rifle's loaded and walk on.

A mile or so south on our side of the river a long stretch of vacation cabins line the riverfront. A paved road with more houses turns inland for another couple of miles. Heaven's Gate, they call it. Thirty sameish-looking houses the white people bought from Progress Corp., more on the way. All that used to be Bonaparte land. And how did Progress get hold of it? I can't stomach too much talking about which Negroes sold which acres for what chump change, or had it stole from them in tax sale, so never mind. The white people don't come down to our part of the river, don't speak to us, don't hunt in our woods. That's fine by me but it does add to this feeling I have that Bonaparte is disappearing. I don't just mean the land they took, I mean like it's actually disappearing. I mentioned it to Carter Lee one time. He looked at me and started quoting Lamentations.

We got people buried all along the riverfront, even way down by the white people. Not a real cemetery with headstones and such, that's up the other end of Bonaparte, on the road to my place. By the river it's just a long skinny boneyard, maybe twenty or thirty graves with simple wooden crosses we used to change out every few years when they got too weather-beaten. We'd go down there and sing over them, tend to the jessamine trellis the old people put up long time ago. Progress bulldozed right over it. You can't tell me those white people ain't got nigger ghosts all up in their wall-to-wall carpet. And think of the poor Negroes, their resting place overrun with white folks, like they ain't had enough of them when they were alive. One time when Ava was little, she said she hoped they had Jim Crow in heaven cause she didn't want to spend eternity too close to the tall people. I had to pop her in the mouth of course, but it was a fair request. Then, heh heh, Caro told her white people didn't go to heaven.

There's still a few graves left down at our end, near Jimmy Mackie's old fish shack at the edge of the tree line where the woods end and the land slopes down to the water's edge. I like to sit down there. That shack leans and is beat to hell, but you can still make out a few streaks of Jimmy's orange paint. The old picnic table where we used to eat our fried catfish sandwiches has held up pretty good. When Bonaparte was plantation, they buried people in any secret spot they could find. You can always tell a gravesite by the vegetation—blood-red pomegranates big as grapefruits, wild daffodils all year round, jasmine bushes. None of the bad stuff, no milkweed or nightshade, though I guess plants are only bad if you do bad with them. There's a happy feeling in those places. If it's a clear night me and Delilah can see the ferry lights twinkling on the Bodine side, and behind that the blue-black tree line curved around their harbor. The spirits come tipping out from wherever they are and sit around us like cats.

They bring little bits of the lives they lived and open them up in front of me, Technicolor and 3D: Riding in the back of a truck holding on to your hat on the way to somebody's do. Leather-smell Sunday shoes in crumpled blue tissue paper. Hard stuff too: a woman alone with sleeping babies set up next to the window with a shotgun, her man hired out way down in Mobile. Starlight, a cup of chicory gone cold. That one could have been mine. Caro was gone so many nights till he was gone for good.

Me and him used to go rowing at night, way over to the other side of the river, past Bodine, and raid the hatchery at Talbyville. It was so many fish they didn't really need to keep a count of every one—but white folks *is,* so they posted a guard who was sleep most of the time. It's they own fault anyway. They dammed upriver and after that the fishing wasn't the same down by us. Anyway, we'd fill our boat and head back to Bonaparte. Sometimes we stayed out too late and went from feeling like it was us two against the world to feeling like we were the last people left on earth. Just when we couldn't take it one more minute, when our arms were cramped and teeth chattering, the boat skimmed around the bend and the Light came into view, leaping orange against the pitch black.

One hundred years one of us lit the fire at dusk and tended it till daybreak so anybody who belonged to Bonaparte could get back home over water. When me and Caro caught sight of it, we rowed harder and flew across the river. Whoever was keeping the Light that night would splash out to meet us and haul in the bass and crappie. We took a couple for ourselves, set some aside to salt and dry, and left the rest with Jimmy for a big fry-up next day. Off me and Caro went down the road, bones aching tired, his arm around my shoulder and mine around his waist. Ava at home sleep on a bed of hunting dogs.

Bygone years. Now it's now, which has a flimsy feeling to it. Caro is gone. The Light is decades dark. That's enough, I tell these greedy old spirits. Sometimes it's too much sitting out here with them grabbing at my ankles. Too damp and too chilly and too much memory, so I creak on up from the picnic table and turn inland toward Carter Lee's post office. It's just one room, but he's always in there late night with the envelopes stacked in neat piles and his table light glowing.

It's a long walk from Jimmy's. Me and Delilah go back through the turpentine woods and out again to the main road, back in through Erma Linner's grazing fields before the clearing on the other side of our main street. By the time I see Carter Lee's PO in the distance I been out so long it feels like I have been exiled from the human race. Delilah takes off running and is swallowed up in the dark soon as she gets past the beam from my flashlight. Then she doubles back to check on me and races out again, in and out of the darkness. I must have come up on Carter Lee's lit-up window a hundred times after a hundred walks but it's always a mercy. I wrote a lot of songs trying to put that coming in from the dark feeling into music. I don't believe I have got it right yet.

You know what it is about Ava? She don't know how to come in from the cold. She's always out somewhere looking in. It makes me sorry. Makes me mad too. She thinks she needs what she don't need, and don't need what she does. Stubborn.

When she nine, ten years old she was so skinny she looked like a spoon, but she had hands like a grown man, callused, with raggedy nails. She spent all her time hanging out back in Caro's shop or out in the woods, pulling half-dead rabbits out of traps with her bare hands. She came home scratched and bloody to the elbows. Things in her pockets little girls ain't have no business with—John the Conqueror, dragon's blood. I used to whup her for it. Caro said they was just trinkets—but he knew and I knew better. Some things are not suited for dabbling. She come in the house at supper and find us waiting for her at the table. She used to look at me like I was a cow, dumb as air. Caro'd say, "Sit on down there, gal." When she told him she wasn't hungry he said, "Well, that's really not the point." Burrs in her hair. She'd push the fried potatoes around on her plate till I told her to go to bed. You couldn't give her an at-home feeling, she wouldn't take it.

I get up to Carter Lee's and tap on the window. Delilah is already out front, huffing like she's mad I only got two legs instead of four. I do believe she thinks human beings are a little pitiful. A wave of warmth rushes out to me when Carter Lee opens the door. The place smells like coffee and newspapers. Carter Lee pours me a cup from his thermos—thick as sap and bitter.

"You got some of these," he says and hands me some letters. Lord, let there be checks! We sit there quiet. Delilah whimpers and settles herself on the floor. Carter Lee does his sorting, even though it's hardly nothing to sort these days.

"These too." He slides me a letter from Progress. "Two this time. Everybody got em." He frowns. "We gonna have trouble about that land," he says.

"Yeah."

"Bad."

Carter Lee runs out of envelopes to sort so we sit looking out his single window at the sky graying up around the edges.

"I don't know how you drink this shit," I say.

Carter Lee lets out one of his snorts that passes for a laugh, just a little puff of air, and tips some more of his coffee sludge into my cup.

"You hear something?" I say.

"Just your old bones turning to dust."

"That's your bones you hearing."

Delilah lifts her head and sniffs the air.

"You sure you ain't heard nothing?"

That time he just looks at me over the top of his glasses. I sit up there a long time with Carter Lee, Delilah snoozing. Carter Lee gets out one of his little miniature houses he sends for from the catalogs, and his magnifying glass, and sets to work. I can't settle. I keep looking out the window even if isn't nothing there but the early sun oranging the leaves of the chinaberry tree. The most beautiful place in the world, is Bonaparte.

PHILADELPHIA

...

Bell Telephone

THE BRUISE SETTLED into a deep lavender. At the Rite Aid the girls at the checkout sniggered while Ava compared concealers on the back of her hand. On the way out of the store she said, "My husband did this to me. You heifers probably won't do much better, if you even get husbands."

She walked back to Glenn Avenue looking for a fight. The thing was, Abemi didn't do anything to her. Or he did, just not the way she made it sound. But those girls didn't know that, and they should have been mad about her getting knocked around. Maybe getting your ass beat is funny and Ava had missed the joke. The bruise throbbed against the rim of her sunglasses; the butterfly wings pulsed like they were beating out a message she couldn't decode.

In the days before the interview with Bell Telephone Ava did everything she was supposed to do: She called about Section 8 apartments listed in the paper. She went to the employment center. They didn't take too well to the black eye. Uh, miss, you, uh . . . they sent her back to Glenn Avenue. She searched the want ads at the library while Toussaint was at school.

The bruise had its own weather. Twice a bright flash detonated in her vision—kaboom!—and there was nothing but white for a few seconds. When Ava was a girl, she saw spirits: white lights in the woods or one of Bonaparte's long dead fishing in the river. The spirits left her, for the most part, when she left Bonaparte. Since the bruise she'd had a constant sense that something was hovering around her. Or could be she had a concussion and her brains were scrambled.

The drugstore concealer, didn't. The bruise was dark and lurid beneath the almond-colored paste. Like she had leprosy under there. That's how the Bell Telephone lady acted when Ava showed up for her interview. She arrived early for her appointment and sat waiting in a lobby for fifteen minutes. A receptionist led her to the personnel woman who stood in the open doorway to her office. Just like Miss Simmons. So many mean ladies standing in doorways! Haha. The woman stared at Ava for a few seconds with her mouth a little bit open. Her turtle mouth snapped shut, then pursed. *Snap snap.* But Ava was determined. She looked nice. Peter Pan collar blouse with sailboats printed on it. Wedge heels. Pumps would have been better, but who knew where they'd ended up. She had hot-combed her hair and filed her nails. She had even put on the gold cross Abemi had given her.

"Good morning!" Ava said brightly, despite all that snapping and pursing. Patricia Benson was her name. Patricia Benson couldn't take her eyes off the bruise. Ava sat across from her at a long table in the too warm conference room. The butterfly was agitated, beating its wings as though it were trying to lift right off her face. No matter.

"Good morning!" Ava said again, more cheerfully this time.

Patricia Benson seemed reluctant to open her folder. Ava would not be deterred. She said, "You'll see from my résumé that I have seventy words per minute typing, seventy for dictation, and over fifteen years of clerical experience."

Patricia Benson nodded and opened the folder at last. "Tell me about your duties at the last position you had. That was— Oh! That was over three years ago?"

"The billing department at Jefferson! It was three years ago; I took some time off because I had just gotten married. Yes! I worked for the assistant director."

Ava was off to the races. She was on a roll. Patricia Benson nodded and took notes. They were doing just great.

"At Jefferson, I . . . I worked for the assistant director as part of the administrative pool. I did . . . I was . . ." Ava paused. Her thoughts flitted away from her. Her hand moved toward the pulsing butterfly.

"Miss Carson?"

"Yes! I . . ."

"Are you all right? Have you had that, err . . . has it been . . . looked at?"

"I think we were talking about . . . about Jefferson."

The butterfly thrashed and Ava's head throbbed.

"Jefferson! At Jefferson, I . . . the assistant director . . . Could I have a little water, please?" she asked.

There was some trouble about getting the water. Patricia Benson got it herself instead of asking the girl at the reception. She was gone for a long time. When she returned, she handed Ava the little paper cup but didn't take her seat again.

"Thank you, Mrs. Carson," she said, walking toward the door.

"Will I?" She stood up very quickly, too quickly, and the room tilted, though not so much that anyone but her would notice. They walked to the doorway. "Thank you! I hope I'll hear . . ." *Snap.* Purse. Nod. "Thank you," Ava said. Patricia Benson was already heading down the hallway.

Ava needed the bathroom. It would be clean and it would be cool, and she could lean her face against the metal walls of the stall and soothe the ache. She took a turn out of the lobby and found the ladies'. It was immaculate and silent. She sat in the stall for a long time, moving her face an inch forward or back along the wall as the metal warmed. It was the cleanest place she'd been since Abemi threw them out. "Please," she said, with her hand over her mouth so no one would hear her sobbing. "Please let it be okay. Please." The concealer smudged and ran in beige rivulets so the butterfly was revealed in little streaks.

Outside was too hot. Rush hour on Market Street. The old

Horn & Hardart was just four blocks away. Those meatloaf sand-wiches! Those sticky buns! She used to take one home on Friday night after work at Gimbels. She shared an apartment with a girl named Rita Fashaw. At work one day a man in the elevator told her to stop eating those buns because she was ruining her figure. She ought to have said, Mind your own business, or, Who the hell do you think you are. But it didn't really bother her if a handsome man thought her figure was worth saving. And it didn't matter, not really. Nothing was heavy then; she didn't owe anything to anyone. Not love, not safety, not tucking in before bed. Ava steadied herself against the side of a building. She stood there a long time before she was stable enough on her feet to go toward the subway. The street quivered in the midday sun.

The Jennys

SCHOOL WAS ALL RIGHT. It wasn't as good as the one in James Creek, but it wasn't as bad as it could have been. Or as Ava told Toussaint it would be. Some of the kids said he talked white, but nobody really messed with him, not even the older boys on the XH bus. Except on Mondays. Monday morning on the bus was sorry business. Half the kids were sullen and exhausted, Toussaint too, worn out from so much time with the grown-ups taking care of them. The other half couldn't figure out why everybody was so touchy. Like if somebody showed off a new haircut or bragged about going to the Sixers game, next thing you know he was on his back with some boy punching on him. You had to be careful on Mondays.

It was a Monday when three new girls got on at McNair Street during the third week of school. All of them with meticulously lotioned knees and elbows and perfect cornrows with clack-clack beads at the ends. They stood in the aisle stage-whispering to one another, "Who these kids?" They frowned. "So dusty."

It didn't take the new girls long to discover that the bus stopped at the shelter before it got to their stop at the projects. And it didn't take Toussaint or the other kids long to discover that two of the girls were named Jenny and the third was their cousin whose name was of no particular note. The Jennys were together all of the time—in the hallways at school, in homeroom, at lunch. The Jennys were after total domination. They knew just how to go about it; some people have an instinct for power. The Jennys got free lunch just like everybody else, but they weren't bothered about that because their hair was always done and they lived in the projects and not the shelter. In the cafeteria they'd go out of their way to find Toussaint and the other Glenn Avenue kids. "You know what's funny?" one Jenny said. "It's the same smell in here as it is on the bus." The other two nodded. "Booty." More nodding.

Within a week the XH bus was divided: the Jennys and the other project kids up front, Glenn Avenue in the back. Toussaint sat in the middle; he wasn't joining anybody's army. The Jennys didn't like that.

"His clothes wrinkled."

"Look at them kicks. Ninety-nine cents!"

"What's wrong with his hair?"

Despite himself, Toussaint tensed. Aha! The Jennys smiled.

"Yeah, why he got that busted-ass haircut?"

"Ain't no scissors where they stay?"

"His mama musta spent the money for his haircut on a bottle of beer."

"He got a Afro like my aunt Jeanette used to have!"

The Jennys fell against each other laughing.

"Hey, Aunt Jeanette! It's me, Jenny. Why you don't speak?"

It was true. It had been weeks since he'd had a haircut. He and Ava even stopped going to Sunday breakfast at the little diner near their favorite park. Ava said it was because they needed to save up. Toussaint thought it had something to do with the big bruise on her face and how tired and dreamy it made her. Now they passed their Sundays trudging back and forth to the cafeteria where Ava looked at everybody with tricky eyes that wouldn't keep still in her face. She had trouble keeping her balance. She was always lying down with a rag on her head. Toussaint couldn't imagine any headache bad enough to make you into a whole different person. He stopped asking about going to the playground or movie night in the TV room. The answer was always no. One time he asked why and she said, "We're never going to get through this if we don't stick together." Toussaint felt like she'd left him alone in a house where the lights were turning off room by room. Ava had taken to collecting old newspapers on her walks around the building. She sat at the desk with the small stack of newspapers, circling an ad now and again. Ma, he thought, staring at her. Ma, here I am. But she never lifted her eyes.

"Hey, Aunt Jeanette!" the Jennys said.

Don't look at them, Toussaint told himself. Don't touch your hair.

One of the girls walked the few steps to Toussaint's seat and bent in front of him. "Aunt Jeanette, it's me!" she said, mouth open, laughing, waving her hand in his face.

That was too much. Toussaint was out of his seat in an instant and the Jenny was on the floor. "Oooh oooh!" the cry went up from the kids on the bus. There were only a few adults at that hour, old folks mostly. They rose from their seats but it was too late. The kids had already enclosed Toussaint and Jenny in a tight circle. He straddled her and made a fist. "Go head," she said. "My brother will fuck you up. Go head." He reared back, but before he could strike the bus lurched and threw him sideways. The shouting stopped.

"Y'all ain't gon start this mess on my bus!"

The driver stood over them, his big stomach poking Toussaint in the face. One meaty hand reached down and grabbed him by the shirt collar.

"You ought to be ashamed of yourself! Beating on a girl."

Toussaint's mouth opened and closed but no sound came out.

"You all right, little girl?" The driver swung his wrecking-ball belly toward the Jenny, who had scrambled onto her knees, face all screwed up for a good, loud wail.

"What's wrong with you, boy?" he said, swinging back to Toussaint. "Get off my bus. I ain't having no girl-beating hoodlums riding my bus!"

Toussaint stood. He was afraid his legs wouldn't hold him.

"She started it," a brave soul cried from the back.

"Lip!" the driver said. "You want to walk too? All y'all can walk!"

Toussaint managed to wait until the bus pulled away before he was sick in the gutter around the corner from the stop. He thought to call his mother, but he'd only get the shelter office and have to wait on the line while somebody banged on the door to their room. She probably wouldn't open it, she never opened it. Or he could call Abemi. Or Cass, who had said he was on his way to Philadelphia. Not that he wanted to talk to him, not really.

"You all right, son?" a passerby asked.

Toussaint nodded.

"Where you going?"

"Glenn and Tulpehocken."

"You better wait for the bus. That's a long walk."

"Which way is it, please?"

"Down that way. But you better wait on the next bus."

Toussaint had already started down the block. "Thank you!" he yelled over his shoulder.

On the way back to Glenn Avenue he used his emergency money to call Abemi. His stomach bucked and churned when he put his coin in the slot. He didn't know what he'd say. He hoped he wouldn't have to say anything because Abemi would sense it was him and he would feel so bad about everything that by the time Toussaint got back to the shelter he would already be there loading their things into his car. He called back the next day, and the one after that, but Abemi never answered. Could be he was out in the yard. Or in the bathroom.

At the end of the week, Toussaint realized that Abemi didn't answer because he was at work. He'd gone on like before, as if Toussaint and Ava hadn't left. As if they did not live in a place for people who have nowhere to live, with no food of their own and no place to walk in after school and say, "I'm home!"

"You could have got suspended!" Keith said.

"You so stupid," Anthony replied. "They was on SEPTA. You can't get suspended if the fight don't happen in school."

Keith, Anthony, and Toussaint were at recess. A week had passed but the fight with the Jennys was still the talk of the playground.

"I don't care if she is pretty. She deserved it," Keith said.

"Yeah. She had that shit coming," Anthony said.

Keith told him the Jennys had tried all that smells-like-ass stuff a couple of days after Toussaint got kicked off the bus, but one of the Glenn Avenue girls had decided she'd had enough.

"You should have seen it," Anthony said. "Kimmy got up in the Jenny's face and said: 'Aww boo-hoo, I'm so scared of little bitty Toussaint. Save me, Mr. Bus Driver. Save me from little-ass Toussaint.'" He paused and looked at Toussaint. "Err, no offense." The Jenny tried some kind of weak comeback but Kimmy faked a punch and the Jenny flinched—of course she did—and that was the end of the reign of terror.

"So, uh," Anthony said. "You ain't gotta keep walking every day."

"I'm not scared to take the bus!" Toussaint said.

"Ain't nobody said you was. I'm just saying it's far, is all."

"Or you could take a different bus."

"Keith, you so stupid," Anthony said.

"What? I just know I'd be tired if I walked that far."

Toussaint wasn't scared. He had been that first morning when he woke at six and went out alone with his stomach rumbling. The walk had taken nearly an hour and he got lost more than once. But he was proud of himself when he got to school. And he felt something uncanny he couldn't quite put his finger on—as though he had walked the streets alone with his backpack before, even though he hadn't. Or maybe it was more like he had finally started doing something he was supposed to be doing all along, like déjà vu except it was the future. It was peaceful. No bus driver or Jennys or even his friends, nobody who knew where he'd come from or where he was going.

The walking got easier the more he did it, but leaving Glenn Avenue was harder every morning. He lingered by the door a few seconds too long, hoping his mother would make a fuss and stop him. Or demand that they eat breakfast together in the cafeteria.

Or at least get dressed to see him off. Instead, she watched him from the edge of her bed in her nightgown. Why so early, she wanted to know. He said something about the watery oatmeal in the Glenn Avenue cafeteria and the good school breakfast if he got there early. She gave him a sharp look, then lowered her eyes and let him go.

Keith and Anthony exchanged glances. Toussaint realized he had not spoken in a long time. "Naw," he said. "I'm not tired. Not that tired."

A Kindly Worded Letter

LULU SIMMONS WAS NOT unreasonable. She understood that the residents were under duress. It is excusable that one of them might arrive late for an interview. But "harried" and "unsuited to an office environment" (a direct quote from Patricia Benson's report)! And to skip two weeks of job center visits. Miss Simmons's first response to unproductive behavior was a kindly worded letter slipped under the resident's door. She wrote Ava's letter herself instead of using the template:

> Miss Carson. I was disappointed to learn that your interview with Bell Telephone went so poorly. In the future, if a problem arises please come to the office. We are here to help. You will remember, of course, that seeking employment is a mandatory condition of your stay here at Glenn Avenue. I have enclosed a photostat of our rules.

Very kindly worded, indeed, Miss Simmons thought, looking it over before sending Renee to put it under the door of 813. None of these people had any sense of the thousand others just like them, out there in some hovel getting beat up by their boyfriends. Or riding the buses all night and washing up in public bathrooms. Families of seven jammed into Aunt So-and-So's/Mama's/Grandmama's one-bedroom. They were a heaviness on her heart. The poor will always be with us—half of them needing a room at Glenn Avenue. She couldn't dally over one when there were so many others. Three strikes was her rule.

Miss Simmons made a point of going to the cafeteria the day after she sent her letter to 813. Ava and Toussaint sat apart from the others at an end table. The boy was stricken, but he held his head up. He had some pluck about him, God bless. The woman was downright bedraggled. It was lunchtime but she had a pillow crease along her cheek. And a great big green-yellow blob around one eye. A fading shiner if ever there was one. Miss Simmons hadn't seen that coming. I didn't figure her for a brawler, she thought. She only sent the ones with polish to Bell Telephone. My God. And she seemed to have abandoned her respectable wardrobe in favor of old dungarees and a tight little T-shirt that may well have belonged to her son.

"Good afternoon, Miss Carson," she said.

Miss Simmons's friend Latrice was always asking if "those women" thought about their children. If they did, they wouldn't end up in that situation, was Latrice's view on the matter. Latrice had a three-bedroom on School House Lane with a formal dining room and a husband that worked for IBM. People certainly do have opinions. Miss Simmons did not have any children. No husband either, or pets. She understood the appeal, but she herself did not wish to be servile. And she liked a clean house.

Miss Simmons fixed Ava with her firmest reproachful stare. "And how are you, Tow . . . Too . . . young man." The boy looked up, a little panicked, and mumbled, "Thank you." As for the formerly compliant Ava Carson, didn't she snarl a little bit? A flash of hostility and then it was gone. Miss Simmons lingered a few seconds longer and tapped her nails against the table. Mocha, a new color in her rotation.

"Too-sahnt," Ava said softly.

"Excuse me?"

"It's Too-sahnt."

Well.

An Electrical Experience

AFTER BELL TELEPHONE, Ava decided to take matters into her own hands. She sat in a phone booth at the library on Chelten Avenue calling through the want ads: Secretary, clerical assistant, collections agent. The problem was, she didn't have a callback number besides the service desk at Glenn Avenue where Sherry the secretary was supposed to answer the phone discreetly and say: So-and-So isn't available right now. May I take a message? Ava never got any messages.

Maybe it was time she applied to McDonald's. She was thinking how people were always saying how *they'd* take any job at all if *their* back was against the wall. Funny how McDonald's and the Wawa weren't overrun with all those noble, hardworking folks; there sure were a lot of people with their backs against the wall these days.

Outside the phone booth a row of overhead lights brightened, then popped like a fuse had blown. Ava felt dizzy. Pain whipped across her forehead. She fainted, maybe. When the worst had passed, she opened her eyes to find she was holding on to the little shelf in the phone booth, her change spilled all over the floor and the blood beating in her ears. She sat up and took a few deep breaths. Her headaches were a visitation, like seeing a ghost, which is an electrical experience and hurts like hell even though people never mention the pain.

She probably ought to see a doctor. Where was Cass with his bag of pills when you needed him? Haha. You love to push a pill, she said to the Cass in her mind. Remember that time when I was at Temple and I had finals and I wasn't going to make it between the studying and working nights and going out with you? And you gave me those little white pills?

Off she'd gone to her exam two days later—energized, everything there was to know about toddler language development organized in little files in her brain. No sweat! But a few blocks from the subway the sidewalk tilted skyward and her heart tried to bang its way out of her chest. She called Cass during his shift at Panther HQ. "I'm having a heart attack," she said. He told her to go to a diner, have a glass of milk and two pieces of buttered toast, and wait ten minutes. She was fit as a fiddle after that, if a little shaky. And an A+ on the final!

When she asked him about the pills later, Cass said: Oh, they were just bennies. Passed your exam though, didn't you? "You bastard," she said. "You quack." That got him. They lay in Ava's bed laughing so hard their bellies ached, they laughed till they were too worn out for anything but sleep. She woke in the night to Cass kissing her eyelids very softly, so softly that the recollection felt like a dream. He could be sweet like that, in the dead of night, or when he showed up one winter afternoon with a mink hat because she'd kept getting colds that year. Maybe, Ava thought, magically, ridiculously, the Panther clinic had been reopened and Cass would be there to cure her of this electrocuted feeling. He was somewhere in the city. Ava could feel him wafting toward her like gardenia on a breeze.

It was time to go back to Glenn Avenue. Ava needed to lie down. She gathered her pencil and newspapers and walked to the bus stop on shaky legs. On the bus her headache ruptured into darts of white light. I am on the road to Damascus, she thought.

Back at Glenn Avenue Ava made her way to the nurse's office. A handful of people waited in folding chairs in the antiseptic-smelling hallway. The worst of the headache had passed but Ava's temples throbbed in time with her heartbeat. Thirty minutes passed, then an hour. The faces in the chairs changed but Ava was not called. A couple of girls with babies came and went. A woman dragged along a kid with a nosebleed.

"Dammit, Mickey," the lady said. "Dammit." She looked at Ava and said, "They gonna say it's my fault. They'll take your kids in here." She put her hand gently on the back of the boy's head. "Tilt your head, baby."

A steady stream of people entered the office with their infirmities and came out cured—or better, at least. It must be satisfying to patch people up, Ava thought. Fixing things. It wasn't so hard to fix things; you just needed the right solution. Abemi, Ava had come to understand in her concussed state, was not the solution. Of course the other thing is you have to be able to stomach the solution. Or figure out how to stomach it, in the absence of other options.

"Next!" the nurse said, calling her at last.

Ava stood. "No, thank you. I'm okay. I think I have to call my mother is what I have to do." And she was gone down the hallway. The nurse didn't blink an eye. Lots of things the residents said didn't make sense to her. She was supposed to report erratic behavior, not to mention all the rule breakers hanging around the building when they were supposed to be out looking for work. But who had the time?

The stretch of hallway by the pay phones was empty. Ghost ship, like everybody had gone overboard and Ava was the last one left alive. She'd have to call collect. Dutchess would accept the charges. Probably. Ava stood with her hand on the receiver thinking of the bus depot in Bodine—the square of sidewalk out front splotched with bird shit from the robins that lived in the box elder out front. She and Toussaint waiting outside the terminal in that searing sun till Dutchess roared down Main Street in the rusty pickup. She'd climb down from the cab and she'd say— Ava placed the receiver back in the cradle. Not that, she thought. There must be some other way. When she turned to go back to her room, she saw Melvin at the far end of the corridor—always lurking—but she went down the lavender corridor before he saw her. Her head was pounding again.

She headed toward the nursery to watch the babies sleep but it was empty as the last day of the world, so she turned up the blue hallway and went out the emergency exit. From there she could leave Glenn Avenue altogether without passing through the lobby. Or she could go back inside through the delivery entrance to the cafeteria pantry. The door was almost always open during the day, but Ava didn't have the energy to swipe anything to calm the rumbling in her belly.

She hadn't gone to breakfast, or lunch either. The cafeteria gave her the creeps, and there was always the risk of Miss Simmons with her nails and her reproach. It's strange in there, is how she explained herself to Toussaint when she sent him to dinner on his own. Toussaint thought it was because everybody was sad. But that wasn't it. It was more sinister. The last few times she'd gone, she would bite into her sloppy joe, or she'd watch somebody mash up peas for their baby and she'd have a sudden sensation like she was doubled. Like there was a second Ava inside her threatening to get loose and— And what? Trash the place? Stab the woman at the next table with her fork? Abemi used to say, "Ava, you are at loose ends." By which he meant somebody ought to have tied her back or tied her together, or maybe hog-tied her.

The garbage stink from the bins by the pantry door made her nauseous. The sky was a smudged mustard color, like dirty fingerprints on a yellow blouse. August hot, and dirty like that. Only it was October and still the heat swelled with portent and menace. Her thoughts came too fast and interrupted themselves. She could go to the Golden Top Bar round the corner if she wanted to . . . she could meet a man . . . she could find *her* lost man . . . they would . . . Ava had a sudden craving for pimiento-stuffed olives but Toussaint hated olives . . . Something moved in her peripheral vision. A big something against the wall near the entrance to the pantry. She should have walked away but she was already so close. Melvin. Melvin with a woman with her face pushed against the wall, navy blue skirt pushed up around her hips, panties pulled to the side. Melvin behind her and both of them grunting: Uh uh uh. Melvin pressed his hand into the back of the woman's turned head. He thrust harder, the woman moaned with pleasure and backed into him, her hands splayed against the wall. Melvin's mouth twisted into a grimace. No, not a grimace, a smile. Eyes glazed.

It began to rain. No tentative droplets to announce the downpour, just sudden sheets of water falling out of the yellow sky. Ava ran around the back of the building to the glass door that opened to her own green corridor. Locked. Inside, a blurry figure, wavy through the rivulets of rain on the glass, moved slowly down the hall. Ava banged on the door with both hands but if it heard her, if it was even there, it didn't stop. She stood at the glass side door shouting after the receding figure in the hallway as if it were her own self that had gotten away from her and left her out there in the rain. Rain soaked her to the bone, through her hair, pulsing warm down the small of her back. She bent her head forward so the drops tapped the back of her neck. Her skin tingled. Her clothes grew heavy, like another body pressed into hers.

"What the hell? I thought you was right behind me." Ava raised her head to find Melvin pushing open the door on which she'd been banging. "Making all this noise!" He glanced over his shoulder. "You know you not even supposed to be in the building at this hour."

Ava rubbed her eyes. She peered around Melvin to look for the figure that had run down the hallway. Gone. Melvin's uniform was covered with big wet splotches.

"Why don't you just make an announcement on the PA? Skirt all hitched up. Shit."

All at once she felt a draft on the exposed stretch of thigh and a tenderness in her cheek where it had pressed against the wall. She peered around him once again.

"I have to go, Melvin," she said, shaking her head, "I have to go," and she walked toward her room trailing rainwater.

He was a few feet behind her, shaking his head too. Strange one, he thought. Damn women in here gonna be the end of me.

BONAPARTE

∘ ∘ ∘

WE BEEN GETTING LETTERS from the county. Taxes due on the store property. Not a peep about that land in fifteen years. Then it burns to the ground and we all of a sudden got back taxes? Mmph. We had a meeting where the store used to be. Everybody tried to say it was too sad to meet up there, but I still think there's power in the ground of Bonaparte. And anyway, I spent two weeks collecting sage and drying it. I burned so much of it you could probably smell it over in Bodine.

I thought we'd meet up and agree quick that Progress was behind this county stuff—trying to trick us into selling up or Everlasting only knows what else. But you know these people round here don't believe in efficiency. Juniata and Memma say, "Maybe it's nothing to do with the fire and the county just lost track of the payments." I know I go on about how them two are stupid cows. But it really is like they got one mouth and half a brain between them. Carter Lee ain't said much. After about an hour I noticed he was noticing what I was noticing, which is that trumpet vine has grown all up and down the ruins of our general store. And bougainvillea. A tepee of flowers. Nature making our store into something new. Making it into the next thing it's supposed to be. For now we got a great big pyramid of orange and purple flowers right in the middle of town. "Kind of like a shrine." Carter Lee nodded cause me and him are always on the same wavelength.

"Look like she back to funny acting," says Memma, under her breath like I wasn't supposed to hear.

"What?" I say. Then they all, the whole assembled company of ass-backward, give each other a look, except Carter Lee.

"What's that?" I say again. They just go on throwing glances at each other like a Frisbee. Then Erma Linner clears her throat and sort of sits herself up tall—don't look me in the eye though—and says, "You just been a little bit . . . They gonna put this plot up on tax sale and you just keep rambling around late at night like a haint and sending letters to Progress but that . . . We got to pay real money to fix this problem."

"Here you go with that! You can't just give in and give them what they ask for. We don't even know if we owe that money. They'll bleed us dry and still get this little bit of land."

"That's just the kind of thinking how you lost them two hundred acres," says Memma.

Then they all get quiet and Juniata hits Memma on the leg to hush her up.

"No, Juniata, that's enough," Memma says. "I'm done with all this tiptoeing! Two hundred acres gone to tax sale! How you let that happen to Caro's land? Yeah, I said it. You got these crazy ideas about who owes you what and which white folks did what and this mess and that mess and you messed yourself right out of two hundred acres. They sent you them notices for two years. But you was in one of your, your episodes. You all the time calling us fools and heifers but I'm finished with your mouth! You don't even deserve to have that land, that was Caro's land—"

"All right, Memma. All right! That's enough," Nip says. Memma gets up out of her seat, eyes glittering, chins shaking.

"Ain't no shrine here. Just a coupla flower vines. All of it bout to be a great big nothing if we keep on listening to her," she says.

"Sit down, Memma. That's enough, I told you!"

"You keep Caro's name out your mouth," I told her. "Don't you say his name one more time." I still got my blade, tucked right in my sock like it always was.

Pauline County stole that land from under me! They was supposed to show me all the accounting. I refused to pay without records and the motherfuckers pounced like hyenas and it was gone. That land is a sorrow of my life. I get on my knees every night and I say, Caro, I'm sorry. I'll never make peace with it. I will go to my grave holding on to what's left. But that bitch need to keep my husband's name out her mouth.

I must have been reaching down toward my blade cause Carter Lee says, "Well, I guess we talked enough for today."

Memma sitting there with her arms folded across her great big titties—look like somebody pasted a whole pig to the front of her. I walked away. Restraint. I got near to my truck and somebody says, You got to be easy with her, you know she ain't . . . Sounded a little like Carter Lee, but I know he wouldn't say nothing like that so I got up in my truck and drove off.

There's still a little money coming in and Delilah and me don't need much. I put by what I can. I got two accounts. I keep one for the land and taxes and such. The other one's for Ava. I been putting away money for her since she was just a little thing. I have everything she might need: land, a house, and money in the bank. She never gonna come for it though. They may as well put it in the coffin with me. Right next to the deeds to this land. Seem like we getting to endings around here.

I went out to the woods looking for Old Rea. Not that I thought she was there, or that I didn't think she was there, you know. After them devils killed Caro, the town council built a guard post in the woods right off the road where they snuck in. At first there was somebody there every night, and the Watchers, of course. My left eye went red two days after he died, right up to the pupil. Everybody said it was a burst blood vessel because my pressure shot up so high. But I knew it was a sign. For weeks I went out to the edge of the woods strapped: two shotguns, pistol at my waist. They had to keep an eye on me because I wanted to ride on Bodine. I would have gone all by myself like some a them Muscogee used to do in bygone days. And look how they ended up, Carter Lee said, trying to talk me out of it. But you know what? Them motherfuckers would ride white folks down even if they knew they would put em all in a prison and call it a reservation. They knew just what would happen if white folks got around to owning shit. Yeah, you right, I said to Carter Lee, look how that ended up.

After two months watching for them I stopped going to the woods. Wasn't exactly my decision. One night after supper I just couldn't get up. My legs turned to wood and my thoughts got thick in my head. I think my heart beat slower. Like I was turning into a tree, which is a beautiful thing, if you want be poetic. I stayed that way a long time. Then, and I know this sounds like horseshit, Ava fed me some chicken and dumplings and I turned human again.

A year later Bodine came for us. Sheriff and all. I put Ava in the root cellar. I was going to go fight alongside the men, but Carter Lee and Beau George made me go down in that cellar. "Take care of your girl," they said. "Caro's gone. You want to orphan her?" I don't think I was as opposed to dying as I should have been. Me and Ava, Memma and hers stayed down there with the turnips and the spiders—I can't stand a turnip to this day. Bodine came by truck and horseback. The gun-smoke smell crept down where we were. Truck engines rumbled the ground, men grunted above us, scuffling and thudding. There was the sound of a hard thing—gun butt, tire iron—*thwack, snap,* against a rib cage. Ava wrapped her arms round my waist. She buried her face in the middle of my back. I was skinny like a telephone pole. There wasn't any comfort in my body for her. No softness anywhere on me.

It was Nip they had beat so bad just above our heads. When we come up from the cellar he was just pulp and moaning, heaped in the middle of the road. Memma's children had to see their father like that. They dragged out Eugene Kirby and Beau George in leg irons. They beat Eugene and dumped him in front of the Oaks. He was dead two days later. Wasn't nothing ever the same after that. Bodine had been trying to come in here for a whole century, but they never got far. Then Caro died and they got all the way in. Sometimes I think Old Rea left her spirit to him, or in him, and when they killed him Bonaparte flickered and dimmed. Now it's hardly burning at all, like a match just about to go out. I know the facts: all our young people left and there's no work here and we all too tired to farm the land. I know that. But still. We were protected here in Bonaparte. Then suddenly we weren't.

Well anyway, I went out there to ask Old Rea for an explanation, but I ended up in that old lookout shack. There's no end to memory places in Bonaparte. I sat in there a long time staring at the little bits of the road showing between the trees. I brought my guitar. Old home week. I hadn't played in so long that after twenty minutes my fingers were tender from the strings. Nothing passed on the road. One hour, two hours, not so much as a fox. Not that I was expecting anything, not really.

"Rea," I said, and then I didn't say nothing more. What's to say? She would already know, wouldn't she, what happened to us.

I started over: "I got a joke for you, Rea."

By all accounts she didn't have much of a sense of humor. I guess I wouldn't either if I was damn near two hundred years old and held together with rags and shoe leather. I couldn't think of a joke anyhow. "Look," I said. "I figured Ava wouldn't come back here, only I want there to be something for her to not come back to. What are we supposed to do with these acres? Just let them disappear?"

I don't believe in sins but that would be one.

"Rea," I said. "I got nothing but wind in my bones, you could play me like a flute."

"It's no way forward. No future," is what I told her.

She didn't answer me of course. The lookout was warm and smelled like dry leaves and earth. The forest rustled like ladies' skirts at a party. I got to thinking I could just stay there with my thoughts and the woods talking at me. I got to thinking I had had my three score and ten. Delilah could go to Carter Lee. I could wait a few hours till they'd all be asleep and nobody would hear the gun blast. I felt better, I won't lie. Lighter. Relieved.

I was in a nice easy doze when Delilah woke me up growling and running to and fro along the tree line. "Hush up, girl," I said. "Hush up, you devilish thing." She stared at me hard, right up in my face. I was getting to my feet when I heard a rumbling. Delilah took off like a shot. Something thundered down the main road. Sounded like five engines full throttle. I went outside and got my rifle up. I'm still an okay shot. Dropping a white boy would be a fine way to finish my days.

The dusk was coming down purple, but the sun was still orange above the horizon. Leaves flipped around on the tree branches like a storm was moving in. It sounded like the Four Horsemen. Felt like it too, the ground trembled. But I was ready. Out of the light came a pale blue pickup, with some kind of weird gold insignia nearly rusted out on the side. Coming in hot, chugging smoke. Well, here it is, I thought. Progress coming like I guess it was always bound to do, all at once to clear us out of here for good.

PHILADELPHIA

. . .

Breaking Orbit

IN NEW JERSEY Toussaint had gone to Coleman Elementary, where everything was new. If a desk broke it was replaced,
and when a textbook got old you brought it to your teacher who
gave you a long talking-to that didn't really matter because in
the end she was going to get you a new one from the book room. The
school library was always open and Miss Gillette was behind the
front desk. You could tell her you had to write a book report about
Superfudge or that you wanted to do extra credit on photosynthesis.
Miss Gillette had too many books, so many books about rocks and
planets that Toussaint could stay up late reading under the covers,
if he was that kind of nerd, which of course he wasn't.

At Taft they shared textbooks so you couldn't take them home
to do your homework. Wasn't much homework anyway. Toussaint
didn't want to touch the books, greasy-French-fry-fingerprinted
and taped along the binding. No Miss Gillette. The library was
just in a classroom, and most of the books were for little kids or
else they were so old they were falling apart. Toussaint was bored.
He had already learned fractions in third grade but at Taft they
were telling them to him again in fifth grade, the easy ones too.
He was tired of the way the other kids looked at him in class,
like he was showing off if he raised his hand too much. It was just

a way to pass the time. Plus, weren't they supposed to know the answers?

He didn't know why Coleman was one way and this school was so different. He thought it had something to do with what made his mother give the stink eye to everybody in the hallway at Glenn Avenue—but that wasn't right because didn't he and Ava live there just like they did? He didn't tell anybody about the shelter either. He wasn't sure why. Anybody can live in one place or another place, or go to one school or another one; it didn't mean anything about them. But he looked down at the ground more since he got to Glenn Avenue. Half the kids at Taft came from the projects and the shelter and there weren't any white kids except for a tall red-faced girl they called Twizzler and a blond boy who kept trying to do cornrows that wouldn't stay in for obvious reasons. They called him Casper. For obvious reasons.

In science they were doing space. Toussaint shared a textbook with the boy next to him, RaShawn—Miss Gregory said: Boys and girls, the science textbooks are *expensive* so you need to *be careful*—who thought it was funny to pretend to stick his gum on the picture of the moon orbiting the earth. Miss Gregory caught him chewing (loudly) and made him spit it out in the garbage can and after that they moved on to the page where the earth was orbiting the sun. Toussaint flipped ahead to the other planets fixed in place by gravity. Toussaint already knew from Coleman that gravity was a scientific fact, but he couldn't help think of the Jedi and the Force and that maybe the Force was with Toussaint too. It was possible that Yoda held the universe together. Could be.

"No stars in Philadelphia," he said to his mother the night they spent on the bench in the bus shelter. She said it was just the city lights that hid them. He was grateful for the lights because he and his ma were out there in the dark with nothing to keep them from the bigness of night. In New Jersey, farmland extended black and flat from the point just beyond the reach of the floodlight at the house's front steps. There was nothing between the black land and the velvet sky except stars. That is the universe, Toussaint had said, holding his mother's hand. But he was just a small New Jersey boy then; there wasn't much to be afraid of. Not like now.

Toussaint raised his hand. "Miss Gregory?" he asked. "What if the orbit broke?"

"What?"

"What if the orbit broke and the moon came off it and just went out into space. Where would it go?"

Sniggers. "Stupid," someone said.

"The moon isn't going anywhere, Toussaint. Gravity is not going anywhere." She paused. "What's gravity, boys and girls?"

"A natural force," the class said in unison.

Miss Gregory smiled.

"But—" Toussaint said. Miss Gregory shot him a look. "Sorry." He put up his hand. "But what if it did? What if whatever makes gravity stops making it?"

"The sun? The sun's gravitational pull holds the planets in place. And the sun isn't going anywhere."

"How do you know?"

"Excuse me, Mr. Wright?"

"If the sun exploded or it just stopped, then the earth would fly away. Anything could happen. Things break."

"The sun is not going to break."

More sniggers from the other kids.

"Please calm down so we can get on with the lesson."

"I am calm. I just want to know if . . . I mean, maybe the sun . . . because it's a star . . . and then . . ."

"The sun is a star, that's true. In many millions of years the star will implode, but that's a very long time from now. So long we can't imagine it."

"You mean, like, 1995?" someone called out.

Toussaint felt tears coming to his eyes.

"So it can happen! You just didn't want to tell us!"

"Mr. Wright! You need to raise your hand when you speak. You need to *calm down*."

"When? When will it happen?"

Miss Gregory sent Toussaint to the principal's office with a note saying he was distressed and needed a place to get himself together for a few minutes. Of course, she taped it closed so Toussaint couldn't read it. He very nearly went to the playground instead, but he was not the kind of boy who went to the playground when he was told to go to the principal's office. He was not the kind of boy who got sent to the principal's office at all, so he went dutifully, heart pounding, anxiety chewing his insides. The school secretary, Miss Stevens, stood behind the front desk. The principal, it seemed, was not in her office. Toussaint sat in one of the hard chairs across from Miss Stevens and rubbed at the place above his elbow that always itched so badly.

"Are you all right?" Miss Stevens asked.

He nodded yes.

"Would you like to go to the nurse's office?"

No. Toussaint would not like to go to the nurse's office. He took a deep breath. He wanted . . . he did not know what he wanted. Answers, maybe. Maybe he wanted answers.

"Miss Stevens," he asked. "How come I got sent to the principal's office for asking a question?"

"You got sent to the principal's office because you were disrupting class."

"But then how come I have to sit here when the principal ain't here?"

"She's *not* here."

"I know! That's why I'm asking!"

"Smart-mouth," Miss Stevens said, sighing. "Just sit your behind down there until the bell rings."

All at once Toussaint realized nobody had any answers to give him. The grown-ups didn't know anything, or whatever they did know they weren't going to tell him, not even Miss Gregory and certainly not Miss Stevens or the principal, who Toussaint swore he could just about see through the frosted glass panel in her office door. Nobody at the shelter could tell him anything. Abemi had said, I'll come and get you but your mother can't come. Cass, who was supposed to be his father, came walking down their New Jersey road out of nowhere then disappeared right back into nowhere.

His mother wore the same pants and top every day; some days she didn't bother taking off the headscarf she slept in. One time he'd come in after school and caught her buttoning up her jeans in a hurry, shirt all rumpled and her pajamas thrown on the bed like she'd only just changed out of them. "You're early!" she'd said, but it was four-thirty so really, he was very late.

Toussaint's stomach lurched. Maybe he should go to the nurse's office after all. She'd ask how he was feeling, put her hand on his forehead, and let him lie down, even if it was just for a few minutes. When he looked up Miss Stevens was scratching under her wig with a pencil. Outside the warm wind made a little cyclone of dead leaves and drinking-straw wrappers and cigarette-pack cellophane. His elbow stung when the skin broke, but he kept on picking at it till the bell rang.

It was the end of the day. He should have gone back to his classroom to pack his book bag and erase the board and sit for end-of-the-day reading time, all of which was a comfort before the long walk back to Glenn Avenue where Ava would say hello too loudly and lock him in a too tight hug. But he did not return to his classroom. He walked through the crowd of jostling kids, out a side door and down the block. The rowhouses along the blocks near the school were shut up tight. All houses for all time were shut up against him.

When his father . . . when Cass had come, he said he was on the way to Philadelphia. He could be in one of those shut-up houses. But Toussaint didn't think so. He couldn't picture him in any kind of house at all. He would get in there and all the chairs and window shades would blow around everywhere because Cass had brought the outside in with him. So many people he'd met who he'd never see again. Maybe Abemi, too. Paul and Jilly. He was going to ask his ma why that would be. He would ask her even if she didn't know.

Melvin's Advice

AFTER THAT FIRST RAINY AFTERNOON, Ava and Melvin were a regular thing. They met in the private bathroom near the nurse's station, or after hours in one of the social workers' offices. Once in Melvin's car. Ava's days lurched forward in a haze of headaches and naps that she dropped into suddenly and completely. She'd wake disoriented in the midafternoon, still in her underwear and a rumpled T-shirt: What time is it? What day it is? I have to call my mother. Today! She'd look around for clean clothes to put on to walk to the pay phone but by the time she dressed the panic had ebbed into murmuring anxiety. The day ran on, always a step ahead of her, till it was night and time to get Toussaint ready for bed and pack his backpack for the morning and tie on her headscarf and lie awake listening to him breathe in the dark.

How did this happen, she'd think in the middle of some long afternoon, Melvin's big soft stomach pushing into her, her cheek against the bathroom wall, or her breasts pressed against the cool top of a desk. Her mind found whatever it needed to get her pleasure. More than once she nearly moaned, "Cass, baby," but she caught herself in time.

Maintenance fixed the broken lock on the private bathroom door but Melvin gave her a key so she'd never have to use those nasty family bathrooms again. He told her useful things she didn't know. For one thing, she could sell her food stamps. "Matter of fact," he said, "I can sell em for you. So you ain't gotta, you know, get your hands dirty."

This was one night when he'd stayed after his shift and Ava snuck out to meet him in the cafeteria while Toussaint slept. They were in the kitchen by the battered metal pantry door. "It's a trick to it. You just jiggle it a little this way," he whispered, rattling the doorknob. "And open sesame." The door opened with a loud click that made her jump.

"See? This way you can save your food stamps. Just like the Acme in here. Only better cause shit's free. I get my—I mean, uh, they got everything you need," he said.

"You come in here too, Melvin?" Ava asked.

"Me? Yeah, right." He sucked his teeth.

"I think you come in here and get some of these big jugs of orange juice for your lady."

"What? Girl, you so crazy," he said, nuzzling into her neck.

"You don't come in here and get a little bit of sugar for your lady and your kid at home?"

He pulled away. She was staring at him in her creepy juju way he didn't care for. "You tripping, Ava." Shouldn't be talking about a man's family. "I got just the thing for you, baby," he said.

Everlasting knows why, but for an instant Ava thought he had something useful to tell her. She felt a little foolish when all he did was put his hands on her breasts. Well, she had something for him, the moron. Ava turned and put her hand on him, just rested it there so he felt the heat of her palm through his pants. He throbbed under her. She liked this part best, when he was panting for her and she stayed controlled and easy. She teased him like that for a long time, asked him how he was going to sell her food stamps and who he was going to sell them to, and how much money he was going to bring her. He said he took a little bitty commission: "Just like the check-cashing place, baby," he said, his voice thickening. Then she teased him until he took it back and said he'd bring her every penny. Till he told her his lady's name was Tammy. "Does Tammy do it like this?" Ava said. "And how about this?" On and on like that until she had made her own self wait so long she nearly forgot why she'd started teasing him in the first place. Till he was panting like a dog. She was going to pull up her skirt and—

And then she saw a roach on the floor near her foot. Ava blinked and kept on rubbing Melvin but try as she might she couldn't stop looking at that roach. All at once, the sight of the giant vats of mayonnaise on the shelves and the canned-food smell made her sick to her stomach.

"Ow, baby!" Melvin said. Ava realized she was tugging and not stroking. Tug tug. That made her laugh a little. Catch a tiger . . . She let him go. Stepped on the roach. The base of her skull tingled.

"I've been seeing things," she said.

"What?"

"I feel like I'm going in reverse, like I can't get forward. I can't get to the next thing only back to the last thing. But it's . . . I get these headaches."

"Girl, what you talking about?" Melvin said.

"I can't keep anything straight since the headaches. I need to make a plan. I have to get out of here. But stuff from last month, last year, twenty years ago keeps coming back around."

"That ain't nothing—you what they call stressed out. You all right. Let me rub your shoulders and—"

Ava pulled away from him and leaned against the shelves with her arms crossed tight over her chest. Melvin shook his head. "Look," he said, zipping up. "I don't like to get all up in people's personal business. But Imma tell you this much—you gotta let shit go or else you gonna end up somewhere way worse than here."

This Is Him?

WHAT PLACE COULD BE WORSE than Glenn Avenue? Melvin was right about one thing: she did have to let shit go. Or at least she had to fess up. Ava was looking for him was the thing. For Cass. He had walked down her road in New Jersey and told her he was on his way to Philadelphia. The son of a bitch. He had walked, unbidden, into the life she had with Abemi and blown it all up in twenty minutes. Then he'd disappeared again. Wasn't that just like him.

She and Toussaint had been in the kitchen garden at the house in James Creek, examining the hard green tomatoes. Ava was saying to Toussaint that maybe the problem was too much shade, or maybe the soil needed— Cass came walking around the side of the house, no fanfare, like he'd just been there the day before.

"The country girl returns to her beginnings," he said.

His gaze was calm and steady. He wore a white shirt tucked into the palest of blue pants. Tall as a willow. Ava brushed at a smudge of dirt on her cheek.

"Cass?" she said. Though he was unmistakably himself.

She was aware, suddenly, of her old jeans rolled at the cuffs and the bandanna she'd tied around her head and the fact that she had not yet washed her face.

"Who are you?" Toussaint asked.

"This is Toussaint," Ava said.

She looked at her son. "And this is Cass."

Toussaint peered up at the stranger, his hand tightening around Ava's. He took in Cass's shoes, dull and scuffed, and the sharp jawline and clean-shaven face, the tawny lion-colored skin and the eyes of the same color.

"This is him?" he said. "This is Cass?"

"I'm him," Cass answered. The three of them stood in a triangle, the tension pinging between them.

"How did you find us?" Ava said.

"Were you trying not to be found?" Cass smiled a sad little smile and stepped forward. He crouched down to eye level with Toussaint. "I'm pleased to see you. Pleased to meet you, I mean. Pleased to see you both." He fixed his golden eyes on Toussaint, who blinked once, twice in his gaze and backed up a little. "I see your mom has you gardening. It's good for us to know how to feed ourselves. I can't get the hang of growing things," he said. "Brown thumb." He rose to standing.

Ava put her arm around her boy's shoulders. After all these years Cass ought to have a little shame. Standing in another man's yard like it was his. Ava cast about in her mind for some words to speak, something more than an animal bleat or a flurry of kicks and punches.

"Did you come from far away?" Toussaint asked.

"Pretty far," Cass said.

"You don't have a suitcase."

Cass shook his head.

"Where do you live?" Toussaint asked.

"I'm on my way to Philadelphia."

"You live there?"

"I'm going to stop there for a while," he said. "I used to live there."

"Us too." After a long silence Toussaint said, "But now me and Ma live here." And with that he broke his gaze with Cass and backed closer to his mother.

"With my husband," Ava said.

Cass nodded. "A husband is a useful thing," he said. "If you have use for one."

He gave her another of his rueful glances, as if he were sorry her life had come down to needing a husband. As if needing one didn't have anything to do with him. Ava had never wanted a child before she met Cass. She had whipped around the cyclone of him for those two years and when it was clear they were done she wanted a baby. Bad. More than anything. Maybe she needed something of Cass to love when he was gone. I want a kid, she had told him after they'd split up. She had not said: Stay. I'll need help. Or, Hang around so you can meet your child. Didn't seem like the sort of thing you should have to be explicit about. Course, she also said she would raise the baby on her own. But anyway, in the end it didn't matter what she said. Not long after she got pregnant, he was sued for malpractice and the board stripped his medical license.

"Where you been all this time, Cass?"

She didn't mean to sound so keening. He disappeared in the early months of her pregnancy. Some people they used to know said he'd gone to New Orleans. Others said California. The last she'd heard he was in the Carolinas.

"Down South, mostly," he answered. He kept his eyes trained on her; she had a watery feeling in her legs.

"Like Alabama?" Toussaint said.

"Lots of places. There too."

"My grandmother lives in Alabama," Toussaint said. "I never met her." He gave Cass a long look. "I never met you either."

"No. No, you never did."

An engine sound drew closer. Ava hurried around the corner of the house. Thank goodness it was only Mr. Leroy, Everlasting bless him, rolling down the sleepy highway on the 4-H tractor, smiling and waving from the seat. Toussaint took off toward him. Who could blame him? His mother lit up like a Christmas tree and this stranger-father shown up out of nowhere with a haunted, hunted gaze and the iron will of him pushing at them.

"What the hell are you doing here?" Ava hissed.

"I came to see you."

"To see us? To see us! What for? You thought you would show up and I would . . . Me and my son would . . . What?"

Cass paused, rapt, watching his son talk to Leroy. When he turned back to Ava he was . . . If she didn't know better she'd have mistaken it for wonder.

"I thought a long time about what I would say to you. I forgot half of it when I saw you and the boy. I had planned to tell you that I am a different man than I was."

Ava resisted the urge to drive her palm into his chest. She wanted to make him bend to her. She wanted to hurt him. Still, in all her fury, tears formed in the back of her throat.

"I have insulted you." Cass shook his head. "I'm sorry. I won't stay. I'm going back to Philadelphia to build something new— a medical practice, to offer services to people in need. Long-term, comprehensive, with a—"

There he was: Cass of the flashing eyes. His words tumbled out of him a little too fast.

He took a deep breath. "I'm getting ahead of myself. I just wanted to ask if you— It won't be up and running for a while yet, but it will be."

"You shouldn't have come here. I'm married, Cass."

"I don't want to disrupt this life you made for yourself." He looked at the neat house and Ava in her muddy jeans. "Not until I have something better to offer you."

Condescending bastard.

He touched Ava's elbow. When she looked up at him the sky behind him was the most extraordinary blue. The watery feeling in her legs surged upward, like it might lift her off the ground. When she snapped her arm away from his fingertips, she wanted them back more than anything. Cass was always like that. A hot needle through the skin and a block of ice to soothe the wound, both and all at once. Dangerous. He needed to go.

Ava crossed the yard toward Toussaint and Mr. Leroy. The older man looked down at the three of them with his head cocked to the side. He raised his eyebrows when he'd put two and two together. "I'm Leroy Jacobs," he said. "I live next door. Friend to the family." He put the emphasis on "family."

"This is . . ." Ava said. "He stopped by on his way to Philadelphia, and . . ."

Mr. Leroy nodded. "Well—"

"Are you still a doctor?" Toussaint asked. He had been silent for a long time, staring at Cass's shoes. "Ma said you were a doctor."

"I'm still a doctor."

"You don't look like a doctor. Your shoes are dirty. Doctors have clean shoes."

"I guess everybody's shoes get dirty if they walk a long way."

"You sure are tall," Toussaint said. "All the doctors on TV are tall. I guess, maybe . . ." His voice trailed off. "Do you have a stethoscope?"

"No, but I can tell if you have the spotted-frog fever by looking at your tongue."

"There's no such thing as spotted-frog fever!"

"Science man, huh? Okay. But I can take your pulse if I feel your wrist."

Toussaint lifted his arm toward Cass, tentatively, like he was offering up his best thing. Mr. Leroy cleared his throat.

"We're just . . . We're just going to walk him down the road a little way. We . . . Could you give us a minute?" Ava said.

"Oh! Oh yeah. I guess this fella has to be on his way. Well, it was nice to meet you there, uh—"

"Cass." He fixed Mr. Leroy with such a stare that the old man looked away.

"You come by later. All right, buddy? And I'll ride you over to see how that hawk nest is doing. Okay?" But Toussaint was spellbound by his father. Mr. Leroy put the tractor in reverse and backed into his driveway. Nosy.

Ava glanced down the road. She couldn't figure how to tell Cass to leave without upsetting Toussaint. She couldn't say she wanted to go with him. Everlasting help her, but she did. But sometimes

Abemi came home for lunch. And Mr. Leroy meant well, but she'd have to manage his big mouth. And it was all too much for Toussaint. After Cass was gone, she'd have to answer to her boy and she didn't have any idea how she'd do it. Her elbow still tingled where Cass's hand had been.

"Do you know how old I am?" Toussaint said.

"Ten," Cass replied.

"Do you know my birthday?"

"December fifth. At eleven forty-three p.m."

"How come you never came around for my birthday if you know when it is?"

Ava reached for her son's hand. He let her hold his fingers for an instant before snatching them away. He turned his back to Cass ever so slightly. "Ma," he said. "Don't we have to eat soon? I'm hungry. Aren't you hungry?" He kicked at the dirt.

"I'm very glad to meet you," Cass said to Toussaint, who did not answer. His voice was soft, resigned. "I'm glad to see how well your mom takes care of you."

He did not say I'll send you a birthday card or I will call you at Christmas. He didn't try to hug Toussaint; he only rested his great warm hand on his shoulder. Toussaint looked into Cass's eyes in spite of himself. He couldn't say what he saw there, or even figure out exactly how it made him feel, but for months his father's face was the last thing he saw before he fell asleep.

To Ava, Cass said, softly, "I'll be in touch. Once I have things more settled. Maybe you'll tell me to go to hell. But I'm going to try."

He passed his hand over his jaw. Ava remembered that gesture; it was what he did when he was gathering himself together, like in the early mornings when the light came in and he was weary and hungover and briefly undefended. "Thank you for letting me see my son."

Ava and Toussaint watched him walk down the road till the slanting sun swallowed him up and there was only gold light where his body had been.

Rambling

AT FIRST TOUSSAINT WAS TIMID in his truancy—scanning the streets for Miss Gregory or his mother or any other adult that might cart him back to school. But the days turned into a week, and then two. He was a quick study: different route every day or he might catch somebody's attention. He learned to sneak onto out-of-service buses at the Ogontz transfer station and how to play sleepy and lost if he got caught. If he walked close behind a woman on the street, people assumed she was his mother. He learned how to make himself nearly invisible in a corner of the library, and that the branch on Chelten Avenue had record players and headphones where he could listen to the same music he listened to with Paul in New Jersey.

He chose records from the bins based on whether he liked the way the people were dressed on the covers. Toussaint discovered liked the old songs too—his grandmother sang old songs but he never saw any records she made. He didn't always understand the lyrics, but he knew what they meant—the words growled, or trilled and joyful the way sunlight looks coming down through high green branches, or heavy like his feet and legs aching after the hours' walk back to Glenn Avenue when he'd already spent his bus fare. The music was a found thing he didn't know he'd lost. His favorite was a lady named Sippie Wallace. He wondered if she was still alive, and if she ever came to Philadelphia to sing her songs in a big concert at the Spectrum, or on the Parkway like they did on the Fourth.

In the third week of his wandering Toussaint found himself in a derelict part of the city where the downtown high-rises gleamed in the distance beyond grim, broken-window warehouses and abandoned factories. These streets ran along stretches of busted chain-link fences and barbed wire that marked the border with the known world. Toussaint crossed over into the high, straw-colored weeds waving in the afternoon sunlight. He arrived at an abandoned viaduct and clambered up a mound of metal trash. The distant railroad shone dully in late morning light. He had a song in his mind that made him smile: *Tonight when I start walkin'.*

On the other side of an underpass beneath the expressway a dirt trail led to a clearing where a tent city had grown up. Toussaint hid behind a low rise and watched. Blue and orange tarps stretched across long metal rods billowed in the breeze. Camping tents, beach umbrellas staked next to shopping carts, cardboard boxes duct-taped and covered over with garbage bags. A lean-to with a bright green highway sign for one wall: WILLOW GROVE EXIT ¼ MILE. The tent people burned fires in big metal drums. People slept sitting up. A man washed a T-shirt in a bucket, and hung it on a line strung between tall metal poles. Some wore all their clothes at the same time with hoods pulled up so their faces weren't visible. Fee fi fo fum. At the bottom of the slope a group of three men talked together; one was a big man with a perfectly white beard on his dark brown cheeks. Black Santa, Toussaint thought and smiled.

"Whatcha doing here?" he called. As Toussaint scrambled backward, the white-bearded man shouted after him, "Little man! Hey, little man," with a voice that made him think of Mr. Leroy and their rides on the tractor. He ran pell-mell for the underpass and hid there. A long while later he reassumed his perch at the top of the rise.

This time the bearded man came up on him from behind and stood over him, blocking out the sunlight.

"If it ain't the little man back again."

Toussaint was too afraid to speak.

"Cat got it, huh?" he said. "Whatcha doing around here? Don't know? Me neither." His laugh was high and squeaky, so strange from such a big man that Toussaint looked right at him in spite of himself. His eyes were cloudy but not mean.

"You got a name?"

Toussaint nodded.

"Well, what is it?"

Toussaint didn't answer. The man shrugged. "Mine's Zeek," he said, and went down the little hill toward the tents without giving Toussaint a second glance.

Zeek sat on an overturned bucket. He produced a ladies' compact from his pocket and proceeded to trim his beard with the other hand. When he finished his grooming, he walked back up the rise. "Still here?" he said and set a pack of Hydrox cookies on the little mound just within Toussaint's reach. Toussaint took them and ran.

When he came back the next day Zeek said, "If ain't old No-Name," and gave him a half-eaten bag of sour-cream-and-onion chips.

"Toussaint," he whispered as Zeek walked away.

He stood and followed him down to the maze of tents. Zeek fed him more treats from his backpack stash and nodded off between long rants about what he called the police state.

"Zeek ain't my government name. I chose that name. I don't do nothing those motherfuckers want—no tax, no nothing. He's right about that. You know Ark?"

Zeek held up a flyer that said COME INTO THE ARK.

"Get it? Cuz you can dry out in there. Hehe. Naw, that's grown-folks jokes. You don't need to know nothing about that. Point is, this brother been coming around three or four months and put everybody's head on *straight*. Pay attention, little man. That over there was the sugar refinery. You know why it closed?

"And this one they got now, Ronald Reagan, he just a cowboy from the movies! I thought he was nice enough, but turns out he's a mean somebody. And that wife. Nancy. She could freeze a man's dick right off him."

Zeek and the tent city men scared him, but after so many weeks of wandering, regular people scared him too—maybe they'd nab him for not going to school or they'd see something strange in him and start asking questions. Regular people were always doing the same regular stuff—on and off buses, bursting out of their houses in the morning and rushing back to their dining room tables at night. And they looked down on people like Zeek on account of he didn't have all the stuff they had. Toussaint didn't either, but he did have his wits about him. Zeek told him so. And he suffered less from the cold than he used to, and could go longer without food if he needed to. He was less regular every day and more like Zeek and the tent men, even if some of them were too loud and a couple of them tried to get him to come in their tents for reasons Toussaint couldn't figure out. "Stay away from that motherfucker," Zeek said, pointing at the one who'd offered him some Ring Dings.

It was true that the men usually wanted something. They wanted a little change, if he had any. They wanted to sit and talk. Toussaint didn't mind since his part of the talking was mostly listening. One man wanted him to hold the end of a belt while he wound the other end around his arm to make the vein pop. They wanted to tell him they had a son about his age. They wanted to show him a picture of their mothers, wives, brothers who were in Ohio or Tennessee or D.C., or ten blocks away or at the other end of the 73 bus route. Their sons all looked like Toussaint. They wanted to show him a trick for sneaking into the service entrances of movie theaters, or show him just how fine it was to sip on a can of something and smoke a cigarette on a clear sunny day. Some wanted to show him their pain: a wound oozing and stinking. "See this? This shit rotting off me like I was already a fucking corpse. You see?" Everybody wanted him to look. Toussaint found out he was a person who could see all kinds of things and most often he wouldn't flinch and he wouldn't run and they liked him for that and he liked himself for it too.

Be Cool

AVA DIDN'T SLEEP ANYMORE, or not much. She was heavy-lidded and near nodding off all day but at night she couldn't keep her eyes closed for longer than an hour. Regrets dove at her like hungry gulls. Like this one: After Cass came walking down the road, Toussaint wanted to tell Abemi. "Because, Ma," he had said, "who is this Mr. Cass to us?" They shouldn't keep secrets from Abemi.

"Can I tell him, Ma?" he'd said. "I think it's the right thing to do."

Ava kissed him on the cheek and sent her son off to do what she should have done, and set her husband up to do the only thing a man like him could.

Across the room Toussaint slept like a sack of drowned rabbits. His lips were red and glistened in the streetlight's reflection coming in through the window. Ava dabbed his wet mouth with the corner of the sheet. She pulled the blanket up over his shoulders. She prayed for him the way the women used to pray in Bonaparte, which was part help me, Jesus, and part pondering the crimson of a pomegranate and part praise song to the Everlasting. In her prayers Ava could see the shape of things to come. She saw her mother's kitchen table on Sundown Road. And a dinner plate scraped clean with Dutchess's big spoon sitting next to it. There was another shape, beneath that one, more felt than seen. In that vision Ava was a brilliant version of herself, vibrant and satiated. Her boy had

put on a few pounds and grown an inch or two. He smiled up at his
father.

Toussaint sighed in his sleep. Ava watched to see if he'd wake,
then went out into the hallway, up to the cafeteria, and out through
the pantry exit door. In the last weeks she had left the building
only at night. She never went far. Up to the corner, once halfway
across the street toward the A&P parking lot, but she'd panicked,
like she'd strayed too far, from what she couldn't say. Now the night
was still, not a car, not a person, not even the wind blowing. A dis-
carded Peanut Chews wrapper on the sidewalk caught her eye. She
put it into her pocket. She had been collecting things: a cigarette
butt she finally smoked after two nights of looking for matches in
the street, a betting stub for Meet Me on the Outside (dog? horse?)
who paid out seventy dollars, a portion of the directions for a bottle of children's cough syrup. That night, she found a phone number scrawled on a torn bit of paper.

Back inside Glenn Avenue, no one stirred. Ava's footfalls landed
softly as she walked to the pay phone. She held the dirty scrap with
the phone number in one hand and dug through her pockets for
change with the other. Calling the number was just a silly something to pass the wee hours—though sometimes the Everlasting
leaves clues. She'd never know if she didn't call. As she lifted the
receiver, footsteps approached from the bowels of the building.
Ava ducked under the guard's desk, a few paces behind the phones.
She peered through the rectangle of space between the floor and
the bottom of the desk.

Feet tucked into plush pink house shoes appeared. "Motherfuckers always want to be late," a woman's voice muttered. One
pink foot tapped. Outside, headlights strobed once, twice, then an
idling engine cut off and the darkened entry area was again tinged
red from the EXIT sign above the front door. Keys jingled. The door
opened.

"What took you so long?" the woman's voice said. "I been coming back and forth for a damn hour!"

"Ain't nobody else here, is it? I swear I thought I saw somebody
when I pulled up. Imma just take a look—"

Melvin.

"Ain't nobody here. I told you I been coming back and forth a hour waiting on your late ass. Can we just get this done fore my kids wake up?"

Melvin's black lace-up shoes approached. His toes poked under the desk, so close Ava could have thumped them with her fist. They smelled, like he'd stepped in dog shit. Pink feet moved to one side. Ava heard crinkling, something being unwrapped, and sounds like paper being shuffled.

"This the whole week?" Melvin asked.

"End of the month," the woman said. I know that voice, Ava thought.

"You got to be kidding," Melvin said. "This ain't hardly worth driving over here for. We coulda just waited and put this in with next week's."

The woman sucked her teeth. I know that voice, Ava thought again. That woman! The one who always—

"Tess ain't trying to have you pull that high-interest shit on her." She chuckled. "You better pay up and get on out of here."

More shuffling.

"That's off by ten," Tess said.

"Is it?"

"Negro!" They both laughed.

"All right, girl. All right. Lemme just count it again." Beneath the desk Ava laughed to herself. This was where her food stamps had gone. Tess, who sold wigs out of her room, and stupid Melvin had a food-stamp-laundering ring! That was funny. It was hilarious. And to think five minutes before Ava had been all set to call a number written on trash from the street to ask the Almighty for a sign. She covered her mouth with her hand. She laughed so hard her eyes squeezed shut and her shoulders shook.

While she laughed the pink slippers and black shoes turned toward each other. The talking stopped. And the counting too. Unzipping. Then heavy breathing and: "Look like you ain't got to rush away so quick after all."

Ava's eyes flew open. She sat up with such force that her head hit the underside of the desk with a thunk. Pink slippers and black shoes sprang apart.

"What the—?"

Melvin's face swung down into view. A high-beam flashlight shined into her eyes.

"Who's under there?" Tess said.

"Ava?"

"Who?" Tess stooped to peer in. "Oh, this bitch? You tryna fuck with—"

Ava climbed out from under the desk, trying to keep her dignity. "I'm not fucking with anything. What are *you* doing?"

"Oh. Ah-ahn. No," Tess said, stepping toward Ava. Melvin put his body between them.

"Let's just everybody calm down. You been down there this whole time, Ava?"

"Yeah, she been down here this whole time! And nasty too. You like listening to people get—"

"Okay, Tess!" Melvin said.

"Your fly's down, Melvin," Ava said.

Tess looked from one to the other. "Ooh! Tess got it now. You just putting it to everybody, ain't you, Melvin?" Tess laughed. "Don't take it personal, girl."

Ava drew herself up to her full height and narrowed her eyes at the two of them. She settled on Tess and said, "You better get down there and get your dollar," nodding toward a bill on the floor.

"Watch yourself," Tess said.

"It's all good. Ava's cool. You cool. Right, Ava?"

"Sure, Melvin. I'm cool."

"See? That's what I'm talking about. She—"

"Tess, why you don't go see about your kids. Imma just talk to Ava here and work it out."

"You do that, Melvin. You make sure it's worked out." Tess picked up her bill and was gone down the hallway.

"She just got a bad temper," Melvin said.

Ava was silent.

"You want to, uh . . . I got the car here. You want to take a little ride? There's the all-night diner. Get some breakfast before my shift starts?"

Ava fixed him in a hard stare.

"Lighten up, girl. It's just business. You gon make a little something something too."

"Then give it to me now," Ava said.

"What?"

"I gave you fifty in food stamps, so give me my fifty dollars."

"Come on, Ava. Ain't nothing to be mad about."

"Give my fifty dollars, Melvin."

"It don't really work that way, like I explained to you."

"The whole fifty."

"All right. Okay. You doing me like the IRS. But I got you."

Ava eyed the wad of cash Melvin pulled from his jacket pocket.

"You selling the food in the pantry too? What about the toilet paper and the light bulbs? Jesus, Melvin." Ava took the money and turned toward her room.

"Be cool, Ava. Be cool now." He watched her go, shaking his head.

BONAPARTE

• • •

THE STRANGER'S NAME WAS Barber. Roared into our place in his blue truck like the wrath of God. I shouldn't've shot him. But then what else was I supposed to do with a stranger riding up on me like the hounds of hell? Carter and Juniata and Erma Linner decided I had to nurse him on account of it was me that hit him. We took him to my house and there he stayed. In my own bed, mind you, propped on a cloud of pillows.

It takes a minute to heal a gut shot. Long time shitting in a pan and sleeping eighteen hours a day. Long time waking up in the middle of the night knocked breathless like the bullet hit you all over again. In the early days he was too sick to say boo to a ghost. I'll hand it to him for keeping hisself together, no screaming and wailing and hardly any cussing, even when we changed his dressing and mashed yarrow and goldenrod over that hole, which musta hurt like hell.

After a couple weeks he was awake more than he was sleep. But he still wouldn't tell us much about how he came to be in our place. I was a little suspicious at him being so closemouthed. Then one morning Carter Lee caught him giving me the side-eye for the millionth time and says, "Take it easy, boy. Dutchess don't never shoot nobody more than once." The whole room bust out laughing which now I see might have scared him. I kept up changing his bandages a couple times a day, though by then he didn't need the wound redressed so often. I guess I felt like it was the least I could do.

"You babying him," Carter Lee said round the third week he was with us. Meanwhile what was he doing? Rearranging all the tubs and ointments and drinking glasses on the bedside table.

"She sweet on him," Juniata said.

"Don't be ridiculous," Erma Linner said. "At her age."

Truth is, we were all a little sweet on him. My house was full of people like it hadn't been for decades. Everybody dropped in three, four times a day. Stayed fifteen minutes, stayed an hour. All of us crowded in me and Caro's bedroom, sat around the bed looking after him.

"It's not so bad," I told him. "I been hurt worse from getting after a feral hog. Feral hog is no joke."

"No, she was not," Erma Linner said. "You never been after a feral hog, Dutchess. I don't know why you want to act like we are the Beverly Hillbillies."

"Well, I been after one," Carter Lee said. "More than one. My daddy used—"

"Hush up, sugar," Juniata said.

"Yeah, hush up, Carter Lee," Erma Linner said. "He's not going to be able to sleep if y'all keep talking."

Fat chance of that. Juniata had given him a lot of her witch-woman dirt water and basically put the nigger in a coma. There we were, four old fools sitting around watching this fella like he was the picture shows.

"Well, he sure is pretty. I'll say that for him," Erma Linner said.

He was pretty. Tall and long and the same wheat color all over. Eyes too.

"Clearly not from round here," said Carter Lee, who isn't prone to stupid observations but I guess that's a thing that can happen to anybody once or twice.

"City," Carter Lee added. "City teeth." Hands too. Smooth with long square fingers.

"You looking at a murder charge if he don't make it," Juniata says.

Dramatic.

"Dramatic," I said.

He was dicty and northern, but he never fussed about anything we gave him, just kind of squinted at all of it. "What *is* this?" he'd say, sniffing at one of those little Juniata jars. One time, when he thought nobody was looking, he stuck his pinkie in and touched it to the tip of his tongue. Of course, we also gave him the tetracycline Carter Lee kept stockpiled in the postmaster's office.

"We're not cavemen," I told him.

He kept changing his story: he was from Baltimore, a week later it was Philadelphia, and one time he got so far north as Buffalo, but maybe that was his brother or somebody. Even his own name seemed like a surprise when we called him by it. To be fair, he had been trying to tell us his name was "Carver" but his face and mouth was swole up at the time on account of his truck rammed into a tree when I hit him. We thought he said, "Barber," and that's who he stayed.

Carver. Barber. It didn't really matter much. I knew both were made up. I still wonder what his real name was. What people who know him call him. If anybody knows him, which I have my doubts about. Used to be we had a steady stream of strangers around here. Bonaparte is a off-the-world kind of place. People turned up here from anywhere or nowhere. Or they came after traveling so long that whoever they used to be was trailing way behind them. Sometimes they were trying to find somebody new to be. Sometimes they needed to be somebody new. We didn't ask a lot of questions unless folk started acting some way that made us have to.

"Leave it at the Oaks" was what we said when strangers showed up. We were talking about knives and guns, but we meant any kind of shit they were carrying. Leave it at the Oaks. I did. When me and Ava stepped into Bonaparte, I left that other Dutchess and all her trouble out there riding the Yazoo from juke to juke. She stayed out there for a long time. I could feel her, a melody hanging in the air.

"I'm not really from anywhere," he told me once he saw I had quit bothering him about it. "Nothing exotic. We just moved around a lot. My father couldn't stand being in one place. He'd settle us somewhere and in a couple of years the white people with their shit got on his nerves, and the black people with their shit, so he moved us somewhere else. He was an electrician. He could work anywhere. My mother didn't say much. She was sick a lot. Living on her own by the time she died, nobody around to mourn her."

Poor woman. I swear unless they let them go hungry or they see her naked or some such, children don't hardly notice these mamas till they're cold in the ground. At least Barber wasn't sentimental after the fact. Posthumous blubbering about a mama burns me up.

"And what happened to your father?"

"Dead." He paused. "My brother, in case you were wondering, is an insurance agent in Cincinnati."

I don't know why that made me laugh. But for some reason that was just so funny coming out of this ginger man's mouth in my house in the second black incorporated town of the state of Alabama. On the verge of our extinction.

"Well," I said when I could breathe enough to talk. "Somebody got to be in insurance in Cincinnati. May as well be your brother. Is his name Herbert? That's a good insurance-man name."

Barber says, "No, Elroy," and he started laughing too.

"How about Marshall?" I said.

"Or Dewey. Dewey of Mutual of Omaha."

That sent us both howling. Only in the middle of our laughing I remembered we was supposed to be talking about his real-life brother, not some Dewey we made up. Shit, I thought, this nigger is crazy.

But I appreciated him letting me in on the joke.

Of course, me and Carter Lee had searched his truck long before that. And his wallet and the little suitcase in the passenger seat. We needed some fresh blood round here, that's for sure, but we didn't get this far being stupid. We found what you'd expect, clothes and such, a little money. Plus one thing you wouldn't: a picture of a little boy who favored him. But we all had sense enough not to ask him about it.

"Maybe that was what set him rambling," Erma Linner said. "His boy died."

I guess we needed to give him some kind of story. We killed off the little boy in the picture to give our stranger a reason for running around getting hisself shot down here in the ass of Alabama. And anyway, seemed like the only person he really hurt was his own self.

One morning I woke up on the sofa and he was gone. I half figured he'd just got better and wandered back onto the road like animals do after you tend them to health. I won't say I wasn't a little sad about it, but by the time I got through checking the house, he was walking through the front door.

"I guess you can't do anything about those fallow acres with just the few of us to work them? But I did notice your cows were in the road."

"Shit," I said. Not because of the cows—that fence had been falling down for years, and they knew to come back at night—but because at his full height Barber was about ten feet tall, with energy coming off him in gold sparks.

We took him all over what was left of Bonaparte. Erma Linner showed him the old schoolhouse and wouldn't you know she got to caterwauling all over the desks. Scratched-up old things, warped from the rain that came through a hole in the roof. I liked the schoolhouse, it felt like an old church. Whitewashed walls gone to the spiders and ivy. Sun streaming in. A hot smell. Barber wanted to know what all the kids learned and how many there were in a class.

"Well," Erma Linner said. "We learnt em on 'rithmetic, heifer birthin', seed plantin', nigra singin'." Erma Linner can be funny when she wants to be. "No, we just followed the state of Alabama curriculum," she told him. "We had Doreen. Doreen Landry. Everlasting bless her."

Doreen was a sweetheart. She ran away from some white woman's kitchen in Bodine and stayed here with us until her last breath forty years later. Doreen could pass so we used to send her to Montgomery every year to get the curriculum for all the grades. She'd buy the schoolbooks too. Even got some donated. White folks are lambs in the field to a kindly white lady looking to educate the skinned-kneed kids in her nowhere town. They are capable of kindness, which means they choose to be murderers and thieves. "We are all animals," I used to tell Ava, when she asked what was wrong with them. "You go out in the woods and look at all the creatures—some are nice and some are dangerous and got a screw loose."

"My daughter," I told Barber, "went to the University of Alabama with her Bonaparte schoolhouse education." I left out how she didn't finish, twice.

"Ava, right? Your daughter," Barber said. For a minute I didn't remember telling him her name but I guess I must have, all that talking I been doing since he got here.

When he wanted to know how we paid for the school we took him to the Bonaparte General Store, the wreck of it standing burnt in the middle of town. I still tear up when I look at it. We went to the pickling and canning house where there is still a shelf of jars, can you believe it, with BONAPARTE PICKLES labels across the front. We told him about the livestock sales. About Caro's furniture-making business. About the kitchen gardens. About the eggs and the henhouses. About how each of us kept 60 percent of what we made for ourselves and the rest went in a group fund to pay property taxes, buy schoolbooks, maintenance on the common land and buildings, emergencies. Barber said, "A cooperative!" Like it was a miracle we thought of it. Then he said it again like he was trying to make sure we knew the word. Juniata looked at him and shook her head. Uppity has a way of welling up out of somebody now and again.

"Till when? I mean, why did you . . . How . . ." He didn't have the heart to finish the question.

We took him down to the river and the five of us watched Progress bulldozing up our people's bones. New houses going up too, closer to us than they should have been. "That used to be yours?" Barber asked.

"Goddamn Progress."

"It wasn't all them. The checks did us in too," Carter Lee said. I wanted to pinch him, even if he was a little bit right. "Every kind of check. Public assistance, SSI. Disability. Eminent domain payouts. The kids left. People who stayed couldn't keep up the store and the pickles and everything else. Fewer people from outside to buy the stuff anyway. Crops selling for hardly nothing—we couldn't compete with these big spreads the white farmers got. They wouldn't give us FSA loans, neither. People were tired."

"And trifling," I said. "We could have kept on. People got . . ."

Carter Lee sighed. "Dutchess, come on. This fella gon go away from here and maybe talk about this place and he should know the truth, not how you want it to be. It was drugs here just like everywhere else, and some of us could have done better. And some of us did our best and it didn't work out anyhow."

Carter Lee turned to Barber. "Y'all was running around up there Black Power this, Black Power that and wearing your hair nappy. We were here trying to keep this land," he said. "We went hungry for the first time in a long time. All the money went to pay the property taxes. We fell behind. Then they started with the checks and we could eat again. You understand? The checks kept us alive. But that was the end of us."

Barber didn't say nothing to nobody for nearly a week after that. I only knew he was here because I heard the door click shut late at night and there was hot coffee every morning. He roamed all through the woods, through the old fields, down by the river. Carter Lee thought he saw him way out by the Progress houses.

He finished his mourning one day and said, "Do you need all those cows?"

I guessed I didn't, so he said, "What do you do with a cow you don't need?"

Sounded like the beginning of a joke to me so I said, "What *do* you do with a cow you don't need?"

Anyway, he sold off five of them to a guy forty miles out from Bonaparte who I would have sworn had been in the grave for years. He came back with the cash and a whole lot of city-boy self-satisfaction. He said he'd re-staked our sign by the Oaks on his way back in.

"Those woods there are particular," I said.

I wanted to tell him about Old Rea, but that's not a thing we do with outsiders, so instead I told him about Eddie.

"We had Eddie the Indian. He used to come and trade way back when everything was still everything around here. He was old, I can tell you. Twice a year he turned up at the general store. He always wore the same work boots and nubby plaid jacket and a wool pullover cap. I don't think I ever saw his hair. The kids was always disappointed the first time they saw him. He just look regular. Like he work at Fosky's, is what Ava said. Too much of that cowboy stuff. You wonder how that bullshit got all the way to Bonaparte. Well so she says, 'What kind of Indians look like they work at Fosky's?' I pinched her good for being rude."

"Eddie was the last of the traders. When Caro was little, there was a few more. They used to come around regular back when his ma'am was a girl. In slave times even more. Bonaparte was a free place. Anybody kind to us was welcome here. This was their land, anyhow. Well, so by the time I got here there were only a few of these fellas left. And then it was just Eddie. He came with all kind of stuff we couldn't get and didn't have: chocolates, almond candy, tobacco seeds. Slinkys. Yeah. And funny little things too. Caro gave me a little tiny bear carved out of pink soapstone with a fish in its mouth.

"The last time he came—we didn't know it was the last time—he said, 'I saw your old woman in the woods.'"

I ended up telling Barber about Rea after all. But as I talked, I could see Eddie's face, wide-set eyes and long deep wrinkles. And I could smell the tang of wet leaves in the November air. I could hear Bonaparte, voices trailing down the main road, kids yelling, the door to the general store squeaking open every few minutes—this was a living place. We that's left don't talk about how it used to be. We got ourselves accustomed to the emptiness and the silence, to the wind blowing the shutters on the abandoned store and the church, the high grass rustling because there's nobody around to cut it—loneliest sound in the world. I started talking about Eddie, and Rea just followed right behind him.

"Eddie said Rea walked out of the woods toward the river. He wouldn't say nothing more no matter how we pressed him. The next spring Eddie didn't come. Never came back again. Then it was summer and they shot my husband. Eddie disappeared and Old Rea went into the river and Bonaparte got all messed up. We got off the track of our own time and back into white people's time. Maybe this place can't exist in white people time, maybe it'll just fade away and stay gone."

Barber nodded. "They disappear things," he said. "History. Poof."

I never had to explain anything to him.

The next week Barber said, "I'm going over to those Progress people to see if one of the contractors wants some extra cash." And sure enough, couple of weeks later my fences were mended. "What about the general store?," he wanted to know. When I told him what happened he went quiet like he had when we explained about the land. Looked like there was a thundercloud all around him. Like he had his own weather. Caro used to get like that. I know to keep quiet and stay out of the way when a man like that is in a funk.

Turns out the Progress fellas were some eager-beaver moonlighters. Barber got them to tear down the burnt shell of the store and haul away the debris. Him and Carter Lee made a nice sign: SITE OF THE BONAPARTE GENERAL COOPERATIVE, 1941–1970. He had them cart away some trees fallen down in the middle of the road too. So weren't the five of us getting around like we hadn't in years, zooming from one abandoned place to the next. Hehheh.

Barber got on a fix-it kick. He left my house early and didn't come back till night when he was too exhausted to stand up. He helped Nip cut some trees leaning over him and Memma's house. He repaired Erma Linner's sagging porch and patched up a hole in her roof while Carter Lee stood down below yelling up all the how-to's. He cleared all the kudzu and weeds out of her yard. A few mean-looking zucchini was coming up underneath all the brush. "I don't want that," she said, pointing at them. "I don't ever want to stoop and pick anything again. I know you have something to say about golden days," she said, eyeing me. "But I don't."

Erma Linner planted marigolds and gladiolas and Shasta daisies in her cleared front yard. She sat on her sturdy new porch looking out at her flowers like that was all she ever wanted.

PHILADELPHIA

...

Three Strikes

IN MID-NOVEMBER cardboard cutouts of turkeys appeared on the walls of Glenn Avenue. Horns of plenty. Pilgrims smiling big dopey smiles and holding axes. Good Lord, had they always been holding axes? Ava sat waiting her turn in a chair outside Miss Simmons's office. It was that hour when the morning sunlight angled up the long corridor and hit brightly on the cinder blocks. Melvin made a point of averting his eyes when Ava glanced at the guard desk. Like a teenage girl, she thought. She wasn't going to spend her time mooning over Melvin, of all people. But Tess. She was another story. Two notes under the door: "Watch your back." Ava hadn't allowed Toussaint out of the room alone for a week.

"Miss Carson."

Ava had not realized she was holding her breath. Miss Simmons stood in her office doorway staring her down. She turned without so much as a good morning, and stepped back into her office with a jerk of her head. I guess I'm a little dog today, Ava thought. She did not stand and Miss Simmons did not return to the hallway. The stalemate lasted so long Melvin stopped his tic-tac-toe game to watch. Finally, Miss Simmons called. "Miss Carson," voice flat as a pancake. It was clear to Melvin that Ava didn't know how to pick her battles. Lulu Simmons never loses.

"You can close the door," Miss Simmons said, without looking up from the stack of papers on her desk. A poster on the wall showed how to save a choking victim. No Pilgrims in here. No siree.

What a mess, Miss Simmons thought. Standing there defiant. Skinny as the light pole. And pale, more yellow with each passing day. This kind of woman is always setting the house on fire while she's still in it. Miss Simmons hadn't figured Ava for that type. What a mess, she thought again.

"Miss Carson, what is the status of your job search?"

How's your day going, Miss Simmons. Mine's been fine, thank you for asking. Big plans this weekend? Ava smirked, nearly smirked, her lip curled. Miss Simmons's eyes narrowed.

"When is the last time you went to the job center?" she asked.

Miss Simmons probably never shook either of the two (two!) snow globes on her desk. Ava threaded her fingers together to resist the urge to pick one up. Mostly, she wanted to go back to her room and lie down. Without Melvin to break up the time the days were featureless and dragging.

"Miss Carson, you are aware that the rules of the Glenn Avenue Family Shelter require residents to search for employment as a condition of their stay?"

"The . . . Excuse me?"

"Are you aware, Miss Carson, that the rules of the Glenn Avenue—"

"Oh. Yeah. Yes, I know."

"All right. So. When is the last time you visited the job center, Miss Carson?"

Six or seven weeks, at least. Ava had lost count, truth be told. No point in going to that place with its line of tired-looked women—never any men; maybe all the men already had jobs—filling out the same stupid forms with the same information day after day. And those beige walls and that depressing stale-potato-chip smell.

"You had one interview, did you not? With the phone company?"

"Don't they keep my résumé and typing test on file? I mean, it's all still there. At the job center, I mean."

"That is not the point. We have rules. As you know." Miss Simmons gave Ava a long, even stare. "Miss Carson, how is your son doing in school?"

"My son . . . What?"

"Miss Carson, are you aware that your son . . ." She paused and looked down at a notice on her desk. "Taft Elementary is his school, is that correct?"

"Yes, that's—"

"Are you aware that he has not attended Taft Elementary School for the last four weeks?"

Ava sat on her hands to keep from putting them to her mouth. Every afternoon he came back to 813 looking windblown and feral and he wouldn't tell her much about his day. On the weekend he was like a caged tiger, pacing and restless and sullen. "I'm so sorry, baby," Ava would say. "I'm so sorry. I wish we could leave here tomorrow. We could go and live in a great big apartment on School House Lane. With all new furniture. Wouldn't that be nice? Or in Mount Airy? A two-bedroom in Mount Airy?"

She'd bought them a small used television with some of the money from her first benefits check. They needed a distraction. To help them weather it out. Till she saved enough for a deposit on a place, till she got back to the want ads, which she meant to do every day but somehow the days rolled over her like mud sliding down a hill.

"Miss Carson?"

"He's been sick," Ava said.

"For four weeks? Did you take him to the nurse's office? To a clinic? You have—I believe you have . . ." Miss Simmons consulted her papers again. "You have your Medicaid card now."

In Jersey, after the child welfare people took Paul away, Toussaint had not gone to school for weeks. Every day he went down the street and sat with that woman Jilly, who never seemed to be fully dressed and who Abemi called a slattern. What a word. "Probably for the best," he'd said when they took Paul. Like taking somebody's child away from her fixed things right up. One afternoon, the last afternoon Toussaint ever spent at Jilly's, Ava went there to fetch him. The front door to her house was ajar. Her son was holding this grown woman's hand. The strap of her slip had fallen down. She said, "I don't want any Holy Roller prayers if that's what you here for. It's nice when he does it though." She looked toward Toussaint. He had been praying that they bring Paul back. Jilly sat staring into the dark corners of the room. A week later she was gone. Just like that. No good-bye, just gone.

"He's in a bad dream," Ava said.

"Excuse me?"

Miss Simmons didn't know anything about real life; she wouldn't if it bit her on the ass, but Ava decided to tell her one true thing.

"He's sad. Everybody in here is too sad to keep on living one more day. Didn't you know?"

Miss Simmons resisted the urge to shake her head. Did she expect the Hilton? Did she think making a mess of her life didn't cost anything?

"Are the bathroom facilities here not to your liking?" Miss Simmons asked.

"What?"

"I cannot think of any other reason that you would steal a key to the staff bathrooms."

"Wha—I—"

"The staff bathroom is just that, for the use of the staff. The lock, Miss Carson, has been changed. You will find the key you have is useless."

Miss Simmons pulled a form from her stack and turned it so it faced Ava. THIRD WARNING stamped in red across the top. Ava hadn't had a first warning that she could recall. She had seen some notices pushed under the door of their room. But there were always papers under the door: changes to the laundry room hours or training classes on how to use Section 8 vouchers. The Head Start around the corner was closing. Letters about what they were going to take away from you even though there wasn't anything left to take. When they piled up, she asked Toussaint to throw them away.

"I didn't steal anything! Melvin gave me that key."

"Yes, well," Miss Simmons replied. "If you do not resume your job search, your stay here will be terminated immediately. You will return to the Cherry Street Intake Center for reassignment. On Tuesday afternoon you must report to the nurse's office for a psychological evaluation. This is mandatory. If you do not report to this appointment, your stay here will be immediately terminated. If your son does not report to school on Monday morning, your stay here will be terminated. His truancy will be reported to social services, which will open an inquiry." She paused. "I know you don't want to be separated from your son, Miss Carson."

Miss Simmons pushed the sheet closer to Ava. Boxes were checked for noncompliance with shelter rules, failure to search for employment, inappropriate use of facilities. Toussaint's name was printed on a separate line, under which "truancy" was checked with a deep red X. She would not weep in front of Miss Simmons. Her hand trembled as she signed, but she would not weep. Her pop's long-ago advice echoed in her mind, *Don't let nobody make you hang your head.* But she could not lift her gaze.

Miss Simmons watched Ava walk down the corridor past Melvin's desk, her fists balled. It would be just the right thing if Ava punched him in that fat mouth of his. "Lulu," he'd said, a few days before, "Lulu, something you need to know about 813 . . ." She'd said, "813? You don't know her name, Melvin? Not much acquainted?" One day one of these women was going to get him and good. Shame it wouldn't be today. Melvin looked back at Miss Simmons after Ava had passed. She sighed. What use would there be in letting him go? They'd send her another one just like him. What a wreck they all were. And only her to clean it up.

The next one was waiting in the hallway, room 316. At least this one wasn't a problem, not really, even if she was still at Glenn Avenue after fourteen months. Now she claimed she was two weeks sober (Miss Simmons had chosen not to take that opportunity to reiterate the house rules regarding alcohol), thanks to a light-skinned John the Baptist type giving speeches about freedom down by some old railroad tracks. Hmmph. These poor souls were susceptible to any sort of person. "Miss Dell," she called, wearily, and stood waiting in her office doorway.

Mama's Little Baby

AVA COULDN'T SAY: If I didn't have Toussaint I wouldn't be in this place. If I were on my own I would have . . . What? Stayed working at Gimbels? I would be the carefree spinster in the secretarial pool, still at that same desk too far from the windows. Or I'd have gone back to Oakland. It was okay there. When you're somebody's mother you can't admit that you can't manage the mothering. You can't say: I am pulled under by a heavy love and me and him are drowning in it. If Ava started down that road, she'd surely end up with Dutchess. She'd end up in the nightmare years after Pop's death with Dutchess biding time until she could put Ava on a bus to Birmingham.

Dutchess had a different story about how things were back then. Her story was the one she and Ava used to believe together when Ava was a little girl. Parts of it were true in the way some songs are true, which is to say the melody makes you feel something real, even when the lyrics don't match up. That story was still there, way down somewhere Ava might catch the faintest glimmer—if she was willing to see it. The story went like this: Dutchess had been rambling around the Delta playing bad gigs till one October day she rolled into Natchez, Mississippi, in the back of a farmhand's dusty truck, broke and eight months pregnant. "That's how you came to the world, baby girl," Dutchess would tell Ava when they did their reminiscing in the living room on Sundown Road before Caro died. "I was alone as I could be," Dutchess said, "but I had you."

Ava was born in a third-story boardinghouse room at the edge of town. The landlady was worried about stains on her featherbed and chucked Dutchess down on the floor to whelp like a dog. Soon as Ava was old enough to hold her head up, they got back on the road. They traveled, car and rail, to all the great capitals: Memphis, Mobile, Jackson, New Orleans. They were flush now and again—plush mattress motel, hamburgers for supper, store-bought dolls kind of flush. Ava didn't go to school, but she learned more in her first five years than a lot of people do in a lifetime. She knew all the major chords, how to do the Suzie Q, she could fall asleep anywhere, even in the rowdiest juke joint in Nashville, she could play "Mama's Little Baby Loves Short'nin' Bread" on the harmonica. One winter they rode freights on the Yazoo line. Ava was colder and wetter than was bearable, but she found out she could bear it. On the coldest nights Ava and Dutchess were rewarded with stars. They snuggled under their blanket and ate salted peanuts while the train click-clacked; they were one heart beating.

On every stage in every rickety roadside shack Dutchess dedicated the first song to Ava. "Do you remember how I used to say, 'This one is for my baby girl'?" Dutchess would ask in their Bonaparte living room, the darkness coming across the fields at the back of the house. Ava nodded, too full of memory for words, too full of the sawdust-moonshine-sweat smell of those little clubs, of the people's shadows swaying and jigging, and the cigarette smoke ribboning over the crowd. Dutchess would push a root beer into Ava's hands before she went onstage: Don't move from there. Hear? Not for hell or high water. Then she disappeared among the bodies, only to reappear, with the stage light shining down on her green dress, bright like new grass. It must have been dingy with travel, but Ava remembered it pristine and glamorous. Her mother's big brown hands strummed the guitar, the body of it shined to glowing. And there she was, sitting on a stool leaned against the back wall, clutching her bottle of soda pop, her heart in flames.

Those were the best times. There were other times: stale

crackers, cold canned beans, penny candy for supper. Not enough money for bus tickets, nobody to put them up, and no money for boardinghouses. "Trouble got us good, for a while," Dutchess said. Reminiscing wasn't a thing Dutchess liked much, but when she got going about those years before Bonaparte a tremor came into her voice. "And after that . . ." she'd say. Then after that: "I spent the last little bit we had to get us to Birmingham." She knew some people there but the people had moved away so they spent the night in the colored section of the bus station. "Do you remember?" Dutchess said. "You were such a little thing." She shook her head.

They were two days without food. Hollow stomach, dizzy head, pacing, doing their business in the bushes out back, Dutchess's hands guiding Ava's through C major, E minor, Dutchess doing card tricks to distract Ava from the rumble in her belly. On the second day a lady from the relief society came along with a tan pocketbook swing-swinging at Ava's eye level and brown logs for legs. Don't be scared, this lady had said, leaning down to greet her. I am Mrs. Weeks. What's your name? It's true Ava was just a little thing, not more than five, but, oh, that woman made her so mad. Could have been the way she looked down her nose at Dutchess in her singing dress. The woman reached out to touch Ava's shoulder and . . . "I mean, you bit the hell out of that lady," Dutchess said. "You gave her the junkyard dog!" She, Dutchess that is, roared. Ava too until their bellies hurt laughing about that relief woman who mistook a couple of wild foxes for backyard strays. "Aww, but," Dutchess said, catching her breath. "You probably shouldn't have bit her. She meant well, poor thing."

They slept in cots in a church basement for a week. Ava got a hand-me-down dress. A dress! The relief didn't approve of the boys' pants she'd been wearing. Dutchess worked in a laundry for a few weeks. Maybe in that moment, elbow-deep in some white woman's slips, Dutchess regretted all her choices. Maybe she wondered if everything she had ever done was wrong. But not for long, just long enough for a few tears to drip drip into the steaming tub. The next week Dutchess bought bus tickets to Selma. She had a plan: she'd play a few gigs at this little club she knew, make a little money. Get back on the circuit. But! Dutchess would pause and look out into the night where her man was a few miles down the road threading clothes wire between the Oaks. "But I never got the chance," she would say. "Caro walked in that little club and I . . ."

"And you forgot the words, right?" Ava would say, on cue.

"I dropped the damn verse!"

By then the dogs would have been annoyed out of their dozing and gathered round Ava on the living room floor. "Do a song, Mama!" Ava would say.

"I ain't gon to sing not a word," Dutchess said, getting her guitar out of the front room closet. *No one to talk with,* she sang in her gravelly voice. She always paused before the hook.

"Who's that?" she'd ask.

"Oh, Mama, come on! That's Dinah Washington."

She sang another, then another, till she stumped Ava on the singer.

"How come you stopped singing?" Ava would ask. "Don't you miss it?"

Dutchess shook her head. "Caro said, 'Y'all, come on out of the cold.' You understand? It was time to put that life away for something better."

Their remembering nights always ended that way: the past flickering gently between them like fireflies at dusk.

"Anyhow, sugar, I wasn't never going to get anywhere. I'd'a stayed small-time playing little joints till hungry did us both in." Ava couldn't imagine Dutchess done in by anything. Dutchess was as colossal in their plain front room as she was on any stage.

The story was very beautiful, but it was half fairy tale, and Ava had a real boy to raise.

Remember Me

TOUSSAINT WAITED FOR the light to change on the corner of Twenty-seventh and Lehigh. He and Zeek had gone to the Mount Peace Cemetery because Zeek said it was good to pay respects. Plus people left a lot of stuff at graves: food, clothes, even liquor. But Toussaint had stayed too long. Even if he got lucky and managed to sneak onto the R5 he wouldn't get back to Glenn Avenue before six. Ava would rush at him when he opened the door, full of questions. He shuffled from foot to foot against the cold.

"I ain't got time for romance, you know?" said a woman waiting next to him.

Toussaint did not know. He wasn't even sure she was talking to him.

"People always want to love up on all they sad stories. I ain't got time for that shit."

The woman told him her name was Clea. She had two sisters, named Meg and Tisi. Had he seen them? He must have seen them before if he was from the neighborhood. "They always got on bright colors like me," she said. She wore a faded red dress. "You sure? We live right down there at the New Dawn Hotel." He shook his head. Clea said, "I guess you want to know why I am out here all by myself when I got a perfectly nice room at the New Dawn, with a hi-fi, ginger ales, and a box of soda crackers I just bought yesterday."

Toussaint nodded though he had not, in fact, wondered why Clea was out here.

"Because those bitches went off with the key and locked me out! Meg tryna get back with her trifling man and took Tisi with her on account of that nigger is crazy. Romance and bullshit." She paused and looked down at Toussaint. "I shouldn't cuss in front of a little boy like you." She squinted. "How old are you? Ain't you supposed to be in school?

"I would offer you some soda crackers but I got to go sit on the steps over there till my sisters get back. I just hope they don't go over there to hear that Ark when they done with Meg's man. From one crazy nigger to the next is how they want to spend their afternoon. Last week Tisi went to see them Arks and when I got up the next morning, she had threw away all the beer! I mean! I went right and got some more but she knew she was wrong." Clea leaned down and looked hard into Toussaint's eyes, "You stay away from him if you see him. Light-skinned, grand talking motherfucker." She brightened. "It's a nice day though. Come on with me. You skipping school? Stay in school."

Toussaint stood next to the red-dress woman with his hands at his sides.

"You always stand around like a closed door?" She laughed. "I used to say that to Meg. She don't talk much. I used to say, 'Meg, why you all the time stand around like a closed door?'"

"Imma give you some advice." Clea lowered her voice: "That's the kind of thing makes people nervous—standing around looking at folks and not saying nothing. People get mad about that kind of thing. If you gon run the streets you got to put people at ease. I'm here to tell you."

"We okay though, cause we got each other, me and my sisters. We fine. It's not everybody so lucky. Hey, lemme see you better. Lemme get a good look at you."

She stepped back and squinted at him like an aunt who hadn't seen him for a long time. Looking into her face hurt his eyes. Something glowed a little in her, just a scintilla of light like she might be silver underneath if you rubbed her skin hard enough. She crossed the street and motioned him to follow her to a stoop in the middle of the block.

"You sure are serious for a little boy. You got to laugh. You got to have a little fun. You know the one about the rabbit who was always getting hisself in the worst pickle and then talked his way out of it?"

Toussaint shook his head.

"How about the one about the fox?" she asked.

"Your mama ain't told you them stories?" Clea said. "Shame." She sighed and looked off down the street. "They mighta left me the key." She paused, then shrugged her shoulders.

"You got a cigarette? You ain't got a cigarette. That's better. You too young to smoke. Don't take up smoking."

She looked almost familiar with her funny sticking-up hair like shards of broken black glass shooting out of her head. And her red dress.

"Me and Meg and Tisi took up smoking when we was girls and you know we shouldn'ta. It's expensive! I wish we never started." She smiled a great big grin.

"Hey. You got a favorite color? Little kids all got a favorite color. You ain't got on nothing but brown and black, like a mole. Colors make me think of music. You got to have music in your heart.

"What songs you know?" She sang, *Remember me as a breath of spring / Remember me as a good thing* . . .

"You know that one? Me and my sisters listen to music all the time. We love dancing too. We dance and sing and cut up. We don't do nothing but carry on. 'Less somebody do something ugly. Some shit they ain't got no business doing. Then we don't laugh no more."

Clea looked past Toussaint and narrowed her eyes.

"You got fifty cents? I got a craving for a little taste while I wait for them two."

There was a corner store down the block.

"How much you got?"

Toussaint pulled a quarter from his pocket and held it in the palm of his hand.

"Aww, that ain't nothing. You can't get nothing with that. I sure hope you wasn't plannin' on taking the bus. You got your mama waiting on you to get home? You got some cookies waiting on you?"

Toussaint closed his hand around the quarter and moved to put it back in his pocket.

"You sure that's all you got?" she asked. "Maybe it's not. You shouldn't tell me nohow. Don't tell nobody what you got." She paused. "But I'll take that quarter if you feel like giving it to me. Then I'll have a dollar fifty and that's enough to buy me a beer. I got a taste."

Toussaint handed over the quarter.

"You can't come buy beer with me," Clea said, standing. "That ain't kid stuff. Not that you a regular kid. Standing around like a closed door. You got to watch out. People see a closed door and all they want to do is kick it down. Mmm-hmm." She turned and looked at Toussaint a long while.

"You better take this," Clea said. She took something from her dress pocket and pressed it into his hand. Off she went toward the store. She had a kind of saunter, which was also a kind of strut, and the best posture he ever did see on a drunk lady.

The pearl handle of the switchblade caught the sunlight when he opened his palm. It took him some fiddling to figure out how it worked. His finger found the little button at the bottom of the handle and the blade flicked open. A thin line of blood welled up along the pad of his finger when he pressed it against the edge. He made a few jabs and thrusts at the air. How it glinted! But he put it away quick because a man across the street was looking his way. The company he kept, well was starting to keep, they sure liked shiny stuff. Shiny *shit,* he corrected himself. He slid the knife into his pocket and held on to it all the way to Glenn Avenue. That night and every night after, he slept with it under his pillow. He kept it tucked into his sock. He had a sense that was where you were supposed to keep your blade.

The Oaks

ON SUNDAY NIGHT Ava told Toussaint they would go to Bonaparte in two days' time. After Melvin left for the evening, they'd slip out the side door and be gone.

"I'm going to meet my grandmother?" he said.

Until that moment Dutchess had been a lady in bedtime stories, from a place called Bonaparte where a woman named Rea lived in the woods and never died and the fish jumped straight out of the river onto everybody's plates and collards and yams that grew like Jack and the Beanstalk. If it was really like that, why did his mother ever leave? Toussaint had never asked because he liked the stories and he liked his grandmother he'd never met and probably never would.

"We're really going?" he said.

Toussaint closed his eyes to imagine it but instead he saw a boy like him, a Toussaint boy, only with longer legs and scruff on his chin. This big-boy Toussaint stood on a narrow country-looking road with a backpack over one shoulder and a scar on his cheek. A few feet ahead of him a lady stood between a pair of trees tall as buildings. Just step through, she said and beckoned. A fog was coming up. Toussaint's legs were so heavy he couldn't move. She reached out toward him. Come on. Walk through. They were close enough their fingertips nearly touched. He wanted to cross over. He couldn't get there soon enough.

"Ma!" he said and opened his eyes to find he was on his narrow bed in room 813, with Ava talking like she hadn't noticed he'd been gone.

"Ma! We're gonna see those big trees!"

"What?" Ava said. "What big trees?"

"The two big trees by the road where Grandmom Dutchess lives."

"How do you know about those trees?"

Toussaint thought he should bring his grandmother a present. Ava had told him she liked guns. Everybody in Bonaparte had two or three. And she liked her piano. And an old guitar she had.

"I told you about those trees?"

Toussaint shook his head. He didn't know why he was crying. Maybe because Bonaparte had been so close and his grandmother was there waiting for him.

"Baby! Baby, what's the matter?" Ava rushed toward him. "It's all right," she said. "I'm not mad at you. I was just confused. I must have told you about the trees and forgot." She lifted his chin with the tips of her fingers and looked into his eyes. "I promise I'm not mad. Not even about school. Okay?"

He wanted to be gone already. He wanted his mother to let go of him. He wanted her to stop looking at him, trying to pick him apart. He nodded. Yeah, sure, she must have told him. He'd have to settle for giving his grandmother something he already had. Maybe his cat's-eye marble. Maybe the switchblade from the lady in the red dress. He wanted Dutchess to think he was a good boy with manners. He wanted her to say, Come on in, like she did in his dream. Tell me all about everything, she'd say.

"Toussaint?" Ava said. He had been silent for a long while.

"We're going on Tuesday?" he asked.

"What?"

"Tuesday?"

Ava nodded her head, slowly. "Tuesday." She put her hands on his shoulders. "You're okay, baby?" She took a deep breath. "Listen, you have to go to school on Monday and Tuesday. So we don't get into any trouble with the people here."

"We're in trouble?" he asked.

"No! No. It's just we don't want to stir up any suspicions so you have to go back. Okay? I'm not going to punish you, baby. That school was . . . You were probably scared half to death of those kids—"

"I wasn't scared of anybody."

"Okay, well. Okay." She stepped away from him. "What were you doing?"

"When?"

"When you weren't going to school."

"I was going to school."

"Honey, I told you I won't fuss. I just want to know what you were doing instead."

"I was at school," he said in a hard, closed-door voice she'd never heard him use. His set jaw looked like Cass's.

"Tousy," she said. More hesitantly than she'd intended. "We just have to get through the next couple of days. We can do that, right?"

Toussaint had gotten through all these Glenn Avenue days on his own, hadn't he? A cold anger burned in his chest and made him want to cry all over again. He crossed the room and opened the door.

"Toussaint?" Ava called after him.

"Can't I just go to the playground?" he said over his shoulder. "I just want to go to the playground."

BONAPARTE

* * *

ME AND BARBER ATE our dinner outside when the weather was good. I sat on my stump with my plate on my knees and he hauled a chair out from the kitchen table. It's twenty years since I cooked for anybody besides me. Now I do it every day. Don't care for it much. Not that Barber asked me to do it. He would eat crackers and sardines every night if it was up to him. Me too, truth be told. But supper gives the days some kind of shape. Something to do because it's somebody else around to do it for.

"What's going to happen here?" he asked me one night after he'd been with us four or five months.

"What do you mean?" I knew what he meant. He knew I did, too. "It's willed to our children," I said after a while.

"Ah." He paused. "And do you think any of them are coming back?"

"You never know what somebody might do."

"Do you think Ava is coming back?"

Now, that wasn't none of his damn business. I was about to get up and go inside when I remembered this was my yard and I wasn't the one who should leave. One thing was clear: this boy never belonged anywhere long enough to call it home. Ava did. Even if she don't act like it. Even if she never set foot on this land again, it's hers.

"Okay. Okay. I'm sorry," he said. "I shouldn't have said that. But . . . Because, because you all have kept this place up. You could keep the land in the family, or in some kind of black family."

I said, "How you come to know about us? How you come to know we were here?"

"People know about this place. You know that."

"Not anymore they don't."

"Dutchess, come on. I've been to Mound Bayou, Eatonville, everywhere—"

"Everywhere there was free black people. Yeah, that's what you said."

"It's the same everywhere, like it is here. Land stolen, forgotten, litigated away. You know that we have lost nearly a million acres."

Who is this "we"? He had sense enough to know every nigger ain't a promise. We do better for each other than they do but that's not always saying much. But, boy, he was on fire about it that night. Up out of his chair, pacing and talking and waving his hands around.

"I understand you don't want to farm it anymore," he was saying. "But there are other things. Timber. Leasing the hunting rights to the woods. Or you could clear-cut some of it and . . . You know there's an institute for solar energy? Making the sunlight into electricity. They just built a whole solar power station in California. You all could put the earnings in a trust with allowances for your kids and grandkids. Independence. That's—"

"Negro, you going to talk to me about independence? In my yard? On my three hundred free-owned acres?"

He calmed down after that. He's not a sulker, I'll give him that. He just sat there quiet with the bad feeling hanging over us. I did too. Which isn't how I generally do things. I'll throw a glass at your head then walk away. I did get a glass all right. Filled it with whiskey and went on back and sat on the stump.

"Those Progress people are waiting for you all to die so they can take every acre of this land like you were never born."

"You think I don't know that?" I said.

The sun was going down behind the trees. A dozen starlings spread out across the sky. He pointed up at them swooping and diving. And we sat watching them against the orange sky. The air had a fresh smell, green and honeysuckle. I guess I am getting old because instead of wanting to fight I felt the sweetness of this old place.

Things change, young fella. The fact that everything alive has to go away is the saddest and prettiest thing in the world. Anyhow, this land ain't his to save. But I would have let him live on it if he wanted to. Me and Carter Lee had already decided we'd let him have one of the empty houses when fall came around. If he was still here, that is.

Two days later was Jesse Day. Really, it's Jesse's Dead Day. That was the name of the last master that lived longer than two weeks on this land. Bonaparte's Fourth of July. Used to be we had a whole parade. Pageant, too. One of the little girls played Old Rea, and another one was Lucinda who whacked Jesse over the head and left him to burn up in her cabin. After the pageant we made a feast: pit smoked ribs and Jimmy would fry up platters of fish. Muscadine wine. Honey cake and every pie you can think of.

We kept it up for a while after the young people left, but it was too sad, just the few of us looking in each other's wrinkled faces like we did every other day of the year. It got so we went out of the way to avoid each other on Jesse Day. I was all set to ignore it like always, but then Barber came along talking bout, "I hear it's a holiday!"

Next thing I know he's hustling me into my truck and we're heading out toward the river. The rest of them was already there at Jimmy's. I could smell the fried chicken before I got down from my truck. Delilah jumped out of the truck bed like there was springs in her legs and ran up to the picnic table, tail high and wagging. Old girl.

"Happy Jesse!"

Carter Lee had on the mothball-smelling Colonel Sanders jacket and string tie we used to give whoever played Jesse in the pageant. Juniata had dressed herself in a faded nightgown to play Lucinda. She made a big show of pretend-bashing Carter Lee across the head with a stick. I think she really did wallop him good one time.

Carter Lee brought some muscadine wine in a cooler. I didn't know he made the stuff anymore. The table was set nice with a checkered tablecloth and a mason jar full of cut flowers from Erma Linner's garden. Halfway through the meal, joyful past Jesse Days came to mind and I wanted to cry. But then I got to watching Carter Lee and Juniata and Erma Linner and Memma, I mean really looking, thinking how we had got old together like a man and wife do if they're lucky. We hadn't none of us ended up in some cold place where nobody knew us well enough to check if we had breathed our last.

There was a sun shower down the river. Towers of dark gray clouds against pale sky over navy blue water. Never made its way down to us. The clouds broke up and faded into blue. That'll cheer up anybody. Even Barber laughed a few times. Everlasting love him; he didn't have much of a sense of humor.

Sneaky bastard brought my guitar. Everybody got quiet when he fetched it from the truck. I don't sing in public no more.

"I don't sing no more," I said. Even though I had been singing on my own down at the guard shack. But that didn't count.

Delilah stopped her trotting round the table and sat down next to me. I guess she figured she ought to stay close in case I threw the guitar at somebody's head. But. Must have been the wine, must have been Barber standing so upright like my Caro, and insisting on things, like Caro used to. Must have been that for a split second the time went into rewind and I could see Ava the year she was Lucinda, running hellhound down the road after some knobby-kneed Jesse. All of it welled up and rushed around in my chest. I plucked out "This Bitter Earth." I was slow and off pitch. But the longer I played the more the memories cooled and comforted me. Carter Lee started humming "You Make Me Feel Brand New" and we all joined in and sang it like we were the Marvelettes.

Sometime during the singing Barber slipped off. He did that from time to time. You'd look up and he was gone. We lit a bonfire in a barrel by the river's edge. Erma Linner rolled herself a cigarette. Truth be told we were getting tired, old farts that we were, but nobody wanted the evening to end. We stood there slapping at bugs and swaying on our heels and smiling and feeling a little drunk and sleepy.

Downriver by the Progress houses an orange light flashed in the dark, not much bigger than a flare but low to the ground. The newest houses over there are a long line of pale rectangles, one just like the next. Nobody lives in them yet. Another ground flare came up. The vacation white people were always setting off firecrackers and bottle rockets and other reckless foolishness you shouldn't do in a dryish summer when you got woods behind you. "Chickens got better sense," Carter Lee would say.

We were shaking our heads and tsk-tsking when the flashes gathered themselves together and exploded into a tall orange light. In an instant it had shot up so bright you could make out the slats in the siding on the house next to it. A thin line of orange whipped across the narrow patch of grass between the burning house and its neighbor. *Whoosh*. Then another orange lick caught the next house. *Whump, whump, whump*. One right after the other up in flames.

"I'll be damned," Juniata said.

"I declare," said Erma Linner.

Carter Lee whistled. "I don't think the Progress put in hydrants," he said. The last house had a dock that stretched out into the river. The fire raced along the wood slats and burned on the surface of the black water. Biblical. I never saw the like. Near two hours passed before the Bodine fire department arrived. By then it was nothing left but smoke.

An eye for an eye. I knew before I got in my truck. And sure enough, when me and Delilah pulled up to our house it was dark and silent. I didn't mean to cry, but a wave of hurt, I mean an actual pain, nearly put me on my knees. I had to hold on to the porch railing till I got my breath.

He left a note on the kitchen table:

Back again before too long. With reinforcements. In the meantime, I owe you all a debt. I won't forget. Thank you. Tell everybody that I'll see them again.

Yours,

PHILADELPHIA

. . .

Seventh Sense

TRAINS STREAKED SILVER through the high tawny weeds along the tracks. Toussaint counted five in the time he'd been walking. The sun was high. It was the morning of his last day ever at Taft. He knew all the stations in this part of the city: North Philadelphia, Suburban Station, Thirtieth Street, and after that Boston or New York or maybe Florida. Florida is a southern state, not just the place for Disney World. It also has oranges and NASA. But Toussaint and Ava were taking a bus to Alabama, not a train, and she'd told him they wouldn't pass through Florida.

The trains and buses stopped at the station and the people rushed out of them like flies trapped in a jar. The city took them in but it was never full. Cass was somewhere among all these people, or at least he said he would be. Now it was too late. Ava and Toussaint were going where Cass would never find them again. Their bus for Montgomery left at eleven p.m. Montgomery isn't a big city like Philadelphia, Ava had told him. And Bonaparte was like James Creek minus the diner and the grocery store and the municipal building and almost all of the people. "Roads and river, fields and woods, and that's all," she said.

Ava had been ragged that morning, scribbling on a scraggly-edged sheet of loose-leaf when Toussaint woke up. He sighed and shifted in his bed but she didn't look at him until he sat up and made a big show of throwing off the covers. "Done!" Ava said, after a few minutes. "I'm going to put this in the mail at the post office. So it'll get there in time."

"In time for what?" he asked though that wasn't what he meant to say. What he meant was: I thought we'd have a morning together to say good-bye, like maybe one last breakfast in the cafeteria even if it isn't very good, or pancakes at the diner we used to go to. People said good-bye when they left places. He wanted Ava to be like regular people so he could be too. Toussaint didn't dare ask if Abemi knew they were leaving. Ava would say, "We talked about this." Even though they had not. And if he persisted, she'd turn into Hard Ava who would not answer his questions or look at him until he changed the subject.

That morning's Ava, frazzly, tired Ava, crossed the room toward him with her dark coattails flapping out at the sides like a bat. "Here's your bus fare. Remember what we said about not telling anybody we're leaving. I'm going to pick you up at the end of the day and get your records to take with us. Like we planned. Right?" She crouched by his bed. "It's just this one last time. By tomorrow morning we'll be on our way to a new life." Then she was out the door. Seconds later her feet passed in front of their window as she crossed the yard on her way to the side exit. Toussaint decided that when he grew up he'd always go out through the front door.

He dressed and ate the cheese sandwich Ava had left for him, but when he got to the bus stop, he couldn't make himself get on. There'd be trouble at school because he'd been gone so long. His friends Anthony and Keith would ask where he'd been all this time. He couldn't tell them he was leaving forever, and even if he did, he wouldn't be able to explain why because he didn't know himself.

He headed down Stenton Avenue. When he got to Germantown, he kept south toward Girard, hoping he'd find Zeek. Zeek wouldn't ask him any questions. The 23 trolley passed, and the H bus, but Toussaint didn't get on those either. He was saving his bus money for a honey bun and a hot milky coffee—a trick to stave off cold and hunger. Zeek said the cold was just an idea: relax into it and it won't make you squirm. Zeek should know because he lived outside all year around. Even when it snowed.

Ava too was on the move, heading toward Stenton to get a bus downtown. There was so much left to do: the post office, the Greyhound station to buy their tickets, Super Fresh for food for the trip. The block had a flimsy, unsubstantial quality, like it was already fading even though she hadn't yet left the city. Or maybe *she* was the ghost, already half gone. She had the taste of blackstrap molasses in her mouth, and the sensation of Dutchess's big spoon clinking against her back teeth. That was a taste of lean, late winter in Bonaparte. Cod liver oil, too. Every child in Bonaparte showed up to school smelling fishy. And didn't we make it through those winters? Most of us anyway? Didn't they make sure we did.

The 23 was packed. It crawled down Germantown Avenue, picking up passengers at every corner. You're all right, Ava. She took a deep breath. You're fine. Thanksgiving was three days away. After Caro died Dutchess hadn't bothered much with holidays. Come to think of it, she hadn't much bothered with them before they got to Bonaparte either. All of Ava's early holidays involved a juke joint. One was always open somewhere and Dutchess would play any day of the year. It was Caro who made Christmas and birthdays; Jesse Days and Easter.

Sure, Ava was nervous about going back to Bonaparte. Of course I am, she'd answered Toussaint when he'd asked her. She stared out the trolley window. If she were on her own she wouldn't go. She'd keep on not hanging herself in a basement, hoarding the weeks and years of life for no reason other than to rack up days. What futility. But she had Toussaint to raise. If she did right by him, he'd never find himself rummaging the dregs of his mind for reasons to stay alive.

A woman with three brimming shopping bags squeezed in next to her. The 23 was so jammed the windows fogged. They stopped for a red light, and there, down a side street, Bouvier it must have been, Ava thought she saw . . . But couldn't have been. She wiped the smeared window. The trolley lurched forward at the green and she craned her neck to look back at the receding side street. But that gait. She was out of her seat, pulling the cord to signal a stop, shoving past the people and their bags in the aisle on her way to the front. "I have to get off! Let me off!"

"Next stop Broad and Erie," the driver said.

"Let me off, I have to get off. My son—!"

Toussaint made a wrong turn somewhere and ended up near Broad Street, so far down the 23 passed him. He could almost make out the crowd milling around the Broad and Erie stop a few blocks ahead. He turned down a side street and walked until the blocks were familiar again. He passed the Hallowed Be Thy Name Church, and the check-cashing place, and the shoe store that hadn't taken down the Buster Brown BACK TO SCHOOL SALE sign. He passed DeeDee's Soul Food where he must have lingered too long smelling the chicken smells because a passerby got herself all set to ask him if he was all right. Grown-ups were always getting ready to ask him something, but none of them ever helped. Toussaint doubled back to the shoe store and trailed behind a lady who came out. Sure enough, the first woman figured he was with his mother and didn't pay him any more mind. Mostly people don't want to pay you any mind, Toussaint had learned. It's just they think they have to, some of them, but if you give them any excuse at all they'll go right back to only minding about themselves.

Abemi had gone back to minding about himself. Toussaint had told him about Cass and that made him hate them. He pounded on the kitchen table until it flipped onto its side and crashed to the floor. The ketchup bottle exploded into glass shards and red goop spatter. "Help me, Ava. Help me, dammit," Abemi said while he mopped at the mess with a wad of paper towels. Toussaint had never seen a grown man cry before. No matter how hard Abemi tried to clean up he just smeared red mess in big circles all over the linoleum. Ava stood next to the stove shaking her head with her arms folded across her chest.

Ava zigzagged the streets searching for Toussaint. She went into a corner store but she knew he wasn't there as soon as she stepped inside. Caro used to say she had a seventh sense. Sixth sense was for spirits, seventh sense was for tracking. She thought she'd forgotten how to use it, but she found herself following her son on pure instinct. People bother the air. You can feel them if you pay attention. After a time, she rounded the corner onto Girard Avenue and there he was. Her copper-colored boy in his brown coat heading fast down the ave. A spring in his step! He was completely unaware of her. She had not expected her Toussaint, so fragile, so tentative, to be happy—no, not happy, at ease—alone in the cold.

He entered a phone booth and picked up the receiver but came out again without making a call. He lingered at a red light near Poplar Street, a couple of blocks from the old Black Panther headquarters. Ava wondered if it was still there, she remembered Cass at his post in the front room. Look at us now. Ava was glad she hadn't told Toussaint that his father was a Panther; glad she didn't have to explain that they'd all been murdered or arrested or were smoking crack in an alley. All that was left were fatherless children, raging widows and everybody scrambling not to fall into a hole where the glory had been.

Ava didn't want Toussaint to be like her pop. She didn't want him to be a hero. Or a wanderer like her, or feral like Dutchess, or burning with thwarted purpose like Cass. But here he was, rambling like his mother and grandmother before him. A woman standing in front of a chicken place took an interest in him, but he got rid of her. Quite a trick! She could see by the set of her boy's shoulders that he was proud of himself for giving that woman the slip. Ava was proud too, if she was honest. But maybe there were truancy officers around. How did it work when they sent child services for your son? Did they nab him on the bus? Or leap out of a car at a stoplight and bundle him inside? She would give Toussaint another few minutes, another little taste of freedom, but she'd have to stop him after that. This was their last day of roaming. Had to be.

Toussaint turned off the Girard Bridge onto an abandoned stretch of Thirty-fourth and scrambled up an embankment, across a shallow trash gully, and up onto the old railroad tracks, glinting dully in the sunshine. This was not a route he'd taken before, though there were the same high weeds. He wondered, as he always did, if they were wheat. He added this to the list of questions he'd ask Zeek if he found him. He wondered if the people at his old school in New Jersey ever thought about him. Miss Palmiere the language arts teacher with all the rings, Jilly who had disappeared. What was it like where Paul was? "Hey, Paul," he said out loud. "Hey, Paul, we're moving to Alabama."

Toussaint stood on a patch of trampled grass. Industrial discard piled here and there: rusting beams, railroad ties, skinny poles that looked like scaffolding. If he knew how, he could build a robot, or some other thing for the future. Or maybe to the future. But Toussaint didn't want the future, and he didn't want now either. He wanted to go back to when he was little, back to the days when he and Ava used to visit the zoo. The fur-and-popcorn smell when they got off the 38 bus. They always took the same route when they got inside: birds, skip the reptiles, primates. Finally, the big cats. He held his mother's hand and watched the jaguars lolling and stretching. Every time it was better than he had remembered.

Ava had lost Toussaint. He clambered over a ridge, down a low hill, and was gone. She crossed some railroad tracks and came to the mouth of a tunnel running beneath an overpass. The stink! Inside was worse—midnight dark and the smell of shit. She rushed toward the circle of sunlight at the other end, crunching over broken glass.

She was a quarter of the way, then halfway, then her foot sank into a hole in the ground and there was a cold ooze at her ankles. She wiped at the wet seeping through her shoe and sliming her toes.

"Nothing but a little water."

A dark silhouette appeared, framed in the light from the other end of the tunnel. "Who's there," Ava called. The silhouette stepped closer. "You shouldn't be in here," she said in a voice that creaked like a door hinge. "Nice lady like you. But since you are"— she clicked open the switchblade in her hand—"what you got for me?" Sunlight flared at the far end of the tunnel and the woman was illuminated, lips pulled back over silvery teeth, a red-orange dress and eyes that shone with a quiet light. A gaze you could fall into like a fevered sleep. Ava stepped toward her. "Thatta girl," the woman said. "Come on over here."

Ava overreached and stumbled when she grabbed for the knife. The woman sidestepped her with a nimble hop, and stood shaking her head.

"If you looking for that boy," the woman said, "he went that way." She pointed to the other end of the tunnel.

Ava lunged again. Her foot caught on the uneven paving; she pitched forward, and went down hard on the broken asphalt. A firework of visions showered down on her: Caro's body under a sky of scudding clouds, Cass in a ball of flames that burned around him but did not consume. Tinseling glass falling around Toussaint.

Her boy. Toussaint was lost somewhere along the stretch of derelict railroad track. She had failed on her watch and now this red-dress woman and her knife would have him. The damp ground was cool against her cheek. Toussaint! Run!

Then darkness.

Family Business

AVA WAS BACK in the last summer of Caro. She and Pop were tracking a poacher, just the two of them with their little sack of cornpone, honey, and a thermos of water. The mist was still thick off the river, patchier as they went farther into the woods, like gauzy puffs ripped from a giant cotton ball and set down here and there among the trees. Pop was skinny but strong as a tree trunk. He could do anything, shoulder any burden, skin anything, build anything. Caro! they called when he walked around Bonaparte. Ava and her pop moved across the forest floor. Ava in front. She could spot a worm moving on a leaf, could see where a groundhog had snuffled a pinecone looking for beetles. She kept low to the ground breathing with the trees until she dissolved at the edges.

A little past noon they came across the first sign of him. Urine against the side of a tree, sometime after that a cigarette butt barely buried in a mound of moist earth. "Cracker don't even have enough respect to carry his trash." Pop set a trap, then another. Ava picked a strand of blond hair from a tree branch, thin as a spider web and glinting in the sunlight. The poacher was moving quickly, zigzagging. Pop said they should get out in front of him. His truck had to be parked somewhere. They could booby-trap his path out and that would be the end of him. That was always the end of them, slinking off, ashamed they got caught by niggers.

Ava caught a whiff of rot in the air. The smell thickened from sweet to sickening. The air tightened around them. Caro felt it too. He took his shotgun off his shoulder and stood with his head cocked to the side, eyes narrowed. They found the pit a mile in from the road: woodchucks, a fox, a possum crawling with maggots. On top a couple of bantam hens, the kind Mr. George said were disappearing from his coops. One was still alive, bleeding from the throat. Pop twisted its neck to stop it suffering. A mass grave of animals killed for no reason. "Why would he do that?" Ava asked.

"Which way?" Pop said. Ava pointed toward a smear of dried blood on a tree a couple of yards away.

"Go on back," Pop said.

"But . . ."

"Keep off the road. Move quick." Then he was gone. Scared as she was, Ava moved fast and quiet through the forest. Halfway home she heard a loud birdcall. After a few more steps it sounded again. She looked up to find her scabby-kneed neighbor perched in a branch above her.

"Buddy LaPrairie!" she said.

He put a finger to his lips and dropped from that branch easy as a falling leaf.

"They made *you* a Watcher?" Ava said. Buddy LaPrairie was fourteen and an idiot.

Buddy shrugged. "I seen you coming a ways back. Where's Mr. Caro?"

"How you know I was with my pop?" Ava asked. "You can't see that far from here."

Buddy shrugged again. Ava said, "We found a pit near the road with a whole bunch of kilt animals in it, kilt for no reason. Plus, the poachers stole Mr. George's chickens! My pop went to tell that cracker to get and stay got."

Buddy looked at her a long while. "When was that?" he said.

"Buddy, how would I know when the cracker stole those hens?"

"Ava, you ain't got the sense . . ." He looked out into the trees and then said, "I mean, when did Mr. Caro get after the poacher?"

"Bout an hour, little less."

"Go to Mr. George. Hightail it. You know how to get there?"

"I ain't stupid, Buddy." Ava figured one day soon she'd be a Watcher herself.

Buddy was back up the tree, birdcalling for all he was worth. Ava ran hard the rest of the way. When she came out of the woods to the edge of Mr. George's land, she was so relieved she plopped down in one of his neat rows of budding peanuts. She needed to catch her breath for a minute. In the woods across the field something crashed in the underbrush. Caro burst through the tree line seconds later, running head down, arms pumping, not twenty feet away. "Pop!" Ava jumped to standing. Caro locked eyes with her and paused. A second. Less than a second. One white man at the edge of the field, rifle high, four or five others behind him. "Run!" Pop screamed. Muzzle flash. Caro fell.

When Ava opened her eyes, she was alone in the tunnel. She blinked in the dim light. How much time had passed? She stood and rubbed her wrist, tender from her fall. In a few steps she had passed into the mouth of light at the other end of the tunnel.

A train rumbled past so slowly Toussaint could see the people inside. Some of the people looked out of their windows, but they didn't see him. He waved and waved with his hands high over his head. Hey hey hey! In the last car a little girl in pigtails jumped out of her seat with her arms stretched above her head like she'd won the gold. Toussaint smiled and walked on into the wind. Sharp rocks pressed through the soles of his sneakers. His toes ached with cold.

The backs of his hands were numb by the time he reached a trail that veered between two rows of abandoned boxcars. The trail dipped where the boxcars cast shadows over the trampled grass. "Yea, though I walk through the valley of the shadow of death . . ." Zeek had said when he took Toussaint there the first time. "I will fear no evil," Toussaint replied softly.

"Church boy!" Zeek said. "You get a lot of women that way. Believe me."

Zeek's flapping blue tent came into view. The tent city was bigger than it was the last time Toussaint had seen it, but there wasn't a soul around. Not even the dogs. He passed through the maze of tents and walked along a gully. He climbed a low ridge and there, on the other side at the base of a long slope—

"Mr. Zeek!" Toussaint ran down the slope. Zeek sat on a milk crate in front of a makeshift grill. All the people from the camp were there, and more besides sitting on milk crates or flattened cardboard boxes spread on the ground. Regular people too, wearing clean clothes and standing apart from the others.

"Zeek!" he said again, stopping short in front of the camp stove. "Zeek?" This time the man raised his head like it was heavy. He blinked, once, twice. "Looka here," he said in a molasses-thick voice. "Look at this right here." He paused a long time peering at Toussaint whom he knew from somewhere, sometime. "You want a sausage?" he said.

Toussaint bit the inside of his lip and shook his head.

"Why not? You don't know better than to say no to a sausage somebody want to give you? You must get a lotta shit for free."

The man sitting next to him shook his head. "Stupid," he said.

Zeek rubbed his eyes and looked at Toussaint again, more closely. All of this took a long time, like he was underwater. "Oh!" he said. "It's you. Little man. What you doing here? Ain't we said you was supposed to go back to school?"

"It's my last day," Toussaint said.

"Last day of what? School?" He turned to the man next to him. "It ain't summertime is it, little man? We sure *is* fucked up if it's summertime."

Maybe Toussaint had made a mistake. Maybe Zeek didn't care if he stayed, or where he went. He turned to go back up the hill.

"Aww, I'm just playing with you, little man. Just messing around."

"I'm supposed to go to Alabama."

"Alabama? Shit. I wouldn't go to no goddamn Alabama. But look, you going or you supposing on going?"

"I'm going. I guess. With my ma."

"Your mama! Mothers do tend to cloud a situation, so far as I remember. But if you got one you should be glad. Most of em mean well." He considered Toussaint for a moment. "You look like you still in the deciding stage."

"I can't decide! I'm just a kid."

"That's some bullshit. You decided to come here and refuse Zeek's sausages, ain't you?" He waved his hand in the direction of the people gathered. "This here gonna help you focus. Helps me, anyhow." Then, under his breath: "Tryna get off this shit."

Toussaint looked to see where the help was.

"You ain't gettin off nothin," the other sausage man said.

"See? That's a negative attitude right there. That's why you not even tryin."

The other man shrugged.

"Mmm-hmm," Zeek said. "Take the sausage, boy. You may as well eat something. It's gonna be a while before he starts. He just come out when he feels like it."

Toussaint couldn't figure out who was coming. "It's my last day," he repeated.

"Yep."

Zeek forked a sausage and passed it to Toussaint. Just then a man a few feet away started in with a hop-skip kind of dance. Zeek's friend chuckled, "He doing the beam-me-up-Scotty shuffle." Someone in the crowd said, "He caught the spirit." A transistor radio clicked on and Rufus and Chaka rose up through the static. The man kept on with his shimmy and everybody laughed. Zeek handed round sausages and somebody else offered a few bottles of beer. More people came—raggle-taggle Zeek kind of people and civilians too, as Zeek called them—everybody smiling and milling around.

"So, you going to Alabama," Zeek said.

"You ever been there?"

"What? You think I been in a ditch my whole life? I been all over. Service."

Toussaint caught sight of a couple of wooden pallets stacked one on top of the other to make a platform at the other end of the clearing. A rusty shipping container sat just behind it.

"How you gonna get there? Airplane? I flew everywhere. I been to Germany and Italy. You know where that is?"

Toussaint nodded. "We're going on the Greyhound bus," he said.

"Greyhound! Used to be niggers had to sit in back on the Greyhound. You know about that? Back long time ago—" He paused, startled. "Uh-oh," he said, looking past Toussaint. "Coming in hot."

All eyes turned to the rise over which Toussaint had come a few minutes before. Ava flew down the hill, her coat muddied on one side. In an instant she was standing over Toussaint, pulling him up by the lapels. "Are you all right?" She batted the sausage out of his hand. "Don't eat that! Who the hell are these people? Junkies? You skip school to hang around with old junkies?" She pulled his coat so hard the stitching tore at the collar.

"Well, scuse you, miss," Zeek said.

Ava stomped her foot on the ground and tried again to pull her son to his feet. Maybe they'd given him something. They stank like dirty hair; sallow-eyed and waxy-faced, a crackhead dancing in the middle of them and this one sitting next to Toussaint so doped up he could hardly keep his eyes open.

"Get up!" Ava slapped Toussaint hard across the face. These filthy people in their liquor-smelling field. How many days had he spent with them and what had they done to him? Ava hit at the air even as Toussaint scrambled backward away from her.

The man next to Zeek looked like he was going to say something but thought better of it. He shook his head and reached for the sausages right behind Ava. She whipped around, fists balled. Toussaint cried softly, his face going red on the side where Ava struck him.

"Please, Toussaint," she said. "Please get up. We have to go."

Zeek stilled the sausage man who shrugged and kept right on reaching for the grill. "I'm hungry, Zeek," he said. "I can't eat nothing on account of they family business?"

"Naw, nigger. You can't."

"I guess I have to . . ." Toussaint said. "I'm sorry, Mr. Zeek."

Mister, Ava thought. Mister!

"You go on with your mama, little man."

Ava took hold of Toussaint's arm and pulled him toward her, more gently than before.

"Take care of yourself down there in Alabama!" Zeek called. "Don't look back like Lot's wife."

Lot's Wife

JUST THEN, a commotion erupted at the front of the crowd. A sound like a drumstick rapping the bottom of a bucket. Hands clapping, too. Ava dragged Toussaint up the slope. A man wearing a white button-down shirt stepped out of the shipping container and up onto the platform.

"Brothers. Sisters. I stand before you a wounded man."

The crowd silenced.

"I know you all recognize a bullet hole when you see one. Who shot *you*, brothers and sisters?"

Ava turned. Cass had unbuttoned his shirt. Red-ridged keloids exploded in a fleshy starfish beneath his ribs on the left side.

"Somebody did. Let me see your backs and the bottoms of your feet. I know what's there. Chemical burns, knife scars, exit wounds. I see the bruised skin inside your elbow. The worry wrinkles across your foreheads. Rent due. Babies. That man and his knuckles snoring next to you.

"Cradle that weak arm. Caress your swollen ankles. I don't want you to lay down your burdens. They're yours. I'm not here to reform you. I don't want to patch you up so you can go out there and make money for the governor and president and the kingdom of the USA."

"Ma!" Toussaint said.

Ava wanted to continue up the slope and over the ridge. She didn't want to stand there with her heart in her throat and her legs frozen beneath her.

"We have to go. Come on, let's go," she said. "Please."

As if Toussaint was the ma and she was the little girl, Toussaint pulled her gently toward his father. She took one halting step and then another. Cass was gilded in the lowering sun; his white shirt glowed, his hair shone amber. His voice rang across the little gulch and the ragtag crowd.

"Look at the sun slashing orange into their glass high-rises. And those trains silver-bulleting down the track. We built those, you know. They told us they are the kingdom, and we are the slaves. That's a lie. Weep for their lies. Weep for the death they bring. Weep because they don't know they can die.

"The kingdom wants eternal life. It wants everything to go on forever just like it is right now. It doesn't want your tears. Crying people ask questions. They want to know what happened to them. The kingdom destroys history and enslaves the future. The kingdom is seamless, it's smooth as the glass on those buildings. We can glide on it from nowhere to nowhere.

"The kingdom is a conveyor. The belt tightens round your arm and the vein pops and the needle goes in and we are swimming in sick oblivion. And while we are dreaming, the kingdom opens its jaws and shovels us in.

"Weep for their cruelty. Then dry your eyes, brothers and sisters. Straighten your backs. Overturn the tables in the temples."

Ava had a feeling like she had been looking for something that had been lost many years ago. It was very close now. She could almost touch it.

"What did they sell you in the temple, brothers and sisters? I bought this."

Cass lifted a bottle high over his head. The brown liquid glowed in the light.

"Gallons of it for twenty years. Chivas and Cutty Sark and Crown Royal could fix anything. But only for the night. That was the catch."

He hurled the bottle against the side of the abandoned cargo container from which he had stepped. The breaking shattered the air. The people flinched. What a waste! That was the good stuff, too. But then they laughed. That's a bold motherfucker. That's a hell of a show.

"Throw away the narcotics of the kingdom, brothers and sisters. It will hurt. It's going to burn like hell. But we'll come out clean. All the rot they put in us, seared away until we are smooth and lethal as spears."

Cass stepped down from the platform and walked among the gathered. Those that had been drinking paused and examined their bottles. He had a point, didn't he? This rotgut was kinda suspicious the way it got hold of a nigger and wouldn't let him go. Course most kept on sipping, but it did give you something to think on.

Sausages lay abandoned on the grass. Some people stole away from the terrible hush and Cass's electric grip. At the center of the crowd a fire burned in an oil drum. A man threw in his half-empty bottle. The crowd pressed in. A Mad Dog sailed through the air and into the burning barrel. Flames shot a foot into the air. The people whooped. Zeek tossed in the tiny brown paper envelope with the skull and crossbones, still a quarter full (quarter full!) of beige powder. Tenth time's the charm! he shouted.

Ava had nothing to throw but she stood as close as she could to the fire, so close the heat seared the tears off her cheeks. Another glass bottle burst in the flames. The sound exploded in Ava's chest—*bang bang bang* like grenades.

1986

...

PHILADELPHIA

. . .

Communion

FIRST, THE CLICK and snip of the shears. Ava sat in a kitchen chair, surrounded by Cass and her son and her newly found brothers and sisters Zeek, Winnie and her sons, Alvin and Nemo—in the small backyard of Winnie's house at 248 Ephraim Avenue. Their fellowship was called Ark. With a *k*. Because they were a refuge from the devastation and deluge of the city. Ava and Toussaint had been in this new life for four months.

Springy brown puffs of hair floated down onto Ava's shoulders, over her ears, past her eyes. The fluff caught on her eyelashes, tickled her neck, and landed softly at her feet.

"You okay?" Cass asked. He cut slowly, sweetly.

She was okay. This was her choice. She had anticipated some other feeling—panic, maybe, or mourning. Instead, little thrills, trills along her spine, tiny ringing bells. Winnie hummed, a no-word wandering tune that kept pace with the clicking shears. It had rained earlier. Earthworms rooted in the freshly turned soil in the yard, a dogwood in the alley bloomed white and pink. Brilliant green moss grew on the underside of the concrete slabs they'd broken up to make room for Ava's kitchen garden. She could already feel the seeds unfurling in the dirt under her feet. Alive, alive.

Cass turned on the clippers. "Ready?" he said. The warm vibration moved in a steady line from her forehead to the nape of her neck. She had a communion kind of feeling, as if she was less separate from the life around her. When she was a girl in Bonaparte, she and Caro had hunting dogs. Ava named them all Pike. Pike One and Pike Two and Pike Three. In the early morning, she would go out with the Pikes. The four of them waited crouched in the underbrush, the forest dripping around them, one single body. Breathing.

The clippers buzzed at her temples. So gentle. So painstaking. Ava could anticipate Cass's movements by the twitch in the fingers of his free hand. Coolness expanded across her scalp in precise vertical stripes. "Done," he said after some time. Ava did not move or open her eyes. The sun came out from behind a cloud and warmed her. She ran her hand over the new velvet of her scalp. Joyous. Up she floated, like a kite—over the rooftops and the streetlights and the tree line. Not free, she didn't want that anyway. Jubilant.

Good Deeds

THROUGH THE WINTER and into spring, Ark waged war on 248 Ephraim. Dear God, what wasn't ripped or rotted or falling down in that house. The roof leaked, the basement was swampy, the bathroom was Cro-Magnon. Winnie had lived there fifteen years, raised her boys in that heap. And she had endured her husband Carl until Cass drove him out like a pig the devil had got. A head-shaped dent was bashed into the plaster in the hallway between the living room and kitchen. Winnie winced every time she looked at it. Ava told Cass they ought to fix that one first.

They'd found a tooth under the threadbare wall-to-wall carpet. One of the kids', but still. Cass strode the rooms, took the stairs two at a time, calling behind him, "Winnie, how long have these water stains been here?" Or "You want us to pull up these floorboards?" The next thing you know Cass was stripped to his undershirt, crowbarring up that mess. Ava and Zeek too, sledgehammering the fusty bathroom. Ava demolished it like it was the one at Glenn Avenue, like she was putting an end to all filth for all time. Yeehaw! She was stronger than she thought. She ripped up linoleum, carried two-by-fours up the stairs on her shoulders. She plastered over that dent in the hallway, so Winnie and her boys could walk around their own house without Exhibit A terrorizing them all over again.

Toussaint wasn't so keen. He complained about the smell when they took up the old linoleum in the kitchen. And about the dust and the fumes from the sealants and shellac. It all gave him a headache; he needed to nap—then he said it was too noisy to sleep. At least, Ava thought, he says something. At least he's here with us. Not like those awful months at Glenn Avenue: his silence, the flat look in his eye. His sallow complexion. Since they'd come to 248, Cass examined him once a week, every week. He'd gained seven pounds. The color had come back into his face. Cass believed boys needed to exorcise their discontents; they needed to throw their bodies at whatever troubled them. Ava got Toussaint to help break down the splintering front porch steps. And, you know, he actually laughed out loud pounding through the rotting wood. After that he volunteered to help most days, especially if there was something to demolish. When the work was too heavy for a kid, he'd stand at some distance from Cass, transfixed by his father's rippling back while he and Zeek put a sheet of drywall into place. One morning Ava caught Toussaint flexing his biceps in the bathroom mirror.

Late in the evenings, when the day's work was done, Cass and Winnie sat at the kitchen table sorting through bills and notices from the city. Winnie wasn't so much meek as she was childlike when it came to the house. "Oh! I don't know. I just don't have any idea," she said in breathy bursts and sad little sighs. "Carl did that." Or "Carl said I shouldn't bother about that one."

Ava stood by the sink drying dishes, trying to keep a neutral face. It seems Carl had paid the bills whenever he felt like it, or not at all. But he left everything in Winnie's name for the tax man and collections agency. Poor Winnie didn't know a thing about her own life. Piles of water bills, arrears notices, letters from the bank, late taxes, notices from the city about the big oak out front and who was supposed to prune it and who was supposed to pay for it. The poor woman was so wound up you could see every tendon pulling in her neck. She never cried though, Ava had to give her that.

Cass told her which bills she needed to pay and which things she could get help with and which things she could ignore. She applied for public assistance and pooled it with Ava's, and with Zeek's SSI.

There were HUD programs and first-time homeowner programs. LIHEAP for the utilities in arrears, and for the heat bills to come. BSR for home repairs they couldn't handle. Cass found a grant to help them fix the boiler and put a dehumidifier in the moldy basement.

He built a dividing wall in the dining room to make a room for his clinic. A free clinic, like the one he'd worked at Panther HQ. For the community, he said, for self-sufficiency. Eventually he'd offer first-aid classes too. Or basic medic skills so the neighborhood wouldn't be so dependent on ambulances that showed up whenever they got around to it. Only thing was, so far as Ava could tell, the people around there had good jobs with PECO or the city and probably felt pretty self-sufficient already. She didn't say that though, instead she said: "Where would we get the medicine, and the . . . you know, the supplies?" Cass shot her a look like, O ye of little faith, and walked out of the room.

By spring the house was nearly finished. Most of the money was too. That was all right; by Cass's calculations he'd gotten the government to pay for six thousand dollars' worth of repairs. "Bastards," he said, every time he and Winnie returned from one of those agencies downtown. But he was never defeated the way Ava had been when she used to go to those places. He was triumphant.

Ava walked the house, marveling at the quiet clean rooms. They'd restored every inch of 248: new panes in the living room bay window, replastered walls along the stairwell and the hallway that ran the length of the first floor. They'd put a new sink in the downstairs half bathroom and replaced damn near everything in the full bath on the second floor. They built new cabinets in the kitchen at the back of the house. New floors in the three bedrooms on the second floor. The boys shared the largest. Winnie's was the midsize room at the top of the stairs. The third wasn't more than a glorified closet, but Zeek didn't need much space. All the floors were shiny hardwood, thank you very much. Cass said Ark should be serene. They took down some of the ceiling lights because Cass said those old fluorescents sucked the vitamin D right out of them. Not to mention they were ugly. The living room was a box of sunlight. All through the house the walls were cream or sand or toasted almond. "Bastards!" Ava said, turning the new faucets in the bathroom.

"What if he comes back?" Ava asked a couple of weeks after they'd finished the last of the painting and the whole place smelled like wood glue and Murphy's Oil Soap. She and Cass lay under the high open window on the mattress in their attic bedroom. Candles flickered in patterned lanterns and cast amber diamonds along the walls.

"What if he comes back?" Ava asked again.

"Who?" Cass said.

"Carl. What if he just shows up?"

He rolled over and looked at Ava like she was the biggest fool he'd talked to that day.

"He won't."

"He might."

Cass shook his head. "Patch," he said.

Ava didn't want to know any more. Patch showed up at 248 one day and never left. He was Cass's man—didn't talk to anybody else and nobody talked to him, except Zeek now and again. Patch had one milky eye and the other one was small and rat mean.

"Anyway, it wouldn't matter if he did come back," he said. "It's all taken care of."

Cass fixed Ava with that cool gaze of his, like he was scanning her for defects. He pulled up a loose floorboard and took something from the cavity beneath.

"Well, that puts me right at home," Ava said.

Everybody in Bonaparte had a strongbox buried in the floor. And everybody had a deed in her name. The one in Cass's hand said, *248 Ephraim Avenue, Philadelphia, Pennsylvania, 19156*. The owner was listed as Cassius Wright. Ava knew enough to keep her expression blank. She didn't know what he was up to in the grand scheme. But she'd soldier for him. She'd keep right on.

"We need a place that's ours," he said. "This is one. There will be others."

He talked on about property and urban cooperative ownership. He used the word sovereign. Look out world, Ava thought.
His voice turned flat and hard, not one ounce of feeling in it—like
he wasn't talking to her anymore, like he was telling all the white
people, or maybe all the people, what he was going to do to them.
He wasn't an easy man. But then he never had been. All at once the
sentiment in him could switch off. Flick. Ava kept her hand steady
when she handed back the deed.

She wanted to ask: Does Winnie know you have her house?
Maybe she did. Probably she did. And if she didn't maybe it was
better that way. Everlasting love her. She was sleeping downstairs
in her not-hers-anymore room snug as a kangaroo in its mama's
pouch.

House Rules

CASS PUT WINNIE'S TV out on the corner. Free to whoever found it first. Zeek said the crackheads would get it but Cass didn't seem to mind. "Commerce," he said, and chuckled. He emptied the basement deep freeze and doled out the chops and burgers to people who lived in the nearby park. No meat for 248, and certainly no liquor. He tossed every trace of processed food.

"But why? You like all that stuff," Toussaint complained to Ava. "You liked *Falcon Crest* and Rice-A-Roni."

It was true, she had. But she didn't need those things anymore. False comforts. In Ark they were about the long haul. Security. Autonomy. They would feed themselves by the work of their own hands. Well, partially, anyhow. The boys weren't much impressed by any of that when Ava unveiled her kitchen garden project.

Alvin, Nemo, and Toussaint crowded on the back steps that led to the yard. "What a mess," Nemo said. He was twelve and had an attitude.

It was a little squalid, that was true—the last broken slabs of concrete hadn't been hauled away just yet, two-by-fours leaned against the rickety fence alongside all manner of buckets and troughs splattered with hardened spackle.

"This is what we're going to eat," Ava replied, maybe a little too grandly, gesturing out at the yard.

"Rocks?" Nemo said.

Smart-ass.

"A garden," she said. She stood in front of them on the bottom step and held up the garden plan she'd drawn. "See?"

She caught a glimpse of her reflection in the glass bottom pane of the storm door: Muscles curved her upper arms and contoured her back. Sexy, she thought. Beneath her jeans, her calves dipped in at the sides. She wore coveralls most days, and wool caps pulled just so over her shaved head. At night she fell into bed next to Cass and slept like a child. She remembered things she thought she had forgotten: how to aerate soil before planting, how to build boxes for raised beds, how to make a cloche out of window screen and old hangers to protect tomato and strawberry plants. It was Ava who said they ought to collect food scraps and mix them into the churned earth in the yard. Any extra they could keep in a barrel with a few worms to be used later as fertilizer. The garden plan was detailed and thorough: pole beans and peas—a little late to plant them but she'd take her chances—closest to the house so they don't shade out the lower plants, blueberries along the side with lots of acid in the soil (coffee grounds, vinegar), summer radishes and broccoli, spinach in the middle.

The boys folded their arms across their little chicken chests, except Alvin who said they would be farmers like on *Little House on the Prairie* and marched out into the dirt.

"We could just go to the store," Nemo suggested.

Ava pushed a garden rake into his hands. "Start over there," she said.

They whined about bugs and Ava fussing at them to keep the rows straight. They disappeared after lunch, so she had to round them up from the roof and the storage nook under the stairs and herd them outside. They'd've died of starvation in Bonaparte. Not one of them knew how to do anything but buy things. Ava still knew what to do with dirt. Toussaint had a knack for it too. When it came time to plant, he dropped the seeds into the ground and patted a mound of earth over each one like he was tucking in a baby.

. . .

The garden was hours of work. Ava understood that their labor would give them discipline and purpose. The problem was that the others didn't know what they were toughening up for. Cass was a doer, not much for explanations beyond his fired-up speeches. That was all right at first. In the early months at 248 they were all so taken with their new lives. But now the boys were restless and grumbly and wanted to go out for pizza—the adults too, truth be told. "Cass," Ava said. "You have to give them something to replace cheesesteaks."

At Meeting a few days later, for which 248 gathered daily in the late afternoon, Cass told them about what he called the food industrial complex. They settled on the living room floor cushions in a semicircle around him.

"Big money in food. Big money in engineering food that stays on a shelf for three months, six months. So what if it gives you cancer, gives you diabetes. Makes your body heavy and your mind slow. Gets you hooked from the cradle."

Ava was different, Cass told them. She was the only one among them raised on real food, no grocery store trash or drive-through burgers. She came from a place where they knew about self-sufficiency. Ava was singular, down to her very cells. She sat a little taller—she had, she understood, something the others could use. She knew things they needed to know, things in her power to give. Or withhold. Toussaint, on the other hand, sat next to his father looking aghast at the banishment of the Quarter Pounder. But when Cass reached over and put a hand on the nape of the boy's neck, Toussaint smiled in spite of himself

"Preservatives, flavor enhancers. High-fructose corn syrup. Addictive as any drug—and all of it added to everyday food—soda, chips, cookies."

Even Cass cracked a smile at that one. "Hehheh," Zeek chuckled. "High off the Keebler elves. I'll be damned. Shoulda tried that first."

"Look," Cass said. "Half our neighborhoods don't even have a real supermarket. What do they sell at that rip-off corner store?"

Cass looked at the boys. They shrugged and muttered like none of them had ever been to a corner store in his life.

"Yeah. You all know." He cuffed Alvin on the shoulder, lightly, playfully.

"We are a bull's-eye people," he said. "They're gunning for us. We can be scared. We can cower and cry. That's one way. The other way is might, is power. What if we understand ourselves as strong, not weak. Powerful, not pitiful. You see?

"First step is our clinic. Real health advice, not just pills. Free. Disruptive to the pay-care system. We get people in there and help them come around to a better way of living. We make this house a homestead and a fortress. We stay sharp so we always know who is a friend and who isn't."

Afternoon sunlight dazzled the room. It shone off their faces, twinkled their eyes.

That evening Cass tacked a manifesto to the kitchen wall:

1. The Fellowship of Ark stands against all systems of black dehumanization and economic exploitation.
2. Ark does not recognize the legitimacy of said systems, their agents, or their methods. Ark rejects the fiction of American democracy.
3. All those who are called to freedom are welcome here.
4. Black people are not defined by oppression, victimhood, or exploitation. We are instead the drivers of the world's economy: sought after, fought for, and essential.
5. Ark cultivates freedom through care of the physical body. Medical care is always free of charge. Medical care includes lifestyle and mindstyle care. Medical care at Ark does no harm.
6. In Ark we do not dull our brains, spirits, or bodies with substances, foods, or ideas that poison us.
7. We do not eat the flesh of other sentient beings. We do

not imbibe the terror of living things at slaughter or we too will be terrified.

8. We are meticulous in our daily activities and in our appearance.

9. Meekness is not a virtue in Ark. The fierce are the inheritors of the earth.

10. We embody and act upon these principles. They inform every aspect of our occupation of this place and any future places. We are ever reliant upon an expanding brotherhood.

Brotherhood

TOUSSAINT, ALVIN, AND NEMO shared a king-sized mattress in their second-floor bedroom. The mattress was flush against the back wall, narrow rectangles of floor on either side lined with books Cass brought in by the boxload. A small window faced the back alley. The boys folded their clothes into neat piles in the closet, beneath which Toussaint had hidden his most precious comic books from Cass. Cass didn't allow comics, or toys. He thought toys were distractions that kept boys from reading and developing into serious young men.

Except for Alvin. Alvin was allowed a whole collection of yo-yos and a Slinky and a stuffed owl so old its beak had fallen off. Alvin had fits. He rocked and shouted when there weren't any seconds at dinner, or if anybody got even a little bit mad at him. Alvin's fits gave Toussaint the jitters but he liked him all right—he was nine even if he didn't act like it, and he knew a lot of yo-yo tricks and was a fast runner, so fast Toussaint nearly lost to him when the three of them raced. Nemo was okay too. He acted goody-goody, but one afternoon he lied about doing chores and went all the way to White Castle. The boys ate the smuggled burgers in the alley behind 248.

The three of them were big boys—practically young men, Zeek had said—too old to be scared about new family, new father, new life. And way too old for sad-sack tears or mooning over stuff they used to have but didn't anymore. Cass said looking backward wasn't the Ark way. So they banished fear. Be gone! But sometimes in the middle of the night, Nemo woke up shaking because he'd heard his and Alvin's father moving around somewhere in the house. It wasn't actually Carl. But there was some malevolent something creep creeping up the stairs. The boys, hearts pinging, huddled together, waiting for the boogeyman to fling open the door and step in with his grabbing arms and sunken-hole eyes and his sharp yellow teeth. Mine! he would shout because the boys were his and the whole place was his and he wanted all of it back. When they had terrified themselves to exhaustion, all three fell into a deep and troubled sleep.

In the morning none of them spoke of their boogeyman nights. They grumbled out of bed at Zeek's knock at seven a.m. Breakfast at seven-thirty—teeth cleaned, heads brushed—at the kitchen table with Winnie and Zeek. Oatmeal with brown sugar every morning. Ava paced the room sipping her coffee. Grown-up talk whizzed over the boys' heads. Their old lives shadowed this new one. Sooner or later, one of them would always say something about how things were before Ark. The mood soured and dimmed, despite the sunlight shining through the kitchen window. Then Winnie would mention Cass and they'd all brighten. The talk would turn to him: He had looked tired when Ava saw him briefly that morning, or he had seemed especially vigorous. He was troubled. He was radiant! The adults talked about him like he was the weather, unstoppable like that.

When at last Cass strode into the kitchen Ava rushed to take his coffee cup and Winnie was on her feet asking if he wanted anything to eat, even though he never did. Zeek beamed at him: "All right, brother! What's good today?" Toussaint ventured a soft "Good morning" and returned to his breakfast. His father was like one of the big cats at the zoo: you couldn't stop looking but if you got too close it would eat you whole. Cass read the day's agenda; then breakfast was over and adults and children dispersed to their chores. Toussaint lingered with the dregs of his oatmeal, dazed. Or maybe dazzled. Nemo always had to come back for him so they could sweep the upstairs hallway and wipe down the bathroom tub and sink.

Rain or shine the boys jogged behind Cass through the springtime park in the midmorning. Toussaint liked the steady thud of the pavement under his feet, and the push and pull of the air into his chest. He would veer off on his own, run a lap around a field, and catch up to the others, no sweat. Back at 248, lunch waited: Winnie's split pea soup or navy beans and rice in a big pot set on the counter next to a stack of bowls and a pile of spoons. Alvin and Nemo's stinky-breath play cousin Mikey came around some days, mostly when he was skipping school, which was most days so far as Toussaint could tell.

At lunchtime the boys were exiled to folding chairs against the kitchen walls to make room for guests. "This here is Martin," Zeek would say. Or Ava might introduce Vera from down the block and her baby, Naima. Toussaint didn't understand why his mother always brought these ladies and their babies. The baby always started up howling and Ava would look at it kind of scared and angry all at once. That's when Cass would place his bowl lightly on the table. "Come on into the exam room," he'd say. At that point it was just an empty room with a table in it. A little while later all three would come out, the baby calm and the mother carrying a little tube of something. When they were out of earshot Ava might say about the mama, "I mean, it doesn't take a genius to buy a bottle of Anbesol." When lunch was over there was cleanup and gardening. The boys had lessons with Cass so he could quiz them on the Mau Maus and Ida B. Wells. There was Meeting, free time, dinner, more chores. The days unfolded in the same way, each with its rhythm. Cass said routine was the foundation of a stable mind.

In the evening Ark strolled the neighborhood. The neighbors sourpussed their little procession, but Winnie went right on with her hellos to everybody they passed, waving so hard her arm was going to fly right off her. All she ever got in reply were half smiles and cold stares. Poor Nemo and Alvin. Mothers were such an embarrassment.

Cass and Ava always walked behind the others. Cass slung his arm around Ava's shoulders in the late April twilight, their heads bent toward each other. A slight, sweet chill in the air, and no mosquitos yet, or not many. Toussaint's stomach was full from dinner, and his legs buzzy tired from running and racing and doing. Sometimes he walked between Cass and Ava: mother, father, boy; ma, pop, son. Mom and Dad. Toussaint tried all the words. None of them were quite right, but a sheltered feeling came over him, if only for a little while.

Toussaint liked Nemo and Alvin more every day. He really did like them a whole lot, but they were his brothers in the same way Cass was his father, which is to say it was a little bit made up. Ava kept on telling him he was taking a while to get used to them because it had been him and her on their own for so long. She said he was only just now learning how to have a family. He had almost gotten used to how she was now, the brown fuzz of her scalp and how big her eyes looked now that there was no hair on her head. But when she started talking like that it made his stomach hurt. He did have a family. It was her.

Red-Handed

THE KITCHEN GARDEN WOULD YIELD, but it sure wasn't yielding yet. Two weeks after planting, and nothing but the tender green tops of radishes. The storebought food was running low too. "Piggy bank's empty," Zeek had said when Ava went looking for petty cash for groceries. Zeek sold Ava and Winnie's food stamps to help pay for the clinic's supplies. They were down to canned veggies, crackers, neon orange government cheese, and a vat of peanut butter. Ava and Winnie were hungry most days, but they ate what was left after they'd fed the boys and those few who turned up for Meeting and stayed for dinner. "Canape," Ava would say, laughing, and hand around the cheese on off-brand Ritz.

That evening, after a meager dinner of grits and the last bag of frozen lima beans, Ava went out into her garden. "Come on, you babies," she whispered to the pole beans. "Come on up."

"Is it working?" Cass said, walking down the center path toward her.

"We should get some chickens," Ava said. "For the eggs."

"We can get some chickens."

His shirt hung loose. If she touched his chest with her fingertips, if she angled herself toward him, he would pull her into the corner behind the planks where no one could see them. He cupped her cheek in his palm.

"We need more food," she said.

"I know."

"Two more weeks till checks."

"I know."

"We should knock off a grocery store."

Cass didn't think much about food. He could have eaten oatmeal every day for the rest of his life. He folded his arms and looked off toward the back fence, already on to something else in his mind. Ava thought, as she had before, that it would be up to her to do the things he wasn't bothered about. Ark was one body, he had taken to saying. Ava didn't mind being the hands.

"Plenty of food around," Cass said, turning back to her. "They just don't want us to know it."

That was probably true, but her kid couldn't eat philosophy. Ava had had an idea. It had come to her as a sad fantasy. She hadn't any intention of actually going to Glenn Avenue. They weren't starving, they could eat more grits and canned peas. Ava could go to a food pantry. But grits and booger-snot peas (that's what Toussaint called them) get old pretty quick, and anyway, it wasn't about the food, or just the food. Going back there had something to do with Miss Simmons and her warning notices, and the roaches and silverfish. And that Glenn Avenue couldn't even get a security guard who wasn't fencing food stamps and screwing all the residents.

Ava and Cass stood in the A&P parking lot across the street. The building was bigger than Ava remembered, as if her mind had shrunk it so she could put it away someplace where it wouldn't torment her.

"We don't have to do this," Cass said.

The traffic light changed from green to yellow to red and back again, then again. Cars sped down Tulpehocken. The floodlights at the front of the shelter cast a cloud of fluorescence into the air. Inside there would be the same old settling-in sounds: A baby crying somewhere down a hallway. Slipper slap against the linoleum floor. Metallic bed-frame squeak. The smell of ammonia lingering in the corridor by the nurse's and Miss Simmons's offices. It would be too hot in the lobby and too cold in the corridors. Those damn mosquitoes.

For some reason Ava said, "Summer will be here before you know it."

Cass wasn't much fazed by a non sequitur, so he nodded and kept on watching the traffic light change.

Ava turned toward the bus stop. "I can't," she said.

Cass shrugged so slightly Ava nearly missed it. The thing is, he would have gone on back to 248 and never said another word about it.

Ava took a deep breath. "Okay," she said.

They crossed the street, rounded the building, and tipped past the dumpsters to the back pantry door. Ava stood with her hand on the knob. It's just a place, she thought. What do I think will happen if I go in there? Things hurt for a while, and then they stop hurting, despite the warning bells pinging in our chests. Some nights when she and Cass were alone, he scored the scar around his bullet hole with a penknife. "It's only pain," he'd say. Of course, he had Ava clean the cuts with iodine. Pain was one thing, but bacteria was a horse of another color.

The door scraped open with some jerking and pulling. When the smell hit her, Ava backed out and threw up by the dumpster. "Just a body registering a complaint," Cass said. Ava wiped her mouth and pushed through the doorway. Stainless-steel shelves, worn linoleum, dingy walls—just an ugly room with a lot of stuff they needed.

She pulled loaves of bread from the shelves, powdered milk, cans of diced tomatoes. Rice, packages of noodles. Industrial-sized bags of frozen string beans, peas, lima beans, and corn. They were running out of room in the fold-up laundry carts they'd brought along.

"We need to slow down and organize," Ava said.

"Okay. Yeah. Lima beans?"

"Three bags."

"You think we need all four bags of this rice?"

"Rice, yeah. Good staple."

Back and forth they went, debating canned corn as if they were at the ShopRite. It was banal and thrilling, standing next to Cass, who could reach the highest shelves, who was not breathing like a bull from the tension of the moment. They loaded the carts till they were near toppling, then moved toward the pantry doors.

Suddenly, acutely, Ava was aware of her and Toussaint's old room out there in the network of hallways. How many of the kids there six months ago were still there now? Was Tess still there? Some other woman and child were sleeping in the room she and Toussaint slept in. Ava tried not to think about it, she wanted to get back to Ephraim. To hell with these people.

"We were in room 813," she said.

Cass nodded. "You told me."

Ava didn't remember telling him particulars, she didn't remember telling him anything about being there except that they were there. She tugged her cart through the pantry doors and out to the trash area, then paused and glanced at the doors that opened into the cafeteria.

"It was that way?" Cass said. "Your room?"

Ava propped her cart against a wall. An instant later they were in the dark cafeteria. That boiled-bean and lunch-meat smell. Kids' drawings still on the walls. What did she want to do in there? Knock on the door of 813 and say, "Hello! Just wanted to see what you've done with the place!" She imagined the new tenants: a crackhead and her teenage son, who wouldn't be anything like Ava's son. This son would be flabby from bologna sandwiches and laziness and would grow up to be useless with a bunch of babies and a welfare check. Just like Ronald Reagan said. The closer they got to room 813, the more Ava was determined to kick in the door and catch them red-handed. At what? At being poor. Haha. Ha. Degenerates. Niggers.

"That's it," she whispered, when they turned down the green corridor. "That's it right there." She sped up but Cass didn't pull her back. He didn't tell her to calm down. When she tried the handle, the door to 813 swung open. A shaft of light cut in from the hallway. The little shelf above the sink was crowded with toiletries: hair oil, some kind of body spray, a pink comb. The room wasn't so barren as Ava remembered. The new people had taped photos to the back wall. They had tried to make the place fit for human beings. A woman was sleeping on one of the narrow beds, hair in hard curlers under a scarf, her whole body spooned around a little sleeping body, like a walnut shell around the tender bit inside. The child stirred. She sat up and stared. Ava must have been monstrous silhouetted in that shaft of light from the hallway. She had caught them, all right. She sure had.

Cass shut the door quietly. But Ava wasn't sorry. No, she wasn't. She was mad. She wanted to run down the hallway kicking down the scuffed-up doors. Liberating all the people. She raised her leg high in front of the door of the next room. Cass caught her. He put both arms around her and pulled her to his chest. "What's the point in that?" he said.

It was true. Where would they all go? Winnie's?

Back in the cafeteria, Ava sat at a table, heaving for air.

"Look at this," she said, waving her hand around. "Did I ever tell you about Miss Simmons? Did I tell you the drains didn't work in the showers and a bloody tampon floated up and hit my ankles? Did I tell you Toussaint was so out of his mind he wandered the streets all day in the cold?"

They ought to burn it down. They ought to round up everybody who was to blame for Glenn Avenue and . . . and . . . And who was to blame? What had got up on its hind legs and brought evil on all these people? And on Ava too. And her boy. Cass liked to say it was the system, but you can't kick the system in the face. You can't slit the system's throat. She kicked a chair. "Don't blow up the house while you're still standing in it," was what Cass said.

They went out the way they'd come in, through the pantry door. When they got onto Glenn Avenue, Ava caught a glimpse of Melvin: feet up on the desk, dead asleep. Jesus. She strained against the full weight of the cart dragging behind her. The labor calmed her. The labor made her think of harvesting sorghum when she was a girl in Bonaparte. It had been enough, more than enough, to tend the land, and feed themselves and whatever souls washed up in their town. And to take what they needed from people who had too much and didn't want to share. That was right and simple. Like her pop used to say, staying alive is the best revenge. Everlasting bless him.

"Okay," she said aloud. Cass looked at her and smiled.

The night bus never came so Ava and Cass walked for three hours back to Ephraim. Ava ached from her wrists to the flats of her feet. Cass took hold of one side of her cart and the two of them trudged up Fifty-eighth Street tugging it between them. A chill rain soaked them to the bone, drop by drop until Ava's teeth chattered. It was like they were the last two people left in the world. Just when Ava thought she couldn't take another step they turned onto Ephraim and there, in the middle of the block, sat number 248, porch light spilling onto the sidewalk like a beacon. They broke into a little trot then, heading for the light.

In the upstairs bathroom Cass peeled off Ava's soaked jeans and T-shirt, rolled down the sopping socks and pulled them gently from her feet. He took off his own wet clothes and the two stepped under the shower. Oh, the warm tub beneath the soles of her feet! The hot water ran over her scalp and down her neck. Cass rubbed wide circles from her shoulder blades to the small of her back. Dawn came up. The white tiles turned indigo in the coming light, then sea blue, then robin's egg. Pink sunrise caught in the swirling steam.

BONAPARTE

● ● ●

AFTER THE FIRE Progress sent around a bunch of police, local *and* state, thank you very much. They knew it was Barber. "Well, now, that sure would be a shame," we said. "He came round here saying he was Lester-Luther-Jenkins-Jones what used to live down round the bend—the one whose cows was always getting loose's cousin. From Detroit."

Detroit did the trick. You wouldn't think these fools would keep getting their backs up about northern negroes. At this point half of all the damn Negroes are northern, but in Alabama the crackers never got over it. Detroit, they repeated, nodding. They kept an eye out to see if Barber would come back. When he didn't, they went on back to Montgomery or wherever. Except for one. A tall skinny trooper with a face like a skeleton. Prowled around plainclothes at night in a unmarked sedan. He didn't come in the long way through the Progress houses like the rest of them did. This fella wanted to come through the Oaks. I couldn't figure why he was so stuck on us. Maybe he did something to us long time ago, or his daddy did or his grandaddy. Not a white person in this whole state that's more than a generation from something foul, and that's the good ones.

Sure enough, me and Carter Lee were out in the woods on one of our patrols when that sedan pulled up and Bone Face got out. You can see he's not right—big huge eyes that reflect everything instead of taking it in. He wandered up and down the road, looking at stuff on the ground, shining his flashlight into the trees. He was fifty feet down, then twenty, then ten. I stayed calm. Mostly. He got closer, peering through the brush and sniffing the air like a hound. His flashlight beam swept right over the hood of the truck. He was so close I could see he had the liquor sweats. Thing is, he didn't see us. Not ten feet away and he didn't know we was there. I twisted Carter Lee's hand so hard he hit me in the shoulder to let him go. A minute later Bone Face was back in his car. We sat in the dark a long while before Carter Lee turned on the truck.

"What I tell you?" I said.

Carter Lee nodded and sucked in some air like he'd been holding his breath.

"Now you see for yourself. He shined that light right on us but he didn't see us."

"We too far back."

"We not that far back, Carter Lee. He was looking right at us." Carter Lee fumbled around putting the truck in reverse.

"I'm telling you. They can't see past the Oaks."

"What you mean?"

"I mean I think a lotta people can't find their way in here no more."

"Aww, Dutchess, don't start that mess again. It's overgrown in some places. We ain't exactly had Lady Bird Johnson here doing beautification. Shit. Barber came and went easy. He knew the way and this fella don't. That's all."

I didn't say anything else. But I know it was more to it. We are fading. Disappearing out of time. But I tell you this, I ain't gon disappear us quicker by letting them get not a one of these acres a minute sooner than it's coming to them.

Next day I got in my truck and drove to Bodine. I ain't left Bonaparte in seven years. I half expected people zipping around on flying saucers. Course, I was only going to ass-backward Bodine so fat chance of that. More likely they went the other way and reinstated slavery or resegregated the water fountains. It's a lot faster to Bodine by boat, but I didn't want Carter Lee and them to know what I was doing. Anyhow, I don't trust the water without Caro. I packed two rifles and a bullet box in my truck. One under the seat, one under a tarp in the back. I had my blade. And I brought Delilah who is better than a straight razor across the throat—she don't like white people and she don't like the government. She started growling low in her throat soon as the Bodine municipal building came into view. Everlasting bless her.

Bodine makes me want to growl too. The center of town ain't but four long streets, laid out tic-tac-toe, highest building is three stories, not counting the spire of the Methodist church. There's a Woolworth's, Rexall Drugs, and Bodine's excuse for a department store called Lawry's, like the season salt, next door to Wilcox Savings and Loan. The whole shitty town has the nerve to smell like jasmine. Ain't that a blip.

You should have seen the white people when I walked into that bank to get my cashier's check. I had rocks in my stomach but I walked in there Leontyne Price. Bill Blass pantsuit in antique rose. Yes, ma'am. Delilah at my side, hip-high and snorting like a dragon. Conversation ceased! I had to take a little from here and a little from there to get the four thousand but I got it all together. I walked into the tax assessor's office and told them I needed to pay the back taxes on 4128 General Store Way in Bonaparte. The man behind the counter was so surprised he turned forty-six shades of pink. He looked at the tax bill then back at the check then back at the bill some more. "Okay. Uh, Miss . . . Dutchess," he says. You believe they still pull that mess? "Mrs. Carson," I told him. He went off in a back office. I think they was back there dusting the check for fingerprints. I waited thirty minutes.

Course, you can always stick somebody in the neck with a hatpin. Delilah got restless and took to pacing. Off to the side of the counter they had a cardboard box filled with soda cans, boy they sure drink a lot of RC Cola, and behind that a bunch of leather binders on shelves labeled PROPERTY RECORDS and PROBATE. I pulled out the binder from 1936. Do you believe they ain't got this stuff wrapped up in a special room or something? Well, they ain't so I opened it up and there it was: WPA Land Parcel Project, Bonaparte, Alabama, parcels 1 and 2 and so on and all our names. Carson, LaPrairie, Duke, Billups, and so on. I keep the actual deed in my strongbox, of course, but it's something to see all these yellow-at-the-edge papers in a old record book.

It was about four hundred degrees in that tax assessor's office. So humid you could drink the air, and these crackers had all our precious records on those shelves passing into oblivion like the minutes ticking by on their wall clock. When the man came out from the back office Delilah got up on her back legs and put her paws on the counter. She gave him a little grin. He says, "Can you call your dog?" "I'm sorry, sir," I said. "Are you afraid of dogs?" Heh. I am telling you, my girl should get an Oscar. On the way out he says, "I didn't know was none of y'all Bonaparte people left! So nice the Progress is building it up over there, musta been halfway to ruin." I took my receipts and walked away. Names will never hurt me. And I took a probate binder just to mess up their wills and testaments to land they got no business with nohow. How about that.

Soon's you get out of Bodine it's pure country. I guess it's pure country while you still in Bodine, but not in the good way. The road is asphalt paved two-lane highway, but you don't pass nothing but Spanish moss and loblolly for miles. Road flat as a white woman's behind. We passed a little place called Albing which only has Fosky's Roadside Supply selling feed and block cheese and beer. On the porch it's always a passel of niggers standing around to look you up and down if they see you not from around here. But they grin nice and tip hats, metaphorically, I mean, if they seen you before. And believe me these niggers don't never forget a face. They ain't seen but a few their whole lives cause they never been anywhere beside Fosky's and the inside of their trucks. After that it's fifty miles of peace and quiet, a shotgun house or two set back in the trees, and a couple of trailers with dice games going out front.

I got the tax receipt PAID IN FULL in my little briefcase on the floor of the truck. Windows down and the wind is cool and the moss-smelling air rushing in. Delilah sticks her head out the window and puts on a good show of wolfing for some kids by the road.

I slow down so they can chase after the truck yelling, "Arooooo," with their heads thrown back and laughing. "Aroooooo!" me and Delilah howl back at em. "Aroooooo!"

The state highway narrows the closer you get to the turnoff to Bonaparte—after the turn it's even skinnier, but Progress paved it smooth as glass. Ten miles of pretty all the way home: the trees canopy way up high so you kinda feel like returning royalty. My shoulders come down from being so hunched up around my ears and the rifle under the seat stops being so present in my mind. But Delilah wouldn't settle. She whined and huffed and kept looking out behind us. In the rearview mirror wasn't nothing but dappled sunshine on the blacktop and green shadows and those silvery puffs the forest breathes up when it's humid.

"Hush, girl. We almost there. Hush now."

In Alabama it's Jesus and them no matter where you tune the radio dial, or else the country music, which is the same thing. Fiddle fiddle and (at last!) there's Minnie Riperton up through the static, like little gold bells.

"See there, D? You like Minnie," I said.

She hmmphed at me and went on looking out the back. Sometimes there's no pleasing this dog. But I was finished with being nervous, I had spent the whole day with my stomach in my throat. I got my flask out of the glove compartment, turned up Minnie, and drove for home. One thing I did was get five photostat copies of the tax receipt. I planned on putting one in everybody's mailbox. Don't want none of those fools on my doorstep except to drop off my fruitcake come Christmas. Don't hurt nobody, now, I can just hear Caro say, in his chuckle voice. If it was Caro he'd'a gone and paid that bill and not said nothing to nobody, but I'm not noble like that.

The road behind us grayed up. Storms roll in around here one minute to the next. You can't live in Bonaparte and not believe in the Everlasting, or Somebody. We got biblical weather here. This one was strange though cause most times storms come off the water, which is in front of us, not behind. On the radio Minnie got to her *Oooh ooh ooh ooh ooh*, that part only dogs can hear, and I guess

Delilah heard it because she started up barking like it was a bear in the truck bed. "All right, girl," I said. "Nothing but wind." Truth be told it kicked up so strong my flask blew off the dash. Sapling trees behind us whipping. And the Spanish moss blowing like daisies on the stem. I went around the curve three miles out from Bonaparte, and once the road straightened, I'll be damned, the sun was back and the wind calmed. Well, what the hell was that, I thought. Maybe it was a small tornado touched down. I'm going straight to Carter Lee, because he has a hobby of meteorology. If there was a tornado he would know.

Delilah howled, no fooling this time. Coming round the bend was a gray fog moving fast like floodwater only it was so wide I couldn't see around it and so tall it blocked out the treetops. Thick like heavy cream advancing on us. Delilah roared and I hit the gas. Maybe it was smoke from a fire even though I couldn't smell nothing. Or. Or? It rushed down the road behind me. Did you ever see a forest fire eat up everything in its way? This was like that, only a big solid mass of foggy nothing, erasing the woods and trees and birdsong. I floored it. Eighty then ninety. The wheel shook in my hand when I hit a hundred. That nothing was a half mile behind me, then a quarter mile, then an eighth. The steering wheel knocked and the engine light flashed. It was right behind me. Pressure built in my ears so I couldn't hear nothing, or maybe it was that there wasn't nothing to hear, like it had eaten all sound. At a hundred and ten I couldn't steer anymore and the hood smoked. Everlasting, Old Rea help me. I looked through the rearview and half the truck bed was disappeared. Delilah strained against the window, teeth bared, her head jerking back and forth. A wisp of mist curled slow, like smoke coming off a cigarette, just outside the cab window. I swear my ears were bleeding but I slammed the gas, and me and that truck were a comet, streaking past our Bonaparte Oaks.

I came to a smoking stop in the middle of the road a few yards after the Oaks. Up ahead the sun was hot and gold as it ever was, and the woods just as feral and fat-green. A wild peacock strutted down the road a ways ahead of us. I sat in the cab breathing ragged, braced for the cold touch of fog on my shoulders, but it never came.

I leaned my head against the steering wheel for a long while before I got the nerve to look behind me. On the other side of the Oaks a gray kerchief of mist twisted in the air. Behind it the road and the trees were all there like they should be, but something was off; like the road was a snapshot of the road, frozen that way forever. I can't tell you what I mean exactly. My ears popped and I heard that I was crying big hiccup tears. And Delilah. Aww Delilah, she had her head back, howling out a dirge.

PHILADELPHIA

. . .

M-80s

"WHERE'D YOU GET THOSE?" Toussaint whispered.

Mikey closed his fingers around the pair of M-80s resting in the palm of his hand. The boys huddled around him in the alley behind 248.

"Like Imma tell you fools," he said, wiping a line of sweat trickling down his forehead. He stuck both hands deep into his shorts pockets. Mikey had started coming around more often. Nobody wanted him to, but Alvin and Nemo couldn't do anything about it. "We been knowing him since we were *little*," Nemo had said.

"So goddamn hot," Mikey said.

"GD hot," Alvin repeated. It *was* GD hot, Toussaint thought.

Mikey pulled off his book bag. The other boys pressed in. "Yo," he said. "Gimme some space." His grubby palm emerged from the depths of the pack cupping four more firecrackers.

"Oh shit!" Alvin said.

"Damn right." After Mikey turned fifteen, he started acting like he should be in charge. Toussaint never paid him much mind because he had stinky breath and he looked like a giraffe on account of being so tall and light-skinned with brown acne scars all over. He acted like he was doing them a favor by hanging out with them, but Toussaint thought he probably didn't have any friends. He spent the day hanging around the park with the crackheads. His mama would beat his ass right in public. One time she dragged him by the back of the shirt all the way to 248 and cussed out Cass and Ava and told them they better stay away from her son. Which was funny, because most of the time Cass didn't even notice Mikey was in the room. But he had his uses, like the M-80s, for example.

"Oh shit!" Alvin said again. Louder this time, and he started up with the too fast circling he did when he got overexcited.

"Alvin! Shhhh. You gonna get us in trouble," Nemo said.

It was late. Late enough that the woman down the street was done fussing at her man, and the guy in 264 had already smoked his bedtime cigarette on the porch. So late the possums were scrapping at the other end of the block. Old Miss Drucker had the night news on so loud the boys could hear every word even though she was on the other side of the alley. Cass had dragged Toussaint over to her house once to give her a cake Winnie made and to tell her the nighttime news was BS and that everything Ted Koppel said was part of the False Message.

Half of the things Cass said were a mystery, and the other half pissed everybody off. But sometimes he said things that echoed in Toussaint's head for days. Like, kids are born brave but the world tells them their courage is childishness so when they grow up, they are ruined. This made Toussaint want to stay a boy a little longer, so he could fix things for his mother before he grew up and was too scared. He was eleven now—still short for his age, but he had hair down there and a little in his underarms. Time was running out.

"My man. Toussaint. Earth to Toussaint," Mikey said. He was flicking the lighter he'd gotten to use for the M-80s.

"Uh-oh. Oh shit," Alvin said. His voice echoed down the alley. A light turned on in the house just behind them.

"Yo, don't be such a retard," Mikey said.

"Don't call him a retard!" Nemo said.

"It's all right, Alvin," said Toussaint.

Alvin marched on, head down. "Oh shit!"

"Alvin. Alvin!" Toussaint pulled a yo-yo from his pocket and pushed it into Alvin's hands. Toussaint thought it was pretty lucky that maybe Alvin would stay a little boy for longer than the rest of them. "Here. Here you go." Alvin popped the yo-yo as far out as it would go, then snapped it back.

"See? It's all right, man," Toussaint said.

"What we gon do with em?" Nemo asked, staring at the firecrackers.

Mikey looked at Nemo like he was a fool.

"Save em." He lowered his voice: "Make our own kind of Fourth of July celebration."

Toussaint and Nemo looked over their shoulders, as if from the other end of the block, deep inside 248, Cass might hear them. When, after much prodding from the others, Toussaint asked if they could have a barbecue for the Fourth, Cass went silent in that way he does, like a pot about to boil. Then he said, "Your celebration is a sham; your shouts of liberty and equality, hollow mockery." He could have just said no. Later, Toussaint found a book of speeches by Frederick Douglass sitting on the bed in the boys' room. The next day Cass announced a block party—to celebrate some sad holiday nobody had ever heard of. At least it would be a party, even if there wouldn't be any hot dogs.

"We don't believe in the Fourth," Nemo said. Then, more quietly: "Anyway, it's only June. You gonna save em all that time?"

"No Fourth!" Alvin said.

"Whatcha mean no Fourth?" Mikey said. "It's such a thing as July, ain't it? And it got a fourth day, right? So, it's a Fourth of July. Stupid." He leaned in to Toussaint's face: "You not gonna snitch on us, are you, Daddy's boy?"

Toussaint couldn't explain that he wasn't sure whose boy he was.

"Ain't gonna tell," he said.

They considered the state of affairs for a few seconds, then Nemo lunged for the M-80s and Alvin fell on top of him. Toussaint stood apart, watching his not-brothers-brothers. He wondered what Keith and Anthony were doing now that school was out for summer. And Paul, too, was out there somewhere. Toussaint didn't belong anywhere or to anyone. Not really. He didn't know what to do with all that feeling so he let out a roar and threw himself into the tussle of flailing limbs and heat and sweat. "Hoooaaahhh," he yelled, climbing off and leaping again.

The man in the house behind them looked out at them through his window and remembered the animal feeling of his own boyhood, out in the summer night with the mosquitoes buzzing and the moths diving into the light around the streetlamps. He smiled, let out a halfhearted "Y'all better stop making all that noise at this hour."

The boys scrambled to their feet. "Sorry, mister!" Nemo said.

"Yeah, sorry," Mikey said. He looked at the other boys and held his finger to his lips. He produced an M-80 from one pocket and the lighter from the other. Alvin pogoed straight into the air with both feet. Mikey flicked the lighter and moved it toward the wick. "Sike," he said. "SIKE!" He took off full speed down the alley and turned onto Ephraim Avenue with the other boys close behind.

"Yeaahh!" Nemo yelled and jumped from the curb to the middle of the street. Toussaint hopped onto a fire hydrant and balanced on his tiptoes, one second, two, suspended in streetlamp radiance. "Watch this, little dudes!" Mikey said and high-jumped onto a porch. "Oh shit!" Alvin said. "Oh shit!" Lights went on in bedroom windows up and down the block. The boys tore down Ephraim. They sprinted two blocks—past Mikey's, where his ma was probably waiting up for him, past the church and the parish house where the lady reverend always sat smoking on the porch. They rounded the corner and disappeared into the darkness of Sixty-third Street where the streetlight was blown.

Block Party

AVA WOKE ALONE on the morning of the party. He's still mad then, she thought, rolling over and closing her eyes. Cass had been dashing around in a frenzy of preparation for the last week. The clinic is the key, he kept saying, more short-tempered by the hour. Maybe it hadn't been such a good idea to have the clinic's grand opening and the block party on the same day.

He'd been in a good mood the evening before. "You know what brought a lot of young people to the Panthers?" he asked. "Gonorrhea! The clap was the best recruitment tool we ever had."

Haha. Jokes! So Ava made jokes too. "Bring your poor, your staph-infected, your ringwormed masses." she said. No, it wasn't very funny—but Cass turned stony and furious. Why, he wanted to know, did Ava hate poor people so much when she was one herself? He assigned her to clinic cleanup for two weeks after opening. The thought of it made her stomach turn: the pus and drip, blood and phlegm, all of those bodies.

But! Today was party day—Juneteenth! A holiday Ava had never heard of. Nobody had, except Zeek, who had heard of most things, turns out. And now she'd overslept, on top of everything else. The lower floors of 248 were already bustling. The party was Ark's coming out to the neighborhood. Our debutante ball, haha.

Cass's vision for Ark was so clear it was nearly a premonition.

He wanted expansion. He wanted territory. Ark would be an open-door community. Ava wasn't interested in seducing the neighbors, or engaging them, or even talking to them. She didn't care, not really, about anybody else's freedom. She cared about her boy and Cass and what they had made at 248. They were lit by their peculiar brand of . . . of what? Zeek said it was salvation. A higher calling. A leap into life. Ava hadn't known so many lives were so flat till she left Bonaparte. Then, Everlasting help her, her life too became a slog of paying bills and watching television. Pathetic gains—twenty-five cents more an hour at a job that bored her stiff, or a tax refund one year—followed by some catastrophic setback. On and on, grinding her into dust. Home was gone and the future was mud and ash. Until Cass. With him, the days were supersaturated, vivid, teeming. She was full of every sensation of life. Ava wanted things to stay just as they were on this last morning of Ark's privacy. Right there, baby, where it feels so good. But she knew the price of the ticket was whatever Cass asked her to pay.

Ava dressed quickly. Downstairs, the boys had hung streamers around the clinic door. Ava put them to work sorting the okra they'd harvested from her garden the afternoon before. And there were the flowers to set out on the porch—a whole box of petunias and zinnias. Black-eyed Susans and red phlox she'd traded for fresh vegetables with the florist down on Fifty-eighth. Ava settled on the back steps and set to clipping stems. Cass was out there, pacing the garden with his head bowed. He might've been praying, but of course Cass thought God was the biggest con going.

Ava and Winnie served dirty rice and black-eye peas, potato salad and cornbread from a couple of long folding tables. A boom box boomed, balloons bobbed from the porch railings. Ava's flowers alternated purple and yellow in pots on the steps. Zeek and Patch stood by the open door, trying to look casual and friendly. Patch made what he probably thought was an effort, but all his smiles were sneers. Zeek was a grizzly teddy bear, grinning and waving the neighbors up onto the porch.

There was a brightness in the air, begrudging goodwill from the fifteen or so neighbors who'd turned up, even if they were suspicious. Ava smiled and ladled. She watched Cass doing his new Cass thing on the steps. He'd got himself up in khaki pants and a button-down pale gray shirt with the sleeves rolled to the elbows like a field doctor in a movie. Toussaint and the boys streaked down the block, round the alley, then back up from the other side, wild-eyed.

"Toussaint!" Ava yelled as he hurtled past. He came to a stop at her side like a ball caught in midair.

"Meharry, that's right. Class of '66," Cass was saying to a mousy couple from around the corner. That's it, Ava thought, intimidate them just a little bit. Cass shifted position so the couple had to look up at him. "Anything to strip a black doctor of his license," he went on. Of course he was reinstated. He was working out at Hahnemann Hospital. "Come on back and take a look at the clinic." Two women Ava had seen at the bus stop joined the couple, and a guy from the house near the corner with its little square of lawn mowed within an inch of its life. Mr. Clements, was his name.

Toussaint bounced on his toes, sweat dripping, and shoveled in a few forkfuls of black-eye peas and cornbread, eavesdropping on his father on the steps behind him. "Hahnemann?" he said, through a mouthful of cornbread. "Hahnemann!" Chewed bits flew onto Ava's bare arm.

"Not now, Toussaint," she said.

"Hush, boy," Winnie said.

Toussaint glared, swallowed, and was gone. "Hahnemann," he repeated as he sped off. Ava shrugged. To make an omelet, you have to crack a few eggs. Isn't that how the old phrase went? Most people just want to get up in the morning and have their coffee, watch *Kojak* on prime time, and go out to a diner on Saturday nights. They want to be unburdened from the weight of their souls and their misgivings and their convictions. They want somebody to take all that from them. Only they need a little convincing, Ava had told Cass. Give the neighborhood the good doctor show, a little respectability, and wave those degrees around while you're at it.

They want reassurance, Ava thought now, looking over the line of them at the food table. They want to see what kind of return they'll get on the investment of tolerating us here. They want ham hocks in their collards. Haha! One woman walked away from the line complaining, "Ain't a scrap of meat in here. Not a neckbone or a nothing." People really don't like free stuff, quiet as it's kept.

Winnie was beaming at everybody like she'd got knocked in the head and come to on Magic Mountain. Do I look like that?, Ava thought. Was I out here grinning like a—

"Well, this is delightful!"

Good Lord! No pun intended. The pastor from that church down the way popped up in front of Ava like she'd come out of a hole in the ground. Like a damn woodchuck.

"Pastor Phil!" Winnie said, just a-grinning. "Welcome!"

The pastor lady practiced one of those religions that black people don't do. She had a bit of the hippie about her: Shortish Afro—a little skimpy on the hair oil—collarless blouse tucked into jeans from the last decade. Wide brown eyes that took up too much of her face. Some people just rub you the wrong way.

"Philomena," she said, extending her hand toward Ava. "But everyone calls me Pastor Phil."

She kept right on smiling when Ava gave her the fish-eye. A few feet behind her, a persnickety, peanut-faced old man—in a sweater and tie like Mister Rogers—stared daggers into her back. "Pastor Philomena?" he said, like there was something she was supposed to be doing. Like he and some other mean little people on the block had sent her to suss them out.

"Ava," she said. But Ava wasn't going to do any of that hand-shake stuff. Her pop used to say shaking hands was a white people thing, like they were testing your arm to see how much trouble it would be to rip it off you.

"I'm glad to meet you," the pastor said. "You're all the rage!"

Peanut Face snorted.

"Rice and collards?" Ava thrust a paper plate out toward her. She wasn't going to stand here making small talk.

"Reverend Parker." Cass. Ava smiled. There he was, gold and towering and come to put a stop to this. The pastor blinked and her whole body wavered, just a split second, but Ava saw it. Cass could turn on a light in a woman.

"Welcome," he said.

The pastor fumbled her plate but her other hand shot out from her side, smile reconstructed.

"Episcopalian," Cass said. "I guess the Church of Christ people on Sixty-sixth give you a run for your money."

The little pastor looked at him like she might figure him out if she stared hard enough. Good luck with that, honey.

"Neck and neck," she said. "But we have black Jesus. Well, some of us do."

"I see you didn't bring him with you."

The pastor chuckled. No, giggled. The little heifer giggled and didn't she tilt her head? Toussaint raced by with the other boys. "Hey, Pastor Phil!" they called. How the hell did he know her?

"It's nice you're doing this. To set people at ease, I mean. Some people around here were worried y'all were a little, uh, Rajneesh."

She sure didn't waste any time getting to the accusations.

Ava set down her ladle. "I don't know who you think you are, coming—"

"We are . . ." Cass cleared his throat. "We are lacking spiritual counsel. People need that. I understand, even if I don't go for it myself. I hope you'll come back. You're welcome anytime."

"Likewise," she said. She turned to Ava as if she knew something about her, as if they were in on something. "My door is always open."

Ava wanted to fling the pot of hot greens at her retreating back. Cass's eyes flared like they did when he was spitting angry. And who could blame him? Smug little thing.

"What the fuck was that?" he growled, bending over Ava, his breath hard and hot against her cheek. "You keep your mouth shut when I'm handling Ark's business."

Then he was gone into the house.

"Ava. Ava! You going to pour greens all over Mr. Clements!"

Winnie said. Ava had dripped pot liquor all over the man's shoes. There was a fuss and a flurry of napkins.

"Always daydreaming," Winnie said with one of her vague smiles.

An hour later, Cass stepped out onto the porch of 248. His speech was casual and easy, just as Ava had said it should be. All were welcome at 248. Anytime. Tuesdays and Thursdays open clinic. A fellowship every afternoon at five-thirty, to digest the events of the day. A meal after their gathering three times a week (first Ava had heard about that). He was just set to announce their carpentry services when a low boom interrupted his speech. Then two more in rapid succession. Ava heard screaming from somewhere beyond the crowd. Toussaint tore around the corner and up the steps toward Cass. The two of them sprinted off toward the alley with Cass shouting for Ava to get his medical bag from the clinic.

When she arrived, a small crowd had gathered around Mikey, who lay on his side in the alley, blood dripping from his hand. Toussaint kneeled next to him. "It's okay, Mikey," he said. "You gotta take deep breaths, man, just take a deep breath." Cool little cat.

"Hand me the tube that says 'lidocaine,'" Cass said. "Saline solution. Gauze, outside pocket." Ava fumbled but Cass was quick and confident. The gathered crowd watched, hushed.

"Damned if he's not a real doctor after all," somebody said to a chorus of mmm-hmms. Then, "What the—"

A police cruiser rolled down the alley, slow and easy like somebody had told them exactly where to find the trouble. Two cops got out, with that walk like they got so much going on down there they can't keep their thighs together.

"What's the problem here?" one of them said, to any face that would answer. "Got a call about explosives."

"Explosives!" a man said. The woman next to him elbowed him quiet.

"What's wrong with this kid?" The lead cop advanced through the circle of neighbors. Ava inched closer to her son.

"Just a little accident," Cass said. "Boys will be boys."

"Is that right? And who are you, Boys Will Be Boys?"

"He's a doctor!" a woman said.

"This guy's a doctor?" the cop said.

"You all right, kid?" the second cop asked. "What's wrong with your hand?"

"Cl-Climbing," Mikey said, steadying his voice. "I was climbing a tree and I—"

"Climbing a tree. You were climbing a tree? Okay. Y'all got a permit for this block party? And I'm going to need to see some ID. Everybody's ID, especially yours," the cop said, looking at Cass.

A murmur went through the crowd. Can't even have a cook-out on your own block anymore? Harassing us at home? One man made a big show of writing down the cruiser's license plate. Another asked for a badge number.

"You know I could write you up for illegal fireworks," the cop said. "You know that, right?"

Ava stepped on a spent M-80 cartridge wobbling near her foot. The cop turned, and his eyes settled on her shaved head and the T-shirt with the sleeves cut off at the shoulder. He took a step forward. Nervous, she thought, and younger than he looked. Ava felt the crowd tense around her, the complaints grew more urgent. The older cop glanced at his partner and shrugged.

"All right," he said. "Take it easy. And wrap it up here. Maybe we need to come by a little more often, just to make sure there's no fire hazards," he added.

They reversed the cruiser in that same slow, insolent way, then drove off down Sixty-second. Soon as they were gone Mikey started up wailing and carrying on. God bless him.

"Okay, Mikey, okay. You're all right. You have all your fingers," Cass said. "Go on home. Come back tomorrow so I can change the dressing."

A man from the middle of the block—Mr. Jones? Or was it Johnson? Anyway, the one with all the plants on his porch—clapped Cass on the back. A lady walked Mikey home, even though, she said, he didn't deserve anybody being nice to him when it was clear he was a fool and he needed a good beating and ifhethoughthewashurtingnowwaittillshetoldhismother . . . Her fussing hung in the air after they turned the corner. Maybe it was the same sameness of a stupid boy getting yelled at for being stupid that eased the mood.

"We don't have to let them do that," Cass said. "We don't have to let them embarrass us. We can . . . Let's go back to our party."

After thirty minutes of forced, self-conscious good feeling, real good feeling returned. Ava sent the boys to bring out more food. Winnie served a pretty layer cake. House number 260 set out some Millers in an ice bucket. Toussaint was so scared of what Cass would do about those firecrackers that Ava figured she'd leave him alone for the time being. Poor thing carried Cass's medical bag back into the house like it was the Ark of the Covenant. Cass took Winnie's place on the serving line, put his arm around Ava's shoulders. Bygones. Like nothing had happened. Ava leaned in to him and called to Toussaint to help ladle up the food with them. Zeek took a Polaroid.

Hours later, long after the party had ended, two sets of headlights shone at the far end of the block. Ava watched from the little rectangle of the attic window. Could have been anybody, of course. But Ava knew it was the police. She thought of waking Cass, but he was so tired. He had lumbered up the attic stairs an hour before, half asleep before he'd gotten undressed.

The headlights flicked off. But an orange halo ghosted where the high beams had been, four cat eyes in the dark.

Night Watch

AFTER THE BLOCK PARTY, the neighborhood couldn't get enough of 248. Word spread about how Cass fixed up Mikey like a doctor from a TV show. *Trapper John, M.D.* right here on Ephraim Avenue! Groups of three or four waited on the porch for Cass's afternoon talks. Two days a week they served community dinner after Meeting, plus lunch on Saturday. On Tuesday and Thursday, the line for the clinic spilled down the front steps and onto the sidewalk: pregnant ladies and old people, too skinny people and too fat people, coughing people and limping people, all waiting under the shade of the big oak out front. One by one Patch let them in and Toussaint escorted them to the white room where Cass waited with his stethoscope and blood pressure cuff and the penlight he shined in their eyes. "Mrs. Morris!" Toussaint announced gravely, then waited in the living room till it was time to bring in the next one.

The house took on a yeasty smell, like dogs' paws and baking bread. Something was always bubbling in the big pots on the stove: vegetable stews Toussaint hated. Or succotash, which he loved, or string beans with potatoes. Two days a week they pickled the string beans and cukes they'd started selling out of carts on the street. Conversation rising and falling in every room in every moment. His mother and Winnie's constant talk in the kitchen and the yard. Zeek and Patch took to hanging out in the downstairs hallway

so a kid couldn't go anywhere in 248 without one of them saying
something to him. The other boys were always shouting down from
the second floor. There were footfalls on the stairs, footfalls above
Toussaint's head. Ava's humming (she hummed now!) while she
weeded or inventoried their supplies and filled in ledgers with what
needed buying and how much money they had to buy it with. Boxes
appeared at the back fence late at night and were whisked down
to the basement. In the early morning Toussaint, Zeek, and Ava—
not Alvin and not Nemo and definitely not Mikey—inventoried the
contents of the boxes: amoxicillin, blood test kits, syringes, tongue
depressors, diazepam, metolazone, insulin, methadone. Where does
it all come from, Toussaint wanted to know. "Resourcefulness," Cass
answered.

Toussaint didn't mind that Meeting kept getting longer, or he
didn't mind much. And he liked serving at community meals. He
was invisible, watching but not being watched, and that suited him
fine. Cass said serving others was a sign of respect. Trust too. He
and Toussaint had stopped eating with the rest of the fellowship.
Ava served the two of them in the quietest part of the evening,
when the visitors were gone and cleanup was done. They sat at the
kitchen table with only the hallway overhead for light. Their meal
was hushed and sleepy. Cass spoke in mesmeric monologues: We
have to get off their wheel. Rain chaos on them from a distance.
Smoke bombs in the ventilation, so to speak. Pipe bombs in the
water mains near City Hall—short-circuit the computers and flood
the lower floors. All those tons of property records, arrest records.
He whistled under his breath. He was dreamy and peaceful. After
the meal Cass and Ava might sit for long silent minutes in the dim
light, fingers intertwined. Or Cass might rest his hand on the back
of Toussaint's neck, warm and warming.

Ark adopted new rules. Cass announced close-cropped hair
for everybody: distinctive, he said, tidy and low-maintenance. He
buzzed Winnie's hair one Sunday afternoon with all of Ark gathered around. Winnie held on to Ava's hand, but she still cried so
hard she couldn't catch her breath and had to put her head between
her knees. It scared Toussaint that his father would make one of

them cry like that. Afterward they had all tried to comfort her. And you know, it had been only two weeks and already the new hair underneath her old hair was coming in. Toussaint told her it looked pretty, which was sort of true. But Winnie couldn't get past it. Toussaint saw her staring at her reflection in the window over the kitchen sink, near tears. Cass let her wear a head tie.

Ark had a uniform now, navy blue button-down shirts, blue pants, or skirts for the women if they wanted them. Ava got Cass to let them wear green too. She told Toussaint that in Bonaparte the old people said wandering spirits would occupy any living thing till they found a body to be in; good spirits took up residence in blades of grass and leaves and the moss on the forest floor. Everybody in Ark wore a green bandanna around their neck or tied around their arm. Patch used his to cover his scary eye.

School let out for summer and some of the kids on Ephraim started hanging around 248. Toussaint and the boys had a routine for the newbies. "This is our yard," Alvin would announce. "It's seventeen steps by twenty-three steps. This is our fence, it's one and a half Alvins high, which is six feet! Higher than any other fences in the whole neighborhood!" Alvin was proud of the fence, which was wooden with wide planks and had been recently installed to replace the falling-down chain-link one. If a kid made fun of Alvin, he was out. If he stomped around where stuff was growing, same. The ones that stayed weeded the garden, or picked pole beans, or sorted out the canned goods Cass was stockpiling for a food pantry. Most of them stopped coming when they realized they'd have to do chores. Or when they got sick of the smell from the compost and the cloud of gnats and flies over the barrels. Toussaint didn't like that so much either even if it was part of the . . . the ecosystem, is what Cass called it.

Loudmouth Mikey was there most days. His mama was sorry she'd talked so much shit about Ark after Cass saved Mikey's hand from falling off on Juneteenth. And there was Lola from a couple blocks away, who spent so much time at 248 that Winnie and Ava started feeding her lunch. Her claim to fame was that her parents got cable TV and she saw a lady's butt and titties on *Conan the Barbarian*. Lucky Lola, they called her. But really, she didn't know up from down. Before she came to Ark, she just spent all her time trying to get her mom to take her to New Jersey to the Cherry Hill Mall. Other people, people outside of Ark, were lost. Cass said they were wandering Wanderers, lost in the wilderness. Lola needed an education. Toussaint and the others taught her to play Nat Turner even though she couldn't have any of the good parts because she was a girl. They did let her be Patrice Lumumba on account of that was a girl's name anyhow.

Some nights, Lola snuck back to 248 after her parents were asleep. The five of them hung around up on the roof. To the others it was just a game, but Toussaint went up there to keep watch over Ephraim. No offense to Nemo and Alvin, but he had more responsibility than they did. Cass had told him as much: My son, my son, he was always saying, like Toussaint might forget.

The block was full of activity in the night hours. Nemo had names for everybody: Miss You Hear Me, Frank, I ain't gon tell you again about this dripping sink/loose step/screen door. Don't nothing work at they house, Mikey said. There was Hoho who was Mikey's age and always sneaking out to a car waiting for her at the far end of the block. Lola said Hoho was gonna end up preggers. For sure. Some nights Pastor Phil walked past and stopped in front of 248 looking up at the house like she was trying to figure something out.

"She got a lot of nerve," Toussaint said.

"Whatcha mean? She's nice," Lola said.

"How do you know?"

"If you go over to the church, she'll make you a ham sandwich for no reason at all. I know you must want a ham sandwich bad, eating all them nasty vegetables all the time."

"Well, I ain't goin over there. My mom says she got a lot of nerve."

Lola shrugged. She didn't care what adults thought. She liked the family in 262 that had four pretty children who wouldn't give the 248 kids the time of day. The oldest was bad—always creeping around late at night, and plus he had to go to summer school. Come to think of it, Lola was pretty bad too.

"Did you ever have to go to summer school?" Toussaint asked her.

"I ain't dumb!" Lola said.

They glanced at Mikey. He had to go to summer school every year, to hear Nemo tell it.

"How come y'all don't go," Lola asked. "To school, I mean."

Toussaint shrugged. He'd been thinking maybe he'd like to go back, but he knew Cass wouldn't let him.

"We gonna go," Alvin said. "When we're ready. But we're not ready yet because at school they doc—indoc—indoctorate you."

"Ain't that what y'all already doing at y'all's house?" Lola asked.

"What you mean?" Toussaint said.

"Mr. Cass says he's a doctor, don't he?"

"He is a doctor!" Nemo said. "He healed Mikey!"

Lola popped her gum.

"He did! You wasn't there so you didn't see it."

"I ain't say he didn't. But Mr. Peeples and the other people at church say y'all don't have the, what do you call it, the license for that clinic and that's illegal and you could get in B-I-G trouble."

"See! That's because Wanderers want to put a price on community!"

"That don't mean nothing, Nemo," Lola said. "That's just a whole bunch of words stuck together."

The boys looked at Toussaint. Like he was supposed to say something. Like he was supposed to know.

"But, uh," Lola said. "I guess uh, yeah, Miss Bettina said Calvin's asthma is better since he went to y'all's clinic. So. You know. I guess, yeah."

The group was silent for a time.

"I'm in sixth grade," Toussaint said a little too loudly. "I mean I would be."

"Where you went to school?" Lola wanted to know.

Toussaint shook his head.

"It was around here?"

"Naw," he whispered. "It was long ago and far away."

"Like a fairy story," Alvin said.

"Where you lived before here?"

"Lot of places. New Jersey."

"I woulda stayed there. Nothing going on around here. We ain't even got a mall close by!" Lola said. "How come your dad wanted to move here?"

His dad. They were always asking Toussaint how come his dad did this, or said that. Here's what Toussaint knew about his dad: He came from somewhere far from here. He was in the army or the navy. He was a doctor and once he was a Black Panther. He was tall enough he had to dip his head when he went through some doorways. He hardly ever broke a sweat and he always looked everybody in the eye. When he came into a room, the room changed. His mother was never Hard Ava with him, or Tired Ava. Wherever Cass was, some part of her was always angled toward him, her foot or her knee or her whole body. Toussaint could have been on fire and she wouldn't've noticed.

Toussaint tried to piece together the fragments of his father, what he said and did or didn't do, how his moods changed from bright to dark, like passing storm clouds. But mostly, he watched his father's body because there was power in it, and the power was something to believe in and something to be like.

"I only ever lived here," Lola was saying. She paused and picked at a scab on her elbow. Lola had more scabs than any boy Toussaint ever met. She would hang upside down from tree branches, she would go after a rat with a hoe. "My mom says she want to go to California but my dad says it's no reason to go somewhere else when we got everything right here at home."

"We were supposed to go to Alabama," Toussaint said.

"Alabama!" Mikey said. "What y'all was going to do there?"

"Yeah, what they got in Alabama?" Nemo said.

"Alabama Alabama Alabama," Alvin singsonged.

Toussaint felt a rising panic. He had said too much.

"Me, Imma get down there to Disney World one of these days," Lola said.

"You shouldn't go there," Nemo said. "That's a Wanderers place."

"What about Mickey Mouse?"

"What about him?"

"He's not a Wanderer. He's a mouse."

"Not a real one."

"I *know* he's not real. I'm just saying he's not a Wanderer either."

"Well, what is he then?"

"In between. There's lots of in between stuff. Most things are in between."

Sometimes Toussaint wanted to tell Lola things, things he hadn't told anybody. But she'd probably just give him a noogie and start talking about the Cherry Hill Mall. Some people are secret about themselves, he had noticed. Some people won't ever tell you anything.

"All I know is Imma get down there."

"Not me. I'm staying right here where I belong," Nemo said.

"Some people are homebodies. It takes all kinds," Lola said, sagely. The others nodded.

A cop car cruised down the block and rolled to a stop in front of 248.

"Shh! Get down!"

Brights haloed up to the second story. Toussaint and the others lay on the roof for a long time. The tar top warmed Toussaint's belly through his T-shirt. He meant to count the minutes that the cops stayed so he could remember for later. But he lost track and woke much later, with Nemo shoving him in the shoulder.

Broken Bottles

BY LATE JULY the city was a hot fug of garbage stink and arm-pits. The whole neighborhood was liable to disappear in the smoke coming off charcoal barbecues and out of tailpipes. Not to men-tion weed, cigarettes, firecrackers. In the middle of any night boys and grown men were out on the block shooting M-80s, triple-bang rockets, black mambas. Toussaint had the jitters. Everybody did except Cass. He didn't seem to care that some of the neighbors had gone back to giving Ark the side-eye. Him and Zeek got in a big man shouting match with Mr. Clements when he complained that the clinic patients were always sitting around on his front steps. Cass, it turned out, was the King of Chaos.

He took Toussaint Missioning downtown to the tunnel to the PATCO line, to the wild parts of Penn's Landing where people lived in tents along the Delaware, to the Frankford El station (even if they got called niggers). He took him to the medical supply store to order stuff for the clinic, to Germantown Hospital with Patch where a guy who came to Meeting handed him a big bag of pill bot-tles in the back alley near some dumpsters. Patch knew all kinds of everybody. Maybe he was the resourcefulness Cass was talking about.

Cass didn't like being underground so they got occasional rides from a dollar taxi, or they took the bus. He'd even Mission there—his swelling baritone muscling through the French-fry-talcum-powder haze of the 63. In 1 Kings the prophet says, *I saw all Israel scattered upon the hills, as sheep that have not a shepherd.* The other passengers would turn and listen, even if some of them gave them the stink eye. Cass was right, you could always get people with a Bible verse.

On these trips Cass told Toussaint all kinds of things. He had been in Vietnam. He had seen ladies missing half their faces lying next to straw-roofed houses. Children Toussaint's age with their skin sizzling off in big white patches. Wanderers visit horror on the world. Wanderers make war to make money, they make war to make babies too. To colonize. Did Toussaint know what that meant? On breaks between Missioning, they would duck into a library to cool off. Cass showed Toussaint books about wars. The pictures in the books were exactly like the things his father had told him. Cass had also been in the Wanderer war in Korea. Another time he was stationed overseas in Italy. He paid every dime of medical school with a thing called the GI Bill. Also, he had been dishonorably discharged for disrupting their Wanderer army and struggled his way through medical school with no help from anybody at all.

Sometimes his father was sad and quiet. Or he would get mad, slam the books closed, and stride out of the library. While they were walking, he might look over Toussaint's shoulder at somebody on the street and say, Have they been behind us this whole time? He would veer down one block, then another so quickly Toussaint had to trot to keep up. Other times Cass would walk slowly with his arm around him, the two of them walking shoulder to palm. Those were the best times, but since Toussaint didn't know when they would happen, he tried to forget them as soon as his father's mood shifted. He tried to empty his head of whatever Cass said because the next day there were always different things. Toussaint lived in the here and now. He kept his mind on what might happen next but never what had happened before.

.   .   .

Toussaint and his father stood on the corner of Broad and Lehigh waiting for the 54.

"We don't have much time," Cass said.

Toussaint sighed. "I guess the bus'll get here sooner or later," he said.

"I mean we won't stay in Philadelphia much longer."

It was early afternoon. Sun thumped the top of Toussaint's head. He could tell that Cass expected him to say something more. But Toussaint was short-tempered that day and plus he had a heat rash on his arm. Grown-ups were always cornering him: We're going here, we're leaving there. Pack up. Unpack.

Boy, it was so very hot.

"In a couple of months, we'll go to the place I have ready for us. This is between you and me, father and son."

Toussaint was weary of secrets. He was sick of mysterious conversations and scraps of information. It took so much effort to push these things to the back of his mind where they wouldn't dog him day and night. In spite of himself he said, "Why?"

"Fruition. We just need a few more to join us."

"Where are we going?"

Cass shook his head. He looked at Toussaint with urgent eyes. "This whole city is a ship taking on water. We have to get out."

With Sad Cass, Toussaint knew to look up into his face, but not into his eyes. He should step a little closer but not touch him. He raised his face to his father, but Cass had already moved on.

"These last months are tricky. I need you to be my eyes and ears. In the house, I mean. You let me know if anything strange happens."

"Like what?"

"You'll know," he said.

They got off near Fairmount. Cass set up near a check-cashing place just down from the Social Security office. He opened their folding table and unpacked a few jars of Ark pickles and preserves for Toussaint to sell to get the people's attention.

"Preserves, ma'am? Homemade," Toussaint said softly, standing in the middle of the street a half block down from Cass. He wondered where Cass wanted to take them. Did his mother know they were going? Passersby on the street skirted him like he was an overturned garbage can. He held out his jar of preserves at a harried-looking lady. "Preserves!" he said a little too loudly. "Preserves!" louder still. He was sick of being dragged around. He made up his mind right then and there. He wouldn't go. He didn't have to go anywhere if he didn't want to. "Preserves!" he shouted. He darted in front of a man heading toward the corner and thrust the jar into his chest.

The man stumbled. "The fuck you doing?" he said. He scowled down at Toussaint. He was young and big with squinty angry eyes.

He pushed Toussaint in the shoulder, but he didn't drop his jars and he didn't look away either. "Oh, now you ain't got nothing to say?" The man would hit him then Toussaint would smash him in the face with his preserves. Or he would take the guy's punch and then another one and another one until he didn't feel anything at all.

"Whoa, whoa. Easy, brother. That's my kid." Cass appeared suddenly, like he'd only just noticed what was happening.

"I ain't your brother," the young man said.

"Toussaint, go back to the table," Cass said. Toussaint didn't move. "It's all right, go on."

"Yeah. Go on before I whip both your asses."

A couple of people stopped to watch. The man poked Cass in the shoulder.

"Take it easy," Cass said. Squinty Eyes cussed under his breath and shoved Cass in the chest with both hands. Cass staggered backward. He held up both hands, palms open. "Brother man," he said. The younger man shoved him again.

Cass was cool. Cass was like, ain't no thing. Then his fist shot out like a cannonball. He hooked the man in the jaw with an uppercut. Gut-punched him with his left fist. One, two. Squinty was on the ground. It hadn't taken ten seconds.

"Oh shit!" somebody said.

"Dammit, Bug!" Another man appeared. "He just a hothead, brother. He don't mean nothing. Come on, Bug, fore you get your ass kicked for real." Cass watched the two of them move off down the block.

"Are you all right?" Cass asked, turning to Toussaint. His knuckles were bruising where he'd hit Squinty in the face. "That's not . . . I mean, you shouldn't solve a conflict with your fists. I shouldn't have."

"Is your hand okay?" Toussaint asked, looking up at Cass. He wished stupid Mikey had been there to see that, and Nemo and Alvin and his mother too.

"It's fine," Cass said. "It's fine. Listen to me. Listen, I shouldn't have hit that guy. He was just crazy. There are people you have to hit but he wasn't—"

"You schooled him!" An older man walked up. "I never seen a preacher knock the mess out of somebody so quick."

Others drifted over. "Y'all giving out tracts between beat-downs?"

There was a lot of laughter then, and more after a lady asked why they were handing out jelly. In no time at all five or six people had gathered. Cass's attention swung toward them like a search-light and Toussaint was abandoned to the shadows. Cass gestured at him without looking.

Toussaint knew the routine: "Pickles! Preserves! Right this way!" While the people paused to consider the offer, Cass began to speak.

A couple of hours later it was time to go. Cass was radiant. He was high wattage and remote, like a movie star. Toussaint wanted to go home, but he didn't dare ask if that's where they were headed.

After a few blocks his father said, "You hungry? You want a hoagie?"

He ducked into a pizza shop. They sat eating their sandwiches on a bus stop bench in the fading light. Toussaint had had high hopes, but they were only cheese—extra hots though, and lots of provolone.

"Umm, is your hand better?" Toussaint asked. He couldn't think of anything else to say.

"What? Oh, that shithead? That was nothing. That wasn't anything," Cass said, waving at the air as if to sweep the whole incident out of existence. He finished his hoagie and stood. "Ready?" he said, without waiting for Toussaint to answer.

Cass walked three paces ahead. There wasn't any way for Toussaint to say the things he wanted to say, no way to ask a question. He wouldn't be able to speak his thoughts the right way, he wouldn't be loud enough. If he called him, his father wouldn't turn around. They passed an overflowing trash can. Toussaint grabbed an empty glass bottle from the top and threw it against the ground so hard it shattered. He was sorry as soon as he'd done it. Too late. Cass doubled back, the gap between them closed in two of his long-legged strides. He set down the folded card table and glared at Toussaint and the shards of broken bottle. Toussaint flinched when his father reached toward him. But Cass picked up a bottle teetering on the trash pile and hurled it against the nearest wall.

"Now we're even," he said.

He reached for another bottle. Then Toussaint, then Cass. Toussaint again. The shards glittered in the light from the streetlamp. Down the block a voice called, "What the hell y'all doing out there!"

Cass picked up the card table and grabbed Toussaint by the hand. The two of them tore around the corner and down the next block. When they couldn't run any farther, they flopped down on a curb holding their bellies, laughing till tears streamed down their cheeks.

The Oath

THE BOYS TOOK a blood oath and sealed it with a cut on each one's finger. The oath demanded they tell each other everything. They would share all information about what happened in 248, big or small—especially big—and no one would snitch on anybody. Mikey was jealous he wasn't in on it. He saw their Band-Aided fingers—Alvin had insisted on Band-Aids—and bullied it out of them.

"Yo," he said, "y'all are bitches. That's girl shit. And if y'all was a real gang you would go out in the park and beat each other down. That's how real men do it."

"Oh, Mikey," Alvin said.

"Chill out," Nemo said, shaking his head.

The oath came in pretty handy on the not-snitching front. Nemo went behind a bush in the park with Corinne Taylor, who lived down the block. Corinne was in the Jack and Jill club. According to Mikey, Jack and Jill was wack and bougie. But Corinne Taylor was pretty, capital *P*, so Nemo didn't care. When he and Corinne got done behind the bush, he reported that they had tongue-kissed and it was okay but more wet than he'd have liked. That would have been all right, but he didn't really like the taste of grape Bubbalicious. Second time he told Toussaint and Alvin that Corinne had a big squishy booty and he could have stayed feeling on it all day. *"All day!"* was what he said. Alvin was jealous, but he didn't have to be upset for long. Corinne's mom found out she was fooling around in the park (and not just with Nemo either, Mikey reported) and sent her all the way down to Georgia because they didn't want her to get knocked up and not be able to go to college.

"She's only, like, thirteen. She's not old enough to go to college," Toussaint said.

"Like I told y'all. Bougie," Mikey said, shaking his head. "People can make plenty of money at the post office."

"It's kind of messed up that they would send her to a whole other state just for hangin out with me."

The boys decided the people in the neighborhood were trippin and not worth their time.

"Don't need them nohow," Nemo said.

"Naw, naw. Don't need them," Toussaint and Alvin echoed, nearly whispering.

"You gotta be able to count on people," Nemo said. "Know they got your back. Like us."

Toussaint didn't think much about what was coming. Now and again vague ideas emerged from a milky future: nobody would be able to tell him what to do, or drag him anyplace he didn't want to go. Maybe he would go to college like Corinne. His mother went to college for a little while. And Cass did too, for a long time, but he acted like college was something bad the government did to him. Toussaint thought somebody ought to be more worried about what he would be when he grew up—not just that he would be a Free Man, like Cass said. Maybe he didn't want to be free. He wanted to be like the *Brady Bunch* kids, who had Mike and Carol to untangle every mess. Toussaint didn't have anybody to ask if he should be more interested in feeling on somebody's booty. Maybe it wasn't normal that he wasn't. But he didn't have much time to wonder because every time he got around to normal kid things, there were bigger, stranger fish to fry.

A few days later what Nemo called the Fierce Debate broke out between Toussaint's mother and father. Snatches of the argument floated down the attic stairs to the landing where the boys stood eavesdropping: ". . . too much," Ava said, and "not safe." Then Cass: "Safe! Come on. It's time he . . ."

"I betcha 'he' is you," Nemo whispered.

"You don't know that," Toussaint replied. "You're a 'he.' We're all 'he's."

"Me too!" Alvin said.

"Yeah, yeah, you too. Shhhh," Nemo said.

"Me too!"

Nemo cuffed his brother on the back of the head to hush him up. Too late. Cass and Ava's voices dropped to whispers.

"Damn, Alvin," Nemo sighed.

"Something's going on." Nemo lowered his voice: "What you know about it?"

Toussaint didn't know anything about it, but he didn't think Nemo believed him. Plus, he felt guilty for not telling the stuff he did know about, like the boxes hidden in the basement crawlspace, even if he didn't know where they got the money to buy all of it. Toussaint wasn't trying to be stingy with telling. It was just that when he most wanted to say something the words got stuck half-way up his throat, like a bunch of people caught in a revolving door. The rest of what he knew was hazy impressions he couldn't make sense of no matter how hard he tried.

"You swore, man," Nemo reminded him. "We got an oath."

BONAPARTE

. . .

"WHAT YOU GONNA DO with that chicory coming up?" I asked Juniata. "And the fig tree dropping fruit all over the yard. Look like the goddamn garden of Eden over there with all the bugs and armadillos and possums and every bird in creation."

Juniata has taken to her bed. It's nothing wrong with her that you can see from the outside. She just don't want to participate.

"Let them have it." She sat up on her elbow. "Everything got to live. You know what I think? I think all this time we never paid enough attention to how stupid we are compared to everything else. Raccoons and doves. Pigs and snakes. Tree roots. If we could hear it talking, nature would say, 'Sit your ass down and stop making a mess of every damn thing.' That's what it would say."

Well, shit.

She laid back down and looked out the window. "Every day is a teaspoon of water tipped into the river. Don't mean nothing, and lost as soon as it gets in there."

"Juniata, don't be poetic," I said.

"Girl, we just here running out the clock."

Wasn't nothing I could say to that so I went on and left. But I did stop and clean up the mess underneath her persimmon tree. Next day I put up a feeder so the ruby-throats would come around. Picked up all the fallen fruit too even though it's too far from the house for her to see. And it's not like there's anybody around to give it to.

I don't know why it always has to be old women that end up laid down and laid out. The men get off the hook by already being dead—heart trouble or kilt by so-and-so or whatever bullshit. Or they get some kind of stupid hobby and spend their last days in a shed. Tinkering. Well, *I'm* not laying down. I'm not the type, but I do understand the impulse. Everybody's tired around here. Even Delilah. I tried to take us down by the Oaks, but when she saw we were going that way she started screaming high up in her throat. I never heard her make a noise like that before. She ripped my front seat scratching and crabbing to get out. I haven't been back over there since.

The riverfront used to be okay, but the other day some white folks in a boat sailed right past me. They looked over where I was sitting near the old graves and didn't do a thing. You know they startle when they see a Negro they not expecting. Well, these white people didn't bat an eye. It was like I was invisible. Things around here have a suspended feeling now; we're a bubble in the tapioca. Progress is out there bulldozing half a mile from Jimmy's shack. Creeping in on us.

I said to Carter Lee, What you think about all this new building they doing. He shook his old nappy head. That wore me out because Carter Lee used to know about everything. Carter Lee used to know if a bird farted in the sky over Bonaparte.

Next day me and him rode out to the new construction. It was Eugene Kirby's place they were building on. The Kirby acres been nothing but weeds since Progress got em in tax sale six or seven years back. I guess they finally got around to *developing* them. That's their word for fencing the goods. Me and Carter Lee looked on from the cab of his truck, not a word between us. Passed our flask a little while and turned around. Anyhow, I had to get home and check on the vegetable stew I was cooking for Juniata. That's the only thing she'll eat, if she eats anything at all. Don't say nothing to that heifer about chicken. Chicken'll make her start up on all the creatures we have done wrong. She'll go on so long she could put poor Delilah off rabbits.

Maybe she's right. Maybe wasn't no sense paying those taxes.

Feels like whatever was going to happen around here already happened. Barber sure did go out with a bang. He got style. I'll give him that. Probably loosed the hounds of hell on us though. Progress gets an opportunity and they put their whole mouth on it, teeth and all. The truth is, we are just a few old coots near the end of our time and Bonaparte is just some acres of dirt. But the other truth is that this was a gloried place, even if it is disappearing. That's not nearly enough consolation. Might not even be enough to keep us drawing breath, but it's something. I got that arsoning Negro to thank for reminding me of that. I go see Juniata every day trying to explain it to her, but the poor thing won't hear a word I say.

There's another thing. The biggest thing: Memma left. Gone. Everlasting knows I can't stand her but . . . She got a letter from her son living in Delaware. Who the hell lives in Delaware, is what I want to know. He said she and Nip ought to go up there with him because they were old, and what were they going to do down in the middle of nowhere, and so on like the kids always say when they write. He has a nice job, that son, and a wife and a little girl that was sick. Sick enough that the son called her on the phone at Carter Lee's PO. Memma said she might die and then she'd have had a grandbaby who was born and died and she would have never even laid eyes on her. She said Barber brought the world into Bonaparte and made her remember about time and how it passes outside of here. She shook her turkey chin. I hate it when these old heifers make you feel sorry with them. I hate when they're right.

They were gone a week later. Poof! They went out overriver with Carter Lee in a blue-gray dawn. Didn't hardly take nothing with them. We stood on the shore waving them on—me, Juniata, Erma Linner. I held Erma Linner's hand cause she was breathing like she was going to fall out. I squeezed it and squeezed it. The boat glided slow into the mist.

Now we are four.

PHILADELPHIA

. . .

Women and Children

ONE A.M. AND STILL STEAMY, but Ava didn't mind. Cass slept with his arm slung across his forehead, a light sheen of sweat on his bare chest. The moon hid behind clumpy black clouds, but Ava and Cass had their own light from the streetlamp shining into the attic. Quiet along the avenue and quiet in the house, Toussaint's snore rumbling up soft from the boys' room downstairs. Ava stretched; the muscles flexed along her back. She was languid and strong, like a creature that might hunt on a night like this. She could have purred it was so lovely. She fell into sleep.

Ava dreamed her pop had come to take her on a joy ride in his truck. She climbed into the cab. Pop shut the door behind her. *Slam. Slam! Slam!* A brightness like a spotlight cut through the blue sky of the dream. Ava woke to shouting on the stairs that led up to her bedroom. Cass sat up, confused. "What the hell are those boys—" More shouting, and closer now. Cass leapt from the mattress. No time to hide the documents he'd moved to the scuttle attic, so he ripped off the fraying string to the hatch door. "Ava—" he said, but just then the bedroom door crashed inward.

"Hands where we can see them. Hands!" they said. "On your knees!"

For an instant Ava thought she was still dreaming because those are things cops say on TV when they raid somebody's house. They say, "On your knees!" and "Hands up!" Ava didn't move until she saw the gun muzzle. In the flashlight glare Cass kneeled with his hands behind his head. But that wasn't good enough for them so they shoved his face against the floor. Two straddled him, cuffed him, and hoisted him up to his feet like he was a side of beef and not a man. Ava's jaw locked, knees locked, thoughts locked. An image of her pop sprinting through that field rose up before her. Toussaint!, she thought.

"Stay down!" a cop shouted. "Lady," he said. "Stay down. Just stay down." She fell backward.

"Ma! Maaaaa!" she heard. The room flew into focus, as though Ava had come hurtling into it from somewhere else. She was standing in the bedroom doorway. Cuffs digging into her wrists. Cass was gone. "Where is my son?," she said. Ava kicked and snapped her teeth. A flat hand hit her in the chest and knocked the wind out of her. While she was bent double and gasping for air, two took her arms and hauled her down the stairs.

The living room was a blaze of light. The cops dumped Ava against the wall opposite the bay windows. Toussaint sat handcuffed on the floor not two feet away. Handcuffs on her child who didn't even weigh ninety pounds, who was slight and narrow-shouldered with round baby cheeks. The other boys were lined up near the window, also in cuffs. Alvin muttered under his breath. Nemo whispered to him through his tears.

"Did they hurt you?" Ava asked Toussaint.

Her wrists twitched in the cuffs. She needed to run her hands over her boy to check for bruises, for blood. He was in his underwear, too shocked to cry. He stared at Ava's mouth. She felt an ooze trickling down her chin. "Oh!" she said. "I'm all right. It looks worse than it is." Though she didn't know how it looked and her tongue was a little swollen, like she'd bitten it. "Did they hurt any of you?" she called to the boys.

Overhead, the cops stomped through the rooms. They thundered down the stairs and through the hallway toward the clinic. Well, that's okay, she thought. The door's locked! No. No, that didn't make any sense. Okay, Ava. Okay, she thought. Get it together. Her thoughts swam away from her. She heard a screeching sound and a crash like an explosion. Nemo cried out and dropped into a low crouch. "I think it's just the clinic door, honey," Ava said. "I think they just . . ." She couldn't finish her sentence. She got onto her knees to crawl nearer her boy.

"Stay where you're at!" a cop shouted.

Zeek was nowhere to be found. Patch either. But Winnie, Winnie was screaming her head off somewhere in the house. Two of them dragged her into the living room lunging and kicking. They forced her to her knees next to Ava. Spit foamed white in the corners of her mouth. She said to the cops, "We are just women and children here."

They had mothers, right? Sisters and daughters. Winnie had shamed them. Never shame a cop, makes them meaner. Winnie didn't have a thing on besides her shower cap and a towel. Her shoulders were wet. Alvin started screaming—no words, just a long, high wail. The cops tensed their shoulders; their jaws clenched. They will hit him with their gun butts. They will kill him.

"Alvin, honey," Ava said. "Alvin. Your mama is all right. Honey, can you hear me? She's okay."

Winnie angled herself toward her son. "Yes, baby," she said. "Mama is all right." Alvin started in with his hoot-screech.

"Shut up. SHUT UP!" the cops shouted.

"He doesn't understand," Ava said. "Let him go to his mother."

A heavy hand on her shoulder pushed her to the floor. Winnie kept saying, "Mama is all right." Alvin kept on screaming. Toussaint curled around himself on his side. He stared straight ahead. He wasn't in that room with them anymore.

How much time passed? One hour? Two? Ava's knees throbbed. Her eyes rested wherever the terror was least. Winnie's skinny little thighs were scored with stretch marks, like she used to be fat and now she was thin. Her shoulders were slight and rounded. "Cover her up," Ava said. "Please just give her a sheet."

Two men walked into the room in plain clothes: baggy suits and gelled hair. Isn't it funny, Ava thought, how some people look exactly like what they are? One of them crouched so he was eye level with Ava.

"I'm Detective Briggs," he said. "Look, Miss . . ." He glanced down at a notebook he'd pulled from his pocket. "Miss Carson. I don't want to be here long, and you don't want me to be here long."

His eyes were green with tiny brown flecks near the iris.

"So," he said. "We got a warrant. But you know that already. What we're going to do is we're going to take all that stuff out of the medical office you got back there. All of it. But this would be a lot quicker if— Jesus!" he said, turning toward Winnie as if he was seeing her for the first time. "Somebody get a blanket for that lady. Jesus."

"She's been like that an hour," Ava said.

"I'm sorry about that. Jeez."

His jugular pulsed. I could bite right through it, Ava thought. She could hang on with her teeth until they pulled her off him, the vein twitching in her bloody jaws. A uniform dropped a sheet over Winnie's shoulders.

"All right. So . . . you want to tell me where you get all this stuff? You got a few thousand dollars' worth of medical supplies in there. Lotta money for a free clinic."

"I don't know," Ava said.

"And, of course, the big problem is, you got an illegal medical practice here. A whole lotta prescription drugs, but no scripts."

And so much more if you knew where to look! Morphine and methadone. Codeine. Down in the crawlspace. Ava gulped back the blood pooling in her mouth. She might be sick. It took all she had to keep her eyes from darting to the open basement door.

"Where do you and Cassius Wright get the money for all this stuff? He's in custody. Mr. Wright. Did you know that?"

Steady, Ava. "I don't know anything about it."

"You sure about that?"

The vein pulsed, plump along the side of his neck.

"I could take you in, you know? Same charges as Mr. Wright. Plus you were resisting arrest pretty good there. But I gotta tell you, I don't want the paperwork. With kids there's so much paperwork. You have no idea." He sighed and stood. "The thing is, we're gonna find out where you got this stuff anyway. Then it's gonna be a shitstorm." He took a card out of his pocket and laid it on the windowsill.

"You make it easier on yourself and give me a call. Think about it."

The boys had cried themselves hoarse. Winnie was limp under the sheet, forehead against the wall. The police went through the front door with boxes of vials and syringes and instruments and drugs. They marched past Ava and the others as if they were a distasteful inconvenience, loitering in the living room crying and carrying on. Ava's neck ached. She blinked against the grit in her eyes, but she couldn't take her eyes off the basement door.

It went on till nearly dawn. "It's your lucky day," the cops said on their way out. The one who uncuffed Ava said, "You need to think about your kids," shaking his head like it was Ava who ought to be ashamed.

The police left 248 trampled and wretched, muddy footprints in all of the rooms, doors thrown open, the contents of the cabinets and closets flung to the floor. Ava could hardly stand. She fell into Toussaint when she'd meant to hug him. She ran her hands all over him as she had wanted to hours before. Her boy was okay, in his body, anyway. Nemo too. Alvin had screamed himself mute. They swaddled him with a blanket, and that helped him stop rocking long enough to drop into sleep. Ava gathered the ruined throw pillows and the five of them sat together huddled beneath blankets. A neighbor came in. She told them Cass and Zeek had been taken to the Forty-fifth District. Nobody had seen Patch.

The pastor down the street helped. She came to 248 later that same morning and set to cleaning. Out of nowhere. At first Ava wondered if it was her that had turned them in. But she was too worn out to refuse help. Pastor Phil cooked rice and beans and cornbread. No Jesus talk, not much talk at all, but she had a way of appearing just where she was needed. Like when Ava was sorting what remained of the clinic. One minute she was tallying and organizing the suture tape, the next she couldn't move—stuck in her mind with cops tromping through her synapses and Winnie's wet shoulders goose-pimpling in the cool of the wee hours. Maybe she had called out, or maybe she was weeping? Well anyway, Pastor Phil appeared and sat with her until she got unstuck. She brought doughnuts for the kids. It took three days, but she gave Ava and Winnie most of the money to make bail. When Cass and Zeek walked out of the jail, Pastor Phil asked after their health, and their swollen jaws and black eyes, and then faded into the small throng of people milling in front of the station.

Cass and Zeek came back to 248 like jail had turned them up, or turned them out. Like jail was a lit match when they were already doused with gasoline. Cass was incandescent. He came and went with a crew of strangers he had recruited somewhere or other. He and the strangers built levered barricades for the front and back doors. They reinforced the back fence and put a fortified lookout station on the roof. Cass didn't say much, but when he stood on the roof looking out at the block, something deadly came into his eyes.

"Somebody turned us in," he said. "Somebody in these blocks made this happen. But you know what? It isn't their fault. Not exactly."

Oh, yes it is. Ava told him, "I hope you get them. I hope you destroy them." She had waited all her life for an avenging angel. Fuck them up, baby, she'd say, breathless on top of him in their sleepless nights.

Winnie was done in. Wouldn't come out of her room. Ava couldn't soothe her. She couldn't do a thing for her. Ava had had her fill of mamas who wouldn't get out of bed. And anyway, somebody had to look after these boys, who were so scared they screamed in their sleep. Toussaint, too. For a week the only sound Ava heard from him was shrieking.

Ecology

TOUSSAINT CONSIDERED his upper lip in the bathroom mirror of Pastor Phil's rectory. He had decided that once his bruises were gone, he would seal the raid behind a door in his mind and it would be like it never happened. Gotta keep moving, is what Zeek said. His lip was nearly healed and the purple marks from the handcuffs had faded to the palest brown around his wrists. All that remained was this problem with sleeping. Toussaint dozed in fits and spurts, jolted awake by the thing outside of the bedroom door. It wasn't the boogeyman from his early days at 248. This something was a seepage, an oily darkness oozing along the floors and up the windowpanes. If he woke in time, if he leapt out of bed and turned on the light, it would slink back to the shadow place where it lived.

Toussaint turned back to his lip in the mirror. He swung open the medicine cabinet. Pastor Phil didn't have anything in there besides nail clippers and clear polish and Bufferin. No lipstick or anything. Pastor Phil was hardly a girl at all. Not that he would have put the lipstick on. Or at least he wouldn't have put it on his lips. He'd have drawn thick red stripes across his cheeks and under his eyes like football players. He imagined himself all painted up. He bared his teeth and growled into the mirror. He stood on his tiptoes and raised his arms above his head: RAAWR. But then he blinked and he was just little-boy Toussaint again. He went down-stairs to find Pastor Phil.

He hadn't told her about his night visitor, but if he was going to tell anybody it would have been Pastor Phil. They were friends now. Even his mother liked her, sort of, after she had helped them so much. But Cass didn't want her hanging around 248, so after he and Zeek got out of jail, Toussaint went looking for her.

"Toussaint?" Pastor Phil had called that first evening he'd passed her porch. "Come sit up here and have a Coke."

He had lost his nerve and booked it back to the house. But she asked again the next day, and the next, till he finally climbed the rectory steps and sat next to her. Pastor Phil had all kinds of stuff they didn't have at 248: cheese and crackers, Little Debbies, bologna sandwiches, grape juice. The truth was, Toussaint had been hungry—they all were. After the raid their routines went right to hell. That's what Nemo said: Look at this garden, it has gone right to hell. Half of what they managed to harvest was pickled for sale—Cass said they needed more money. The leftovers weren't enough for the six of them plus all the guys his father brought in. They didn't have meals together anymore. His mother would holler that the food was ready and whoever was in the house would grab what they could and retreat to some corner with his plate balanced on his knees. 248 was on grits and okra and barely enough of it. Toussaint felt guilty about filling up at Pastor Phil's but then she told him to bring the boys. Now the three of them came most days between chores.

In the rectory dining room, there were a bunch of leaves and rocks and twigs laid out on the table. The day before, Pastor Phil had taken some of the Sunday school kids on a field trip. Toussaint had never heard of a Sunday school field trip, but then Pastor Phil did all kinds of weird stuff. She'd taken them to Pennypack Park, which was on the other side of the universe in the Great Northeast—that's what everybody called it. Toussaint didn't think it was so great. He and his mother had stayed in a motel there. On the last morning, they'd had breakfast at McDonald's before they went to Cherry Street. Toussaint knew his mother wanted to give him one last special meal even though they didn't have any money, so he had tried to be cheerful while he ate his McMuffin. Really, he felt like he was going to throw up. And then he did, throw up, behind a bush. But he told Ava he was going to do a pee.

He didn't tell Pastor Phil any of that, because she too seemed to want to cheer him up with all her talk about the park. She said it was full of ecosystems because there was a forest in there and a lake and mushrooms and caterpillars.

Ecosystem was a word Toussaint's father used. Did that mean there were a lot of rats in Pennypack Park, Toussaint wanted to know.

"Rats?" Pastor Phil said.

"Yeah. Ecosystems have rats in them, like at our house."

"You have rats at your house?" Pastor Phil looked a little alarmed.

"In the garden. Because of the compost barrels."

"The what?"

"Compost barrels. Where we put the leftover food so we can put it on the ground for fertilizer."

"Oh," she said slowly. "Oh. Well, I guess that would be attractive to rats." She paused. "But also, maybe to birds too?"

Toussaint sighed and shook his head. "Man, I don't know which one's worse. We got pigeons everywhere. We feed them too. And they make nests and have babies. They shit . . . err, I mean, poop— all over the neighbors' cars. Then they come and bang on the door all mad because of the poop and because they say our house stinks."

"Huh. Do they come in the house?"

"The neighbors?"

"The rats."

"Naw. I mean, not really. Not really."

"Huh," she said again. "Maybe the rats go in other people's houses? And maybe that's why they're angry. That and the smell, I would guess."

Toussaint shrugged.

"People are scared too," Pastor Phil said. "Because of the . . . because of what happened."

Toussaint didn't like to talk about the raid. It made him seize up; he couldn't breathe so good. Could they go outside and sit on the porch? But Toussaint couldn't stop remembering once he got started. The night came to him in flat pictures, like postcards: His father dragged out with his hands behind his back, kicking whoever he could reach. Then slam, the police bashed his face into the wall. Cass's mouth smashed and bloody like hamburger meat. His mother crying. Much later there was a blanket, and something hot with honey in it handed to him by the lady who lived next door. That lady hated their ecosystem and wouldn't hardly speak to them, but she came to see about them anyhow.

Pastor Phil sat facing him on the porch steps. She looked him right in the eye. Always. That was why he ended up telling her things he didn't mean to tell. Like now.

"And then you came," he said.

She nodded. Her eyes were very bright, maybe crying-bright, so she lit another cigarette. Pastor Phil was always smoking which was a thing ministers weren't supposed to do. And she kind of talked to herself when she forgot you were in the room. She was always on the porch looking out at the street. Plus, she ate all her meals outside and all of them were sandwiches. When anybody she knew passed by, she waved her hoagie at them like she'd forgotten it was in her hand. Good afternoon, Mrs. Morris. Good evening, Mr. Peeples. Pastor Phil talked like she was in a black-and-white movie. She never cussed.

"How come you only eat standing in doorways?" Toussaint asked.

"Oh. Do I? I guess I never really got a good domestic sense of things." She laughed. "I'm like a squirrel or something that doesn't quite belong indoors. I don't much like cooking. Or anything like that."

"My mom neither," Toussaint said.

"No, I suppose not," she said slowly. "What about you?"

Toussaint considered the question. "I don't know," he said. "A big soft bed with cozy blankets is nice. And lasagna. I like lasagna. I don't know about other stuff."

He looked at his hands.

"Well!" said Pastor Phil. "Let's eat some Ruffles and find out if we like them better inside or out." She hopped up and darted into the house.

When she returned, they took up positions in the rectory doorway, jostling each other and passing the chips back and forth. Giggling.

Men Talking

CASS WAS MERCURIAL. He stalked the rooms of 248 scowling, looking to catch somebody doing something he didn't like. Then the next morning or evening or afternoon he was all smiles, patting the boys on the back and paying everybody compliments.

"This okra stew is delicious, Ava," Cass might say.

Only it was never very good; it wasn't good at all, on account of it was okra and plus Ava couldn't really make anything besides eggs and cornbread. Winnie was in charge of the cooking, but Winnie was . . . Winnie was in her room and wouldn't come out. Alvin and Nemo sat on the floor by her bed most of the day. They wouldn't let Toussaint in for more than a few minutes. "Only family except for visiting hours," Nemo said, closing the door. And just like that, they weren't brothers anymore.

248 was tense. Cass shut the house early and tight, usually right after Meeting unless he had a crew working on what he called their defense system. Most nights Ava sent the boys to bed soon as they choked down the last mouthful of dinner. Then Zeek and Cass went off with Patch to patrol the neighborhood. They wouldn't let anyone else go with them.

When his father was gone Toussaint went up to the attic bedroom to snuggle with Ava. He wanted her to help him understand what had happened to Ark. Cass and Zeek were out looking for informants, she told him. She refused to go with them. "I can't stand to look at those people, Tousy," she said. "Traitors," she called them. "Liars. And after we opened this house to them. That they would betray us that way." Sometimes tears welled, all the way to the red brims of her eyelids, but she didn't let them fall. "You stay away from those people, these so-called neighbors," she said. Toussaint nodded. He was lying low. But he knew he wouldn't be able to keep that up forever. Something was brewing.

Sure enough, one night when 248 was at rest, Zeek led him out of the house and down Ephraim. Cass waited at the entrance to the park. He never smacked at mosquitoes or fidgeted, even at ten o'clock on a summer night. He stood just outside streetlight glare, hands at his sides. The three of them walked into the park, past a couple of guys with their grill set up next to the NO BARBECU-ING signs on the lawn. Past the basketball courts where some boys cussed over the dead batteries in their boom box. Past an old man selling roasted peanuts and sodas out of a shopping cart.

"Hey," Cass said. "That seems like a good idea."

"A salt peanut ain't never a bad idea," Zeek agreed.

They bought bags of peanuts and a not-so-cold-anymore Welch's grape for Toussaint. The three of them sat on a bench passing the peanuts while the men talked about a big deal appointment. Maybe it was that same night, or maybe it was the next night or a week away. Toussaint didn't feel like piecing together the bits of information, so delicious were the salty peanuts puckering his mouth and the cool wash of fizzy sweetness after. He nodded along to the baritone rhythm of their conversation. A bass-line thudded behind them. Maybe those dudes got their boom box working.

"*You* gonna be all right, little man," Zeek was saying, his hand startling and hot on Toussaint's shoulder. "You not going to lose your way. You got your dad here."

"He does have a special sensitivity, doesn't he? A clarity," his father said. Cass's eyes pinned him; suddenly Toussaint was the center of everything.

"I had it too, when I was your age," Cass said. "I always had the sense that an end was coming. Like I was born right when the clock was about to chime. Time's up! All the good things were always drying up by the time I got to them. Silly things, you know, like my high school football team was number one in the state till a little while before I made the team."

Toussaint couldn't imagine his father playing football, or doing anything regular.

"Listen," Cass said. "We're going to do something a little heavy. You have to trust me."

"You know who Frank Rizzo is, little man?" Zeek said. He was all wound up and Toussaint didn't know why. "You know what he did to your dad back in the day? And all of them in that house? Dragged out at gunpoint in their underwear, like, like . . ." Zeek's voice shook. "That's how they treated em, the men of the Black Panther Party. Strong men. Men with principles! Pulled them out of they own HQ and lined em up against the wall, balls out. Like they did slaves. They wasn't doing nothin! They was protecting the neighborhood."

Zeek waved his hands around. "The picture was in the paper. On the front page!"

Cass laid a hand on Zeek's shoulder.

"That was a long time ago, Zeek," he said.

The older man took a deep breath. This, Toussaint had noticed, was how men should comfort each other. A hand on a shoulder; a thump on the back.

"Your father ain't tell you none of this. But you need to know. That's how they finished the Panthers, that kind of shit and worse. Your hear? That's history. Don't you forget that name, Frank Rizzo. He was the police chief. Rat poor South Philly motherfucker. What I'm saying is, we got to defend ourselves so they can't make us animals."

Toussaint didn't really know what Zeek was talking about. He had never heard of Frank Rizzo and he didn't really know what an HQ was. And yet he felt a bitter sadness. The last of his peanuts caught in his throat.

Cass said, "There was a boy there that night. Lived at HQ. Not a whole lot older than you—sixteen, seventeen. Wallace was his name. Young Pup, I used to call him. They split his forehead so deep you could see his skull. Wouldn't call an ambulance." Cass shook his head.

"But you! You have rebellion in your blood. You're a fighter. From a strong line." He put his hand on the top of Toussaint's head. "I don't even believe in that in-the-blood jazz, but I believe it about you."

He looked at his watch and stood. "We need to be getting on."

The park turned to wilderness as they walked in farther—few streetlights, then none at all. The concrete sidewalks gave way to asphalt paths that had cracked into wobbling black chunks. Knotty, fairy-tale-looking trees stretched toward each other high above their heads. Constellations shimmered through the breaks in the treetops. Orion! Toussaint felt a little giddy. He lost his balance. His father whispered that there was more oxygen where there are a lot of trees, and it made you a little giddy. Toussaint figured that was why lost-in-the-woods kids in stories always got caught by the witch. The ground was spongy beneath his feet. To think the city was back there somewhere.

Two men met them at the edge of a clearing. A man named Leo clapped his hand on Zeek's shoulders like they had known each other a long time. They continued into the fable woods until they came to a still, dark place. Once the men had staked their flashlights in the ground, Leo pulled a long, slim trunk from a tent pitched a few feet away. Toussaint wondered if he and the other man lived there, and if it was just those two or a whole city of them living among the trees. No one said much. Leo set the trunk at his feet and his thick brown fingernail flicked open the latch to the trunk: two revolvers and three shotguns lay inside. Toussaint blinked hard. Then again. When he opened his eyes the second time the case was closed and Cass was handing over a roll of bills.

"You might want to go out a different way than you came in," Leo said. "Just in case."

We can't just leave, Toussaint thought. We can't just go back home, like nothing has happened. But Cass was cool and unbothered. Zeek too. Toussaint didn't want to be a pussy, like Mikey was always saying. He willed his heart to slow down. Even his grandmother had guns, he reminded himself, and she was an old lady! Leo led them to another clearing where four or five tents were set up at the edge of the field. Leo and the other guys were a tribe of woodsmen just like Toussaint had guessed. He looked at his father, but Cass didn't seem very impressed. "We bunk here," Leo said. "You can stay if you want."

A few old geezers sat around a pot bubbling on a camp stove. Zeek knew all of them. There were daps and claps on the back and "I don't mind if I do," at the mention of the stew. A bottle passed round. Cass refused it the first time and the second, and even the third, but then, just as Toussaint was nodding off on the bedroll they'd given him, his father raised the bottle to his lips.

Legacy

IN THE MORNING they went to a place in the woods where they could shoot targets drawn on the trees. Leo and Cass held their guns with a practiced hand; they widened their stance, they bent slightly at the knee and in the elbow. Toussaint clutched the pistol when Cass handed it to him. It was heavier than he thought it would be, and awkward in his grip. The bones of his shoulders rattled when he fired, but the pop was immediate and satisfying. He squeezed the trigger again, then again. Only after, when he looked down at the bullet casings shining dully on the mossy forest floor did he feel afraid. Even so, he had to fight the urge to reach out and stroke the rifle muzzles. Leo understood. "Pretty, aren't they?" he said.

Toussaint imagined Leo was Rambo, double-fisting grenades with a machine gun on his back. *Blam blam.* Toussaint knew a kid who had a gun, an older boy named OB who hung around the park. One afternoon behind the bathrooms OB pulled a gun from his waistband, Clint Eastwood–style, to show him and Nemo and Mikey. If you had a gun you had to drop somebody with it. That's what OB said. Drop anybody who comes for your shit. Toussaint hadn't seen OB around for a while.

After target practice, Cass zipped the guns into a duffel bag. "Come back anytime," Leo said. "I always got what you need."

Zeek stayed behind. He was going to catch up on old times. Cass gave him a long look. "Watch yourself," he said.

Cass and Toussaint made for a clearing on the other side of the woods.

"Necessary evil. You understand?" Cass said as they headed out. "We'll only tell the others if we need to use them."

When would that be? And why? They walked out through the woods, along the gnarled paths, and stumbled into an abandoned water main, cavernous and long, with a glimmer of daylight at the far end. There was a hushed feeling like they had come into something else's territory.

A few minutes later they emerged onto Harold Street. The strangeness of Leo's woods burned off in the heat. Now it was endless broken-pavement blocks of tired trees and houses all with the same sagging porches. Cass walked ahead, with the duffel bag bumping against his shoulder and a dark blot of sweat widening across his back. Shimmering heat rose off the pavement. Toussaint aimed loogies into sewer grates to pass the time. Miss, miss, hit.

"In here," Cass said at last. They descended a few steps and entered a cool, dim room swirling with cigarette smoke. Old guys with their guts hanging over their belts sat on rickety barstools. All the old man eyes turned to them.

"No kids in here," a short woman said from behind the bar.

Cass took a twenty from his pocket. "Just a quick one," he said.

The woman shrugged and put a glass on the bar. When Cass had shot back his second, he turned to Toussaint.

"We're going to have to leave sooner than I thought," he said.

Toussaint slurped from the can of Coke the bar lady had given him.

"Where are we going?" he asked.

"To our legacy." Cass held up two fingers for another glass. He finished this one in long swallows: one, two, three, gone. "My mother died in a rented room. They chucked everything she had in a dumpster the next day. They throw you away unless you do something about it. You understand?"

Toussaint nodded. Cass's eyes were wet. Toussaint wanted to do something for him, or say something that would help, but he didn't know what that could be.

"I'll miss it at Winnie's," he said softly.

"I owe you an apology." Cass shook his head. "I miscalculated. But you don't have to worry. I know how to set it right."

Cass reached over and patted Toussaint on the knee. By the time he'd finished his fourth drink the metal had returned to his gaze. The bar lady turned the dial on the radio till the static settled into a scratchy song. *I got to keep moving / Blues falling down like hail* . . . The old men at the bar smiled and Toussaint did too—this was one of the songs he knew from the records at the library with the grainy photos of ladies in fancy hats. Toussaint sang along, *If today was Christmas Eve* . . .

One of the old men swiveled on his stool. "Looka there," he said. "What you know about that, young blood?" He chuckled. "What he know about that?" he said to Cass.

Cass raised his glass to the man. The bar lady pulled out a box of cassettes and played song after song. A kind of church feeling came into the place. The men sang along, or whistled under their breath. "You got any Screamin' Jay, Yolanda?" one said. "How about Count Basie? I know you got Count Basie." A rectangle of sun filtered through the small high windows at the front of the bar and fell on Cass's smudged blue shirt and the ginger stubble on his chin. The bar lady gave Toussaint a sleeve of saltines to ease the grumbling in his belly.

It was dusk when they came out onto the street. Cass stumbled on a broken slab of sidewalk and chuckled. He steadied himself against a tree and took a couple of deep breaths.

"I know a song," he said. "I learned it from a friend of mine." He sang a few bars of "Muddy Water."

That was a library song too. A flock of black birds wheeled over the rooftops—way, way up. Bonaparte birds, like his mother had told him about. He had a funny feeling, like something kind had its eye on him. Just for an instant, though, and then it was gone. His father resumed his long-stride, way-ahead walking. He never stumbled again, not one time, in the hour-long walk back to Ephraim.

BONAPARTE

. . .

THERE'S A SONG I used to do on the road. Keeps coming in my head in a peculiar kind of way, like somebody's humming it right in my ear. Been keeping me company, crazy as it sounds. But I can't recall the lyrics. Dammit, how did that song go? Something about water. That was it!: *Muddy water in the street / Muddy water round my feet* . . . Lord Jesus. All those floods. It's a wonder the whole Negro race wasn't drowned.

Everybody in every juke loved that song when I did it. Half of them cried. Hell, I choked up in the middle of it more than once. I don't think much about that stuff that happened back then. It's plenty to be sad about in the here and now. I don't care for childhood reminiscence. Truth be told, most of what I remember from my girlhood was high water and awfulness. Except for Mother and Daddy, Everlasting rest their souls. Bessie and Ma and them were always singing about floods like the one we were in. Those girls told it like it was, but the problem was, they sang it so it was pretty. Not silk-scarf-and-summer-night pretty, but pretty like the saddest thoughts are pretty. That's what a song does, that's its job. But that sheen music puts on a thing, that's nostalgia. And I hate it because it makes ugly things beautiful.

What *I* recall about high water was people dropping like flies from fever. I remember there was a lot of rain, weeks of rain, and finally the levees broke and we rowed out of Orville, where I was born and raised until the age of thirteen. My daddy had us in a boat early on, so we weren't stuck on a roof or watching the houses float down the Tallahatchie like other folks. Before they got to the Red Cross camps, people were in canoes, or on river rafts that drifted and drifted, or on hilltops sticking up over the surface of the water.

Some made it to shacks on high ground, but most of us were in tents the relief gave us, jammed together like maggots on bitty stretches of land more like swamp than dry ground. No water—or little. No food, or little. Powdered milk to mix with . . . with what? And half the time the white folks only gave you rations if you went digging out mud in town. We had every kind of thing: typhus and dysentery and cholera, but we just called it the Fever. Those camps were the worst place I have ever been, everybody shitting everywhere and pissing everywhere and throwing up and bleeding on those little spongy patches of land.

Women had their cycles, you know. I was never so disgusted by my own body. We had pallets the relief gave out. I was on that pallet with a plague of flies all around me. I couldn't get off it because the first few days we was there they didn't have anything for girls on their monthly and there weren't rags or anything to spare. A circle of blood spread around me, from my knees up to my back. I was beyond shame. You don't think about things like that—when people tell you about wars and disasters, they leave out body shame. A body won't stop doing even when the world is ending; it just keeps on. Nasty machine.

Before we got to the camps, when we were rowing, we saw a man up in a tree with a baby tied to him. He was up at the tippy top, the rest was underwater. We were five in our boat, riding low. Daddy wouldn't take the man and the baby. "One more and we sunk," he said. All of a sudden, he was pushing my mother off him and the boat was rocking and pitching. She clawed his neck and one of the oars splashed into the water. "Give us the baby! We can take the baby!" I remember it had a dirty pink bonnet. I thought the man was sweating because his face was streaming water, then I saw he was crying.

Crying man, you gonna use up all your water crying like that.

You better save your water, I wanted to tell him. The baby looked down at us with big big eyes, honey-brown face, pointy chin. Mama fell back in the boat and we nearly turned over. The crying man held on to the baby and nodded his head. He kept on nodding and watching our boat inch away with Daddy rowing with one oar. There wasn't anybody left in the world, just the flat water and the crying man and the baby with her big eyes and my mother wailing across the universe, "I'm sorry. I'm sorry."

I only hit that sound she made one time. I busted my voice for a week. I was at a little joint in Tupelo. I was down in it—I was one thing with the notes and I hit Mama's wail. My voice shattered the air for miles and miles, it flew across town breaking everything.

Almost everybody on our spongy piece of relief camp got Fever. I bet we just needed penicillin. I don't know if they'd invented it yet or if they had and the white folks just didn't give it to niggers. I have meant all these years to look it up, but somehow, I don't. Maybe I don't want to know that curing us would have been that simple, maybe that would just be too heartbreaking. I can't stand the heartbreak of the whole stupid human history—all those years of knowing nothing about nothing. All those brutal centuries. The white folks were bad, they were a terror. If you wanted to leave the camp you had to have a tag they gave you, pinned to your chest. They were a curse. And niggers were fools. Niggers have always been fools, beautiful fools. Me too.

In one little corner of the camp a doomsday Bible-thumper set up shop. The flood must have washed him right out of the pulpit—still wearing his preacher suit, a tie he had wrapped around his forehead, and a pair of good brogues. He had a head half eaten with ringworm. He was calling out with his big baritone, "Ah, sinful nation . . ." All the usual crap, he was hooping good, brimstone and all of it, and then he says, "God gave Noah the rainbow sign, / No more water the fire next time." We all knew that old song and some started singing. I guess it made us feel better, a little bit of poetry. But excuse me, I wanted to say, this flood we in now, plus that one makes two floods, thank you very much. Anyway, there we all were singing in the middle of that godforsaken swamp—beautiful, fool niggers. And we just keep right on!

I can't get shut of memories these days. I wish whatever they're trying to tell me would just come on and be plain about it. Course, you gotta be careful what you wish for, so I guess I shouldn't try to hurry it along.

PHILADELPHIA

. . .

Now or Laters

"GOOD AFTERNOON, Little Brother Toussaint!"

A woman Toussaint had never seen before stood next to Winnie and Ava in the kitchen. New people had replaced the neighborhood people. They seemed to know him, but he didn't know them. These new, after-the-raid people talked to him too loud for too long. Or they were sugary nice for no reason. Or they ignored him until Cass walked into a room and then they gushed all over him. The new people didn't just come to Meeting or the clinic anymore. They invaded all of 248's private places: the kitchen, the upstairs bathroom, the garden at night. Toussaint steeled himself before walking into a room, just like he had at Glenn Avenue.

"You remember Miss Rhonda, don't you?" Ava said, setting a soup pot on the stove.

Winnie and this lady beamed at him. Winnie was flushed and sweaty, still in her faded blue nightgown even though it was two in the afternoon. Something had happened to the grown-ups. They smiled too wide when there was nothing to smile about. Their eyes glittered but it wasn't because they were happy. It gave Toussaint the willies. The days dove at him like a swarm of bees—too fast and too many of them to do anything but duck. Late nights Cass and Ava argued up in their attic. Next day it was as though the fight never happened. And it wasn't just the pretending about the arguments. In Ark things disappeared, big chunks of the world beyond their walls vanished like they'd never existed at all: kids from the neighborhood stopped coming around. The books Cass put in the boys' room were different; now there was a long pamphlet by something called the Weather Underground, and books about a thing called a kibbutz and about survival living. Toussaint didn't want to poop in a bucket or make antiseptic out of boiled pine needles. He wanted to go to sixth grade like he was supposed to.

"You want a snack before your garden shift?" Ava asked him now. She stood with one hand on her hip, the other stirring a pot like Jilly used to. Jilly wouldn't like it here, Toussaint thought.

"Five minutes, then afternoon chores. Okay, baby?" Ava called as Toussaint left the kitchen with his glass of lemonade and a cornbread end Ava had sprinkled with salt just how he liked. Ark was flush that week; who knows how long it would last. Toussaint wanted a quiet place to savor his snack. A few minutes of nobody looking at him and nothing to do. But the downstairs half bathroom was occupied; Zeek and some other man were talking excitedly in the living room. The hallway was full of clinic patients. "Hey there, Brother Toussaint," one said. Toussaint spun around and stuck out his tongue. He walked fast in the opposite direction.

"Where you going?" Ava called.

Toussaint was already through the back door. He sat on a folding chair, nibbling his cornbread and sorting himself out. That's what Patch said about people before he did something scary to them. I need to sort him out, he'd say. Or: That one there can't sort himself out. The house heaved behind him, but the yard was empty and still. Almost peaceful, even with the bugs and the smell.

"There you are," a stranger lady called from the back step a few minutes later. Toussaint jolted upright and spilled his lemonade. "Winnie said you had a basket of okra ready for me." Toussaint threw his cup into a row of strawberry plants, his last bite of cornbread too. "Where you going? Boy, I asked you a question," the woman shouted after him, kept on shouting even after he'd slammed the back-fence door behind him.

Out in the alley, Nemo and Alvin worked the food pantry shed. Not much in there but some stray cans and stale loaves of bread. They'd already given out most of the surplus, and there wasn't any more to replace it. Mikey was there too.

"Where's the fire, man?" Mikey said.

"What?" Toussaint asked.

"Where's the fire. Cause you was walking so fast and that lady . . . Never mind, man."

Toussaint stood squinting with his hands on his hips.

"Hot out here. How much longer we got?" Mikey said.

"*You* ain't gotta stay out here, Mikey," Nemo said. "We're the ones working. Right, T?"

Nothing moved in the alley. The backs of the houses and the neighbors' chain-link fences and the patchy grass were pale in the high sun. Toussaint sat on the pavement tossing stones at an oil stain. It was all so ugly. Heat lay on top of him like a body.

A rough-looking young-old man shuffled around the corner. The boys eyed him silently until Mikey said, "Yo, get outta here. Fucking basehead."

Toussaint looked him over: cracked lips, stained too big shirt and too big pants. He *was* a fucking basehead. But still.

"Come on, man," he said wearily. "We're not supposed to talk to people like that."

"He ain't gonna eat nothin nohow," Mikey said. "He just want to sell it."

Toussaint shrugged. He nodded at Nemo, who handed the man a loaf of bread and some canned peaches. Probably Mikey was right. Probably he wouldn't eat it.

"Big man, huh? Calling the shots," Mikey said. "Why y'all always listen to him?" he asked Nemo and Alvin.

"Cause Toussaint always knows what to do!" Alvin said. "Right, Nemo? He always knows!"

Nemo made a big show of loudly rearranging the cans.

"Quit it, Alvin," Toussaint said.

Alvin's smile faded.

"Aww, come on, Alvin. Don't cry."

"Yeah. You can't be a retard *and* a pussy," Mikey said.

He nudged Toussaint in the shoulder and busted into one of his *skeet-skeet* chuckles. He had, Toussaint noticed for the hundredth time, tiny square teeth that were too small for his mouth and needed brushing. Alvin got out his yo-yo.

"Where's Lola at? Y'all seen Lola?" Nemo said, just for something to say. He was right: Lola hadn't come around for a minute.

"Why, you want to bone her?" Mikey said.

Nemo shook his head. Nobody could understand why Mikey had to act like that. Toussaint figured it was probably why he kept getting left back. At least he got to go to school. And he didn't even appreciate it. A woman and her daughter came up and got some hot-ass canned goods. The alley returned to quiet. Too hot even for the flies.

"Alvin!" Mikey said. "Yo, Alvin. Whyn't you run to the store for me and get some icey pops and Now or Laters?"

"Don't want Now or Laters."

"I ain't ask you what you want. Go get me some Now or Laters."

"Leave him alone, Mikey," Toussaint said. A line of sweat trickled down his back. He wanted to peel his skin off and leave it in the alley. He wanted to float up over the clouds where it was dark and cool.

"Why he can't go down the street? He too busy?"

"I don't want to!" Alvin repeated.

"He could go down the street, Mikey. But he doesn't want to go down the street," Toussaint said.

"Oh, *doesn't* he?" Mikey sucked his teeth. "Your Highness. You so uptight. You know what you need? Your pops need to get you some," he said. "My pops took me to get some when I was your age."

"Your pops ain't come around since you was a baby. Why you always gotta talk shit?" Nemo said.

Toussaint's back itched like ants were biting him. Ants on his arms and back and the backs of his hands.

"Your pops is always chilled out," Mikey said. "I betcha he get some on the regular. And not just from your moms. She probably just one of his—"

Toussaint launched himself at Mikey. The other boy fell backward onto the concrete. Toussaint was on him with his fists.

"You don't ever shut up. You need to shut up. You need to fucking shut up." Nemo didn't pull him off. Mikey had it coming.

Kicking Up Leaves

"WHY CAN'T STUFF GO BACK to how it used to be?" Toussaint mumbled. He fiddled with a sliver of wood sticking up from the bottom step of Pastor Phil's porch. He didn't know what he wanted to go back to. Was it Abemi? Couldn't be Glenn Avenue. Maybe it was 248 before the police came? Not really. He didn't want any of those. He didn't much care where he lived, he just wanted his mother back, and for everything to stop changing.

"It's like if you kick up a pile of leaves," Pastor Phil said. "Eventually the leaves will settle, but not how they were before they got kicked."

"Why?"

"I don't know."

Pastor Phil was always straight up with him. He told her how the days were familiar and strange at the same time, like a TV show he had seen before but suddenly all the people in it were different. Weird guys—guys that stared at him out of the corner of their eyes, guys who took too long in the bathroom and came out sleepy—were at the house at all hours, even though they had long since finished reinforcing the entrances and exits. Zeek was sweaty and irritable or dreamy and remote and spent too much time in his room. 248 was grim. Toussaint felt like he was in a prison—there were two-by-fours across the doors and security bars on the ground-floor windows.

Ava snapped at Toussaint if she didn't like the way he'd done his chores. That wasn't fair because there were weeds everywhere in the garden, which meant she wasn't doing hers either. One time she left a pot of beans cooking so long smoke filled the kitchen. Then she hollered at everybody for not reminding her to turn it off. Winnie hollered right back. Cass walked into the middle of it and slammed his fist on the table. "Stop!" he shouted. Then he left and nobody saw him for a whole day.

Toussaint told Pastor Phil about that too. He told her almost everything. He left out the guns, of course. That night on her porch they were talking about his grandmother.

"Were you disappointed that you didn't go and see her?" Pastor Phil asked.

Toussaint shrugged.

"I was going to give her my cat's-eye for a present."

"Do elderly ladies like marbles?" Pastor Phil said. Toussaint blinked and looked down at his hands. "Oh! Sorry. It's the thought that counts. Not that a marble isn't a good present." She sighed. "I'm sure she would have loved it, I mean."

"I thought about learning to play the harmonica so I could play one of her songs for her. But I ran out of time."

"That's very beautiful. She would have liked that."

"Ma says she's mean and hates everything and lives in the hut of her memories. But . . . I don't know. Maybe she was mad at Ma. Ma does a lot of things that make people mad."

"Everybody does," Pastor Phil said. "Me too." She nudged him with her elbow. "You too," she said. "Your grandma lives on a farm down there?"

"A great big one!" Toussaint said. "With cows and chickens and everything. And the river's full of fish. My grandfather is buried down there. He was like the mayor of the town, like the king. Everybody loved him. He was in charge of everything."

"Kind of like your father," Pastor Phil said.

"Yeah. Yeah, I guess so. Kind of."

"What happened to him?"

"Some white people shot him."

"Oh. Oh dear. Well, that's too close for comfort."

"Huh?"

"Nothing. Just talking too much." She stubbed out her cigarette and lit another. "You ought to write to her," she said.

"To my grandmother?"

"Yeah. Fill her in. Introduce yourself, you know? I can send the letter if you don't want your mom—if you don't have postage."

"I don't know her."

"Well, maybe you can get to know her."

"Why?"

"Security."

Toussaint considered. He thought Pastor Phil was going to say something about how Dutchess was family and you had to know your family. People were always going on about that. Outside of Ark, not having a family was one of the things Toussaint was supposed to feel bad about.

The next day he snuck a peek at a letter he'd found in the shoebox where his mother kept their important papers. In the letter Dutchess said something about a place she was keeping for his mother. He supposed it was the same place Ava had been talking to him about all his life. The envelope was smudged with fingerprints, but he could make out the return address written in his grandmother's round, loopy hand. He copied it onto a piece of paper. That night, Toussaint dreamed that a lot of people were waiting for him in a place down by a river. Five nights he dreamed of that place, and on the sixth day he wrote.

Lazarus

THE ADULTS OF ARK were gathered in the kitchen of 248.

"Something is in you and it has to come out," Cass said. "All of us have something. Some malignancy. Secrets. An overdeveloped sense of individualism."

"Seeking out old comforts." His head swiveled on his neck till his gaze settled on Zeek. There was a coolness about him lately. He even blinked less.

The head swiveled again and stopped when Ava was in his sights. "A tendency toward self-sabotage.

"What we're doing here, brothers and sisters . . . what Ark is doing is helping these people see that their lives have been made wretched. That there's a system that controls everything they do and say, who they can be, what they can have. That's hard to swallow. We have to be an example. Strengthen our own frequency. Tune out our own static."

It was midmorning. Soon visitors and gawpers and clinic patients would arrive. Ava was exhausted—she'd slept two hours, maybe three. None of them had much time for sleep anymore. She'd done her watch shift on the roof with Cass from eight p.m. to four a.m. then come down for breakfast at seven-thirty. Now she was so tired her throat was scratchy, like a cold was coming on. They didn't have any coffee, hadn't for weeks. Cass wanted them to get their get-up-and-go from vitamin B$_{12}$—mainlined like speed-balls. Cass shot them up on a rotation. Clearly, Winnie's turn had come that morning. She was standing at the sink washing dishes with enough pep for a busload of cheerleaders.

Zeek sure hadn't had his. He was worn out and fidgety at the other end of the table. Ava wanted to go over and squeeze his grizzly old head. But he didn't take hugs anymore. He kept to himself when he wasn't with Cass or Patch. Everlasting bless him, Zeek had something to fess up to, and everybody knew what it was. Except Winnie, who didn't want to know about anything.

"Ava," Cass said. "What is it you want to tell us?"

She startled, dropped the pen she'd been twiddling. The room's eyes were on her.

"I . . . What do you mean?"

"This is not the time for defiance," Cass said. "Put aside your pride," he said.

Ava shook her head. She didn't know what he wanted from her, and truth be told she was too tired to give it to him. One thing was sure: she wasn't being proud. Some part of her was curious to see what this latest Cass thing would do to her.

"Incomplete commitment," Zeek said, suddenly perked up. People with something to hide sure are good at pointing fingers.

"Doubt," Cass said.

Ava felt a little shaky. She was beginning to understand that she should be afraid. How did Cass know the things he knew? Just yesterday she had watched from the attic window as Toussaint walked down the alley alone. He flinched when he reached the back fence, like he was bracing himself before he passed through the door. She wanted him to have a pack of regular boys to hang around with—hamburger-eating, basketball-in-the-park boys. School-going boys.

Now Cass approached her. She thought he would strike her, but instead he lifted her chin with his fingertips. He hugged her so tightly she stumbled to one side. Over his shoulder she saw that tears had come into Winnie's eyes. Like she was watching Jesus heal a leper. Or more like watching him bring back Lazarus, that poor man. What must he have been like after being dead, then not

dead. Not quite alive, that's for sure. But Ava was—alive, that is.
Oh, she was so alive the blood burned in her veins.

"All this resistance only hurts you," he whispered. "You who
have so much."

He sent the others away and guided Ava into the tiny walk-in
pantry in the corner of the kitchen. It wasn't really a room, not
even a closet—more like a human-height cabinet, not two feet
square. He left her standing in there with the door ajar.

"Don't move."

A few minutes later he eyed her through the slit in the door.
He didn't leave the room; she could see his shadow on the kitchen
table. A little while later he looked in again.

"On your feet," he said, when he saw she was leaning into the
shelving.

Oh. Standing was her punishment. Plus the paprika and onion
powder and tin-can pantry smell that roiled her stomach. Cass
went off again, for much longer this time, though she could hear
him moving around the kitchen. Ava's legs began to ache.

After a long while, Zeek appeared. That was worse, somehow,
just as Cass knew it would be.

"Why?" she asked.

Zeek thought she wanted to know why she was being punished.
He said, "It's good for you." But what she meant was, What has
happened to you? Cass was supposed to be cruel. He was supposed
to inflict lavish pain and pleasure, it was all he'd ever done. But not
Zeek. "Not you, Zeek," she whispered.

He didn't say anything more. But when he came back some
time later, he gave her a little cup of salted lemonade. "Help with
the cramps," he muttered.

Ava's legs throbbed, then numbed. Her mind flailed, casting
about for something to hold on to. She began to think about things
that had been lost: two of Toussaint's baby teeth she'd saved in a
little jewelry bag, his first report card, a picture taken on Chest-
nut Street near her first job in Philadelphia, still a country girl
in a powder-blue skirt and jacket, with matching hat. A score of
Dutchess's—in B-flat. A forest-green travel case with silver trim,

the bright yellow kitchen in New Jersey with the window above the sink. Those matching fox coats Dutchess had, delivered all the way from Marshall Field's, in the middle of summer one flush year when Pop was still alive. There is no record of us, she thought. Nothing to lift gently from a box of keepsakes and unwrap from its tissue paper—*Careful!*—and pass delicately to Toussaint. No record to show where they had been and what they had done and who they belonged to. Everlasting help us! Help us.

Cass came for Ava hours later. She had collapsed by then, legs a leaden tangle sprawled across the threshold. She had not gone to the bathroom on herself, but the pain in her bladder was excruciating.

"Toussaint?" she asked.

"Missioning."

She could not walk up the stairs. Cass carried her like a baby. He undressed her and laid her in the tub. When he walked away she urinated painfully against the white porcelain tub. She stank. The pee smell mingled with the acrid must from her armpits and between her legs. Cass insisted on washing her. She was humiliated and indebted at once. When it was over he wrapped her in a towel and laid her on the attic mattress.

She woke in the dark. Cass was lying next to her, reading something by dim lamplight. The house was quiet. In spite of herself, she wondered who was on watch on the roof. She wiggled her toes; sat up and rubbed her calves.

"All right?" Cass said. Hopefully, like he'd given her an aspirin and wanted to know if it had kicked in.

Ava lay back on the mattress. The room had a gray tint, and she wondered for a moment if something irreversible had happened to her brain during those hours in the pantry. She blinked and the attic went from gray to grayer, then black and . . . "Ava," Cass said softly from far away. Her thoughts drifted like a mosquito landed in a puddle, wriggly like that, and buoyed along the surface of the water.

When she blinked again, Cass was standing in the doorway.

Her pelvis ached from holding her urine so long and from having been kicked. Only she hadn't been kicked, she didn't think. But she ached like something was coming out of her. She closed her eyes again. The pain was a childbirth kind of pain, or maybe she was dreaming of labor, the waves of it whipping along her lower back when Toussaint was born. Cass had appeared outside her room in the hospital, when she was woozy and cesareaned. Sliced open and sewn together. He had a habit of showing up on the other side of agony. But he hadn't been there, of course.

"Ava," he called again. "Ava?"

She swam up through the dark. The room had righted itself into streetlamp glow and window and rumpled sheets. Cass lay beside her, his face oranged by the lamplight.

He'd go right on, wouldn't he? And she would go on taking it, right up to the moment she couldn't. Until that night, she had not known such a moment existed. Downstairs one of the boys called out in his sleep. Ava brushed Cass's hand with hers in their attic bedroom. Tears slid down her face and pooled on the pillow.

"It's all right," Cass said. "It'll take some time."

BONAPARTE

. . .

I NEARLY THREW Toussaint's first letter in the trash before I opened it. What on earth, I thought, after Carter Lee gave it to me. The name in the return address was Toussaint Wright. Progress has turned to pure petty meanness, mocking us with letters sent in the name of rebel slaves. That's a nasty prank.

Course, it wasn't a prank. But it was the meanest trick anybody ever pulled. I cursed Ava after I read it. I was done with her, which is its own sad shame because ain't much to be done with. All we got to show for the past twenty years of mother and daughtering is a couple dozen phone calls and some postcards.

I went and sat by Caro. "I can't take this," I told him. "This is too much for me."

All these years I had been thinking me and her were the last of our line. When we went it would be like none of us ever existed, not even Caro.

"Remember how long we tried to have a baby?" I asked him.

I was so ashamed that I couldn't. I'm still sorry. It was almost worse how you didn't get mad, never made me feel like it was anything missing at all. "Darling, sugar, heart of mine," you said. "We got Ava. We got Ava and this land and all Bonaparte."

Look at it now. Acres of nothing. When you died everybody around here had some shit to talk: Of all the men in this town he's the one should have had some babies. Should have had a child to carry on the line. They wouldn't say so when you were alive, but they all thought I was a stray you picked up at a juke with no kin and a yellow child got God knows how. They weren't wrong. It's not so hard to imagine what savage thing could happen to a young traveling woman that would leave her with a light, wavy-haired baby. But that's mine to take to my grave. Point is, there wasn't no future after they killed you. We didn't have a "next." Then I got the boy's letter. All this time with ashes in my mouth, and for the last eleven years there has been a little boy named Toussaint. She must hate me.

"She must hate me good," I said to Caro. "I know I wasn't perfect but I didn't deserve that."

I was having a fine time howling and crying. Then Caro says, Hush. I heard him like he was sitting next to me. Hush. Cool and sweet against my ear. We have a grandbaby! A next generation. You just said it yourself. Hush, girl.

I went on home with Delilah and soaked the dishes piled in my sink. I picked up the ashtrays and the junk in the front room and tried to get my mind quiet enough to figure something to say to Toussaint that wouldn't scare the mess out of him. The more I tried to keep my thoughts on him the more they went every which way. Maybe we have already taken Bonaparte as far as we are meant to carry it. The next leg of the journey is for somebody else. Ava acts like she ain't got good sense, but she got plenty, that's her problem. Maybe she hid the boy from me because she wanted to save him from the weight of his inheritance. Well, baby girl, you can't stop some things. Some things just are.

Me and the boy been sending each other cassettes. I sing to him. Talk to him, tell him about this place. It's nice. Feels like I ain't rattling around this whole town with just Delilah and three old fogies for company. I put all my memories in those tapes. Some of them I'll never send. Some of them I'm saving for when he gets older.

In the evenings I chip away at my paperwork. The legalities and all of that. I'm putting my house in order, so to speak. I wish I knew about the boy—my grandson! how about that!—before Barber cut out of here. There's a lot of papers that need ferrying between here and there. Ava's going to have to get her head out of her ass and sign all this stuff. It's something troubling me though, I can't find the deed and title. Looked in my strongbox too. They're around here somewhere. I mean, they got to be, right?

She got a new man now. Toussaint says he's his real father. I guess if that's what Ava told him, it could be true. Sometimes you got to tell children what they need to hear. Everlasting knows I understand all about that. I just don't want this man causing trouble for my grandboy. Toussaint says he's too big. That's how he described him: so big nothing can be in the same room with him. Might be the boy ain't got to worry. Ava's men don't tend to stick around. She always was a vine looking for something to grow itself around. But I know this cat Cass better keep his wits about him. You got to watch out for a vine—you think it's holding you up, but half the time it's choking you out.

PHILADELPHIA

...

Mercy for Onesimus

"I'LL JUST SAY we ought to keep an eye on the people that go to that clinic."

Mr. Peeples stood when he spoke and cleared his throat like there was a lot more where that came from.

"Okay, everybody," Pastor Phil said. "How about we get back to verse five!"

Toussaint was hidden in the broom closet in the church basement. He sat on an overturned bucket and peered through the cracked door at the ten people gathered for Wednesday Bible study.

Of those ten people, at least half used to go to the clinic themselves. Not grumpo Mr. Peeples, but Toussaint recognized a man with high blood pressure sitting closest to the door in a beige track suit. There was chlamydia in the middle row drinking a Mountain Dew, and an ankle sprain up front.

"It's not just the clinic," somebody else said. "Seems to me it's people coming and going from there at all hours."

"They're not like they used to be. Not that I ever liked them much," another man said. "But they would speak, you know? I passed that house the other day and Cass and the other one with the bad eye didn't say not one word. Watched me all the way down the block. Gave me chills."

Things weren't so bad as they were saying. It was just Ark had to be more careful now. Toussaint thought everybody had taken things too far. Cass too. Cass said most of the people in the neighborhood were collaborators, informing on Ark to the police and maybe even the mayor. Mr. Peeples and them were pains in the butt, but Toussaint didn't think they were spies. Lately he was confused about what was real. Nobody else at 248 seemed to think Cass was exaggerating about anything, not Zeek or Winnie. Not his mother for sure. It was just Toussaint tied up in knots in his mind.

Toussaint sneaked into Bible study because he thought it would be like when he used to go to Sunday school in New Jersey. He wanted to hear about miracles, about God gathering all the world's creatures—that would include him, Nemo and Alvin, his mother, and even his father—and lining them up to be saved two by two. He wanted to hear that angels watched over them, warrior angels who pulled swords from their wings to set things right. Sometimes Toussaint was scared that his father was an angel.

Instead, Pastor Phil was talking about a book called Philemon, which Toussaint had never heard of, and a man named Onesimus, who Paul told Philemon to be nice to when he got back to town after being in jail. One lady said that didn't mean you had to let any kind of people come around and do whatever they wanted. People had to be accountable, they had to have respect for their hosts. Toussaint thought she was talking about the police, who had come into his house and done anything they felt like to him and his mother and father. His throat tightened with tears. He felt that way a lot when he was around Pastor Phil. She was the only person who had said, I'm sorry that happened to you. And: That must have been very hard. His stomach growled. He'd had plain grits for breakfast that morning, then more grits with canned corn for lunch.

Then Mr. Peeples said, "Three bikes missing in the last two weeks. I think we all know who took them."

One woman said she found human waste, not the liquid kind, in her front yard. Pastor Phil tried to steer them back around to welcoming prodigals, but the Bible study people didn't want any more mercy for Onesimus.

Why weren't the Ark kids in school, they wanted to know.

Should they report them to child protective services? Or the police? Why were they on the roof day and night, spying on everybody?

"And that smell!" Every head nodded. The smell was something.

"Maybe we're being a little too . . . not much like Paul," another woman said. "I know that smell is bad and they act strange. But I think . . . I think the smell is old food they use to make some kind of fertilizer for that raggedy garden they have."

The garden wasn't raggedy! Well, it didn't used to be.

"Why can't they just buy some MiracleGro like everybody else?"

"I know. They're not the best neighbors. But, I mean, they not doing anything so bad. They're just selling preserves and pickled beans. And they're always neat and clean."

"My car windows got smashed last night. Stole my car radio."

A hush fell.

"But that probably wasn't anything to do with Ark. Crime is up all over the city!" A couple of people nodded. "And," Pastor Phil reminded them, "they served lunch every day for the neighborhood kids who needed it."

Uh-oh. The Bible studiers tensed. Ark's lone defender stood up so fast her chair wobbled. "Kids around here don't need free food. Everybody around here owns their house. Feeds their own kids. You're new here, so maybe you don't understand that."

Pastor Phil returned to Philemon. Toussaint could tell by her fidgeting that she wanted to be done already, to be on the rectory porch smoking her cigarettes. Mr. Peeples said the point was that Paul was asking Philemon to free Onesimus.

"Clearly," he said, "it's a passage about slavery. The scripture says, 'no longer as a slave, but better than a slave.'"

A chorus of vigorous mmm-hmmms went around the room. Pastor Phil didn't drag things on too long after that. While the people were busy gathering their things, Toussaint slipped from his hiding place, ran upstairs to the sanctuary and out the main doors.

It was dinnertime. Maybe magically there'd be cornbread or potato salad, and maybe Zeek would be awake enough to eat it. And Alvin wouldn't hoot or slam his hand against the table a million times. Maybe his mother would say, Enough is enough. Let's go down to your grandmother like we were supposed to all those months ago.

"Hey! What you doing here?"

Toussaint nearly tripped over Lola, who was sitting on the bottom step looking so . . . *regular.* "Lola?" he said. Her part was arrow straight, with long twists on either side. Her summer dress didn't have a single stain, and her elbows were Vaselined to high shine.

"You went to Bible study?" she said. When she swiveled to face the church doors, the balls at the ends of her twists swung around and hit her in the temple. She swore under her breath. Toussaint smiled—same old Lola.

"How come you out here?" he said.

"My mom said I ain't have to go with her if I waited in the church. But it's too hot in there." She lowered her voice: "They finished?"

"Guess so." Toussaint put his hands in his pockets. "Hey, you want to come over to my house? To eat?"

"Well," Lola said, glancing back at the church door. "Naw. I think Imma head home. With my mom, I mean."

"Oh. Oh, okay."

"Yeah. I, uh, I heard about . . . I mean, with the police and all."

Toussaint looked down at his tennis shoes.

"Is everybody?" she said. "I mean, Alvin and Nemo, are they . . ."

The church door opened with a bang and the adults spilled out onto the steps. Lola jumped to her feet. One of them said, looking at Toussaint, "Isn't that—?" The next instant Lola's mom—turns out she was the one with poop in her yard—swooped down the steps like a mean bird. "Young man," she said in a tight voice. She snatched Lola's hand and marched her onto the sidewalk.

"Bye! Bye, Toussaint," Lola called.

Her mother shook her by the shoulder and bent to whisper something. But you couldn't stop Lola. She looked back and waved even though her mother yanked her like she wanted to pull her arm right out of the socket. Good ol' Lola, Toussaint thought, wiping at tears. You can't stop Lola.

Weak Link

TWICE CASS RETURNED to 248 with bruises across his knuckles like he'd been in a street fight. His moods were turbulent. They whipped around the house, overturning pots and furniture and people. "Where is Toussaint?" he would shout from the second-floor landing. Then the two of them would head out into the early morning, or the midday sun, or the late evening, with Ava calling from the porch steps: Be careful! Watch yourselves!

The hours of their absence were interminable. Her boy was always tired when he returned, and tight-lipped about where they'd been or what they'd done. "Baby," she'd ask, as gently as she could manage, "anything you need to tell me?" All she ever got in return was one of his sighs. But at least he'd stopped screaming in his sleep. He smiled sometimes, way more than in the weeks right after the raid. That was a good sign, wasn't it?

"The boys are okay, don't you think?" Ava asked Winnie after one of these outings with Cass. "Oh yes. Just fine," Winnie said, all exclamation points.

There wasn't any use in pressing the point. Winnie had only just gone back to getting up in the morning and changing out of her nightgown. She was different though. She even had a new smile— a jack-o'-lantern grin that flared and disappeared. Her hair was growing in too. Corkscrew whisps escaped from the bobby pins she used to hold them back. Cass didn't say a word about it. Cass let Winnie get away with anything. Maybe he felt like he owed her, for the house and all.

Ark was in a rough patch, that was sure. But Ava was keeping things together, bare cabinets and all. All the money went to what Cass called the Independence Fund, with some left over to replace the clinic supplies the cops had taken. Ava could handle Cass's moods and his mysterious coming and going. She wasn't even too worried about him sneaking a drink. He didn't do it often, she'd been tracking. The man was allowed a weakness, right? What Ava couldn't stand was how distracted and withdrawn he'd become. He wasn't all there, even when he was sitting right in front of her. He didn't seem to notice that everybody was scared the cops would bust in at any moment. Scared they might try to take the kids. Scared about Cass and Zeek's impending court dates. Cass wouldn't talk about any of it. After he and Zeek got done turning 248 into Fort Knox he was done with the raid and the cops and anybody who mentioned them.

"Zeek has priors, you know," Ava said one night up in their attic room.

"I know."

She kept her voice calm: "We need some kind of plan."

"There is a plan."

"Okay. So, what is it?"

"I don't have to explain myself to you."

His voice was hard. He looked through Ava like she was a windowpane. That made her fingers twitch, made her a little buzzy in the temples.

"I guess you haven't noticed we're running out of supplies? I guess you don't have to explain yourself about that either?"

She'd meant to say it all more kindly, she really had. She had been rehearsing how to tell him that the groceries were low and everybody was still hungry after meals, especially the boys. But you know what he did? He picked up a book and started flipping pages like she wasn't in the room. Ava tapped him on the shoulder, just a tap. A light little tap.

"This is your show, dammit," she said. "So run it!"

Cass roared a long bellow from deep in his throat. His hands were up, like he might . . . He didn't, of course. He wouldn't.

Winnie knocked on the door. "Please," she said. "The kids."

Ava slept in the boys' room that night. On her way out of the attic, she felt Cass's gaze on her back, like he was assessing her to see if she was the weak link in the pack. Like, would he have to leave her behind in the woods or what.

He didn't say much to her after that night. He came up to the attic late and woke her to have sex with her hands pinned behind her back. Ava thrashed and moaned and wondered why it was so extra good when he thrust into her like he wanted to screw her right out of existence.

Travail

TOUSSAINT DIDN'T VISIT Pastor Phil every night like he used
to, and he didn't stay long when he did. He didn't stay long anywhere anymore. At 248 he was jumpy and restless: his father always
summoning him, cornering him. He and Ava's fights erupted most
every night now. Toussaint felt better at Pastor Phil's, where it was
quiet and he didn't have to be so watchful, but then a cop car would
cruise by the rectory and he was out the front door, sprinting into
the darkness to warn everybody at 248, the pages of his grandmother's most recent letter strewn on the floor behind him. Pastor
Phil said he was like a war veteran. Vets remembered terrible things
that happened to them a long time ago and the bad stuff scared
them all over again. She recommended prayer and deep breathing. That didn't do any good. Nothing did any good except his
grandmother's letters.

Pastor Phil kept them in a big wooden cabinet at the rectory
so Toussaint could read them whenever he wanted to, even if she
wasn't there. Plus nobody could snoop them like they would have
at 248. Some of the letters came with cassette tapes Dutchess
recorded. His grandmother sure didn't hold anything back. She
cussed and called all her neighbors every name there was and told
about how when she was a traveling music lady she had been all
over in the whole South.

"And I was so fine," she said. "With a ripe ass like two melons shoved up the back of my dress!"

Boy oh boy. Toussaint couldn't tell if she forgot that he was a kid or if she just didn't care. She wanted him to go down to Alabama. He would carry on his grandfather's legacy, is what she wrote.

"Everybody wants a piece of you," Pastor Phil said, and gave him one of her try-and-be-strong looks. "Heavy is the head."

"Huh?" Toussaint said.

"Nothing. Nothing important. Have some more cheesy crackers."

Toussaint knew what she meant; he just didn't want to talk about it. He figured that once he got to Bonaparte his grandmother would calm down and stop talking all that deep stuff. She and him could just go fishing like she said they would. Toussaint was working on a plan to talk to his mother about it. Cass could come too. Maybe. If his grandmother said it was okay.

Some of Dutchess's tapes were like sermons. Other times she was just mad about everything. Sometimes she told long stories in her deep voice that she could make sound like different people. She should have been in the movies. One tape was about a place she stayed when she was little after her house got washed away in a flood. It was the saddest story Toussaint ever heard, but he listened to that one again and again. She had been a kid like him when it happened. But things worked out okay in the end. Dutchess said Toussaint was from a long line of noble scrappers.

"Sometimes," she said on the tape, "they was just trying to stay alive. Keep their kids alive. But Imma tell you that's a whole lot of effort. That was everything they had. And all of it aimed right at you. Before you was even born. Ain't that something?"

Dutchess called God the "Everlasting." Did Pastor Phil think the Everlasting answered prayers?

"Sure! I mean, your grandmother wrote to you, didn't she?"

"I didn't pray for that."

"Oh. Yeah. Well, you know what I mean."

Pastor Phil said God was unfathomable, but God heard her. And Toussaint too, and all the billions of the living. God might respond in hours or days. Or it might take years, or it might seem like there wasn't any response at all, but that wasn't true. It was just that sometimes people couldn't understand what God said. *For my thoughts are not your thoughts; nor are your ways my ways.* Pastor Phil said that a lot. Then she'd stare misty-eyed out of a window, especially if it was nighttime. She told Toussaint that waiting for God could be agonizing. But God sits with people in their travail. She and Toussaint prayed for God to sit with 248, and with Ava and Winnie and Alvin and Nemo and Zeek. Pastor Phil asked God to help Cass "contain his impulses," which meant something scary that Toussaint wished he didn't understand. Anyhow, it comforted him to think maybe God was up there somewhere, listening and taking it all in. Deciding.

Toussaint always wrote his grandmother back. Even if it took him a few days because he kept having to stop his letter writing to go back to 248. In his last letter, he'd included a snapshot of himself, Cass, and his mother. The three of them were on 248's porch steps at the block party. He had folded in a church flyer so his grandmother could see Pastor Phil even though she was stiff and formal-looking in her collar, which she never wore except on Sundays.

A couple of weeks later, Toussaint arrived at Pastor Phil's for one of his midnight visits. She ran down the steps to meet him.

"Kid! Kid, where've you been?" she said, waving her cigarette around. She put her hands on either of his cheeks and nearly got him in the eye.

"Toussaint," she said. "Your grandmother called."

An Urgency

CASS ANNOUNCED THAT one of them should get a part-time job. Well, it was about time. Ava didn't say that out loud, of course. Cass took everything the wrong way. He'd have thought she was trying to stir up trouble. Ava volunteered for the job. Not *you*, he'd said. He chose Winnie, of course, because she was docile like a cow and as trustworthy as one. Within a few days she was working twenty hours a week at a mom-and-pop stationery store on Sixty-ninth. Just in the nick of time! If there was one thing they needed around the place it was ballpoint pens. Haha. Ha. Fridays were payday. Ava figured Winnie must stop at a check-cashing place on the way home because by the time she got to 248 all she had was her pay stub and an envelope of cash. Two paydays had passed and still no more food in the cabinets.

By the third Friday Ava had had it. "You gave him all of it?" she asked Winnie.

They were in the garden gathering what they could for dinner. So many weeds clotting her perfect rows. Ava tried to remember the exact moment the garden got so overgrown. Maybe it was when she'd taken over the cooking while Winnie was laid up. Or when the boys began disappearing after meals and there was no one to help with upkeep. Thing is, it was never going to yield enough to feed everybody, especially after Cass started bringing around so many strangers. It was just a little kitchen garden with too much expected of it. Now there were weeds in the makeshift greenhouse, weeds choking out all the good plants. Rats had figured out there were snacks to be had, and chewed right through the cloches. You had to stand on the back steps clapping and stomping your feet to shoo them away. Ava slapped at a mosquito on her neck. It was so humid nothing moved, not even time.

"Winnie," Ava said again. "Did you give him all the money?"

"Of course I did," she said over her shoulder. "Why wouldn't I?"

She'd got herself in a huff. "I wouldn't cheat him out of one single cent," she said.

And that's just how he got your house from under you. Not that Winnie would have done anything besides live in it, which is exactly what Ark was doing—and she sure wouldn't have been able to fix it up like they had. Winnie moved down the row of okra.

"These just don't quit!" she said. "We can have them with potatoes. Or I can make grit cakes. Everybody likes those!"

They didn't. Nobody liked those wet-paper-towel grit cakes.

"We only have half a bag of grits left. And we're almost out of potatoes," Ava said.

One evening Ava found Toussaint and the boys eating crackers and spray cheese in their room. Took them all of a minute to fess up after she threatened to tell Cass. Now they were all living on Philomena's peanut butter crackers and canned fruit cocktail, smuggled into the house and eaten in secret while Winnie was at work. Even Alvin kept the secret, which wasn't so hard because he didn't talk much anymore. No more happy hooting and yo-yo slinging after the raid.

Cass had forbidden them from going to the grocery store right around when Winnie got her job. I'll take care of it, he'd said. He did. Sometimes. He might come home with a big bag of brown rice, or a sack of sweet potatoes, or some flour. Once it was two shopping bags with a whole lot of what he called rice and peas. Plantains and cabbage too. It wasn't half bad. He got it from the Jamaicans with the hair. The boys gorged themselves. After the meal, everybody sat out back, happy and sleepy.

"We should do this every week," Ava said.

It was just a throwaway comment, just a nothing, but the table went silent. Uh-oh, Ava thought. She looked down at her hands. They were her childhood hands, rough and ugly, with raggedy nails. A few months ago, she'd been proud of her working hands, but now she hid them under the table.

"Anybody else unhappy with this food we just enjoyed?" Cass said. Nobody dared look at him. They sat for a long time under the silence he'd slung around them like a noose. He got up without saying anything else and left through the door in the back fence. "You always got to stir the pot. Don't you, Ava," Zeek said. Winnie shook her head and carried the plates inside. They left Ava sitting out there on her own.

Now Winnie wouldn't shut up about grit cakes. Chirp, chirp. "Winnie!" Ava said. "Stop with the damned okra! These kids—"

Winnie whirled around, face twisted. "Don't you talk to me like that!" she said. "Don't you act like you're worried about the kids. You don't think one minute about these kids."

She's just upset, like the rest of us, Ava told herself. She doesn't mean to say I don't care about my son. She's just out of sorts.

Ava took a deep breath to keep herself calm. "Look, Winnie. I just meant that we need more food and now that you have this job—"

"Let me tell you something. It's not easy to do what you're asked to do when you don't know why. A whole lot harder than acting up every time things aren't how you like them. A lot harder than having a hissy fit because you happen to look up one day and notice the people around you aren't doing so good. Because you all the sudden decide you're going to pay attention."

She stared at Ava, full of contempt.

"Everything all right out here?" Cass appeared in the back doorway.

Winnie dropped her shoulders. "Oh, it's fine. Fine, Cass!" She smiled. "We're just out here fussing about what to do with all this okra. A big stew, I think, but you need so much rice with stew. We're low."

"I'll run to the store and get you some rice, Winnie," Cass said. "We'll have a feast tonight!"

"Yes, we will." Cass looked right at Ava.

He sees into my guts, she thought. He can read every thought in my head. He stood in the doorway, hands loose on the doorframe. "Won't we, Ava?" he said.

His eyes never left her face. She looked away, embarrassed at how much she still wanted to please him. "Yeah, baby. Yeah, we will," she said.

Late that night Cass shook Ava awake. He kneeled next to her, fully clothed. "Come on, Ava," he said softly. She thought the cops were back and sprang to standing. But it was quiet in the house, and on the street, and everywhere except in Cass's eyes.

"Come with me," he said.

They entered Winnie's room with hardly a knock. She got out of bed as though she'd been waiting and followed Cass into the hallway in her nightgown. They stopped for Zeek. Cass shook him and shouted and finally thumped him on the chest with the side of his fist. Zeek came up gasping from whatever depths he was in. Last, the boys. They gathered on the narrow landing and filed down the stairs. The boys walked in front, rubbing their eyes and turning to search for their mothers' faces in the dark.

When they got to the living room, Cass wouldn't let them sit. "I need you sharp for this," he said. "You know they're watching us. You've seen them tracking and recording."

Police cruisers once, twice a night. Parked cars with men in them no one had seen before. Ava had noticed; everyone had.

"We're at a critical point," Cass said. "We're in an urgency."

A faint light shone in from the kitchen at the other end of the hallway.

"We have to be more vigilant. First thing: No more toxic store-bought food. I know you're sneaking it in." He looked at Ava and the boys. "That stops now."

Had they left a wrapper somewhere? Had the boys been careless about their hiding spots? Or—

"Second: No one goes out unless they check with me first. I'm scaling back clinic hours. The only people who come in here are the ones I screen.

"Big changes, I know," he said. "Don't be scared." He put his hand on Zeek's shoulder. "Be invigorated. Renew your commitment!

"Feels good to be enlightened, right? To know we have saved ourselves and spread our message. But you forgot it's not free. We have to earn it. There's no place for self-satisfaction. No place for cowardice. No place." He looked around the room. "For anyone who's only half in."

Cass switched on the overhead light. Ava blinked in the sudden brightness. Butcher paper covered every window. Butcher paper over the three smoky glass squares at the top of the front door. Plastic sheeting duct-taped over the radiators and the old iron heating vents in the floor. In the middle of the room, on the lone, wide floor cushion: two pistols, three shotguns. Winnie gasped. "Oh!" she said, waving her hand at the guns and the windows. "We can't have those . . . I don't . . ." Then: "I'm sorry. Please, I just . . ." She covered her mouth with her hand.

Guns weren't so bad. Ava knew guns. They weren't anything to get so worked up about. Ava stared at them. She was suddenly weary, as though she had walked a long way only to find herself at the place she'd started. Toussaint burst into tears.

"Stay where you are," Cass said when she moved to comfort him. "Stay where you are, Ava, and listen." Ava kept on toward her boy. Cass intercepted her and led her back to her place next to Winnie.

"We are in danger," he said. "We will boil the water before we drink it."

He'd gotten rid of all of the radios except for one, which he'd locked away in the hall closet. He listed banned radio stations. The stations broadcast messages—they called it advertising—that burrowed into minds. "Brain stem, cerebellum, cerebral cortex."

His talk seeped into their mouths and ears and noses and rose over their heads. Hours passed. The boys nodded to sleep on their feet. Cass shook them awake. Each time anyone changed position, Cass swatted at them. The swats turned to shoves. The shoves became slaps. Not my son, Ava thought. Not Toussaint. Cass stared Toussaint down hard. When the boy could no longer hold his gaze he said, "Look at me when I am talking to you." But he didn't touch him.

Dawn came in dull brown through the butcher-papered windows.

Alvin sobbed. "Please, Mama," he said. "Mama, please. I'm tired. I'm tired, Mama."

Hummingbird Cake

WINNIE TOLD CASS she wanted to make something special. They needed to lift morale and it was clear nobody was going to do it but her. Winnie understood. The burden of the whole community was too much for one man. Cass was trying to save their lives! He couldn't look after their every mood too. So he didn't always go about things with the gentlest hand. But he was a vessel. A vessel isn't perfect. He needed to know they were with him, even his errors. "I want to make a cake," she told him, "but I don't have eggs. Or butter. And I'd need some pineapple. Canned'll do."

"Well, Winnie," he said. "That seems nice, it really does. Maybe you can make another kind of cake. That stuff at the store . . ."

"Oh, I know, Cass," she said. "I know."

God bless him, Winnie thought. Poor man never had a grandmother or anybody to make him anything good to eat. To nurture him that way. He didn't have a homemaking spirit. Ava was about as useless in that department as a bucket with a hole in it. She'd had her run of the place while Winnie was down those few weeks, which had made things so much worse. Alvin and Nemo still weren't doing so good. Winnie couldn't forgive herself for putting her boys through that. Ava had looked after them, in her way. But, my goodness, when she saw the state Winnie was in the day after the raid, she sure had turned right around. Didn't come back to check on her not one time. Ava knew how to get things done, but she didn't know how to care for anybody. Except Cass. For Cass she'd walk through fire.

Winnie had to explain to Cass that there wasn't any good cake that didn't have butter. She was gentle because you never know what sort of thing might remind people of what they don't have, or what they lost along the way. The next morning, she came down to the kitchen to find a box sitting on the counter: SPECIAL DELIVERY FOR CHEF WINNIE. Inside were three pounds of butter, a dozen eggs, milk, and canned pineapple. Winnie got to work late that same night after everybody else was asleep. Night baking gave her peace. It always had—way back when she was a girl working in her grandparents' bakery on Ogontz Avenue. That was before Carl. Carl walked into Ginny's Cakes and Bakes when Winnie was twenty-three years old. He ordered half a dozen sticky buns, and when he put his money in her palm it was live wire all the way to her toes. They were married four months later.

Thank God nobody in Ark ever asked her about him. Winnie didn't have anything to say about Carl. Sometimes—even now that he was long gone—she felt his presence on the back steps. He never made a sound coming in the house, but when he threw his jacket over the kitchen chair, the metal zipper tapped the wood. *Taptap.* When she had one of those Carl flashes, when she felt him climbing the stairs toward her, she would concentrate on Alvin whispering in his sleep down the hall and remember that this was now and that was then.

Carl didn't have his name on the deed to the house, mostly so he wouldn't have to pay for it. "Take it," Winnie told Cass all those months ago. "Take whatever you want. Just so long as me and my boys can always live here." Winnie didn't want to have anything Carl might want. But she prayed. She prayed she and her sons would never see him again. She prayed no other woman would get herself mixed up with him. She prayed he wouldn't die alone on a corner with his liver rotted spongy. Winnie didn't have her thick, pretty black hair anymore. By the time she met Cass it was brittle and broken off and shot through with gray. And that's all Winnie could say about Carl.

The neighbors didn't understand her life in Ark. Mr. Clements stopped her one day and said, "Winnie, why are you letting those people use you?" That was the first time he ever asked her anything. When Carl was there, she used to come out of the house limping, scarves around her neck in the summer, big sunglasses in the evening. She had her jaw wired shut twice. Mr. Clements never said anything about any of that. But Winnie didn't want to be mad at anybody. She was done being mad. It only breaks you down and makes you tired. And the person you're mad at is just going about their business, easy breezy.

"Mr. Clements," she said, "Cass hasn't taken anything from me I didn't get back times two." He gave me back my life, she thought. But she didn't say that.

He wouldn't have believed it anyway. The block thought she was brainwashed. But weren't they all? Victor Clements was single—worked sixty, seventy hours a week at PECO, and he petted and cooed over his Buick like it was a woman.

Winnie served her hummingbird cake on a Tuesday evening. Nobody was ever so surprised. The kids whooped and clapped their hands. Zeek said, "Well, that is beautiful. You almost hate to eat something so beautiful." It was a pretty thing: three perfect layers, with lavender buttercream icing and lilac petals all around the sides. Nemo told her she had outdone herself. He said such funny things sometimes. And her baby, her Alvin, grinned ear to ear and swayed his whole body like he used to when he was happy.

They hardly ever sat outside together after the raid. The police had taken away their ease in each other's company, stolen their trust in one another. Cass had got himself a whole army. Strange men all over the place looking at Winnie and Ava in their nightgowns. It seemed to comfort him at first. Cass was calmer with the new crew, but after a few days he started looking narrow-eyed at those guys. He accused one of them of stealing some papers from his room. He said the fella was stealing their future. Patch and Zeek took the man out to the alley late one night. Winnie heard them beating him. *Thump, thump, thud.* Every beating sounds the same. Flesh to flesh, flesh to bone, softer, harder, silence. Winnie threw up in the trash can by her bed. That was a week after the raid. A few days later Cass had gathered a whole new bunch. Then those guys were gone, and so on.

No strangers for her hummingbird cake! Not even Patch, who was a brave and serious man but he sure did give Winnie the creeps. Music drifted in from over the fence. "The Ohio Players," Toussaint said. *Rollercoaster* . . . he sang and nudged his mother. Ava said, "Winnie, this is the best cake I ever ate." Winnie figured that must have been hard for her to say, so she was proud of her for it.

"A dance with the lady of the hour?"

Cass bowed and held his hand out to Winnie. She didn't know he could dance; she didn't know he had it in him. Everybody was relieved to see him smiling. After their dance he went in the house and came back with the radio.

Zeek got Ava doing some kind of fox-trot, probably because he hadn't danced with anybody since 1945. Winnie danced with Toussaint, then Ava twirled Alvin and Nemo and showed them how to do the hustle. Ava and Cass kept trying to avoid each other but they couldn't hold out. Winnie was glad to see them getting along. But, Lord, the bedroom feeling between those two. They weren't even touching but Winnie felt like she should tell the kids to look away from grown-folks business.

People think a little thing like a cake doesn't matter much, but a hummingbird cake will make anybody glad. The gladness might not last long. It might not even last a day, but you have to take uplift when you can get it. Even Carl was tamed by a little beauty for a day or two. Winnie got one of her feelings like he was outside the back fence. She wasn't scared this time, just sad. But she went on and scanned the alley through the back-fence door. Empty as the day is long, of course. It really was good, her cake. Maybe the best she ever made.

Cicada, Frog Song, Wind

"WHAT'S THIS PLACE I'm calling?" Dutchess asked. "Who's is it? I know it ain't yours."

Dutchess sure didn't waste any time. Ava steeled herself. Maybe she had it coming. Maybe she'd had it coming all these years she'd kept Toussaint a secret. Still, Dutchess didn't have to come out swinging.

"It's a rectory. Not far from where we live. Tou—" Ava stammered. "Toussaint comes here to see this pastor lady."

"My grandson."

"Yeah."

"My grandson you didn't tell me I had for eleven years."

"I'm . . . There's no . . ."

"You right about that. No point at all now."

In the next room, Philomena had put a plate of food in the small rectangle of space she'd cleared for Toussaint amid the stacks of paper on her dining table. He sat forking in his spaghetti, but his whole body was swiveled toward the doorway and his mother just beyond.

Dutchess inhaled deep and long. Ava could feel her mother gathering herself on the other end of the line. Marshaling herself for whatever battle she had called to wage.

"You go to a rectory in the middle of the night?"

Here we go, Ava thought.

"Yes."

Dutchess had to sit down. Ava's voice came over the line tinny and small but it was her. She'd always had a deep voice for such a skinny little thing. The night pressed against her. This old hide can't keep it out, she thought, lowering herself into Carter Lee's desk chair. Outside his postmaster's shack the night was rolling: cicada song, bat-wing beat, tree-branch squeak, tide out, moonlight icing the surface of the river. Her bladder squeezing, her chest tightening, the blood *thump thump* in her ears, her breath too fast. Oh, the night was rolling.

"So. You summoned," Ava said.

She intended it as a statement, cool and calm, but her voice rose at the end. Two minutes in and she had already made her first mistake. Dutchess was half hound. Dutchess could smell trouble. Not that Ava was in any trouble. Not that she was under any obligation to explain all her whys and wherefores. Keep it together, she thought.

"What's it like over there where you and the boy live?"

"What do you mean?"

"I mean, is it a house or an apartment? Just y'all three or . . ."

"It's a community of people living together, we take care of each other like— But you already know that. Toussaint must've told you."

"Yeah, he told me."

"So why . . . Okay. Look. What's going on? All this cloak and dagger."

"Ain't my cloak and dagger. I'm not the one lives with somebody they got to sneak away from at one in the morning."

Sneaked away she had. But how the hell did Dutchess know that? I don't have the stomach for this, Ava thought. I could just hang up and be done with it. But there was Toussaint, peering around the doorway. Expecting. The light back in his eyes for the first time in months.

"What do you want," Ava whispered.

"I want to tell you that the man you living with is a con man and a hustler and goddamn thief. That's what I want. I called to tell you something you need to know. That nigger was here. Called hisself Barber."

"Barber? I don't know any Barber."

"I'm telling you that nigger, your man, was here in Bonaparte." Liar.

"Before you ask, I know it's him cause Toussaint sent me a picture of y'all three on a porch." She added, "House number 248." Better to include every detail. So Ava couldn't wiggle out of it; so she couldn't rearrange the truth into something she liked better.

Ava turned her back to her son and put her hand over her mouth. A gasp slipped out through the spaces between her fingers.

"Is everything okay?" Toussaint called. "Ma?"

"Yeah. Yeah, baby, everything is all right. We're just talking. Everything is fine."

"That's my grandson?" Dutchess said.

Just a few feet away. My grandson. Hoohoo, this night is rolling.

"That's Toussaint?"

"You need to shut the hell up. Just stop talking," Ava whispered hard into the phone.

Dutchess stopped. They both did.

"Well, damn," Dutchess said.

Philomena steered Toussaint toward the porch. "But I don't want to miss my grandmother!" he said.

"You won't miss her. Your mom won't let you miss her. She's going to tap on the window when they finish so you can come in and talk to her. Right?" Ava, her back still turned, raised her hand in assent.

"But I . . ." Toussaint's voice faded. The front door clicked shut.

"You not gon let me talk to him?" An old lady voice. Mournful. Pleading. "Ava?"

"Of course. Of course you can talk to him. He just went out on the porch."

Dutchess sighed down the line. "Okay," she said.

Why did she sound old all of a sudden? Leave it to her to go and turn into an old lady. Wasn't it just like her to pull some shit like that.

"When?" Ava said.

"Huh?"

"When was this guy there? My— Toussaint's father's name is Cass, not that name you said."

"Cass. That's what you call him? Don't suit him," she said and sighed. "He left bout a year ago, on Jesse Day. I don't think he woulda stayed long as he did if I hadn'ta shot him. He was here a few—"

"You what? You shot him?" Ava shook her head. "Where? Where did you shoot him?"

"I didn't mean to. He was coming in by the Oaks, I thought he was Progress and I—"

"I mean, where on his body!"

"I know you better stop yelling. I got him in the gut, under his ribs. But I told you it was a accident. Anyway, clearly the nigger doing just fine. Shit."

Ava sat on the edge of the couch, her hand clammy around the receiver. She had a spinning feeling like she did when her pop died. Like when she left Bonaparte for the last time, like when that peculiar woman attacked her in the tunnel near Cass's grimy field of glory.

"He was all right to us. Up until he wasn't," Dutchess went on. "He helped. Ain't nothing but weeds and rubble round here now. He mended fences. Literally. He got some people to haul away the— You know Progress burnt the store?"

Silence.

"Hello?" Dutchess said.

"Yeah." Ava's voice was low and muffled. "Yeah. I'm here."

"Oh. Well, I, uh. I'm sorry. I guess, it's a, uh . . . a shock."

If Ava hadn't been so close to falling through the floor she'd have laughed. Dutchess never could comfort anybody worth a damn. A shock. Haha. Yeah, you could say.

Dutchess was still talking: "It was bad enough when Memma and Nip left. Then I figured out how that nigger did us and I—"

"Memma's gone?"

"Huh? Yeah. Delaware. Ain't that a blip. Stupid old thing. Just us four now."

"What do you mean?"

"You know it's just us here, Ava."

She did. But in her imaginings Bonaparte was filled with people. And always Memma and her big butt waddle rolling along Sundown Road. Memma who had saved them with her pot of dumplings in the worst winter of their lives. Memma, gone. Suddenly Ava could see Bonaparte as it was: four worn-out old people, with all the weight of the place on their gray heads. And all those empty fields and untenanted houses, oblivion closing over them. Over me! Ava thought in a panic. Over me!

". . . We knew he wasn't who he said he was. But it was a miracle for a live human being to show up here. It was almost worth it, if I weigh what he brought us against what he took. Maybe I would have let him get away with it, but—"

Ava realized she had missed something in Dutchess's telling. She had missed the part about Cass taking something.

"Get away with what?" she said.

"Shit, girl. Is you listening? The land! I told you. He took the deed! And the title."

"The deed! Come on. You don't know that. You don't know that he took anything. And even if he did, what would he do with a couple of pieces of paper? He can't *do* anything . . ."

Ava went on, feeling sicker by the second. She knew. In her gut she knew Dutchess was right.

"Ain't no point talkin around it," Dutchess said. "I got a letter, couple weeks back—confirmation of a request for ownership transfer to a Cassius Wright, with a copy of the transfer application. He forged my name on that form, Ava. I got the letter right here. You understand?"

"I'll be damned," Ava said. Her stomach pitched around her insides. "I'll be damned."

"Yeah."

But that's our land, Ava thought. Even if I never step foot on it again. Even though I won't ever see it again. That's ours.

"It don't matter, I'm sorry to say, but it don't matter if that man is the boy's father. He's a liar and a thief. That's Caro's land."

Pop. He read the newspaper nearly every day. He'd walk down the road from Carter Lee's post office with the week-old paper—all the newspapers in Bonaparte were a week old—tucked under his arm. How long had it been since Ava remembered him alive? When she thought of him, he was always killed or about to be. Always, ever falling dead into Mr. George's field. But now his loping walk came back to her, and how he was most always smiling. "Got to keep up with the BS," he'd say and tap Ava on top of the head with the folded paper.

"You hearing me?" Dutchess said. "Time to stop living like the future is a dream. Caro didn't think it was. And your son. He got hard reality in front of him. Months and years, not dreams."

Dutchess could feel Caro out there in the night. Urging her on: Steady, baby. You doin all right. You doin fine. And she could see Ava—stubborn and childish, playing make-believe with her not-Caro man. Her Cass/Barber. She could see him too. The shimmer on him like scales on a king snake. I understand, Dutchess thought. I understand he has to do what he has to do, but not to me. Not to us. And anyway, he was going to die some kind of bad way, like her Caro had died.

"Men like your Cass," Dutchess said, "don't live long."

"No. No they don't," Ava said softly. "You at Carter Lee's? Can you put the phone to the window?"

The static on the line had cleared. The window sash creaked as Dutchess pushed it fully open. Outside sounds swelled into Ava's ears and hummed in her throat, unfurled in her chest. It'll break my ribs, she thought. Bonaparte is going to bust me right open. Cicada, frog song, wind, like it had always been. Dutchess behind it all saying, "This night is rolling. You feel that, Ava? You feel it?"

After a time Dutchess said, "Hey, girl. Girl, you listening? I need to explain some things. I'm getting this mess straightened out about the property transfer, but I got a lot of papers I need to send. I'm moving most of it to the boy's name. All right, so first . . ."

· · ·

By the time Ava tapped on the window, the sky had a greenish tint and Toussaint had fallen asleep on the porch. She knocked a little harder and he was on his feet and in the living room in an instant, the phone pressed against his cheek.

"Grandmom? That's you?" he said. Then: "Aww, don't cry. You shouldn't cry.

"You got my marble?" he asked. "It takes so long for stuff to get to where you are . . . Well, I guess we could. I want to come . . . Are the birds still there? Yeah. The birds at night. My mom told me. I want to see em . . ."

Idling

AN ENGINE IDLED SOMEWHERE out on Ephraim. The sound rumbled up to the attic of 248 where Ava had been lying down for four days. Cass had said she needed to rest. He said something had gotten into her. Apparently, he thought it would get out of her if she were locked in a room. That wasn't quite true. Ava wasn't locked in there. She could leave whenever she wanted to. But, of course, he would be downstairs. "Are you feeling better?" he'd say calmly. "How are *you* feeling," she might reply—maybe *you're* not feeling so hot on account of Dutchess put a curse on you from the witchiest corner of the world. But, of course, she wouldn't say that. Cass would look her deep in the eye. And Winnie would be standing behind him, chopping something or slicing something. Anyway, with a knife and her sweet smile. Cass's appraisal, his diagnostic, would turn Ava inside out. He could always find disease. He was a doctor, after all. Then Ava would have to turn around and climb the stairs right back to her bed.

Ava squinted at the daylight filtering through the sheets she'd hung over the attic windows. Light made her headache worse. The pain dizzied her, mixed her up, like when she had her butterfly. The engine out on Ephraim revved, *vroom vroom,* like a sound in a children's book. She had been trying not to close her eyes. When they closed, she was plunged into a dream about her room at Glenn Avenue, lying on that narrow squeaky bed. The migraine surged. Her eyelids fluttered shut. In the dream an engine idled, just beyond the Glenn Avenue playground, behind the jungle gym and dumpsters. Thank God it didn't wake Toussaint. The engine grew louder and Ava lifted herself onto her elbows to see what it might be. She did this in real life too, there in her and Cass's room. God knows she'd rather be at 248 than Glenn Avenue. She'd rather be at 248 than anywhere else. Which probably made her a little crazy, given all the givens.

Four days before, after Ava talked to Dutchess, she'd ransacked the attic looking for the deed and title to her land. She hadn't found them. But that didn't mean they weren't there. She did find two thousand dollars in cash, which she took to mean that Cass must have other things he shouldn't have, taken from other places he shouldn't have gotten them. She was too worn out to clean up after the ransacking so she just sat down in the middle of the mess.

Cass came into the room. "Go on and look," he said.

Who knows what he thought she knew. Maybe he was trying to find out. Maybe he wanted to get caught. It is a relief to get caught, to get called out, to be told to *stop this shit right now.* Ava could have given him that. She wanted to, she truly did. Instead, she gave him herself. When they finished, she stayed on top of him for a long time. She kissed him deeply and tenderly. She meant every second of it. That spooked him, so he got up fast and shook himself like a dog. That was when he said she should stay in the attic and rest until she felt better.

"It really is going to be all right," he said, kneeling by the mattress. "You're allowed your doubts. You'll conquer them and come out on the other side."

That sure would be nice.

On his way out of the room he said, "You know, don't you, that what belongs to one of us belongs to all of us."

Toussaint snuck up to the attic with tidbits of food and news, and a lot of questions Ava didn't have answers to. That morning he'd told her a big fat envelope had arrived for him at Philomena's; full of papers with his name all over them. They made a plan for Ava to sneak over there to sign what needed signing. But she didn't know if she'd manage it because of the idling. Plus, she didn't really mind her confinement, it was peaceful in its way. And her head ached so.

Ava tumbled through the worst of her memories: Those hours in the root cellar when Bodine came for Bonaparte. She had wrapped her arms around Dutchess and felt her mother's body strain away from hers. If she hadn't held on Dutchess would have cut loose, she would have joined the fighting and made Ava an orphan. Maybe, she thought now, that wasn't the right way to look at it. Could be Dutchess felt like all that was left to her were the bullets in her shotgun. Maybe she figured her choices were death or vengeance. But she didn't choose either. She stayed down in the cellar sweating and straining against Ava's arms. Much as she wanted to do anything but. My son needs a future, Ava thought. Cass can't have it.

She sank back onto the pillows. Glenn Avenue returned when she closed her eyes. The hidden engine grew louder. The idling was closer and vibrated in Ava's legs and chest and rattled her brain. Toussaint slept on, more heavily than before. The idling had drugged him, he slumped on his side like they got him with a tranquilizer dart. Down the hallway, Miss Simmons and Melvin and Renee and Tess didn't seem to hear the roar. Tess said, "Tess sure wouldn't just lay down. It's always some bitch just laying down." She was right, some bitch always was. It's a wonder anything ever got done. Tess said, "Tess don't wonder. You want to buy a wig? You want some food stamps? Twenty for ten." All of them were down the hallway going about their business. Ain't studying bout me, Ava thought. Like they used to say at home. Steadying about me. She put her hand across her mouth to keep the vomit in. All at once she realized that it was her. She was the engine. Idling. In the waking world, in her and Cass's attic, Ava swung her trembling legs over the edge of the bed and stood. The room quieted. She was steady.

. . .

Downstairs, Meeting was in full swing. Ava paused to watch from the hallway. Everyone was there who was supposed to be, except her, of course. There were a couple of others too: a Temple professor who used to be a skeptic but had, a few weeks before, started sleeping in the front room on Cass's command. Even Mikey had turned up after being banished for a few weeks. Cass was very beautiful. Especially beautiful. The hollows in his cheeks suited him. He was saying, "We are in the time that remains." Remains to be seen, Ava thought. But that wasn't what he meant. What he meant was that Ark was in a waiting time, between where they had been and the paradise he planned for them. "The time is brief," he said.

But the paradise to come was Ava's land, Caro's legacy, stolen, and the trip there would be funded with Winnie's property—also stolen, even if she didn't think it was. Cass would keep right on; he wouldn't ever stop pulling things into himself. It was his nature. You can't blame a thing for following its nature. You might even love it more, for being so powerfully itself.

Ava slipped out the back door and through the garden. *Tip tip tip.* When she got to the alley, she felt a stab of alarm and patted her pockets. Then she remembered she didn't need any change to call 911.

They Won't Hurt the Kids

"IS THIS DETECTIVE BRIGGS? You were at that house at 248 Ephraim Avenue a couple of months ago? In West Philly? Well, I . . . You left your card . . . No. No, I don't live in that house. I just, I got your card and I didn't know who else to call because you know we have called the police a few times and nothing . . . Well, the one guy. The . . . uh, the leader, Cassius Wright? He has a gun. Him and the other one, with the bad eye? They threatened me. They pointed guns right at me . . . Just a few minutes ago. I was going by that house and . . . Peeples is my name. You all come quick, okay? . . . Yeah. Yeah. Okay. I have to hang up now."

Ava placed the receiver in the cradle and leaned against the wall of the phone booth. Well, that's done, she thought. Maybe we'll have burgers for dinner. Ha! Haha! She slid open the phone booth door and her knees gave out. Right there on the corner of Sixty-second and Hazel. She couldn't work out the right combination of hands and legs to push herself back up to standing. Panic slashed through her chest. She wanted to warn him, to burst through the front door of 248 yelling, Cass, get out of here, they are coming for you. And you, Zeek, and you too, Winnie, and, Everlasting help her, the boys. She felt her betrayal like a tear in her body, right between the shoulder blades. But this wasn't the time for wounds. They would come and she and Toussaint could not be there when they did. She took a deep breath, heaved herself up, and took off running toward 248.

Ava slipped back into the house the way she'd left it: down the alley, sticking close to the houses so the roof watch wouldn't see her, quietly through the garden and in the screen door. 248 was oddly quiet. Meeting had ended early. Muffled voices floated down from the upper floors. Ava figured she had ten minutes, maybe less. She would get Toussaint and grab a few of their papers she kept under the mattress in the boys' room. There wasn't time to warn Winnie and Zeek, and anyway they would tell, wouldn't they? They'd take her by the arms and march her right back to Cass. But the boys. The boys she could bring out of there on some pretense—sandwiches at Pastor Phil's. Or she could say . . . Her thoughts scattered. Calm, Ava. Calm.

The commotion upstairs grew louder, then quieted. Footsteps approached on the stairs so she ducked into the hallway closet. The time ticked down. Eight minutes. Then seven. Never mind the papers. Get your boy and go. The footsteps moved past the closet. After a few seconds, the doorway to the half bathroom clicked shut. She heard the pull cord for the overhead light and the whir of the exhaust fan.

Ava's hand trembled on the knob as she cracked the door to peer out at the hallway. Nownownow! She was up the stairs to the second-floor landing. Alvin and Nemo sat on the bed in the boys' room. Ava put her finger to her lips. But Nemo stood, shaking his head, waving his arms. Shh-shhh, she mouthed again, but he advanced toward her. In the instant she realized he was warning her to turn around, Cass appeared a few feet away at the bottom of the attic steps.

"Ava," he said, gently, easy as poured milk. "Where you been?"

Look him in the eye, Ava thought, or he will know.

"I needed some air," she said. "It gets so close up there."

"Why didn't you say anything? Zeek could have walked you outside. Or Winnie."

"I was scared you would—that you wouldn't let me, so I just—"

"You snuck off, like a kid breaking curfew."

The police would be on their way by now. Five minutes, maybe less.

"You're not well, Ava. You shouldn't be outside, you know that. What were you doing?"

"I just wanted some fresh air. I walked down the—"

"Ma?" Toussaint appeared at the top of the attic stairs.

"Ma?" he said again. His voice shook.

"Baby?" Ava stepped around Cass to go up to her boy. Cass blocked her path. She darted in the other direction. Cass intercepted.

"Ma!" Toussaint took a few steps down the attic stairs. As he drew closer Ava saw his eyes were red, his face tear-streaked.

"Get out of the way, Cass," she said.

"Go back into the bedroom like I told you, Toussaint," he said. No more gentle, bedside-manner Cass. His voice was all iron. "I need to talk to your mother a little while."

"Get out of my way!" Ava pushed him, both hands against his chest. He didn't even lose his balance.

"What were you doing out there, Ava?"

She bent at the waist; she would run at him and knock him down. Just then a pair of arms circled her shoulders from behind and lifted her off the ground. She kicked but the grip held firm.

"Stop! Stop. I'll go back upstairs. Don't hurt Ma! Zeek, why would you hurt Ma?"

Why would you hurt me, Zeek? Ava thought. What has happened to us?

"They're coming," she said.

"What? Who's coming."

"The police, Cass. That's what I was doing. I called the police."

"She ain't call no police," Zeek said. "I don't believe it."

Ava held Cass's gaze.

"I believe it. I believe she did," Cass said.

Toussaint ducked around Cass and ran to his mother's side. "Stop it, Zeek," he said, reaching up to rest his hand on Zeek's forearm. "Please stop."

Zeek's gaze softened. He loosened his grip just enough for Ava to break free.

"Run!" she shouted. "Run!" Ava reached behind and grabbed Toussaint's hand. The two of them sprinted for the stairs. "Boys!" she called as they sprinted past Alvin and Nemo's open bedroom door. Ava and Toussaint were at the landing, then halfway down the stairs.

It was the loudness that caught them off guard. The incredible volume, as if the sirens were inside the house with them. Everything stopped: Ava and Toussaint, Zeek and Cass, the boys, even Patch, who had appeared at the bottom of the stairs, Winnie behind him. Alvin put his hands over his ears against the siren shriek.

"What have you done?" Cass said. He was mournful. His heart was broken.

She drew her boy close behind her. "Let us go, Patch."

But Patch never let anything go. He slammed his palm into her breastbone. Ava tried to get to her feet. She tried to say, "At least let the boys pass," but she couldn't catch her breath.

A voice boomed over a bullhorn: "Come out of the house. Come out with your hands up."

Ava struggled to her feet. "Send the kids out," she said. "They won't hurt the kids."

Another siren approached, car doors slammed. That would make maybe four cop cars, she figured. Or could be they were so loud it sounded like more. That was possible.

"They won't hurt the kids," she repeated, more quietly this time.

"What's wrong with you, Ava?" Cass said, shoving past her to pull up the hallway floorboards. "Did they knock the sense out of you in the last raid? They will shoot these children point-blank. You know that."

He lifted the duffel bag of guns from a hole in the subfloor.

Zeek and Patch rushed forward. Each man took a rifle, calmly, efficiently. They'd been practicing, Ava realized. They'd rehearsed this moment. Their reckoning, at last.

Zeek and Patch ran up stairs.

Sirens sounded from the back alley and the street in front. Red and blue smudges of light pinwheeled across the living room through the butcher-papered windows. The sirens cut off and the bullhorn voice boomed again: "Come out of the house with your hands up." Ava heard voices in the street. The neighbors had gathered to watch the police drag Ark out of 248.

"Go to the basement," Cass said to Toussaint. He shook him by the shoulders. "Do you hear me? Go. Stay there until one of us comes to get you."

Toussaint gripped Ava's hand; his eyes fixed on the wheeling lights. Here was her boy, only eleven, nearly the same age she had been in the root cellar with Dutchess all those years ago. It all just keeps right on.

"You coming?" Cass said to Ava. The shotgun was light and easy in his grip. He offered it to her.

She would go. There wasn't any other option. No choices remained. Ava would go up to the roof with Cass and have her long-awaited revenge for her pop, for Bonaparte, for everything she had lost. Winnie and the other boys were already in the basement. Winnie could take care of them. Yes, Winnie would look after them. Ava stepped toward Cass. Her son tugged her hand. Just once. Lightly. She felt the tremble in his fingertips. Cass gazed at her. Almost patiently, almost lovingly amid the chaos of sirens.

She looked at him and shook her head. Dutchess had given her that much. Mama, don't go, Ava had said. And Dutchess hadn't gone. Cass nodded. His hands, those long square fingers, grazed the side of her cheek. Then he was gone, up the stairs two at a time.

I will not see him again, Ava thought. She and Toussaint ran for the basement.

Fire

THE FIRST SHOT SAILED over the squad cars and lodged in the wooden siding of 248 Ephraim Avenue. Later, the police would say Ark had fired first. They would say one man, Cassius Wright, whom they knew to be the leader, had fired from a second-story window. Later still, they'd revise that account to say he had not shot first, but they'd seen the muzzle braced against the window frame so they had fired to disable the gunman. The people of Ephraim would say the man in the second-floor window had aimed his first bullets over the squad cars. Not at them. Just to let them know, they would say. They would say the police, seven squad cars at least, all opened fire at once. They would say they remembered when the man fell backward into the house and the gun disappeared from view. But he held out, they said. He held out a long time. Hours.

Spent casings rained down on the avenue—two hours, three. The cops in their cruisers had enough. They called in special forces. SWAT launched tear gas. After the tear gas, flash-bang grenades. In response, a Molotov cocktail hurtled from a shattered window in 248 and exploded in the middle of the evacuated block. Gunfire resumed with the *poppoppop* of an automatic rifle from the SWAT team in the back alley. Bullets shattered the doorframe and the jars of Ark pickles and the kitchen table. They tore into the propane tanks rigged to the stove.

The boom set the dogs howling up and down the block. A fireball blew out the kitchen windows and set the back fence aflame. The flames shot up the back of the house to the roof. Police watched from behind the barricades they'd erected to cordon off the area. They heard screaming from inside of 248. "Do something!" shouted the residents of Ephraim Avenue. "You can't just let it burn!" they shouted. But the firefighters did not turn on their hoses or rush forward with pickaxes and oxygen masks, not yet.

Two people ran out of 248. Ava carried Toussaint on her back into the gunfire. The back of the boy's shirt smoldered. Ava did not loosen her grip on her son. Her mouth was open. Somebody shouted, "Dear Jesus, stop shooting!" Toussaint's head lolled to one side. Ava bent forward at the waist so that her back was a flat plane on which Toussaint could rest. A gruff white voice called out an order, the bullets ceased. When she was far enough from the burning house, she got to her knees, then lowered herself onto her stomach on the asphalt. She spread her arms and legs, careful not to topple her boy.

Ava bled from her side and her shoulder. Police officers rushed forward, rifles drawn, and circled woman and boy. Two pointed rifles at Ava's head. A cop dropped a blanket over the boy, who groaned at the burns on his back. They picked him up and ran with him to a waiting gurney. Ava wanted a last look at her son, whose weight she could still feel, more even than she could feel the burns on her hands or the bullet in her shoulder. When she moved, they pressed a rifle muzzle into her temple. Paramedics rushed into the cordoned-off area. They placed an oxygen mask over her face and lifted her onto a stretcher.

Ava saw Toussaint lift his head. "Please," she said to the medics. "Please." Her mouth was charred. Pain seared down her arm and through her back. She felt the blood rushing out of her. "My son," she whispered. "Please."

The men carrying Ava paused. They looked from the boy to the woman. The police waved them toward an ambulance parked at some distance from Toussaint, but the medics took her to her boy instead. His arm hung limply over the side of the gurney.

There were white patches on one side of his face where the skin had burned away. His eyelashes were singed off. But he was breathing. His fingers twitched. Ava took his hand and his fingers curled against her palm. His eyes opened and fixed on her before closing again. "He's asleep," the paramedic told her. "We gave him something for the pain."

"Sleeping?" Ava asked. The medic nodded. Ava held her boy's hand for as long as they'd let her. She knew she would not be with him again for a long time. Pain surged with such intensity she couldn't contain it so she followed it out to where it was brightest and there she rested.

1988

. . .

PHILADELPHIA

. . .

TOUSSAINT WOKE JUST AFTER DAWN in the stinging cold of 248. His eyes adjusted to the dim light shining through the holes in the roof. Smoke-blackened plaster lay in broken heaps on the floor, alongside a moldy blanket and every cigarette butt in the world. Someone had graffitied FREE THE THREE on the wall along what used to be the hallway to the kitchen. The three were Toussaint's mother and Winnie and Zeek, all at Holmesburg.

Ava's most recent letter lay beside Toussaint on the floor, fallen from his hands when he'd dropped to sleep the night before. He'd come to 248 because she'd asked him to. Toussaint is the kite and Ava is the string. Even now. The letter read:

Dear Tousy,

Your grandmother called. Again! She's been trying to reach you at Philomena's place, but she says you haven't called her back. I know you're not there all the time, but I guess she gives you the messages when you come around? Did she tell you I've been calling too? It would have been so much easier on you if you'd gone to live with her. You're sick of hearing that. I can see you frowning. I can hear you saying, Aww, Ma. Not this again.

Did you ever get over there to that last place in Olney where DHS put Alvin and Nemo? I was glad they didn't separate them. They need each other. Winnie told me a cousin of hers is coming to get them. After all this time! She's taking them to live with her in Ohio. Maybe you want to say good-bye. Or maybe they already got in touch with you. I gave Winnie the number where you were, but I don't know if she passed it on. You know I'm not her favorite. Haha. I'm sorry. That's not very funny. Sometimes I wonder if you don't answer my letters because of my bad jokes. I'm kidding. Again. I miss you every day.

I need to tell you something. My lawyer says the city is finally going to tear down 248. They're going to raze it to the ground like they should have two years ago. I have nightmares about that house. Not like it was when we were there, but as I imagine it is now, burnt out and terrifying. I know the people in the neighborhood will be glad when it's gone.

I don't blame you if you don't want to see it again. But I've been thinking maybe you need to say your good-byes. Me and Zeek and Winnie have to move on the best we can in here. But Alvin and Nemo are leaving. You should too. You have somewhere you are wanted. Somewhere people have been waiting for you.

Go to Ephraim one last time and tell Cass whatever you need him to know. Then you get on the bus and go to Bonaparte. Don't spend your life chasing ghosts. You have to be free of us, Toussaint. You have to live.

Love always,
Ma

Out on Ephraim the sun was up, full and cold. Toussaint hitched his backpack onto his shoulders. A flock of sparrows twittered overhead. Toussaint watched them circle and land in the upper branches of the old burnt tree. He walked toward the bus stop on the next block. The 42 ran all the way downtown. Almost all the way to the Greyhound station. He wouldn't even have to transfer.

BONAPARTE

∘ ∘ ∘

WE GOT BUT FIVE, six starlings left these days. They don't much like all the shooting since I leased the hunting rights to the back acres. Still, it's enough of them to mean something. Toussaint'll understand when he gets here. Ava too, when the time comes. If I'm still around to see her. But the boy. The boy has everything he needs—map, money, tickets. You know this damn mist is something. Me and Delilah come out here every day right around dusk and wait outside the Oaks. Just in case he has some trouble finding his way in.

Acknowledgments

For her indispensable editorial advice, my deepest gratitude to Jordan Pavlin, who would not settle for less though the road was long. To my patient and stalwart agent Ellen Levine, for taking such good and expert care. I am indebted to the New York Public Library's Cullman Center for Scholars and Writers, an oasis for the mind and spirit, for its generous gift of time and support. Thanks to the Bogliasco Foundation with its lapping waves and tranquil beauty. To the Civitella Ranieri Foundation for a stunning place to think and write, for its warm hospitality and even warmer community. To the American Academy in Berlin for its Fellowship—literally and otherwise—and incredible generosity. To Aspen Words Writers in Residence for offering solitude when I needed it most. To the Blue Mountain Center. To the Iowa Writers' Workshop for kinship and sustenance. And to the brilliant young minds there who taught me more than I taught them.

For their support and friendship, I am unendingly grateful to the incomplete list of folks to follow: Marilynne Robinson, Emily Raboteau, and Jericho Brown. Jenna Johnson, Angie Cruz, William Johnson, Farah Jasmine Griffin, Brigid Hughes, Lan Samantha Chang. To Miriam Feuerle, Hannah Scott, Andrew Wetzel, and everyone at Lyceum Agency for hanging in there all these years. To Papa G, who waited and waited with humor and wine. To Lucy Mingo and the town of Gee's Bend for inspiration and aspiration. To Philadelphia, where my imagination lives. Last and most, to Christina Cooke for everything she is and was and will be.

ABOUT THE AUTHOR

AYANA MATHIS's first novel, *The Twelve Tribes of Hattie,* was a *New York Times* best seller, an NPR Best Book of 2013, and the second selection for Oprah's Book Club 2.0, and has been translated into sixteen languages. She is the recipient of fellowships from the New York Public Library's Cullman Center, the Bogliasco Foundation, the Civitella Ranieri Foundation, and the American Academy in Berlin. Mathis is a graduate of the Iowa Writers' Workshop. She was born in Philadelphia and currently lives in New York City, where she attends Union Theological Seminary and teaches writing in Hunter College's MFA program.

A NOTE ON THE TYPE

This book was set in Hoefler Text, a family of fonts designed by
Jonathan Hoefler, who was born in 1970. First designed in 1991,
Hoefler Text was intended as an advancement on existing desktop
computer typography, including as it does an exponentially larger
number of glyphs than previous fonts. In form, Hoefler Text looks
to the old-style fonts of the seventeenth century, but it is wholly of
its time, employing a precision and sophistication only available to
the late twentieth century.

Typeset by Scribe,
Philadelphia, Pennsylvania

Printed and bound by Berryville Graphics,
Berryville, Virginia

Designed by Cassandra J. Pappas